"Fast, relentless, and impossible to put down. Landon Beach's *The Cabin* is a must-read for fans of Ted Bell, Clive Cussler, and Bryan Gruley."

- The Real Book Spy

"*The Cabin* has all the elements of a great espionage thriller along with a dose of introspection on the state of the world at large. If you're looking for an intelligent, high octane read, you can't go wrong with *The Cabin*."

- Chris Goff, author of RED SKY

"Landon Beach spins a great yarn—while deftly illuminating more significant issues."

- Jesse Stoddard, Writer, Speaker, Entertainer

THE CABIN

Landon Beach

Landon Beach
Visit my website at landonbeachbooks.com

Printed in the United States of America

First Printing: August 2019
Landon Beach Books

ISBN-13 978-1-7322578-2-5

For John Thomas and Barry Beam—two missed men who wore the badge with distinction, honor, fairness, and compassion.

And, for Generation X.

THE CABIN

"A nation that wants to project its power beyond its borders needs to see over the horizon, to know what is coming, to prevent attacks against its people. It must anticipate surprise. Without a strong, smart, sharp intelligence service, presidents and generals alike can become blind and crippled. But throughout its history as a superpower, the United States has not had such a service."

-Tim Weiner, *Legacy of Ashes*

"Why Americans believe that conflict is good within their own society and yet bad between societies is a fascinating question which, to the best of my knowledge, no one has seriously studied."

-Samuel P. Huntington, *The Clash of Civilizations and the Remaking of World Order*

PROLOGUE

BERLIN, DECEMBER 2005 – PART I

The spy was late. CIA Officer Jennifer Lear sat inside a toasty café drinking a cappuccino, *Die Welt* open in front of her. She was at a table for two against the front window and right next to the door. Outside, the snow fell as if there was an unlimited supply, and Berliners wearing dark heavy overcoats and knitted hats made their way along the Kurfürstendamm. She felt a hint of sympathy for her partner who was outside weathering the freezing temperature a block away. A feigned yawn and stretch gave her the opportunity to glance at the clock on the wall above a booth with two loud Germans arguing over a game of chess. 7:02 p.m. Her agent, Sari, had never been late, which would give Lear the grounds to call off the meeting right now. But, Sari would be doing a surveillance detection run, and the weather might be slowing her down. Lear and her partner had decided on a 5-minute window. Sari now had 3.

She moved her toes up and down inside her hiking boots. Her feet were sore from her own hour-long surveillance detection run with her partner, performed to make sure that no one was following them before she entered the café. First, they had driven around for a half an hour to spot anyone tailing

1

their car. Then, she had gotten out and started to walk while he parked the car up the street in front of a bookstore. As soon as he exited the car, a third officer emerged from the store, took the keys from him, and drove the car out of the city. For the next half hour, Lear had strolled the shopping district while her partner followed from a distance.

The door chimed, and Lear took a sip of her cappuccino to see who had entered. Damn. It was a heavyset grandmother with a scarf over her mouth. The woman shut the door behind her and moved toward the café's bar. Lear set her cup down. *Where was her agent?*

CIA Officer Brian Turner shivered beneath his wool coat. The wind whipped against the snow on the ground, dusting it up like a snow blower and then scattering the flakes in a narrow blast pattern. He crossed the street and began to look in store windows. He pondered, he nodded, he abruptly stopped and acted like the deal he saw advertised on the storefront was too good to be true, and he kept watch on his surroundings to make sure that nothing interfered with Officer Lear's meeting. He had last seen their agent at the rendezvous six months ago, and he wondered what information she would have for them this time.

The corner of the awning above the storefront he was currently "browsing" gave way, dumping a pile of snow directly on his neck and coat collar. As he brushed the snow off with his gloved hands, some of it slipped under his shirt and ran down his back—*Jesus, it was cold.* The summer meetings were much more pleasant. Why did he keep getting assigned to winter meetings? Lear only handled one summer meeting and one winter meeting a year; the rest of the time she was probably at her cover job or working as an analyst at Langley. He was stationed in France, which made it easy for him to accompany her to Berlin. They were posing as tourists for a week and were enjoying all Berlin had to offer: the Gendarmenmarkt, the Brandenburg Gate, the Reichstag, the Berlin

Television Tower, the Berlin Cathedral, Museum Island, and the Berlin Wall Memorial and Documentation Centre. Then, on a pre-arranged day and time, they would meet up with their agent. The usual protocol called for Lear to live in Berlin under the cover of some state job at the U.S. Embassy. Once the CIA had an agent for her to run, she would coordinate all of the meetings using classic tradecraft—dead drops, chalk markings, the opening of a window at a certain time, etc. But in the last decade, this had become more difficult to pull off since most foreign countries now watched *every* employee of the embassy. Updated techniques were needed to effectively run agents and gather intelligence. Using officers once or twice a year for the face-to-face meetings had proved effective. The Berlin station personnel would set up the meetings, but when the meetings actually took place, known officers were followed and unknown officers like Lear and Turner were not—allowing them to slide into a café or take a stroll in a park to meet with their agent. They would exchange money and other items for information, forward it to the Berlin office, then go on acting as tourists for a few more days.

Turner entered a store directly across from the café. The warmth inside restored him. He took off his gloves, smiled at a salesperson, and meandered through an aisle of clothes until he was facing the window. He could see Lear sitting at the table. The other chair was empty. Something was wrong.

He turned toward a rack of men's coats and picked up the sleeve of one to study the price tag, which also gave him an opportunity to glance at his watch. 7:04. Four minutes late. If Sari didn't show in one minute, they would leave. A no-show agent was a pain because of the time devoted to the meeting's set up, communication, and surveillance detection run, but it didn't necessarily mean that anything was wrong. Perhaps the agent was being followed and had to abort. Not a problem, they'd set up another meeting. But still...

He let the coat sleeve go and gave the street a quick survey as if to check the conditions outside. The snow continued to pour from the sky as shoppers walked the Kurfürstendamm. The agent was nowhere in sight. Less than a minute left. He felt uneasy.

Officer Lear finished her cappuccino and dabbed a napkin across her lips. Convinced that her agent was not going to show up, she started to slide her chair back away from the table. It had only moved a few inches when the door to the café opened and Sari entered.

Lear bent down and tightened the laces on both of her hiking boots. The floor looked like it hadn't been swept in months, and the snow tracked in had turned the dirt into a wet grime. She sat up. Placing her elbows on the table top, she rested her chin on her hands and stared out the window disinterestedly as if she'd be there to pass another hour.

Sari joined her at the table.

"Guten Abend," Lear said, still looking out the window.

Sari affectionately rubbed Lear's right arm. "Alles klar."

Lear turned her head and released a smile. "Ja, alles klar, danke." She took out a handkerchief and surveyed the café as she wiped her nose. Nothing seemed out of place, and no one was paying attention to them. Lear put the handkerchief back in her pocket.

Sari had spotted the folded newspaper on the table. After a pause, she laid her large purse next to the paper and began to search the middle pocket with her left hand. With precision and timing, she slid her right hand between the folded sections of *Die Welt*, as if to stabilize the purse, and then removed it, joining her other hand in the search of her purse's contents.

Lear pretended to be annoyed with Sari's searching until Sari finally pulled out a pack of gum. Lear's face said: *about time.*

Sari offered her a stick, which was accepted, then took one out for herself.

Lear said, "Danke," and put the green piece of gum into her mouth while Sari placed her purse on the floor. Lear slid the newspaper into her backpack with her right hand. With her left hand, she took a small cookie tin out of her coat pocket and placed it inside Sari's purse. The tin was filled with cash. When they had started exchanging information, Sari had asked for more specific items—an original Michael Jackson Thriller record, two cartons of Treasurer cigarettes, a Gucci scarf—but now she just wanted cash.

"Bitte schön."

Lear relaxed. The Berlin exchanges were always quick, and the signal that everything was fine was communicating in simple German phrases that any tourist would know. If there was anything wrong and they needed to split, Lear was to say a long sentence in English, and, if there was anything wrong on Sari's end, she was to say a lengthy sentence in German. Lear didn't know why Sari was late, but she was convinced that, whatever the reason, all was well. She made eye contact with her agent and then, using her right index finger, rubbed her watch face in two slow circles.

Sari patted Lear's arm. It was time to get going.

Lear rose from the table and pushed in her chair. She said, "Gute Nacht."

"Bis dann," Sari replied.

Lear put on her backpack and headed for the door. The two Germans playing chess had escalated their insults as Lear slid by their booth. She pulled on the door handle and heard, "Wir fahren morgen mit dem Zug nach Hamburg, wenn ich dich wider sehe, lieber Freund." *We'll take the train to Hamburg tomorrow when I see you back here, dear friend.*

Lear looked over at Sari, gave her a nod, and then exited the café.

Outside, she noticed Turner leaning against a lamppost across the street. After tilting her head back and looking at the sky, as if pondering whether to venture out or head back inside, she took a pair of reading glasses out of her right coat pocket, examined them, and then put them in her left pocket.

Turner's heart started to beat faster, and his situational awareness became even more acute. Lear had just signaled him that something was wrong. But what was it? It appeared that the meeting had gone smoothly; it definitely hadn't been rushed. Surely, Sari would have signaled trouble as soon as she entered the café, but the two had sat down like old friends. Had Lear seen something after the meeting? He put his hand inside his coat and felt the handle of his 9mm. He slid his fingers down the barrel and felt the silencer attached—the pockets were extra-large to accommodate the handgun. At the same time, his eyes swiveled left and right, then up and across the rooftops. Nothing seemed out of place. He looked through the café window. Sari sat, reading a paperback. She seemed in no hurry.

His eyes met Lear's, and she turned left out of the café. This was the direction they had agreed upon if there was danger. He let her get a block ahead and then began to follow. In another block, he would cross the street and—

There. A man wearing a driver's cap and carrying a shopping bag from an upscale clothing store entered the sidewalk from an alley. He took a little too much time searching the crowd of fellow shoppers until he spotted and began to follow Lear. Trouble.

Turner kept his eyes on the man. After a few paces, the man made a second mistake and turned his head to the right, keeping it fixed for a moment in the direction of another man who was across the street. The second man was half-a-block ahead of Turner and walked with a smooth, confident stride. He had on a black overcoat with a scarlet scarf, and his mop of salt and pepper hair blew in the wind.

Then, the second man veered off the sidewalk and entered a store; the other man continued to follow Lear. Turner saw his opportunity and crossed the street, cycling his eyes between Lear, the man following her, and the storefront where the second man had disappeared. As he passed the store, he did not see the man inside, but he only had a second to scan. There was no time to double check, and he could not reveal himself by stopping and looking in the storefront window. He focused his attention solely on Lear.

From a corner inside the store, the man with the overcoat and red scarf watched his fellow agent follow the woman. He waited an entire minute until they were far away down the sidewalk. He approached the window and scanned both sides of the street. Confident that he had not been seen or followed, he exited the store and headed back toward the café.

Turner began to close the distance between himself and the man following Lear. Up ahead was an apartment complex, and if he could walk past both of them like he was in a hurry to get somewhere, then he could warn her. It was his only chance. He sped up.

Lear saw the apartment complex looming two blocks away. Should she dart into the main office, take an elevator up, walk all the way down the hall, take the stairs down, and then exit out the rear entrance? It was a simple evasion technique, and they had discussed it last week when they arrived and again this morning. She wasn't sure if she was being followed, but Turner wouldn't be far behind. He would join her in the building and they would go from there. The one thing she could not do was turn arou—

"Apartment plan," a voice said next to her, and before she could turn her head, she saw Turner running past her. Ten yards ahead, she saw him look at his watch, shake his head, and then swear loudly in German. He continued to run—past the apartment complex, past another store, and across the next intersection.

Now she knew something was wrong. Twenty yards until the entrance of the apartment complex. She maintained discipline, never speeding up or looking around, and her hiking boots continued to crunch though the freshly fallen snow.

Ten yards.

She put her hand inside her coat pocket and fingered her own 9mm with silencer attached—she hadn't fired a gun since the range, right before she left the United States for the mission. She had never fired at a human being before.

She reached the double glass doors and entered the apartment building. Then, she picked up her pace and strode toward the elevator—the doors were just about to close. She slid her hand between the doors, and they opened. An elderly German couple frowned; she apologized. The doors closed, and she saw the 11th floor's button was lit. The elevator started to climb; she pushed the button for floor 3.

Turner watched as the man followed Lear into the apartment complex. Then, he stepped away from the outdoor restaurant table he had slid behind and scooted around the space heater before heading back toward the apartment complex's back door where he would take the stairs up to meet her.

Lear exited the elevator and made her way swiftly down the long hallway. At the far end was a door with the sign reading "Ausgang" above it that led to the stairwell. Almost clear. She would go down the stairs, out the back door, and head straight for the waiting car, which would be two blocks away. She knew the car would be there because if everything had gone as planned, they would have already been picked up on the other end of the Kurfürstendamm; her team would have switched to the alternate pick-up location immediately when she and Officer Turner hadn't shown up. She continued to hustle toward the door.

* * *

Turner entered the stairwell and was already on the second flight when he heard the door below crash open. He looked down and saw three men with guns drawn enter the building. They saw him and started racing up the stairs. Then, he heard something that made his insides turn: They were shouting at each other—in Russian. He ran up the last flight to the door numbered 3.

Lear grinned as she moved to within ten feet of the stairwell door. *Piece of cake.* Then, the door burst open. It was Turner.

"Run!" he said.

She stopped, confused. "Brian—"

"Now!"

She turned and sprinted away down the hall.

STATE HIGHWAY 250, NEW YORK

THURSDAY, JUNE 29, 2006

"We're almost to our little bungalow, babycakes," Iggi Hilliard said to his wife as he tapped his fingers on the steering wheel. "Gonna seduce your ass before our company arrives."

Maria Hilliard's large sunglasses stayed focused on the *People* magazine she held in her hands. "Keep dreamin'," she said. "Plus, you just got some last night, and you're lucky you got that." She grinned. "Don't you need a few days to recover?"

He started to roll up his window.

"No," Maria said. "I like to feel the breeze while we drive by the lake."

"C'mon. A little AC, please? It's hot out and not even 9 a.m."

"No," came the final answer behind the magazine.

He rolled his window back down and then observed his reflection in the rearview mirror. His brown forehead was dotted with perspiration, and the black hair that rose four inches from his scalp became wet as he wiped the sweat from his forehead through his hair. His thick full beard was helping to hide the tell-tale signs of weight gain on cheeks and neck. Monday nights filled with beer and snacks at the bowling alley followed by all of the goodies each press box included during football weekends hadn't helped. His playing days were long gone, but now he got to do the next best thing: get paid to watch games, get fed free, mostly delicious, food while he watched and took notes, mingle with prime-time coaches and players and sometimes interview them, and then write it all up for the *Democrat and Chronicle*. "So my thirty-three-year-old body doesn't look like Donovan McNabb's anymore," he said. "I recover just fine."

Maria let out a giggle, "You're damn right it doesn't. You've got your own bowling ball starting to form." The wind blew through her black wavy hair. "This air is heaven."

Iggi took his left hand from the steering wheel and began to rub his belly, which, he had to admit, was out over his pants and close to the wheel. He was sitting though; when he stood up, it all evened out. At least that's what he told himself. "Didn't you notice last night, how I used this to my advantage? It kept my rhythm smooth like a pendulum." He pointed to his gut. "This thing is a weapon."

She dismissed his argument with, "Uh huh," and kept flipping through her magazine.

The road curved to the left, and the trees began to thin out as lakeside houses began to sprout up. Beyond the properties, Lake Ontario was a sheen of cobalt. A few triangles of canvas were spread out on the water like signposts on a road that stretched in every direction. *You'd never get me on a sailboat.* Too slow. Too boring. Too much work. Powerboat or nothing. Slam the throttle down and let's go already.

Maria put the magazine back in her tote bag.

Shoot. She's going to start talking about the weekend.

She looked past him at the lake. "I can't wait for you to meet Cal."

"How come I've never met him before?"

"Well, he's been a little busy since 9/11, don't you think?"

Right. He was a cop. A Detroit cop. "I forgot," Iggi said.

"Well, he's my friend," she said. "So be nice."

"I can't promise that," said Iggi. "He's got to prove himself."

"Why?"

"I can't believe you're asking me that."

She took off her glasses and looked out her window at the passing road signs. "I'm sorry," she said. "I promise he's good."

Iggi exhaled. What does *good* even mean? "We'll see."

She gave his right forearm a quick rub and then put her glasses back on. "Haley isn't seeing anyone right now."

Man, she switches topics fast—always has. "The birthday girl is single, huh?"

"Ridiculous, right? But she's so introverted, I don't see how she's ever going to meet anyone," she said. "I mean, I'm her one friend at school, and if I didn't go down to have lunch with her once a week, I think she'd just stay in her physics lab and no one would ever see her."

Iggi rubbed his beard as he thought. He'd been distracted the past few weeks going back and forth with his editor on the phone over the book manuscript. The editor wasn't pleased with what he had called the 'nuclear missiles' Iggi had shot in the opening chapter about the culture of losing in the Detroit Lions's locker room and the irony of a fierce man-eating lion serving as the franchise logo. The editor was also unsure of the title: *Not with a Roar but a*

Whimper: Three Decades of Ineptitude. He wondered why Iggi didn't write a book about the Bills instead—at least they *had gone* to the Super Bowl four times in a row. Iggi had replied, "New York is where I make my living, Robert, but Detroit is where I'm from. I don't shit where I eat." Anyway, he hadn't had time to think of this weekend—let alone the guest list—until they were getting into the car.

Usually, they invited Maria's college roommate and her husband to stay with them over the July Fourth weekend, but the couple was unavailable. Like the professional athletes he covered, Iggi liked routine. Maria liked to say he needed someone to give him a routine. Left to his own devices, without some game or season to prepare for, his daily journey became unpredictable and inefficient. Now, he was being asked to help host two people he didn't know. Of all years, why did the Fourth have to be on a Tuesday this year? That meant that the guests would be arriving on Friday and departing on Wednesday. In sports parlance this was like playing man-on-man defense for the entire season and suddenly being asked to play zone defense in the championship game—and the championship game was going to take three overtime periods to decide. And why *these* two people? Well, he could somewhat understand Maria's invitation to Cal. Some childhood bonds lasted a lifetime. But Haley? The quiet-as-a-mouse math and physics teacher whom he had seen only once? Twice? Anyway, the last time had been at a bar last year during a boring, end-of-the-year faculty get together, which he had escaped by inventing a work emergency while using the restroom and then delivering his lines with feigned regret and surprise to the huddled group of worn out teachers.

Great. A Detroit cop and Haley. Wait a minute.

"I know what you're up to," he said, giving the steering wheel a tap like a coach giving a player a pat on the butt for a good play.

"And what is that?" Maria said.

"You're at it again. Trying to play matchmaker with our guests."

Maria picked up her plastic cup of Starbucks iced coffee and took a sip through the straw. "We'll just have to find out about that."

"Jesus," Iggi said. "Is that all this weekend is? Some booty call?" He paused. "Are you sure Steve and Val can't make it?"

"Let it go," she said.

Iggi shook his head in frustration. "I just want it to be like it always is. Besides, you're leaving me in another week to go 'teach for America' for a month. Can't we have one summer where someone else goes and helps the damn kids?"

"Not a chance. I need my time away doing the Lord's work."

"What about when we have kids? Will you leave then?"

She grinned. "So, now you're thinking about us having kids again?"

"Anything to get my mind off this weekend. I really don't wanna hang with new people."

"You know my girl is beautiful, but her life is so damn boring! I've gotta get her out of her funk. Being with us and meeting Cal will be a good thing. And Cal? His divorce was finalized this past fall, so he's back in the game."

Iggi cracked a smile.

She took another sip of her coffee and then set it down. "What?"

"You know you make my ass weak when you use sports to describe life," he said. "This weekend is going to be a disaster."

"It's going to be fine." Maria checked her watch. "Besides, tonight is all ours."

Their SUV climbed up a hill and then started down the other side. At the bottom, the woods thickened around them as the road curved away from the lake.

Maria's family had immigrated to the United States from Cuba over one hundred years ago, initially settling in Tampa, Florida, before moving north.

The towering log cabin had been in her family for three generations, set in the middle of three wooded beachfront lots, and had been constructed by her grandfather Miguel Ernesto Torres in the spring of 1961 after Kennedy's narrow election win, for which Torres had helped get out the vote and was compensated with manila envelopes stuffed with cash. As a fellow World War II veteran and Roman Catholic, Torres had wept tears of joy when it was announced that Kennedy had won, and he had wept tears of sorrow when it was announced that JFK had been shot and killed in Dallas. These were the only times that Maria's father had ever witnessed his father cry, and it had become a family legend—brought up, quietly shared, and then passed down within the log walls of the cabin: "Las dos veces padre lloró"—the two times father cried.

Miguel Torres had wanted a home for his family that would serve as its heart—a pulsating center where celebrations would be held, yet also a sanctuary that would sustain them through life's challenges. However, he had warned that the physical structure alone would never sustain them: 'A house on the beach does not solve any of life's problems.' What would sustain them was gathering at the cabin and drawing strength from each other. This had been his vision, and the house he had built was an architectural masterpiece.

The log home's great room had floor to ceiling windows that allowed for a sublime sight of Lake Ontario, and there were three bedrooms upstairs all with lake views. Besides the great room on the first floor was a den, kitchen, walk-in pantry, and dining room. The addition had been built in 1987 and included a first-floor master suite, entertainment room, wine cellar, and sun room.

Her grandparents were gone, and the house now belonged to her parents. But they lived in Boston and rarely used it, whereas Maria and Iggi lived only an hour away from the cabin and spent almost every weekend there. Some weekends Iggi would be away covering sports, and she would have time to herself. She rarely had company as her younger brother and his family didn't like the water and had no interest in visiting what had been the family's rallying point for forty years. They were in Boston too, and, as much as her two nephews loved Aunt Maria and Uncle Iggi, they had been spoiled—ruined?—by the fast pace of Boston compared to the solitude of the cabin. If her grandfather had still been alive, then he might have cried a third time knowing this. Friends? There had been a few teacher retreats there, but those had tapered off when her colleagues started having children. The advance from Iggi's book had provided them with enough money to buy the house from her parents. Maria suspected they would be willing to part with it because there were good memories there, but too many echoes whenever they visited. Perhaps because she was another generation removed, she didn't have her grandparents' presence haunting her down the hallways, up and down the staircase, or in every doorway. Her father wasn't an emotional man, but she knew it hurt too much for him to be there with his parents gone.

The woods surrounding the cabin extended for fifty yards toward the road and around thirty yards to the right and left. The neighbors had not sold their extra lots. The houses could not be seen; only by sitting on their beach or swimming were they aware that they had neighbors, and that was only if the neighbors emerged from their residences or had company. The closest town was Bay Harbor—five miles away and far enough to make it a pain if an item had been left off the grocery list by accident. While sitting on the back deck looking out at Lake Ontario in complete silence, she often thought that if there was ever a stretch of property for a celebrity to disappear from the spotlight, this was it. She teased Iggi that he needed this place to hide when angry fans read his honest column every week. He joked back that if the Lions fans ever found the cabin, they might burn it down.

Her routine during the past school year had become more of a Friday countdown every week—watching the clock like the students until the final bell rang. After trying to convince young 12th grade minds that books like *Beloved*

16

and *One Hundred Years of Solitude* should be cherished and pondered, she would exit the brick fortress moments after the bell and speed out of the school's back lot. It took fifteen minutes to navigate the city traffic until she hit State Highway 250. Once on 250, it was just under an hour to reach the grocery store in Bay Harbor where she'd stock up for the weekend and then travel the final miles to her getaway. If the weather permitted, she would lower the windows and turn up the radio. She wished a nurse could be sitting in the passenger seat taking her blood pressure at that exact moment.

Iggi parked the car in the handicapped spot closest to the big doors that welcomed shoppers into Danny's Market. From the glovebox, he removed a white and blue press pass encased in plastic with a black lanyard wrapped around it. He unwound the lanyard, found the knot he had tied to shorten the length, and then used it to hang the press pass from his rearview mirror.

"Cha Ching," Iggi said.

"You're ridiculous."

Iggi whistled the theme to Monday Night Football as they exited the vehicle. "If a cop happens to drive by, it looks just like a permit."

Maria adjusted the purse strap on her right shoulder. "How long have you been doing this?"

Iggi patted his round stomach. "Ever since this little guy started to form."

Maria peered around the parking lot, expecting a patrol car to pull up any minute and arrest them. The lot was quiet. "Let's get this done," she said, pushing his hand away as he tried to hold hers.

Iggi shivered as they crossed through the A/C boundary and approached the grocery carts. His hands hovered over a cart's handles.

"Oh, C'mon!" Maria said and grasped the handles.

Iggi pulled his feet back just in time to avoid them getting run over. "Shit's cold in here," he said.

Recently, 'Beer Caves' had started to sprout up in gas stations across the country, and Iggi got a kick out of going in and freezing his ass off for a minute while grabbing cold beer—*nothing* beat cold beer—and watching his breath escape into the atmosphere. But Beer-Cave temperatures in a grocery store? Guy must be paying a fortune to keep the place cool.

"Let's *go*," said Maria, looking back at him.

They made their way down the familiar aisles with Maria maneuvering the cart around other shoppers like a racecar driver. *She's worried about my press pass being used to park in handicapped parking. Such a rule follower. Relax, girl.*

He walked alongside the cart and nodded as items like steak, hamburgers, hotdogs, chicken, and bratwurst got added to the cart. *Hell, yes. Time to grill. Thank God Maria tackled everything else in the kitchen.*

She threw in spaghetti, garlic bread, Caesar salad, potato salad, baked beans, macaroni salad, Ruffles potato chips, pickles, lunch meat, bread, onions, mushrooms, bacon, eggs, ingredients for homemade waffles, a massive bag of Dunkin' Donuts coffee (his favorite), vanilla ice cream, and—his eyes got greedy—ingredients for Maria's special raspberry pie.

They turned the corner and went down the final aisle—drinks.

Non-negotiables first: Into the cart, he placed two cases of Bud Light and a 12-pack of Pepsi (Coke could go to hell), while Maria put in a 12-pack of Diet Pepsi and directed him to load up two cases of bottled water.

They paused. "Now, what wine should we go with?" Maria said.

"Don't tell me they're wine snobs," said Iggi. "This is the Fourth of July; beer is where it's at."

She rolled her eyes and walked past him.

"What? Am I right, or am I right?"

She picked up two bottles of merlot and two bottles of chardonnay and put them in the cart. "It's what our *guests* want that is important. Cal will drink beer with you, but the wine will go with dinner."

"There isn't a thing in this cart that beer doesn't go with."

"Waffles?"

"Watch me," Iggi said.

She looked at their full cart. "Let's check out and head next door."

"What's next door?"

"Dorne's Liquor Store. Cal likes Scotch and Haley and I are having Margaritas on the beach." She maneuvered the cart around a young couple arguing over a bottle of wine. 'It doesn't finish well.' 'Not enough body.' 'They've probably never even tasted a Malbec.' *Christ.*

Iggi shook his head. "I thought you said he'd have beer with me."

They reached the end of the aisle. "He will," she said over her shoulder. Seeing the coast was clear, she crossed the main aisle and arrived at the checkout counter. Iggi took a *Sports Illustrated* off the rack and put it in; Maria grabbed *People*, *Bazaar*, and *Redbook*.

"These won't be around too much longer will they?" Iggi said looking down at the magazines.

"I'm afraid not," Maria said.

Iggi started loading items onto the register's conveyor belt. "Want me to go next door while you pay?"

She searched her purse for the checkbook. "No, let's go together."

"What were you thinking for dinner tonight?" he said while hoisting one of the cases of Bud Light out from underneath the cart's basket.

"I was thinking about a spinach smoothie."

Iggi's eyes narrowed. "What?"

She pinched his arm. "Just kidding. How about we pick up pizza and wings from Miss J's?"

He picked up the second case of Bud. "Now you're talkin'."

* * *

They exited Dorne's Liquor store and headed for the SUV. The sun was rising higher and the muggy heat was suffocating.

"What was all that shit about single malt versus blend the owner was talking about in there?" Iggi asked, pushing their overflowing cart.

Maria held a side of the cart with one hand and a black plastic bag containing the scotch, tequila, and margarita mix in her other hand. "I don't know," she said. "Just that the single malt was better or something."

"It sure was more expensive," he replied. "What in the hell does that guy know? And since when do people introduce themselves by giving their age and middle name?"

When the towering figure had approached them in the store, Iggi had momentarily slipped into his sports reporter character and asked if he had ever played football.

The man had rubbed his beard—every bit as big as Iggi's—and said, "No. In my forty-seven years of life, I've stayed away."

Maria said, "Great, Mister—" and searched for a nametag.

"Rick Gregory Dorne at your service," he said.

"Okay, Mister Do—"

"Rick," he cut her off.

She nodded. "We're in need of a little help selecting a bottle of scotch for a friend."

With his hands behind his back, the right wrist held by the left hand, Rick thoughtfully nodded and said, "If I'm asked."

Iggi and Maria looked at each other and then back at Rick. "Um, you're asked," she said impatiently. "What should we get?"

This was the wrong question to ask. Rick went on a three-minute-long history of scotch peppered with bar war stories of him drinking particular brands of scotch until closing time at hole-in-the-wall establishments in New

Jersey. It was, "I'm an old bar horse myself—grew up in 'em," and "I know my way around a bar stool," followed by, "It was three against one, and I kicked all their asses." His last tale ended in a wide grin and the triumphant declaration, "I *know* how to navigate a bar." Simultaneously, he placed a seventy-five-dollar bottle of The Macallan in Maria's hands. Iggi had watched, mesmerized. Rick had placed his hands behind his back once again and said, "A Detroit cop...Yeah, in my humble opinion, he'll love this, darlin'."

"You have got to be kidding me!" Iggi shouted as they neared the vehicle.

"Uh huh," Maria said. "And *you're* payin' for it."

Underneath the driver side windshield wiper blade was a yellow ticket.

2

Haley Girard sprinted the last hundred yards and crossed the finish line of her driveway. The afternoon heat seemed to make the blacktop underneath her shoes pulsate in rhythm with her heartbeat as she put her hands on her hips and walked on down to the end of the cul-de-sac. Her quads and calves burned as she got her breathing under control with each step. None of her neighbors were out, which was just as well. Small talk bored her and most of the residents on Orchard Drive were around ten years older than her, married, and had children. There was one other single person, Mike something-or-other, who was her age but worked from home for a computer software company and was never seen. Actually, most of her neighbors and their children were never outside. Here it was 5 p.m. on a late June day in the summer, and the neighborhood was a ghost town. When she was growing up, the kids never seemed to be anywhere but outside—riding bikes, playing tag, jump roping with friends, and playing sports of any kind. Now, it seemed like the kids were never anywhere but *inside*. She looked around at the neatly trimmed lawns that surrounded the end of the cul-de-sac. A sprinkler system came to life, and she acted like the strip of grass between the road and sidewalk was a tiny stream and hopped over it onto the sidewalk. She paused for a moment as the sprinkler twitched toward her. Then, she walked through the spray of cold water and basked in its relief. Despite the heat, the afternoon miles had been easier than the morning miles today. She didn't know why.

A neighbor poked his head out from behind his front door and then pulled it back inside when Haley spotted him. She continued around the sidewalk and headed back toward her home—no one else emerged from the street of houses.

Inside her kitchen, she poured a tall glass of water and dropped two cubes of ice in from one of the two trays in her freezer. A box fan that she had set on the wicker seat of one of her kitchen table chairs took fresh air from an open living room window and blew it toward another fan set up at the end of her main hallway, which took the air and moved it to the bedrooms. It was warm air, but at least it was circulating. One day, she'd have central air put in, but right now she couldn't justify the electric bill for just three months. Fans and open windows hadn't inconvenienced her when she was a kid. Except for the windows that she had open to help the air flow, she kept the shades drawn and the lights off in her house, which kept things cooler and helped her maintain her privacy. Although, with the lack of neighbors outside, she was sure that she could walk through the house in the nude with the shades open and there would be no one to see her.

She took a long sip from her glass of ice water and sat down in the middle of the living room floor where she set her water glass aside, spread her legs, and started to stretch. Increasing to two runs per day since March had paid off. Her energy and focus had returned, and she was sleeping better. The doubling of her protected time for stress relief had allowed her to sweat out the disappointments, frustrations, anger, confusion, fear, and nightmares. Her weight was now less than before December. The depressed months of January and February where she had put on fifteen pounds and finished off bottle after bottle of chardonnay upon completing each teaching day seemed far away. Her only social events in the past few months were the occasional dinners with Maria.

And now she had been invited by Maria to spend the July 4th holiday with her, her husband, and a childhood friend that Maria hadn't seen in years, who was single, "And I repeat, single," Maria had said to her. Wonderful. More new people to meet. She had thought about cancelling but had been advised to stay busy and connected or suffer the fate of January and February all over again. When faced with that choice, she had decided to accept Maria's invitation.

She finished her stretching routine and headed down the hallway. She'd shower, have a light supper, pack for the trip, and then continue reading this month's book, *The Kite Runner*. Her first baby step to break out of her introverted fortress in early March had been to join a book-of-the-month club at her local library. So far, it hadn't been too bad. She wasn't interested in analyzing fiction and wasn't looking for much conversation either. It was more about being around people and away from her home. The club bylaws stated that you didn't have to talk if you didn't want to but that conversation was encouraged. During the first few club meetings, she had nodded and quietly consumed her tea and cookies after the obligatory round robin introductions and hellos. "Hi, I'm Haley," were the only words she had said. The club would be discussing *The Kite Runner* at the end of July, and as she looked at the book on her nightstand while she entered her bedroom and started to undress, she realized that she was actually looking forward to the next meeting. Maybe she would offer an opinion this time—or, maybe not. She stepped into the bathroom and closed the door behind her, locking it—she hadn't let go of that habit, not yet.

As the cold water began to needle her skin, she was completely unaware that a car had gone past her house, driven down to the end of the cul-de-sac, turned around, stopped at the end of her driveway for a few seconds, and then driven away.

The fire crackled and popped in the cabin's massive hearth. It was the short span of time at night where the light cast by the fire across the room equaled the dimming sunlight cast across Lake Ontario. Iggi sat on the maroon rug that covered most of the living room's wooden floor. His back was against the brown leather couch, and in his hand was a glass of scotch.

"Maybe that Dorne guy knew his stuff," Iggi said, taking a sip. "This stuff is gold." He turned his head to the left and peered out the towering glass windows at the calm surface of the lake. "See? Now why can't it stay this way all weekend? Just you and me."

Maria sat in the recliner and drank from a stemless wine glass. "You're gonna have to get over it. They're coming tomorrow."

Iggi frowned and went back to staring at the fire. "I've been re-thinking the situation. I can handle Miss Introvert, but do we have to have the cop here?"

Maria crossed her legs, and the old recliner groaned as she reached over and set her wine glass down on the end table. "Give the guy a break," she said. "Trust me, you two are going to be fine."

Iggi rubbed his hand across the smooth dimples in the glass. "Where did you say he grew up?"

"Detroit. Same as you."

"I *guarantee* it wasn't the same Detroit I grew up in."

"Are you saying that *I* didn't grow up in that same Detroit?" she asked.

He drained the rest of his scotch. "No, I didn't mean it like that."

"He was there for me."

Iggi looked out the windows again. "How?"

3

DETROIT, APRIL 1985

Nine-year-old Maria Marcela Torres walked along the cracked sidewalk toward her home after another boring day of school. The zipper had broken on her backpack, and almost half of her green-colored Trapper Keeper stuck out the top, threatening to escape if she went any faster.

"Keep up," she told her younger brother, Marco.

Marco adjusted his thick glasses once again and kept his eyes glued to the ground. She knew he was scared of walking home, but at some point he had to get over his fear. Their father had told them that he'd been in many fights growing up and that it was a part of life. For Dante Torres, the rule was simple: If a fight cannot be avoided, then you fight until you finish it. Period. He had tried to continue his father's tradition, which was to ask his children when they sat down to dinner at exactly 6 p.m. every night, "Did you get into a fight today?" If 'no', then they would say grace and eat. If 'yes', then he would ask,

"Did you win?" Their mom, Sofia, put an end to the tradition after the first night. However, their father would still check in with them when their mother wasn't around.

She walked for another block and then looked back again. Marco was falling further behind. *C'mon.* She stopped. They were three blocks from their one-story yellow-colored house with brown shingles—two more blocks down this sidewalk and then one block to the right. If there was one part of the path home that scared her, it was the next block. There was always a group of teenagers standing at the corner passing around a weird-smelling cigarette. There were usually two white boys, one white girl, two black girls, and one black boy who was older than the rest. They were always calling him "Junior" because he'd had to repeat 8th grade in his junior high school. She didn't know if he minded the nickname. His older brother had been shot and killed on that corner one humid summer night five years ago—right in front of a ten-year-old Junior. Maria could still hear his mother's screams that night from Junior's driveway.

After witnessing her brother get made fun of by the group one day, she had approached her father. "Ignore 'em and get home; you're not big enough to fight them yet," he had said. She had wanted to tell her mother, but her mother didn't get home from work until 5 o'clock each day. Yes, her mother could soothe Marco, but there was nothing she could do to help the situation. Neither could Maria's father; he didn't get home until a quarter to 6 every night. She would learn later that she and her brother were "latchkey kids," like most Generation Xers, but, for right now, she just thought that it was normal to come home, lock the door, get herself and Marco a snack, do her homework while he watched TV, and wait for their parents to get home.

Maria vowed to avoid the bullies. She found that if they left right after school, they could make it home before Junior and his friends made it out to the corner. But today her brother had taken his sweet time in the bathroom after school, and they were late.

"*C'mon*, Marco. You wanna get made fun of again?"

Marco bent down to tie his right shoe.

"Ugh!" she said, and ran back and helped him tie his shoe faster. "There. Got it? Now, let's move."

When she turned around, she felt a lump in her throat. Junior was leading the crew out of his house to take up station on the corner. She grabbed Marco's hand—it was shaking. "Don't look at them," she said. "We'll just walk past them and get home." They steadied themselves and pressed forward.

The wind was cold, and there were still patches of snow on the ground. Once again, a Michigan winter was holding on, refusing to thaw into spring. They crossed the street and were ten yards from the group when she heard Junior say, "Well, if it ain't the little spics from 'round the corner. Haven't seen you little worms lately." He took a puff from the funny smelling cigarette and passed it to one of the white boys. "Where you two been?"

Maria gritted her teeth. She knew the slur and hated it, but if they could just get past them... They avoided eye contact and started to walk around the group. Junior stepped in front of them, blocking their way. He put his hand on Marco's shoulder. "Hey, I'm talkin' to you!" he shouted.

Marco started to tear up.

"Leave him alone," Maria said. "We're heading home."

"Shut up, *chica*," he said. "I just want to hear the little man answer me," Junior said, smiling. The group laughed, and then the white girl said, "They're both scared shits, Junior. Don't waste your time."

Maria tried to pull Marco around Junior, but he pushed her back.

"Don't touch me!" Maria said.

Junior's smile disappeared, and he moved in front of her. "Oh yeah, what you gonna do about it? You thinkin' you gonna be singin' 'We Are the World' next week on the playground and shit. Girl, you ain't goin' nowhere."

Then, she heard a voice. "Hey, leave 'em alone."

Junior spun around and the crew parted. Maria could see a white boy of about thirteen sitting on his BMX bike with one foot on the pedal and one foot on the pavement. He put the kick stand down and approached the group.

"Who the fuck are you?" Junior said.

The boy wore jeans and a hooded Detroit Tigers sweatshirt. And as he got closer, Maria recognized him—his family had moved in down the street a few weeks ago. His dad was a cop. She'd never been this close to him though, and she now saw that he was almost as tall as Junior and looked strong. But those weren't the things that distinguished him; it was his brown eyes and the stare he was putting on Junior. He wasn't flinching.

"My name is Cal, and I'm telling you to leave them alone."

The two white boys moved back, sensing Cal's determination. The black girl spoke up. "C'mon, Junior. Waste his ass. This your block."

Junior made a fist with his right hand and started to walk toward Cal.

One of the white boys spoke up, "Man, Junior, watch it. His dad's a cop."

Junior paused. "That true?" he asked Cal.

"What my dad does has nothing to do with this," Cal said. "You're being a bully."

"You asked for this," Junior said and then lunged at Cal. He took a monster swing at Cal's head but his arm whiffed through the air. Cal swept his legs out from underneath him, and he fell, his back landing squarely on the street.

Suddenly, Cal was on top of Junior and had him in a head lock, pressing Junior's arm down over his mouth and nose, suffocating him. Cal's eyes were dull as he stared down into Junior's wide-open eyes.

With their leader down, the group split, leaving Cal, Junior, Maria, and Marco.

Junior started to shake from lack of oxygen. Cal held his grip for one more moment and then released. Junior gasped for air, and tried to sit up but couldn't. Cal hovered over him, and once Junior got his breath, he put up a hand. "Okay, okay."

Cal backed away. Then, he looked at Maria and Marco. "Head home."

"Thanks," Maria said, and then she took Marco's hand and they were off.

Junior sat up, and Cal offered him a hand.

"Man, you got to be kiddin' me," Junior said.

"Why's that?" Cal said.

"'Cause, you should've finished me off." There were tears coming down the sides of his cheeks.

Cal looked around. The neighborhood was quiet. He squatted down next to Junior. "You tryin' out for the baseball team next week?"

"What?"

"I'm new at our school, but I saw you pitching at the park after school a week ago. I didn't see anyone get a hit off you. You're good."

"You watched? How come you didn't play?"

"Had to keep helping my mom unload. We've still got a lot of stuff in our garage to get moved inside, and my dad isn't home much."

Junior shook his head. "I just got taken down on my own turf. I don't know if I can ever face my crew again."

"You don't have to," Cal said. "They're not much of a crew anyway. They chickened out after the action started. Forget them. Come try out for the team with me, and you won't have time to hang out with those losers after school anymore."

Junior wiped his face and stared at Cal like Cal had cat ears. "Man, it don't work that way."

"Who cares how it works. C'mon, let's try out." Cal looked around at the small deposits of snow. "It's barely warm enough to play."

"Can't disagree with that. What position you play?"

"Catcher."

Junior coughed. "Of course."

Cal put his hand on Junior's shoulder. "You get to wind up and throw the ball at me as hard as you want to for six or seven innings. Good deal, right?"

Junior smiled and nodded. He put out his hand. "Deal."

Cal shook it. "What's your name?"

"Jared."

"Let's practice at my place tomorrow after school." Cal pointed to a one-story white house with red shutters two blocks down. "Bring your glove."

"Okay. We straight."

They stood. As Cal turned to get on his bike, he heard the thump of the bass coming from an approaching car. It was a black Cadillac Seville with gold-plated rims and the rear tires jacked up. There were three high school-aged black boys inside. He waved; they ignored him. As he pedaled away, he heard one say, "Junior! Get inside, my man. We got work to do." Cal looked back and saw Jared get into the back seat. The car door slammed shut, and the Cadillac swerved around Cal as it accelerated down the street—the bass growing softer and softer.

NEW YORK, THURSDAY, JUNE 29, 2006

"Great. Another story about some white person saving a black person," Iggi said.

They were both sitting on the floor now, leaning against the couch.

Maria scooted a few feet away so that she could turn and face him. "You're wrong. Life has always been about people helping people. We all need saving, Iggi. I may not have grown up in the richest neighborhood, but I grew up in one where every neighbor sure as hell knew each other and was there for each other no matter what the color of his or her skin.

"Cal's dad made a huge difference in the neighborhood. Yes, he was a police officer, but the man influenced events by loving and serving his neighbors. It turned the tide. Daddy and he became friends and got all the neighbors together for cookouts, parties, you name it. No one had any money. I mean Cal's parents were the best off, and that was with a stay-at-home mom and a dad that probably made a little over twenty grand to put his life on the line every day; that was considered rich in my neighborhood. So, because no one had money, we all got tight and stretched every dollar. When it was someone's birthday, we all chipped in for the party. Didn't you ever notice that it was always the same kids around the cake for each birthday picture of mine?"

Iggi shook his head no.

"Anyway, the adults took responsibility for making sure we were safe, doing what we were supposed to do, and keeping us on track."

Iggi interrupted. "The group on the corner didn't mess with you again?"

"Never again," Maria said.

"Junior—"

"Jared," she corrected him.

He paused, surprised at her protectiveness. He started again. "*Jared* could have been anyone picked from a handful of my classmates when I was that age," Iggi said. "What happened to him?"

"He and Cal made the baseball team, and from then on they were inseparable. In high school, it became football in the fall, basketball in the winter, and baseball in the spring. They were always at Cal's house drawing up plays or practicing.

"Early on, there was this Cadillac—full of rough kids, gang-bangers—that rolled through. Jared used to run with them, which is another reason why I was scared of him."

Iggi leaned forward. "In my experience, those guys just don't go away."

"Cal's dad was ready. No one knows what he said to those boys, but they never showed up again. A year later, we heard that one of the boys had been found shot to death inside the car—the outside riddled with bullet holes and left in an empty lot on the other side of town. Cal's mom got close with Jared's mom, and they used to have coffee every morning on folding chairs in the driveway—no one had a porch. They would alternate days for whose driveway they would sit in. Either way, we waved and said hi to them as we all walked to school together: me, Marco, Cal, Jared, and another girl named Keisha."

"What happened to the kids who were hanging with Jared on the corner the day Cal showed up?"

"They tried to pull Jared back in, but he said no. So, they just went a few blocks over and started doing, and later selling, drugs there. One of the white boys got strangled to death on the orders of a bigtime Detroit dealer a few years later when it was discovered he was skimming money off the top. The other white boy is currently serving life in prison for Murder One. The black girl, her name is Melody, did just fine. Her family moved to Kalamazoo, and she ended up attending Western Michigan. She's an Elementary School Principal in Lansing. The white girl got pregnant—at 14—a few months after they switched neighborhood hangouts; I have no idea where she's at now."

"Where's Jared?"

"Assistant baseball coach at Central Michigan University. He's married and has two little boys."

"How do you know all of this? Didn't your family move out of the neighborhood when you were in high school?"

"Jared's mom keeps us informed—still lives in the same house. And Cal—" She started to tear up.

Iggi touched her shoulder. "What?"

"Cal's parents passed away. His mom to cancer, she was a heavy smoker, and his dad—" Maria took a breath, "—died in the line of duty."

Iggi started to rub her shoulder, but his face was stoic. "What happened to his dad?"

"I don't know. Cal doesn't talk about it."

Iggi became transfixed by the fire for a moment. Crackle. Pop. A log finally breaking down and falling over, sending sparks up.

34

"Cal got divorced around the time his mom was sick, and he moved back home to take care of her when he wasn't on patrol. After she died, he decided to stay in his old house."

"How's the neighborhood?"

"Not what it was when we were growing up, but Cal has a lot of his father in him. He watches over the neighborhood kids the best he can, and he goes over and has coffee with Jared's mother at least once a week."

"Did he have any kids with his ex-wife?"

"Thank heavens, no." Maria gave him a wicked grin. "I hate that bitch."

"When did you get so tough?"

She smiled. "When haven't I been tough?"

"All right, you've made your point," he said.

"Correction, *many* points," she smirked.

"*Many* points," he nodded and let out a laugh. You didn't get on Maria's bad side. No way, no sir. "I wish we would have talked about this before," he said.

"I know you don't like to talk about your years in Detroit, so I never brought it up."

Iggi's face went back to stone, and he nodded.

"But now, after all he's been through, he needs to be around friends."

"Well, he's still a cop."

"Jesus, Iggi, have you heard a word I just said?"

"I have," he said, "and I'm glad things worked out for your neighborhood. But that doesn't change what happened to *my* neighborhood."

"I know that. But Cal's a good guy."

The muscles in Iggi's face neither gave an approving nor a disapproving look—just an even front. He said nothing in return.

The fire continued to burn and warm the great room. They cuddled and watched the flames slowly die as the night came on.

5

SEPTEMBER 11, 2001 – 8:00 P.M.

The phone rang in Haley Girard's apartment. She hit the mute button on the television and continued to watch the news footage of the horrific day as she made her way from the living room to the kitchen. She paused in the middle of the carpet, retreated to the end table next to the couch, and grabbed her empty wine glass. The phone continued to ring, and she picked up her pace across the living room floor.

She had been in front of her second period physics class introducing the semester's Rube Goldberg project when one of the assistant principals had knocked on her door. She was a third-year teacher, which meant after one more year with no problems, her job would be protected as long as she continued to get decent evaluations and didn't get into trouble with the law. To some outside of the teaching profession, tenure after three years meant that as long as you had a heartbeat and showed up, you were good to go. Haley knew better, although it *was* next to impossible to fire a tenured, marginal teacher who showed up day after day. She had been nervous because this particular assistant principal never showed up unannounced to her class. Had she made a mistake? Did they know about the party the previous weekend at her fellow teacher's house where things had gotten out of hand? A joint had been passed around, which she had not participated in but had watched from her perch on the back-porch swing as others puffed away and then digressed into psychological babble about the value of an education. Had a parent called to complain about her class standards? Was she about to be fired? It had been worse than all of those fears. She had returned to her class to let them know that school would be let out in an hour. Then, she had turned on the television set in her room and saw the second World Trade Center tower crumble to the ground. Tears had not come, which had surprised her. What should have been an outpouring of watery emotion had turned into rage behind her eyes, which narrowed. Her jaw had started to pulsate. With her body warming with each passing second, she had looked out at her class full of students who were speechless as they stared at the television.

Approximately a glass of merlot remained in the bottle on the counter, and Haley began to empty the wine into her glass as she picked up the phone.

"Hello?"

A voice that sounded like it had endured an hour of sobbing spoke, "Haley, it's Brooke."

Hearing Brooke Saunders's broken voice sent Haley's mind racing through the possibilities. Did Brooke, her college roommate, have a medical emergency? Doubtful; they were both in their mid-twenties. Had one of her parents passed away? Please, no. Could the bad news be unrelated to today's events? Possibly. Perhaps something bad, but not tragic, had happened within the past few hours, and the horror of today was magnifying it. Or, did Brooke's news have to do with the events of today? Damn. Was it someone they knew? Who? Oh, God. Was it Nate? Haley knew they were getting serious—as in *marriage* serious—but why would Nate Martin be anywhere near New York, or D.C., or Pennsylvania? He was a school teacher like her and Brooke. Someone else? Time to find out.

"Hi, sweetie. What's wrong?" She immediately shook her head. *I am the world's worst comforter.*

"Haley, I just got off the phone with Kelly's mom."

"Kelly *Smith?*"

"Yes."

"What's going on?" God. Damnit. Why couldn't she think of anything better to say? Kelly Smith, the third musketeer for she and Brooke, was now a financial planner in Cortland, New York.

Brooke started to choke up. "Kelly was visiting a firm in the south tower this morning for training."

"Oh no," Haley said.

"The firm had offices above the floors where the plane hit, but her mom hasn't been able to reach Kelly on her cell phone," Brooke paused. "Oh, Haley. I don't know what to do."

Haley put her glass of wine down and thought. "We don't know anything for sure at this point, Brooke. Maybe her phone's battery died or there's no reception where she is. Or, maybe she got out and hasn't reached a place where she can phone anyone yet. I heard on TV that there are hundreds of people unaccounted for. Right now, we have to hold on to the hope that she got out."

There was silence. On the television was footage of a group of New York City firefighters, covered in ash, searching through the World Trade Center wreckage.

"Okay," Brooke said, sniffling.

"Let's keep each other informed if we hear anything."

"Do you have a cell phone?" Brooke said.

"No," Haley said. "But I have a phone next to my bed and one here in the kitchen. I'm not going anywhere tonight. Do you have a cell phone yet?"

"I bought my first one about a month ago, but it doesn't get good reception. Nate refuses to get one. I don't know why I bought it actually, I'm a teacher for crying out loud. I didn't see the need for it, but I was in the store and figured that this was where the world was headed, so I—God, why am I talking about this now?"

"It's okay," Haley said. "I think I'm in Nate's camp, but I understand why Kelly needs one. The financial game is high stakes and high stress. Let's pray that she calls someone soon."

Brooke seemed to feed off of Haley's strength, and she said in a calmer tone, "Okay. Okay. Thank you for being there for me."

"I'll let you know if I hear anything," Haley said, and the call ended.

She took a gulp of wine and started to watch the television again. It was hard to look away; in fact, once she had gotten home, she hadn't even left her apartment's living room all day with the exception of bathroom breaks and getting wine and food from her kitchen. She was still dressed in the slacks and blouse she had worn to school. She started to move toward the couch when it hit her. Her answering machine. Next to the phone in her bedroom.

She set her wine glass on an end table and walked down the hallway, more butterflies in her stomach with each step. *Please, no.* She entered her bedroom, turned on the light, and went around the foot of her bed until she reached the nightstand on the far side of the room where the phone and answering machine were. She felt a clammy sweat start all over her body. A red number '1' was blinking on the machine. She swallowed and pushed play.

"Haley, this is Kelly—"

Dear God. She could hear raised voices and commotion in the background.

"I'm in the South Tower of the World Trade Center. I can't get through to my parents so I'm cycling though contacts trying to reach someone. Look, I'm in the Sky Lobby on the 78th floor, packed in waiting for an express elevator to take me all the way down. I should make it on the next elevator. My battery is running low, so I might not have a way to call anyone until I get to safety. We started to evacuate—"

Haley breathed a sigh of relief. Everything was going to be okay.

"—about ten minutes ago, and I'm—"

Haley heard the voices in the background getting louder, then screaming, then...for a brief instant before the call ended...the sound of an explosion.

She sank onto the bed and started to cry while gripping the comforter with both hands, squeezing and pulling.

After calling Kelly's parents, Brooke, and then her own parents, Haley Girard walked over to her desktop computer in the corner of her living room and sat down. Her eyes were puffy but determined. She opened her internet browser and typed:

HOW TO JOIN THE C.I.A.

6

DETROIT, FRIDAY, JUNE 30, 2006 – 1:00 A.M.

Detective Cal Ripley popped a Dexedrine tablet, took a chug from his bottle of water, and swallowed. The other seven members from Detroit's Joint Terrorist Task Force (JTTF) did the same; they needed to be awake and alert. The unmarked black van carrying the team rolled down East 8 Mile Road past the Northeast Water Treatment Plant, and Cal checked his weapon, a .40 caliber Glock 22. The others followed suit, except for Dyson Westover, Cal's partner, who was driving the van. Bautista and Cherry, the team's FBI members, each carried a .40 caliber Glock 23 Smith & Wesson; Higgins and Horvath—H & H—had pump action tactical shotguns and grenades; Gore had a fully automatic Uzi slung over his shoulder and Sampson had an assault rifle slung over his. The team wore flak jackets, cameras, and radio headsets with ear buds and microphones. They were also equipped with tasers, OC pepper spray, handcuffs, and expandable PR-24 batons.

Bautista was Latino, Cal and Cherry were Caucasian, and the rest of the men were African-American, which mirrored the demographics of Detroit's police force. Cherry was the lone female.

A quarter mile behind them was a caravan of other police vehicles, each one slowly peeling off at different intersections to set up a perimeter surrounding the site where Cal's team would rush the house on Fairport Street, just south of Collingham Drive.

It had taken weeks of surveillance and intelligence gathering to zero in on the house, a herculean effort triggered by intercepted internet chat room posts outlining the plan for a major terrorist attack in Detroit. The attack would be within the next few days. The year prior, Detroit's 13 precincts had been consolidated into 6 Districts, and Cal and Dyson had worked the District where the house was located for the past year. When the internet chatter had been picked up and decoded, Cal's boss, Captain J. Brendan Montgomery, had handed Cal and Dyson off to JTTF for the job at the request of Agents Bautista and Cherry.

"Turning onto Fairport," Dyson said into his headset, and the van completed a smooth turn.

Cal, seated in the passenger seat, nodded. He looked back at the team seated on two benches across from each other in the modified van. Bautista gave him a thumbs up.

The target was a one-story brick home with white trim, like many on Fairport, that was just over a thousand square feet with two bedrooms, one bathroom, kitchen, living room, and an unfinished basement. There was a sliver of grass that ran the length of the street, separating the street from the sidewalk, and then a small yard before the two steps that led up to the front porch. The two other entrances were from the driveway on the north side and a back door on the east side.

Without the data provided from the chat rooms, finding the gathering place for the suspected terrorists would have been nearly impossible. Once the street name was deciphered, then the search had yielded one home that stood out from the rest: bought with cash in 2004 by one Matthew Jones. Jeff Rohrman Properties, who had handled the sale, had closed up over a year ago. Mr. Rohrman had not been located, and no records had been found.

The JTTF had found a rental one block down and had moved two undercover officers posing as newlyweds into the house. For the past two weeks, they had gone from door to door introducing themselves to their neighbors and casually asking about the one-story house owned by Mr. Matthew Jones. Up until a month ago, none of the neighbors had seen Mr. Jones or anyone else in or near the house since the 'For Sale' sign had been taken down two years ago. Then in May a Ford Taurus had been seen in the driveway. Two middle-aged men wearing baseball caps had exited the car and entered the house from a side entrance around 10 p.m. one evening, a neighbor said, but the car was gone the next morning. Then, there had been a brown van that must have parked in the driveway during the night because it wasn't there when the neighbors went to sleep but was there in the morning. No one was seen during the day, and the next morning, the van was gone.

Spotters from the rented house radioed in that the Taurus was in the driveway. There was no sign of the brown van. The in-place back-up JTTF team members emerged from the rented house's back door and made their way swiftly across the street and down the sidewalk until they had eyes on all doors and windows of the target house.

Dyson slowed the vehicle as the target came into view. He could see some of the back-up team members in position. Cal hit the button, unlocking the doors, and put his hand on the passenger door handle. In the back of the van, Higgins grasped the rear door handle. The rest raised their weapons.

Two houses away...

One house away...

Dyson pulled the van onto the grass section, put it in park, and shut the engine off. The team exited in a flurry. H & H headed for the front door, while Cal and Dyson headed for the side entrance with Gore backing them up and covering the northern and western sides of the house. Bautista and Cherry sprinted for the rear entrance. Sampson took position in the backyard to offer support and cover the eastern and southern sides of the house.

In position now, Bautista gave the command, "Go."

H & H broke down the front door and threw concussion grenades in. A lightening flash, a bang, followed by the sound of broken glass. Then, H & H were inside the living room and saw two men down on the floor, both reaching for automatic rifles that had fallen onto the ground next to them. The living area was sparse with only one couch and two cots where the men had been asleep. As they moved toward the downed men, another man appeared in the hallway and raised a handgun at them. Crack! He lurched forward as if hit by a linebacker from behind. His body fell, exposing Bautista and Cherry standing ten feet behind him with their weapons drawn. H & H each took a man and handcuffed his hands behind his back and then zip-tied his ankles together. Higgins trained his shotgun on the two men—one was Caucasian, one was African-American. Horvath headed toward Bautista and Cherry. When he arrived at the body, he knelt down and examined the man's features. Middle Eastern? Maybe. Maybe not. He moved past the body and down the hallway.

Cal and Dyson entered through the side door off of the driveway and were met by a 9mm. Cal yelled for the man to put the weapon down, but the man squeezed off a round, hitting Dyson in the center of his flak jacket. Cal fired back, and the man dropped to the floor.

"You okay?" Cal asked.

44

Dyson looked down at his chest where the jacket had stopped the bullet. "Yeah, I'm fine." They heard more shots from the hallway, then a massive shotgun blast, followed by silence. Horvath appeared in the doorway off the kitchen.

He radioed, "Two down in the hallway, two tied up in the living room. One was trying to make it to the door that led to the basement."

Cal nodded and then heard Bautista on the radio, "Both bedrooms clear. One bedroom has clothing and three backpacks. Bring in the dog. Anything outside?"

Both Sampson and Gore radioed, "All clear out here."

The back-up team's leader said, "Perimeter clear."

Through the window, Cal could see a technician with a bomb sniffing dog on a leash exit the front door of the rented house and head for the target house.

Cal met them in the front yard, and they entered the house through the porch. Inside, the dog went to work. Nothing in the living room; nothing in bathroom or kitchen; nothing in the bedrooms or the backpacks—Cherry started to search the contents carefully. Then, the dog stopped outside of the door to the basement. Bautista and Cal were now behind the technician and dog. The technician said, "She's got something." He handed the dog's leash to Cal and checked the door for any explosives. Then, he slid a thin probe with a camera on the end underneath the door and rotated it around until he was sure that there was nothing on the other side. He withdrew the probe and nodded to Bautista. "Clear."

Through his earpiece, Cal heard, "Still no sign of the brown van from any of the checkpoints."

Bautista acknowledged and then asked, "Can anyone see into the basement windows?"

Outside, two back-up team members moved to the two basement windows and crouched down, shining their MAGLITEs inside. "My window is covered by paper," one of the men said. "Mine too," said the other.

Cal handed the leash back over to the bomb technician. "Ready?"

"Entering the basement," Bautista said.

Dyson walked up to Cal. "Be careful, partner."

"Will do," Cal said.

They all took a step back as Bautista slowly opened the door...

...nothing happened. Breathe, Cal told himself. Bautista flipped on the light switch, and the technician looked down the stairway, searching for any tripwires. Confident that there were none, he proceeded forward. Bautista followed, and Cal brought up the rear.

They descended the stairs quickly; the dog was pulling on the leash, sniffing like crazy and starting to whine. They reached the bottom of the stairway, and Cal and Bautista cleared the small room.

"Sweet Jesus," the technician said as he approached a large table in the center of the room. The dog sniffed all around the table, whining.

On the table were city maps, explosives, timers, wiring—a bomb maker's workshop.

Cal walked to the table. On one of the maps was a handwritten date: July 4th. "Shit," Cal said, looking up.

"What's this?" Bautista said, walking toward something in a corner below one of the paper-covered windows.

The bomb technician started to follow. The dog's nose snapped in the direction of Bautista; she started to whine.

The technician halted. "Wait!" he shouted to Bautista.

It was too late. Bautista felt the slight tug against his right foot as he stepped forward and tripped a wire. For a split second nothing happened, and then an explosion took off both of his legs. His torso and head smacked

46

against the concrete floor, and a pool of blood quickly formed around the severed thighs. His dead body twitched side to side.

Cal stumbled forward, his ears still ringing from the explosion, and keyed his microphone. "Agent down! Need a medic now!"

It was 3:45 a.m. when Cal walked into Captain J. Brendan Montgomery's office in Detroit's police headquarters. At six-foot-five, Montgomery towered over most of his force, but Cal was just two inches shorter and every bit as built as Montgomery. "That's good police work tonight, Detective Ripley," Montgomery said, handing Cal a glass of bourbon. The men did not clink glasses. They just drank.

"I heard they found the van," Cal said.

"Abandoned and wiped clean. We'll get 'em though. Already have some leads."

"I should have done something," Cal said, staring into his drink.

Montgomery put a huge hand on Cal's shoulder. "You *did* do something tonight, Ripley. You prevented a major terrorist attack in Detroit. Problem is, no one will ever know about it. Got to keep it under wraps—drive the public crazy if they knew about any of this. Ignorance is bliss; our brothers and sisters in Boston, New York, DC, Atlanta, Orlando, and LA have already stopped attempts like this. We just joined the club. Our officers are already making up some bullshit story to the neighbors. Thank God the explosion wasn't too loud."

"I meant—"

Montgomery cut him off. "I know what you meant. There's nothing you could have done for Bautista." He finished off his bourbon. "And you better get something through your head right now."

Cal looked into his eyes.

"This war is going to continue to have costs, Ripley. Now that it's happened in our own backyard, it's a little more real."

"Did Bautista have any...any family?"

Montgomery's tone softened a hair. "Wife and a kid."

Cal's eyes filled. "Christ." He paused to wipe his eyes and gather himself. "I should be the one to notify them," he said.

"No, son," Montgomery said. "The FBI has it; they like to take care of their own, like we do." He moved over to his desk and picked up a clipboard. He studied the printed-out spreadsheet. "I see that you're scheduled to take leave starting," he took a quick peek at his watch, "today through the 6th."

"Yes, Captain," he said. "But, now—I should be on duty for the 4th."

Montgomery set the clipboard down. "You've worked every 4th for the past 5 years, and with what happened tonight, you need to get away for a few days. Believe me, it'll all still be waiting for you when you get back." He walked toward Cal again. "Where are you headed?"

There is no talking him out of it. "I'm driving to New York. Got a childhood friend who has a cabin on Lake Ontario, just outside of Rochester."

Montgomery nodded. "Good. I don't wanna see your face around here until the 7th."

Cal shook his head in surrender. "Yes, sir."

He arrived home at 4:30 and undressed. Sitting on the edge of the bed in just his sweatpants, he petted his German Shepherd, Rosco, who kept trying to lick his hand. He thought of Bautista and Bautista's family. Suddenly, he missed his ex-wife and hated himself for it. He leaned over and wept.

7

FRIDAY, JUNE 30, 2006

The smell of fresh coffee wafted up toward the ceiling and down the open second floor hallway. Iggi followed his nose like a bloodhound toward the stairway. *The goddamned company gets here today.* Were there any moves he had left to play to avoid this whole gathering? He stopped at the top of the stairs and gazed out the living room windows at the flat sheen of blue water beyond the beach, calling to him. He could slip down to the garage, grab his kayak, and be gone before Maria noticed he was up. No, that would eventually come back around to bite him. She wouldn't call him out on it directly when he returned, but she would exact revenge slowly for the rest of the visit, which would make things even worse. Bad idea, even though kayaking was the only type of physical exercise he did besides sex and bowling. He rubbed his round belly. After punishing his body while playing football from middle school until his junior year in college, when he quit, he was done with working out and more than happy to write about the thrill of the hit, the recovered fumble, the pass break-up, the bruising run, or the miracle touchdown heave instead of living it himself.

Two kayakers entered his field of vision from the left and paddled with smooth even strokes, slicing their crafts through the calm water of Lake Ontario. Another thirty seconds ticked by, and they passed in front of the house, heading east along the coast. There were no other boats or people in the water. Not even a mile out toward Cedar Island—three square miles of heavily wooded cedar trees that was not only a stop for birds migrating south but also the proposed site for a wind farm where 75 wind turbines would provide electricity via an electrical transmission line to Bay Harbor. The New York Power Authority was still considering the proposal from a private company named Ontario-New York Island Power, but he had heard that the chances of it ever being approved were slim. It wouldn't be the first private-public battle on Lake Ontario. The latest debacle had been the cancellation of the Fast Ferry nicknamed *The Breeze*, a 284-foot boat that had transported passengers between Rochester and Toronto. When the private company that owned the ferry got into debt, the city of Rochester purchased the ferry. Then, less than a year later, the mayor had pulled the plug on any further funding; it was rumored that the ferry had lost around 10 million dollars during that period. What a waste of public funds. Iggi had even taken the ship, re-named *The Cat*, across the lake to cover a sporting event in Toronto last fall.

The kayakers were now out of view, and the scent of the coffee took him out of his trance. His watch said 9:30. There *was no escaping the vacation from hell.* He placed his hand on the knotty pine bannister and followed the stairs down. After pushing off the bottom step, the old wooden floor creaked with each pace as he made his way across the living room.

"Good morning," Maria said from the kitchen.

The aroma was even stronger down here—Dunkin' Donuts, his lifeline. *She's trying to get me in a good mood.* "Good morning," he said, entering the kitchen.

Maria turned away from him and walked to the coffee pot at the end of the counter. She had a cream-colored tank top on that had inched up her torso, exposing the smooth brown skin along the top of her hips and lower back. Below that were her tight-fitting cut-off jean shorts, the ones that drove him wild. *Now he wished they had made love last night.* The conversation had become too serious, which had submarined the mood and wasted the opportunity to be in the house alone. Now, with visitors, sex would cease to be spontaneous. Even if it was scheduled, the coupling could be derailed by an unforeseen knock on the bedroom door by a house guest wondering where extra toilet paper was.

She poured him a cup of coffee and brought it back, placing it in his hands. "Sleep well?"

He had. "Yeah." He took a heavenly pull from his cup as she pulled open the dishwasher. Inside, he was surprised to see it full. "I thought we were just using paper plates while the company was here?"

She took two plates out and put them in the cupboard above and to the left of the sink. "Yes, but on Haley's birthday night, I want to use these. Thirty is a milestone, and my mom's Pfaltzgraff dishes are around that age. I thought it would be a nice touch."

What? "I see," he said. He looked down at his watch. *You just checked it a few minutes ago, dumb ass.* "When are the troops arriving again?"

She continued removing dishes from the bottom tray and stacked them on the counter. "Sometime this afternoon," she said. "I already told you that."

He rubbed his eyes and took another sip of coffee. "Do I have time to take the kayak out to Cedar Island and back?"

She stopped. "Maybe, if you help me with these dishes, lazy bones."

He set his cup down and started to take the silverware out. "My father would have *never* done this shit," he said.

"Well, thank God you were born on this side of 1970 then," said Maria. "World's changin', baby."

Iggi rolled his eyes. After placing a handful of forks in the silverware drawer, he slid behind her and placed his hands on her hips. His enormous beard started to rub against her upper back while he kissed her neck. "Do we have time for anything else?"

She held firm. "Not right now. I've still got to make the beds and wash and dry the towels. And—"

He continued to nibble on her neck. "And what?" He grinned. Don't interrupt the master at work.

She stepped away. "And, I've already showered and dressed for the day." She put a finger to his lips. "Maybe tonight."

He reached for the jean shorts again. He was crumbling. *Don't beg, asshole...Jesus, that smile.* He caved. "Pleeeease?"

"No," she said. "Let's finish the dishes and then you can put the kayak in the water and work up an appetite."

She's got me, and she knows it. He bent over and picked up a spoon.

At 4 p.m., Haley Girard pulled her Chevy Blazer into the Hilliard's long driveway, and the vehicle meandered down the narrow path. Secluded. *Perfect,* Haley thought. After a slight turn to the right between two large rock piles, the blacktop straightened once again and eventually ended at a vacant rectangle of concrete in front of the cabin's 2-door garage. Where to park? In front of the door farthest away from the house? As a guest, that would be the most polite. But what if they had parked their car behind that door so that she could pull in closer to the house? Did they drive together or separately? And what about the other guest? Was he already here? *Stop overanalyzing! Park the damn car.*

She stopped her Blazer in front of the outer garage door. As she turned off the vehicle, she allowed herself a look at the cabin. A lot bigger than she thought it would be—and more beautiful. Rustic? Yes. But run-down? No. Don't hesitate. You need this time away. You need...*friends* right now. She grasped the handle. Everything is fine. She opened her door.

It was quiet outside, but a breeze off the water had managed to wrap around the house and touch her face as Haley stood up and stretched. She inhaled the fresh air through her nose, held it, and then exhaled through her mouth. After two more cycles, she began to relax. Control your breathing. Your thoughts: Let them come in and let them go out with your breaths. She closed her eyes. Breathe in—

The sound of a door opening followed by the jubilant shout, "Hey, gorgeous!" broke her concentration. Like dark shades being raised in order for a room to face the morning sun, Haley's eyes opened and saw Maria Hilliard prancing toward her. She managed a, "Hi," back before Maria collided with her.

Maria embraced her and squeezed hard. "You ready for some fun, birthday girl?"

Haley gave her a polite squeeze back and then attempted to disengage from the hug. Maria was having none of it, and continued to hang on.

Maria's husband Iggi walked through the open doorway and onto the concrete porch. She had only seen him once at a boring after-school social hour, but she remembered his thick black hair, which stood straight up and his coarse beard, which had only grown longer since she had last seen him. He met eyes with her and gave her what she could only describe as an 'Iggi for Mayor' smile.

Maria finally released her. "Let's get you inside and settled."

Iggi made it down the steps and to them. He reached out his hand and Haley shook it firmly. "Nice to see you again, Iggi."

"Great to see you too," he replied.

She caught Maria giving her husband an approving look. What was that all about?

"Where are your bags at, lady? Let's make this man here useful," she jabbed an elbow into Iggi's chest.

"I can get my own bags," Haley said.

"Uh, uh, uh." Maria said. "He's got it. Besides, he knows what room you're staying in."

Haley opened the trunk.

"The blue room, right?" Iggi said.

"Incredible," Maria shook her head. "No. The red room."

Iggi smiled again. "My bad," he said. "I got it."

"Thanks for having me over," Haley said, grabbing a small plaid suitcase and putting it on the concrete. She almost convinced herself that she meant it. Then, she pulled out a matching messenger bag and closed the trunk.

"That's it?" Iggi said, eyeing Maria. "Piece of cake." He picked up the two pieces of luggage and headed for the house.

Haley reached inside her SUV and pulled out her purse and a gift bag, which she handed to Maria. "For the weekend," she said and closed the driver side door.

"You shouldn't have."

"C'mon. Open it up."

Maria did and pulled out a bottle of merlot and a bottle of chardonnay. There was also a card inside. "This here is a statement, lady," Maria said, putting the bottles back in the bag. "I wondered which Haley I would be getting this weekend, and you just answered it." Maria pointed to the bottles. "We picked up a few of these too, so now I know it's on." She gave Haley another hug and then a surprising kiss on the cheek. "Let's get inside and see if my unreliable other half found the right bedroom."

Haley gave a little laugh.

Maria seized upon it. "I've already got you laughin'."

Haley looked around. "Has your other guest arrived yet?"

Maria gave a wicked grin. "No, Mr. Wonderful isn't here yet."

"Nothing is going to happen, Maria. You said he was recently divorced."

"Pfft. Like a year ago," she said. "You're fine."

"I'm here to relax with my friend," Haley said.

"He'll be here anyway." Maria winked.

They started to walk toward the front door when Haley stopped, fished through her purse, and then locked her car with her key remote.

Maria put a hand on her shoulder. "No one's going to steal your stuff out here."

They headed inside.

At the end of the Hilliard driveway, a black GMC Yukon pulled in, paused for a few seconds, then backed out and drove off in the direction it had come from.

C.I.A. HEADQUARTERS, MCLEAN, VIRGINIA
APRIL 2002

D r. Leiko Narita, the C.I.A.'s Deputy Director for Intelligence, sat down in a leather chair across from a matching couch where sat her head of the Office of Scientific & Weapons Research, Rolfe Judas. She passed Judas a blue legal-sized fastener file folder. "Why in the hell should I care about Haley Girard?"

Judas ran a hand through his black mane, which he refused to cut, and then worked his hand down to his thick salt and pepper colored beard—the kind a biblical prophet would have been proud of.

She'd seen the tic a thousand times. *C'mon. Out with it already.*

"She's going to be part of my special project," Judas said. On the coffee table between them was a tray with a fresh pitcher of coffee, a cup of creamer, a cup of sugar, two spoons, and two black coffee cups on matching saucers. "Coffee?" Judas said.

It's my office and he's offering. He needs something. Narita nodded, and Judas poured two cups—black for Narita, cream and loads of sugar for his. She cradled the cup in her hands. "I don't get it," Narita said, motioning to the blue file folder. "She applied online right after 9/11 like a thousand others—college roommate was killed in the south tower. Her background check was fine, boring in fact, and completed in less than a month. Twenty-five years old. 5'8". 125 pounds. Excellent scores: 4.0 GPA in high school. 32 in reading, 34 in English, and 36 in both science and math on the ACT. 4.0 at Western Michigan University for both undergrad in mathematics and Masters in Math Education." She waved a hand dismissively. "She's a high school math and physics teacher in Rochester. End of story, Rolfe."

Judas took a sip from his cup and grinned. "Which is exactly why I want to hire her." He sat back against the cushions. "We've been thrown into a whole new ballgame. The old ways will not do; we learned that the hard way. We need to get creative, and I think I've put together an option that could pay dividends down the road."

Narita crossed her long legs, and the navy-colored polyester pants she was wearing slid up her right ankle, exposing a small section of brown nylon. "I'm listening."

"We've recruited and hired educators before. Mostly, they come from the professor ranks and are contracted to work for us over the summer, sitting in claustrophobic rooms pouring over large amounts of data or in labs working out calculations and running experiments. At the end of the day they submit their findings to us on paper pads that are locked in safes for us to use as we see fit. They never know what we do with their work, but they are paid well for it and usually come back each summer to work some more for us. Right?"

She nodded.

"Now, you take young Haley Girard, here," he patted the blue file. "Based on her scores, we should have recruited her while she was still at Western

Michigan, but, hey, we thought we had enough analysts until...well... Now, we can't get enough analysts."

"You want her as an analyst? Fine. Hire her. Why are we talking?"

"I want her as an analyst at first, but then I want to use her and other educators who fit the mold as officers." He paused.

On purpose, she thought.

"Think about it. We have plenty of officers right now for most of our operations during the year, but with an educator-officer, we'd have someone way off the radar we could use during Thanksgiving, Christmas, Spring Break, and the entire summer. While all of our traditionally trained officers would be more familiar, these officers would be a tremendous asset to run drops under cover as tourists. For example, Teacher A saves up some money, decides to visit Mexico City, or Tel Aviv, or Rome, or Rio de Janiero, or Copenhagen during one of his or her vacations, and during the visit he or she performs a dead drop for us or meets with one of our agents. Then, he or she continues on with the vacation, comes back home, and goes back into the classroom like nothing ever happened. Once we get a reliable number of educators, we just rotate them so that they go on a mission once every few years. The cover is perfect. Teachers teach abroad all the time, and single teachers travel a lot over vacation." He studied his fingernails for a moment.

He's trying to give the idea time to take hold in my brain. Effective move. Now, he'll try to switch tactics and downplay the new roles.

"We wouldn't be training them to run agents like Tolkachev or Gordievsky, for Christ's sake, just providing a fresh face to handle the exchange."

Kudos. And now I'll play along. "And Girard is single."

"I'm always amazed at how much you can pick up from a file in just ten minutes."

Kissing ass never hurts either, and that started with the coffee offering you sneaky sonofabitch. Narita gave a slight grin, and she knew he would take it as a good sign. She could fool him and drop the hammer right now, but the truth was he had her attention. She took another sip of coffee, and he mirrored her by raising his cup.

"Her Myers-Briggs Type Indicator is INTJ, so she'll keep to herself and won't get too close to anyone, which also makes her a good candidate."

She set the cup down on the saucer with a *clink*. "The training?"

"We train them like every other officer, except we work even harder to keep their identities secret. In just over a month school will be out for the summer. I propose that we contact Ms. Girard—she's our only current teacher applicant out of thousands—and have her fly to Baltimore in June. In Baltimore, she'll check into a hotel and stay for one night. After she checks out, we'll have a car waiting for her in the underground garage. The car will take her to Langley, and she'll start her training. At the end of the summer, we'll reverse the procedure, use a different hotel with a pre-paid room under another name, and then she'll leave the next day and fly back to Rochester out of Reagan."

"What's her story for being gone all summer?"

"Mission trip. No K-12 educator will ever ask her about spreading the word of the Lord to a third world country over summer vacation. In fact, they'll ignore her, which is even better."

She pulled her glasses out of her white blouse's pocket, put them on, and then picked up the blue file and opened it. "So, this would be a pilot program with Ms. Girard as the test case?"

"Yes," Judas said.

She raised her eyes above the rim of her glasses at him. "Absolutely no recruiting until we see how she does this summer. And this stays between us. I'll notify the D.C.I., but only you and I will discuss the new program. Understood?"

"Yes."

"Funding?"

"All ready to go. I have approval of our discretionary off-books budget by the same small armed services subcommittee that I used last year. Wined and dined them at my townhouse—bastards cleaned out my brandy—but didn't tell them how we were going to use the funds."

"Good," Narita said.

"The money has already been transferred—a mix of unvouchered funds and untraceable moolah hidden in the Pentagon's budget. I plan to divert half of the cash in the account to fund the project."

"Authorized. Since only three people will know about the mission, we can't ask the computer in the basement to select a random name for us. We'll have to come up with it. Any suggestions?"

"Socrates."

An educator but also a method for examining topics by generating questions that, when discussed correctly, lead not to answers but only more questions. Perfect. "Agreed. Got any ideas for her legend?" She almost knew for certain that he did.

"How about this? Jennifer Anna Lear. Here's my thinking. She was born on July 2, 1976. From 1970 to 1984, Jennifer was the most common name in the United States for a girl. That takes care of the first name. In the Arthurian legend, Anna is Arthur's sister; Girard's brother's name is Arthur Richard Girard. Normally, we'd make a slight adjustment to her last name so that if someone pronounced it, then she wouldn't give herself up by responding to it since it was so close to her legend name."

"But we're not going to do that."

"No," he said. "We're breaking completely from Girard. Other than Lear being my favorite Shakespearean play, Haley is the middle child in her family. Arthur is older, and her younger sister is named Sandra. In the play, the middle daughter is named—"

"Regan," Narita interjected.

"You've read the play?"

"We had little choice in our re-education camp in Colorado during World War II. Other than the King James Version of the Bible and the Constitution, the only other book we were permitted to have was The Complete Works of William Shakespeare."

Judas sat forward. "I—I had no idea. We've worked together for almost twenty years."

"You've heard of order 9066 no doubt?"

He slowly nodded. "Pardon me, but I would have never guessed that after how this country treated you and other Japanese-Americans that you would have joined the C.I.A. to help *defend* the United States."

"Life is complex. Wouldn't you say?" She removed her glasses for a moment. "As for the twenty years, it's easy to forget that we all have private lives—people we were before we came to work for The Company."

His right eye made an ever so slight twitch, and he rubbed it.

He's wondering if I know that he likes men as well as women. No problem on this end, Rolfe. You love who you love, and I'll tell you that right now if you go there. Life is short, especially with what we do. Keep hittin' it, you beast.

He recovered. "How old were you?"

"I was almost 6 in 1943 when the government removed us from Sacramento and bused us to the internment camps."

"You read *King Lear* when you were six?"

"No, but my father did. Besides playing cards and keeping the stove fueled in the long rows of abhorrent barracks they forced us to live in, my father read. He had gone to the University of Southern California where he studied business, so he had never taken a Shakespeare course before. He chipped away at the book night after night under the one 60-watt lightbulb in our apartment's ceiling. Once he read *Lear*, he shared parts of the story with my brother and me before we went to bed at night."

Judas cut in. "He didn't tell you about Gloucester's eyes, did he?"

"C'mon. Give him some credit, Rolfe," she chided him. "No, that was one part he left for me to discover in college."

Judas wiped sweat off his brow. "But you never forgot the characters."

"Never. The entire experience will never leave me. I wanted to play baseball with the boys at our center, but girls were not allowed. So I studied instead. By the time we moved back to California in 1945, I was ahead of grade level. By the fall of 1955, I was enrolled as a freshman at Stanford majoring in Literature with a focus on the Renaissance. Thanks to dad, the Shakespeare bug had bitten me, and I couldn't get enough," she waved her hand. "Well, you know the rest."

"No, I don't," Judas said. "Tell me."

Why not? "Stayed there until I finished my doctorate and then got hired by Berkeley."

Judas raised an eyebrow.

"I know," she said. "I was good, but not *that* good. I looked at who was also applying, and there is no way I should have been hired. I later found out that it was due to some disingenuous initiative. Apparently, certain members of the department felt guilty for how Japanese Americans had been treated during World War II, and they hired me ahead of four other highly qualified individuals—two white males, one African-American female, and one Native American man. I didn't waste it, though. I stayed and achieved tenure in five years—no speed record, but no slouch either." She paused. "However, I couldn't get the experience of what happened to my family out of my mind. I never wanted another American citizen to go through anything like that. The conventional wisdom was to stay at Berkeley where I could make a difference, but I had come to believe that world crises are not prevented in any liberal arts departments. Now, an economics department like the University of Chicago's?

Sure. Let's face it, Friedman is the greatest intellectual of the twentieth century."

Judas searched his memory. "Friedman said, 'A society that puts equality before freedom will get neither. A society that puts freedom before equality will get a high degree of both.' Right?"

Narita smirked. "You *have* learned a thing or two."

Judas blushed. "C'mon, it's Friedman."

"True," she said. "So, I shocked my department and left Berkeley. Years later, I heard that when they found out I had risen to a leadership position in the C.I.A., they tried to erase me from any record that tied me to the university."

"No disrespect, but I'm surprised the C.I.A. hired you."

"Yeah, they were pretty much convinced that I was either a Japanese spy or a communist mole from Berkeley trying to infiltrate and disrupt The Company, but I eventually won them over." She paused. "Fast forward to a few months ago. I was about to submit my retirement papers, but then September changed my mind. There's still work to be done before I can walk away."

Judas remained silent.

She put her glasses back on. "So, in honor of the Bard's *best* play—I'm with you; *Hamlet* can go to hell—and the fact that our girl Haley Girard is the middle child, her last name will be Lear."

"That was my thinking," he said. "We should also screen potential officers to pair her with. Having them become familiar with each other while she's at The Farm will help speed up the process. Plus, if they have chemistry, we can even play the boyfriend-girlfriend or husband-wife angle on the operations."

"My instincts tell me that you already have someone in mind."

"I do."

"I admire your creativity, Rolfe. The path forward for this country and for the world is going to need some." She closed the file and uncrossed her legs.

"Notify Ms. Girard of her employment opportunity through the usual channels and make arrangements for this summer. You'll meet with me once a month in here to keep me updated. No electronic communication whatsoever. Take handwritten notes, lock them up, and then destroy them when you no longer need them. The same goes for Girard and the officer you have in mind."

"Yes, *ma'am*," Judas said.

9

FRIDAY, JUNE 30, 2006

Cal Ripley knocked on the front door to the Hilliard's cabin. It was just after 6 p.m.; the holiday traffic out of Detroit had made the trip even longer. He was on his fourth cup of gas station coffee and would attempt to be energetic and happy, but the truth was that he was exhausted and still shaken up from the previous night's raid. He had overslept, not shaved, and had been late dropping off his dog at the boarder's. The door reflected the outfit he had thrown together at the last minute: a pair of cheap camouflage cargo shorts, running shoes, and a white Fruit of the Loom t-shirt—all grabbed from the dryer because they were clean. His Ford Bronco sat at rest in the driveway behind him.

The door opened, and the familiar face of his childhood friend slid into view. Maria wasted no time in giving him a huge hug, moving him side to side, and then giving him a kiss on the cheek. "Got my boy back!" At 5'2" and wearing straw sandals with tall heels, she was still not close to eye level with his 6'3" frame.

The smell of alcohol escaped along with her greeting. Gas station coffee now seemed the vilest beverage in existence; he could use an adult drink.

She stepped back and looked him up and down. Next to his feet was a small duffel bag. "Ready to relax?"

"Sorry I'm tardy," he said.

She shook her long slender finger back and forth. "Not needed," Maria said. "All that matters is that you're here."

"It's good to be here," he lied.

An African-American male, perhaps six feet tall, walked onto the porch.

Cal put out his hand. "Iggi, right?"

Iggi took his hand and gave it a firm squeeze while nodding.

"Nice to meet you," Cal said.

Iggi broke off the handshake and continued to stare into Cal's blue eyes. Maria's hand wrapped around Iggi's back, and he said, "You too."

Behind Iggi emerged a woman he guessed was Haley. He made casual eye contact with Maria, and Maria raised her eyebrows once. She had told him that Haley was nice and reserved, but she had left out the fact that she was also beautiful. The word sexy came to mind as well, but it was more of an assured, athletic, and almost youthful energy that seemed to emanate from her approach. She was around the height of his ex-wife, maybe 5'8", but whereas his ex-wife's hair was auburn, Haley's was blonde. His ex-wife wore designer clothes; Haley had on salmon colored capris and a white tank top, which exposed a deep, natural tan. It was evident that she was outside a lot.

Iggi and Maria moved to the side.

Haley raised her hand before he could. "Cal?"

He nodded.

"Haley."

66

Don't be awkward. You're wiped and haven't even thought about dating since you came home to a half-empty house. Right now you need...food? Food. Think of something...

"Dinnertime!" Maria said. "We've already got it started."

You are a saint, Maria. He bent down and grabbed his bag.

"C'mon. I'll show you to your room, and then we'll get some food in all of us," Maria said.

He saw her elbow Iggi. Iggi responded, "What can I get you to drink, Cal?"

Make it easy. "Whatever everyone is having," he replied.

"Haley and I have been working on a bottle of chardonnay and Iggi's tackling some Bud Light," Maria added.

"Bud Light works," said Cal.

He saw Maria give Iggi a look that he thought said, 'See? I told you so.' What was going on?

Haley and Iggi headed back in. Maria said, "Follow me."

"So, what do you think of him?" Maria asked Haley.

They were in the kitchen putting the finishing touches on the spaghetti dinner. Haley was making the Caesar salad, and Maria was stirring the sauce on the stove.

"I don't know. I just met him," she said.

"I admit that I was giving him all of my attention, but I did see you pause to watch him pick up his duffel bag."

"Where's the box of croutons?" Haley asked.

"Second shelf down in the pantry."

Haley walked over and opened the pantry door.

"You're not *answering me*, lady."

Because you're pushing already. Relax. He's handsome, yes. But quiet too. And yet, there's something about him. What was it? His square chin? His possible vulnerability from being divorced in the past year? The way his hand felt when they greeted each other? "Let it play out a little, Maria," she said with a grin to appease. It worked.

"I know I'm right," Maria said.

Iggi entered the kitchen and grabbed plates to start setting the table. "I brought Cal a beer, said he was going to grab a quick shower before dinner."

"Got it," Maria replied while refilling her wine glass and Haley's. "We've still got about ten minutes." She started stirring the sauce again.

Haley took the box of croutons out of the pantry and went back to work on the salad. After sprinkling parmesan cheese on the lettuce, she took a sip of wine. "I haven't had a sit-down dinner with more than myself in a while."

"Do you wonder if people do that anymore? When I was growing up, we had dinner as a family every night."

"We did until I was around 13. Then, my older brother started high school sports, and we all started eating at different times, mostly on TV trays watching the day's episode of *Another World* that my mom taped."

Iggi returned to grab bowls for salad.

"Well, when we have kids—"

Iggi almost dropped the stack of bowls.

"—having dinner as a family will be a priority." She turned to Iggi. "You need help with those?"

"Nope, nope," Iggi said and headed back to the table.

"Kids?" Haley said.

"Yeah. You ever going to have any?"

"I've got to be with someone first." Shit. She had just opened that door—

"Exactly!" Maria said, her eyes motioning upstairs.

Haley took another drink of wine, attempting to regroup. She found some cover by shaking the croutons from the box and onto the salad. Acting as if the salad would be judged on a cooking show, she focused on putting the precise amount of dressing across the maze of lettuce, parmesan cheese, and croutons.

Iggi made another trip into the kitchen and gathered the silverware while Maria threw a noodle at the wall next to him.

"Can I do anything to help?" came Cal's voice from behind Haley.

"Well, that was quick," Maria said.

"Habit," Cal said.

"You look refreshed, Detective Ripley," Maria said a little louder. She took the noodle off of the wall and threw it into the sink. "Go ahead and grab our drinks."

Haley turned around and saw Cal standing a few feet away, picking up Maria's wine glass. He had changed into a pair of jeans and a navy polo shirt— the bands stretched tight around his arms. He had also shaved and combed his hair. Then, she caught a whiff of him. Cologne...what type? Or was it the soap, shampoo, or body wash he had used in the shower? Whatever it was, it smelled good, and she carefully handed him her wine glass as he put out his hand.

He took the glasses and headed to the dining room.

"Detective?" she asked Maria.

"Detroit," Maria said.

"Just a minor detail," Haley said.

"I had to keep something a surprise, lady. We all lead boring lives compared to him." She leaned toward her and lowered her voice. "Don't tell Iggi I said that."

What would you do if I told you I worked for the C.I.A.? It would probably knock you flat on your ass, lady. Detroit detective. He's been on the job for at least four or five years then.

Cal returned and she studied his straight posture. It wasn't like he had a corncob stuck up his rear, but his walk wasn't lazy either. He moved in steady strides—purposeful, but not rushed. He didn't have nervous eyes; they were sharp and observant. A little tired though, which reminded her of her own.

He's seen some things. But how old was he? There hadn't been any gray in his beard earlier.

He spoke to Maria. "Your hubby said you had some red wine. I think I'll make the switch. He said he's staying with beer."

"The Bud Light is in the fridge, and the wine is in the rack above that counter," she pointed.

Cal navigated around the kitchen island to the crisscrossed rack.

"There is merlot and cab, sweetie, and could you grab the other bottle of chardonnay out of the fridge for me and my girl?"

"Yep." He pulled a bottle of red, not bothering to see what it was, and set it on the counter.

"I'll get you a glass," Haley said.

Cal made eye contact with her. "Thanks," he said. He reached the refrigerator and removed a beer and the other bottle of wine. "Opener?" he asked Maria.

Haley already had it in her hand along with a wine glass. "Accounted for," she said to him, showing him the corkscrew.

Maria concentrated on pouring the boiling water with the noodles into the colander over the sink. Above the stove, the microwave's timer started to beep. "Garlic bread is ready."

On instinct, Cal and Haley both moved toward the stove. Their bodies touched for the first time. His scent was stronger, and she noticed his height more now.

"Sorry," Cal said and moved away.

"I've got the bread," she said.

"Iggi!" Maria shouted. "Get your buns in here and help."

Iggi jogged into the kitchen. "What? I just got done setting the table."

Cal moved past him with the wine and beer. Haley stole a glance as he disappeared around the corner.

"Get Haley an oven mitten," she said.

"Where in the hell do we keep those?" he said.

"My God. Take this," she said handing him the colander.

"Have we already passed the sweet spot of human being cohabitation?" Maria asked the group, circled around a large bonfire on the beach. The dark cabin loomed behind them at the edge of the woods.

Iggi took a long pull from his can of Bud Light—half-a-dozen cans littered the sand at his feet. "Explain."

"What I mean is, have we passed the point where we have just enough separation from each other but not too much; enough human contact with each other without distractions; enough authentic interactions to keep us coming back for more; just enough options like TV, movies, books, travel, sports, and music to provide breaks and escapes but within limits; just enough family, friends, and acquaintances for life balance, mentorship, and companionship while still preserving the opportunity to meet new people?"

"No. I don't think we're past it," Iggi responded. "If we were, then we wouldn't be here together."

Maria turned to Haley. "What do you think?"

"I think this is why I teach math and science and not philosophy," she said.

Shit. Cal had been hoping Haley would get dragged further in so he could nod, maybe give an affirmation, and then move to the next topic. Unless he did something, it would be his turn next. Discussing deep subjects with people he barely knew was not a place of comfort for Cal Ripley. Small talk over dinner was one thing; sharing belief systems over a bonfire at night while—*be honest*—getting laced with alcohol was another. It was their first night together too. "Ah, that's a cop out, Haley." The moment the words escaped his mouth, he regretted them.

71

She set her wine glass down in the sand and turned toward him. "Just lightening the mood a little, Cal. I'll answer, but you go first, deal?"

Damnit. He had to answer now. He cracked open a fresh beer—another mistake, don't mix your alcohol...well, too late now—and took a chug. "Cell phones, the internet, and artificial intelligence will eventually lead to our downfall." Their eyes were glued to him now. He concentrated on the fire. "We're right at the tipping point. If we let these machines upset the balance that exists between the items you listed, Maria, then we're done. Once past the point of no return, it will take some sort of event to shake up humanity and then take a long time to re-normalize after the event—if we survive it."

Haley wasted no time jumping in. Must have hit a nerve. "I'm with you, but finish the thought."

"You finish it for me," he said and chugged his beer.

"Let's say that event occurs. Then we're just in *Canticle* territory."

"What does that mean?" Iggi said.

"*A Canticle for Leibowitz*," Haley said. "It's the only book that your wife ever assigned that I read. Everyone should read it, and I never say that because I'm not a big reader."

"Get 'em, chica," Maria said, refilling her wine from a fresh bottle she pulled out of the cooler.

"What's *Canticle* territory?" Cal said.

"What it means is that life is cyclical; human beings are destined to repeat history, even if it is apocalyptic. We will continue to do things because we can and won't stop long enough to ask if we should. Whenever we destroy most of the human race and our world, we'll immediately start over, and the clock will start ticking away until we regain the knowledge and technology to do it again. And, at some point, after enough times of doing it, there won't be anyone left to resume the cycle." She picked up her wine glass and handed it to Maria. "Cal, was that a cop out?"

Um, no. Hell no. Now, I've got to read that book. "I think we nailed it together," he toasted.

Iggi stood up. "Baby, can you come with me for a minute? Got a question about tomorrow."

Maria raised an eyebrow, but followed him toward the house.

They stopped at the edge of the backyard.

"You gotta get me out of here," Iggi pleaded.

"What's the problem?" Maria asked.

"*What's the problem?* I'm bored outta my mind! I can't take another night with these two."

"Shhh. Keep your voice down," she ordered. "It's going really well I think."

"Everybody is lit but me, and you keep bringing up topics like we're around some damn circle in your classroom. Can we talk about something normal?"

"Bring up anything you want. I'm not stopping you."

"I don't know. Do they know I'm a sports writer?"

"Haley does. I'm sure Cal still likes sports. I actually thought that was the one thing that would get the two of you to bond." She rubbed his belly and then pinched his rear. "Now, get that fine ass back over by the fire and start talkin' shit about the Lions. Then, I'll swoop in and brag about your book. Got it?" She laughed.

He couldn't stay mad and chuckled too.

"And man up and start drinking like the rest of us. You get back in the game tonight, and we'll all go bowling tomorrow night. I'll put everybody on your turf. Hear?"

His face lit up like an adolescent who had just discovered masturbation. He kicked the sand in triumph and started toward the house. "Grabbing more liquid," he said over his shoulder.

"That's my baby," she said and headed back to the fire. But not too fast. Haley and Cal were talking.

"So, you're a science and math teacher?" Cal asked.

"I am," Haley said. "And you're a Detroit Detective."

"Armed and ready," he joked.

She adjusted her skirt, exposing her sinewy tan legs as she crossed them. After dripping spaghetti sauce on her capris, she had changed before coming down to the fire. Fine by him.

She smirked. "You're also a fellow humorist, I see. I like that."

Damn, I like her smile. "Found that it helps diffuse tension much better than logic," Cal said.

"Well, I can't go *that* far," she said. "But the principle is sound."

"I've had one too many beers for principle tonight," he said and finished the one in his hand.

She opened up the cooler and threw him the last can of Bud Light. "Last one, Cal."

He grasped the cold can but frowned. "Can't do it."

She looked at him, puzzled. "Why?"

He laughed, shaking his head. "Principle."

"Get out of here," she joked back.

"No, I'm serious." He raised the beer while still grinning. "You don't take a man's last beer. My dad taught me that."

"How so?"

"I had just turned twenty-one and was with him over at a neighbor's house being the gofer for them while they built a shed in the backyard. I was offered a beer and took the last one out of the refrigerator. After my first gulp, my neighbor told me to grab two more for him and my dad."

"Uh oh," she said.

"Yeah. I told them that I had taken the last beer, and it was then that I was not so nicely informed by my father that you never take a man's last beer, even if it is offered to you. I've followed it ever since." He tossed the can back to her.

Over her shoulder she could see Maria meandering back toward the fire and Iggi heading inside. Cal followed her eyes.

"Hope we didn't scare them off with our end of the world banter," Cal said.

"I doubt it," Haley said. "I don't think Maria gets scared off."

Of course. Better stop trying to be witty. In fact, witty left you four beers ago. "Good point."

They each sat back and refocused on the fire. It became quiet except for the crackle and pop as another log slid down, succumbing to the heat. The onshore wind had picked up, and a natural rhythm set in as every few seconds the waves broke and slid up the beach.

Maria returned. "Don't stop talking on my account. I could see the two of you chattering away down here."

"Iggi pack it in for the night?" Cal asked.

"No, sir. Went to get more libations."

"Okay, new topic," Cal said. "Kids."

Maria sat down. "Don't tell me you've got a surprise," she said to Cal.

"None that I know about," he winked. "But you and Iggi—any plans?"

"I think we're ready," she said.

Haley jumped in. "If it's anything like what my older brother has gone through, then you're in for some surprises of your own."

"How so?" Maria said.

"Well, he always thought that our parents were harder on us whenever we would visit our grandparents. I hadn't thought about it, but, after I did, I agreed with him. We talked about it and came to the conclusion that they were harder on us in front of their parents to prove to them that they were raising us right.

This allowed our grandparents to be easier on us and spoil us; they let their guard down. We were the prototypical extended family; it was us and our grandparents versus our parents."

Maria nodded. "I follow you. It was pretty much like that in our family." She grinned. "Listen to you talkin' up a storm."

"You keep giving me wine!"

They all laughed.

"But, here's the twist. My brother and his wife decided *not* to do this with their children when they visited my parents. Let's just say...tension." Haley swirled the wine in her glass and then took a long drink.

"Don't leave us hanging!" Maria said.

"Right," said Haley. "My brother and his wife are calm and peaceful people. They're not trying to make some overtly defiant statement like, 'We're going to raise our kids *our* way,' they're just not going to treat them differently around family." She paused. "My parents don't know what to do. They totally expected to have the same relationship with their grandkids that my brother and I had with our grandparents. Now, every time my brother and his family visit them, they're thrown off. And, most recently, there have been instances of them being jerks to their grandkids in some weird attempt to show my brother and his wife how to be parents."

"Expectations," Cal said. "That one word can change things faster in life than anything else I have observed."

"Thanks for the heads up," Maria said to Haley. "I think I know how my parents will be if Iggi and I ever have children, but I guess I can't say for sure after hearing what you just said. It makes perfect sense. Looking back, I feel like our Greatest Generation grandparents and Baby Boomer parents were locked in some epic contest to see who would win out in the race to raise us."

"And every Gen Xer both benefitted and suffered because of that," Cal said. "Our grandparents built modern-day America, but not without blind spots. Our parents rebelled, brought to light important social issues, but also became self-absorbed. And here *we* find ourselves, sandwiched between two behemoth generations—Baby Boomers and Millennials. Unapologetically, we're the indispensable bridge, holding things together—the last adult generation that remembers what life was like before the machines." He started to tick the fingers off on his right hand. "We're a pretty good mix of tradition, flexibility, loyalty, and defiance." He crossed his legs and thought he caught Haley checking him out. "The question is: Who will our kids take after?"

"You still think you'll have kids?" Maria asked.

Cal was silent.

"I'm sorry. That came out wrong," she said.

"No worries," said Cal. "And, yeah, I haven't given up yet on becoming a father. But I also know that not everyone gets to have kids."

Maria went to set her wine glass down, but it slipped out of her hand.

As her glass fell, she was aware that it would not break when it landed on the sand. Glass, like life, shatters when it hits or is hit by something hard. Pieces can be swept up; sometimes, if the pieces are large enough, they can be put back together. If the pieces are not swept up, then they become a danger for anyone who approaches them—glass cuts. Once a piece of glass is shattered, then it can never return to what it once was. A new piece of glass can replace the old one, but it will never be exactly the same. For Maria Hilliard, the shattering took place a few days before the turn of the century—an event that no one knew about. There was *one* situation where she might have to tell Iggi.

She'd be six now.

* * *

Landon Beach

DETROIT, TUESDAY, DECEMBER 28, 1999, 2:30 P.M.

The frigid December wind stung 23-year-old Maria Torres's cheeks and nose as she exited her car wearing a Detroit Tigers baseball cap and sunglasses. She was certain no one would recognize her but wasn't taking any chances. She was living in Rochester, New York, and working as a high school Language Arts teacher, so she had decided against any of the Rochester clinics. In fact, there were plenty of other places between there and Detroit, but she had grown up in the Motor City before her family left for Boston when she was a sophomore in high school. It felt more like home than Boston.

Unsure, reluctant but committed, she began to walk toward the one-story brick building. Normally, there would be demonstrators, but today's temperature was *5 degrees* Fahrenheit—even activists had their limits. She found it hard to take steps as she contemplated once again what she was about to do. The script running through her mind had not stopped since she gathered up the courage to make the phone call a week ago.

The trouble had started in late November when she informed her fiancée, Mark, that she was seven weeks pregnant. There had been no 'How are you doing?', no 'Oops, but I'm excited', no 'We'll be just fine', no physical comforting, no reaction when she started crying, no question like 'When do you want to tell everyone?', no 'Do you want to have the wedding early?', not even 'Let's talk about this.' The subject of children had come up while they were dating, but his attitude had been more of a 'Yes, but not until later' type. She knew he would be surprised, but did not anticipate his strong reaction. She had been raised as a Christian and wanted to the keep the baby; he couldn't handle it. "We're just starting out. We'll lose all of our freedom if we have this child," he had said. The fighting had started immediately and had not let up. He moved out of their apartment a month later. His last words were, "I don't want to have anything to do with you or the child."

Out of shame and embarrassment—she would later forgive herself these emotions—she had told no one about the baby or break-up. Less than a week later, she went to her first trimester screening and had a blood test and ultrasound. Both had raised red flags. Her blood test results showed that her protein levels were abnormally high, and the ultrasound revealed that there was increased fluid behind the baby's neck. These meant that the baby had a possible chromosomal disorder and/or heart defect. The ultrasound technician was also able to get a clear picture of the baby's genitals, and told Maria that it was a girl.

Even though Mark had left her, she still called him to deliver the news. After a silent pause, he said, "I think you know what to do then. Don't call me again." She had called back two times after that, but he had never picked up. On the third call—this December morning—she was informed that his number was no longer in service. Later on, she realized that there had been other warning signs from him that she had overlooked: his 5'4" Napoleonic complex, his need to control her with statements like 'I don't ever want you to talk to him again,' after a kind male co-worker had gone out for coffee with her to discuss a student who needed help. And there was the hair. He wore it shoulder-length and pulled it back into a—what had he called it? A man-bun? The style wasn't a big deal, but it was the fact that he wanted people to *know* he wore his hair long that made him annoying. The constant un-bunning of it, pulling it back a dozen times when two or three times would do, and then putting the hair band in. She had gone along with it as lovers do when they are blind—'He's a free spirit,' and 'He's so reformist—borderline avant-garde,' and 'He's just a beautiful human being, brooding, an intellectual.' What she really thought was: You look like a teenager—if you played with my clitoris as much as you played with your hair, I wouldn't notice how ridiculous you look. Sex had also been mostly one-sided. After Mark left her, she vowed it would never be again.

She entered the musty, dreary lobby of the Women's Center, signed in on the clipboard at the front window, and took a seat in the waiting area. Across from her sat a woman, perhaps forty, who had a blank stare on her face along with a twitching knee that wouldn't stop. A few seats down from her was a teenaged girl—gosh, maybe 14 or 15—who was crying along with the woman holding her, who Maria presumed was the girl's mother. In the far back corner was the sole male in the waiting room, a white college-aged kid who was holding the hand of a woman at least two decades older than him. He kept running his hand through her hair and whispering something to her. They shared a quick kiss, and she went back to leaning her head on his chest.

She wondered briefly what all of their stories were. What exactly had happened? And how did they all come to this day? After observing them for another few minutes, she decided that she did not want to know any of the answers. Outside, snow began to fall. Who else would come through that door today? Who had already had the procedure done here today and left through those doors? Who would be coming tomorrow? Who was here yesterday? And who would get pregnant today and be here in another 6-12 weeks?

Her appointment was for 2:45 p.m. During the consultation, the doctor had told her that the procedure—called a vacuum aspiration, or suction abortion—would only take 5-10 minutes. She couldn't believe it. The hours of lovemaking with Mark, the weeks of morning sickness, the nights of reading *What to Expect When You're Expecting,* and the growing life inside of her that she would now be ending. 5-10 minutes...forever. Her eyes filled, and she placed her fingers underneath her sunglass's lenses and wiped her eyes.

The door to the waiting room opened. "Ms. Smith?" a staff member said. This was the name they had agreed upon during the consultation to keep her identity private.

Maria wiped her eyes and stood up.

"This way, ma'am," the staff member said.

She took one step, then another, and after a few more, she was in the hallway. She started to sweat and feel lightheaded. The door closed behind her.

"Baby?" Iggi said, sitting down next to her.

She continued to stare at her wine glass, the rim coated with sand like salt on a margarita.

He gave Haley a look: *What's going on?*

Haley shrugged.

"Baby?" he said to Maria, raising his voice.

She snapped out of it. "Sorry," she said. "You get the drinks?"

He patted the cooler. "All filled up."

Cal was working on a fresh beer and Haley had a full glass of wine again.

Maria picked up her glass and wiped the sand off of the rim. "Fill her up," she ordered Iggi.

As he poured the cold wine into her glass, he wondered what she had been thinking about. Being unresponsive while studying a fallen wine glass was the last thing he'd imagined her doing when he returned to the fire. Everyone drops a glass from time to time, but her stare bothered him. She hadn't just been distracted: That was a stare where the body was present but the mind and soul were on the other side of the world. What had they been talking about while he was gone?

He put the cork back in the bottle and stowed it in the cooler. Okay, what was the plan again? Right. Start talking about the follies and failings of the Detroit Lions—his specialty. He sat back and watched her take a sip, recline and look up at the stars, and then close her eyes. *C'mon, sweetie, come back to life. I can't get this started without you.*

"Is that a boat out there?" Cal asked.

They all looked out at the water.

Iggi squinted. The fire was disrupting his night vision. "Can't tell," he said, getting up from his chair and walking toward the water. Cal followed.

Barefoot, they covered the ten yards of beach between the fire and the water's edge and stood facing Lake Ontario. Iggi listened while his eyes adjusted. There were no sounds of a motor or even voices. Then, he heard a swishing sound as Cal entered the water up to his knees.

"Cold?" Iggi said.

"Yeah," Cal said. "Feels good though." He pointed. "You see it?"

Iggi's eyes followed Cal's arm. Perhaps fifty yards offshore, he could now see a small boat silhouetted above the dark horizon under the star-filled sky. There was no movement aboard and no lights. "What kind of boat is that?" he said. "And how did you spot it?" *Sweet Jesus, I'm asking a cop for information.* Snap out of it already.

"They should have their running lights on, or if they're anchored, their anchor lights." Cal concentrated. "It's a cabin cruiser, maybe thirty-five, forty feet."

I just kayak, man, I don't know shit about boats. "We should see someone aboard, right?" *There—that's safe.*

Cal held up his index finger and fixed it at the cruiser's bow as a point of reference. The boat crept past his stationary finger, heading further west. "Well, they're not anchored," he said, lowering his hand. "I don't see anyone topside either. Strange."

Maria and Haley approached the men. "What's all the fuss about?" Maria said.

"We've got a boat out there with no lights on and no one onboard," Iggi beat Cal to it. *Boom!*

Haley joined Cal in the water.

After the women's eyes had time to adjust to the darkness, Cal helped Haley locate the boat while Iggi helped Maria.

"Well, it is the 4th of July weekend," Maria said. "That's when the crazies come out. This coast will be full of blitzed boaters starting tomorrow."

"Why don't they have their lights on?" Haley asked Cal.

Why is she asking *him*? Iggi noticed her move closer to the big detective, and he hadn't missed Cal holding her arm a few minutes ago, guiding it until she found the boat. *Maria has to be eating this up.* He saw his wife staring out past the boat. This is what she wanted for them! *What gives, baby?* When they were alone, he'd have to find out what had thrown her off.

"I don't know," said Cal. "They're just drifting."

"Think they're in trouble?" Haley asked.

Before he could answer, they heard the faint sound of a motor carrying across the water. Then, the navigation lights came on, and the boat picked up speed.

"Might have stopped for a little *fun*," Cal said, his face clear in the moonlight.

Did the sonofabitch just wink?

Maria laughed.

Thank God. She's back. Enough about this stupid boat already. "More fire time?" Iggi said, wrapping his arms around her.

Haley and Cal made eye contact but then looked quickly away.

Haley stepped back up onto the beach. "Well, it's been a good first night." She yawned. "I'm going to hit the sack."

What?! No way we're callin' this a night right now. I just filled up the cooler!

"Can I bring anything back up to the house?" Haley asked.

Hell yes, everybody take your shit up...when it's time, and it isn't time yet. He went to say the toned-down version of his thought but was drowned out by Maria.

"Just leave everything. We'll be back down here tomorrow." She looked at Iggi. "But *you* can bring up the cooler."

He knew the right move was to acquiesce—suck it up and start over again tomorrow—but he felt cheated of his promised moment to shine. "I just loaded the damned thing."

Cal exited the water. "I'll help you carry it up. I've been drinking your beer all night."

Before Iggi could reply, Maria grabbed his arm. Her squeeze told him: Watch your reply. His lips parted and slipped into a toothy politician's just-been-re-elected smile. "Thanks," he said.

Soon they were all past the fire, and a few steps later their feet hit the soft blades of the backyard grass. Iggi and Cal set the cooler down on the back deck. To the right of the two steps that led up onto the deck was a tub of water and a towel. One by one, they all dipped their feet into the bucket and then wiped them off. Iggi was last.

Cal, Haley, and Maria entered the house.

Opening the cooler, Iggi took out an ice-cold Bud Light. *Gonna have at least one of these blues before I go to bed.* "I didn't load this bitch for nothin'," he muttered, closing the top. As he went to shut the sliding glass door behind him, he poked his head back outside and took one last glance out at the water. The others didn't seem to be giving it a second thought, but something didn't sit right with him about the boat they had seen. He searched the horizon, but the boat was gone.

The cabin cruiser rested at anchor in 20 feet of water approximately two miles west of Rochester. The anchor lights were on, and two of the four men aboard had hit the rack about twenty minutes ago. The other two were seated in the stern, talking in Russian.

The agent, only known to the other three men as Gregory, sat on the port bench and tipped back his tumbler of vodka and ice. He smacked his lips. "What's wrong?" he said.

The older man, Vladimir—Gregory guessed 60—sat behind the helm and drank straight out of the Smirnov bottle. He finished his chug and said, "Why didn't we just take care of her at her house?"

He knew the real reason but wasn't about to let this over-the-hill sack of Siberian dog shit know what it was. "Timing, comrade. Timing."

The bottle was back at the old spymaster's lips.

From his reputation, Gregory should have been cautious, respectful, maybe even uneasy around Vladimir. But those assassinations—euphemistically referred to among the KGB as acts of heroism—had taken place decades ago and on different continents where the rules of morality and ethics were taken as seriously as flatulating. This man had overseen the hanging of a double agent's entire family—one by one as the traitor and other family members were forced to watch—in 1981 at a house in Beirut. The vision made Gregory's stomach turn. If this was what happened in the 'Paris of the Middle East', then he never wanted to be stationed there. Now Vladimir was old and had become a slave to the bottle.

"Tomorrow?" the old man questioned.

Gregory drained his vodka and held out his cup for more. Vladimir poured.

"Perhaps," Gregory said.

Vladimir said nothing and drank.

Gregory looked at the shoreline in the distance—darkness with clusters of white lights spread out in both directions. *It might be tomorrow. It might be the next day. We dispose of Officer Lear when I think the time is right.*

10

ROME, JULY 2003

The American Academy in Rome was created in 1911 by combining the American School of Architecture, founded in 1894 by architect Charles Follen McKim, and the American School of Classical Studies, founded in 1895 by the Archaeological Institute of America. J.P. Morgan, John D. Rockefeller Jr., and Henry Clay Frick all donated to McKim's vision for a retreat for artists and scholars to pursue their crafts in a serene, inspirational, and relaxed environment. If there was ever a place for the great minds of America to gather and then contemplate, collaborate, and create with complete artistic and intellectual autonomy, then Via Angelo Masina 5, 00153 Roma ITALIA was it.

For the lucky thirty or so who are awarded the Rome Prize Fellowship, a year of communal living with free room and board and dedicated study space awaits. All meals are prepared and delivered by the Rome Sustainable Food Project—all one has to do is show up to an immaculately set dining table either in the historic dining room during the winter months or the fabled Cortile during warmer weather. There is no air conditioning in the apartments, single and double rooms, study bedrooms, or studio suites—ceiling fans, a cold shower, glasses of ice water, or a refreshment from the Academy Bar are the only means to cool down. The experience can be life changing for an early to mid-career professional.

And as it tends to happen when intellectuals and artists meet and mingle, research is done about who is who "in the zoo." Brain trust and creative power of this magnitude are not immune from the desire to determine one's place in the intellectual stratosphere. For even at a utopian oasis of creation, collaboration, and innovation where everyone has earned the right to say 'I belong here'...some still believed that they belonged there more than others. The list of prior fellowship winners—now members of The Society of Fellows—is legendary. And if one was to dig back far enough into the archives, he or she would find that of the two fellowship winners for the Renaissance and Early Modern Studies in the year of 1966, one was a young Japanese American female professor named Leiko T. Sato, PhD, from the University of California at Berkeley.

The enemies of America knew that this same professor who had worked studiously on a new biography of Shakespeare during October 1966 to late July 1967 was now Dr. Leiko Narita, the C.I.A.'s Deputy Director for Intelligence. And for that reason, they more than likely suspected that The Company would never place officers at The American Academy in Rome.

They were right; no C.I.A. officer had ever used the Academy as a cover before.

Until now.

Mrs. Jessica Stein looked out through the open window of her apartment in the Villa Aurelia. The temperature was 5 degrees warmer than Rochester—

around 89 during the day and a few degrees under 70 at night—and she wore a plain Spanish orange-colored summer skirt with a faded olive t-shirt and no bra. She would miss the sounds, smells, and sights of Rome. It was Monday morning, and they were leaving the Academy this weekend.

Her husband, Professor Andrew Oliver 'Ollie' Stein, PhD, took a seat at a round wooden table and began to write in a leather journal with a Cross pen. He wore denim-colored linen pants, sandals, a white linen button-down shirt, and sported a heavy black beard. His hair was over his ears and ran all the way down his neck.

She heard him, took in one more refreshing breath of air, and then returned to the living room. "You've perfected the expatriate look, Ollie," she said to him.

"Someone's got to educate the citizens of the world," Stein said.

She watched as his eyes moved from the ceiling fan to the large couches on either side of the wooden coffee table and then back to her.

"I don't want to leave," he said.

He'd been at the Academy since the beginning of May; she, since the beginning of June. "How's the novel?" Jessica said.

"Stalled," he replied.

The novel was the means to discuss the new agent, Sari, they were running. And in just one prior meeting, Sari had already produced a Kilimanjaro-sized load of intelligence—all roads *did* lead to Rome. 'Stalled' meant that they would not be meeting with her this morning. Her next question was to be about how he would overcome whatever difficulty he had encountered in the writing of the book. "Characters not behaving?" she said.

He brought the end of the pen to his lips. "In a way," Stein said. "I'll hack away for a few more hours. Perhaps, I need a break from it this afternoon."

She now understood perfectly. The meeting would take place at two o'clock this afternoon: 'I'll hack away for a few more hours' meant two hours, and 'Perhaps, I need a break from it this afternoon' signaled her to add the two hours to noon, hence, 2 o'clock. "A good idea," she said. "You've been at it non-stop since I arrived, and I'd like to see something in Rome beyond the back of your head bent over a notebook."

"You know I get difficult when I'm near the end," Stein said.

She approached him from behind and placed her soft hands on his shoulders. Starting with her thumbs, she began to massage his tight muscles. The end of their mission was finally in sight.

It had started in the fall when Judas had made contact and asked her to visit Langley over Thanksgiving. Having never been activated during the school year, she had been hesitant. But after some smooth talking from Judas, she had agreed. So, while the majority of Americans were sleeping off the hangovers that accompanied their participation in the biggest bar gathering of the year—Wednesday night before Thanksgiving—she was flying high over New York on her way to the meeting in Virginia.

The briefing was quick and direct. She would travel to Rome and stay with Officer Turner at the American Academy after the school year was over; he'd arrive in the beginning of May, when the Visiting Artists and Scholars Program term started, and she would stay with him as his wife until the term finished at the end of July. Having Turner be awarded one of the coveted Rome Prize Fellowships would invite too many questions and be almost impossible to establish a credible academic history. However, Visiting Artists and Scholars came and went all year long, and a stay for an up-and-coming novelist who was a professor at one of the growing number of university online programs could be arranged without drawing any attention. And so intellectual giant, Renaissance man, trusted professor, and daring novelist Ollie Stein, PhD, was created.

When their time at the Academy was over, they would return to an apartment in Norfolk, Virginia, where Turner—Professor Ollie Stein—would resume his duties as an online Creative Writing Professor for Southern New Hampshire University. Officer Jennifer Lear—Jessica Stein—would continue in her cover as his wife. Two weeks later, Ollie would escape to Saratoga Springs, New York, and once again immerse himself in his unfinished novel, *Treasures of Lust*, at Yaddo until the end of August. And while Ollie was taking his breakfast and dinner communally and having his lunch packed for him by the Yaddo staff, she would take a road trip to visit her husband, the struggling and starving activist-professor-artist...and just happen to stop at a café on the way to debrief with Judas. After spending a weekend at a hotel in Saratoga Springs to lift Ollie's spirits, another C.I.A. officer who looked very similar to her would join her at her hotel room, assume her identity, and check out the next morning to drive the car back to Norfolk. Meanwhile, Officer Lear would leave the hotel from a back staircase and walk a few blocks to be picked up by a car that would take her to the airport. She would fly home to Rochester after spending "a tremendous summer in Cameroon spreading the word of Jesus Christ" and get ready for a new school year.

The Steins neared the end of their surveillance detection run, which had been taking place over the past two hours. Their agent, Sari, was no doubt doing her own run, attempting to 'go black'—completely shaking any surveillance, if there was any. For the past few months, the Steins had established routines on the weekend: this bar for a drink, that market to look at goods, this restaurant for pizza and wine, that nightclub for dancing, etc. Today, they turned the market and bar into cover stops: Anyone who was following them would see the stops as normal routine. Certain that no one was following them, they swiftly slid out the back of the bar and into a hotel lobby. They walked down a hallway toward the room that had been reserved a few

90

weeks ago for another female Company employee. Stein performed a special knock combination on the door, and it opened. Inside, they changed clothes, and, after months of sporting the thick beard, Stein used the trimmers in the bathroom to take it down to a five o'clock shadow. Then, she trimmed the back of his hair and he cut six inches off her hair. She hated it. 'Why the change in appearances today?' she had asked. He had told her that today's meeting required extra measures.

After seeing their transformations in the mirror, they put on sunglasses and he slipped on a hat. This had taken five minutes. When they arrived back at their apartment in the Villa Aurelia later, they would make sure to complement each other on their new look from a delightful stop at the parrucchiere. Before opening the door to let them out, the female Company employee handed her the tote bag and him the backpack and introduced them to two other officers who were dressed exactly like they were now. Twenty minutes after the Steins had left, the two officers would change appearances and leave through the back entrance while she checked out of the hotel and then headed for the rendezvous to meet the Steins and retrieve the tote bag. Everyone gave a thumbs up, and the Steins left the hotel.

Now, they were at their final turn. Jessica said, "95?"

Stein replied, "95."

The rule of thumb that every field officer followed was that you didn't proceed to the next stage of a mission unless you were 95% sure that you were black. Stein's reply told her that they were good to go.

They made their final turn, and the Colosseum rose before their eyes as they travelled down Via di S Gregorio. To their left, the remains of the Roman Forum stood in silence—some of the structures seemed to be threatening to topple over with the push of a hand.

"With creations like these that *still* stand," Jessica said, pointing to the Colosseum, "it makes me wonder how a civilization like Rome falls."

With his sunglasses now in his pocket, Ollie Stein raised an eyebrow for a prolonged beat. "Someone hasn't read her Gibbon," he said. Then, he gave her a patronizing pat on the shoulder. "Like many great societies, Rome was not conquered by barbarians at the gate. It fell from within."

I wish he would break character. We're black. Lay off the persnickety professor bit. In fact, he'd been nothing but an egotistical sonofabitch since she had arrived. A horrible thought came to her mind: What if this wasn't a character? She ignored his reply and kept walking.

He continued. "Whereas the Greeks were built on art, literature, and philosophy, the Romans were political animals. You can see it in their architecture. The forums, amphitheaters, and arches all speak of grandeur, power, and the spirit of empire."

"Well, when your claim was that you were the moral and cultural epicenter of the world, the architecture kind of goes without saying doesn't it?" she shot back.

"Patriarchy, organizational strength, and their functional ethos were never going to produce just pure beauty. The angles, entrances, and breathtaking expanse all serve as *the statement*. They couldn't escape themselves, and that flaw eventually turned Rome *on* Rome."

Perhaps he was right, but what an ass. The couple continued on in silence.

At the visitor entrance, they paid for an audio tour. Ollie didn't wait and entered the immense arena ahead of her. From one of the workers, she took a green-colored device the size of a flashlight with a speaker at one end and buttons at the other and caught up to Ollie.

"What in the hell is that?" Stein said.

"We walk to different locations inside and push the corresponding button on this," she pointed to the device, "to listen to information about those particular places."

Stein frowned.

"What did you expect?" she said.

"Would it be too much to ask for an actual human being to give the tour?"

She held up the device. "These allow for more people to take the tour, and, hence, *professor*, the Colosseum does better business." *I can dish out uppity sass as well as you can.*

His look back at her said...hold on, was he *impressed?* She started to walk around the first level. Stein followed.

Halfway around the circle, she stopped at the railing where she had a clear view across what had been the wooden floor of the arena. She consulted her chart and pushed the appropriate button on the magic wand. Ollie got close, and their ears—his left and her right—were a few inches from the wand's speaker. Soon, a voice explained that below the wooden floor were stalls where animals were kept. They looked out and saw a maze of passageways and rooms underneath what had been the floor. The voice continued on and talked about the large opening directly across from them where those who had perished in the arena were dragged out. Jessica maintained her stoicism, but her eyes floated up to Ollie's face. *Did he just wince?* Now, it was she who grinned. The recording stopped, and they started to walk around the lower level again.

Jessica's large tote bag was open and hung from her left shoulder. Ollie meandered to her right, seeming to search his soul for what had happened in this god-awful and epic structure of glory and death. *It should be any minute now...*

Then, it happened. She felt a slight tug on her shoulder as a woman wearing a long yellow summer dress and straw hat brushed up against her. The woman was carrying an identical tote bag by the long straps in her right hand.

"Excuse me," she said, not making eye contact. This meant: You now have the material.

Behind her sunglasses, Jessica's eyes slid down to the open bag and could see a small white envelope on top of the teal-colored summer sweater she had packed. "You're fine," Jessica said back to the woman. This meant: Material received.

Sari stopped at a section of railing up ahead and set her tote down. It was novelist Ollie Stein's turn. He stopped next to her and removed his backpack. Jessica kept walking. After setting the backpack on the ground between the tote bag and the railing, he spread his arms and did an exaggerated stretch of his chest muscles; Sari knelt down, her dress and hat concealing what she was doing, and placed the backpack in her tote bag.

Finished with his stretching, Stein left the railing and caught up with Jessica. They slowed to almost a stop, which allowed their agent, Sari, to speed up. *One last piece of information...*

"When in Rome," Sari said over her shoulder as she passed them. Less than a minute later, she stopped at the next section of railing and pulled out a map of the Colosseum and began to study it. The Steins walked past her. After twenty or so yards, they both exhaled. Sari's words had meant: All is clear.

"Champagne?" Stein said.

"Of course," she replied. "But first, a picture."

They stopped, and Jessica pulled out a Cannon Rebel camera from her tote. Ollie backed up a few feet and leaned on the railing, striking a pose of deep contemplation—as if the future of the Roman Empire depended on his next directive.

She snapped the picture and then zipped the bag shut over the camera, sweater, and envelope. "You are now officially a part of history."

"Let's hope it's an important part," he said, referring not to the picture but to the envelope inside the bag.

They continued the tour, listening to the magic wand, nodding, pointing, even holding hands at one point—the happy couple touring what was once the greatest civilization the world has ever known. Not once did they see the yellow dress again.

A half-mile down the road from the arena, the Steins got on a bus, and Jessica sat down next to a woman who had boarded the bus a few people ahead of them. She complemented Jessica on her short haircut and went into a boring tale of how she was visiting Rome for the first time herself and hoped to see the Pope tomorrow—'I just *love* Saint Peter...Seen the Basilica yet? Michelangelo's dome? No?...I *gush* over Bramante and Raphael too—oh, not much into the art scene? Too bad. Mind you, we're in the great cradle of Western Civilization.'

A half-hour later, the Steins exited the bus near the American Academy. The kind and annoying lady continued to ride—holding Jessica's tote bag in her lap as the bus pulled away.

The Steins entered their room. Jessica's clothes were stained with sweat, and she examined her hair in the living room mirror. How long had it been since it was above her shoulders like now? Middle school, perhaps. Stein fell into the couch and took off his sandals.

She moved away from the mirror, closed each window in the apartment, and pulled the drapes closed.

Loudly, she announced, "That stylist did wonders with our hair. Your cut is making me tingle. Ready to get it on?"

"Oh yeah," he replied, just as loud.

She walked over to the bookshelf behind the couch and opened the disemboweled copy of *Bleak House* that they had hidden a small safe in. She entered a code, and the safe opened, revealing a 60-minute Maxell tape. Reaching under the couch, she pulled out a tape recorder. She plugged it in and turned the volume on high. After inserting the cassette, she pushed play. Soon, the sounds of her and Stein engaging in seductive conversation, followed by foreplay, began to fill the room. These sounds would soon be followed by the echoes of intense lovemaking. She chose Side A of the tape today. A week ago, it was Side B, which contained a dominatrix flavor mixed into a full-blown romp-a-thon. They had made ten tapes at Langley. Two other employees had done the lion's share of the work, but the voices needed to be their voices, so she had been given a script of things to say or yell that varied from the sweet "I love you" to things she had never even thought to utter while having sex. The sound engineers had taken over, and the tapes were ready for any mission where they would be posing as a couple. Today's tape was number 7. One night, when they had nothing confidential to discuss but had to keep up the appearances of a couple deeply devoted to the intricacies and pleasures of the Karma Sutra, they had opened a bottle of wine and listened to the tape from the kitchen, having to bite their tongues to keep from laughing. It was almost certain that they were not being bugged, but they stuck to the program.

They slipped on their noise cancelling headphones and sat on the floor, waiting. Side A of the tape would take thirty minutes, and then they could shower and press on.

A sense of exhilaration filled her. She had successfully completed her first mission. They had gone over everything on paper the night before: each cover stop, each street, the hotel layout, the amount to cut from her hair, his hair, his beard trim, body language to use after they changed clothes, all the ways in and out of the Colosseum in case the operation went south, what to listen for from Sari, etc. She watched as Turner-Stein sat across from her with his headphones on and his eyes closed. Every few minutes he would check his Ironman Triathlon watch to see how much time they had left before they could shut off the tape. She remembered him arguing with Rolfe Judas about the watch. Judas claimed that a professor should look like a professor. 'Get a decent timepiece, Officer Turner.' Turner had said that he had a professor in college who had taken off his Ironman in front of the class and thrown it across the room where it hit the cinderblock wall. The professor had walked over, picked up the watch, and put it back on. 'Indestructible,' he had said. When Turner added 'I'm an online professor, Rolfe,' to his argument, Judas had given in, and the Timex had made the trip across the pond.

She ran a hand through her short hair. They'd be leaving in a few days, and she thought about becoming boring Haley Girard again. After the debrief at Langley, she'd go to a salon and get it professionally trimmed before returning to Rochester. At school, she'd have to explain the hair—if anyone noticed. Who would? Maria would. She'd tell her that it was time for a change and hear something like, 'About time, chica. Can we do something about those clothes you wear?' Sitting on the soft carpet, feeling the cool breeze blow down from the ceiling fan, she decided that she didn't want to be Haley Girard yet. She preferred cosmopolitan Jessica Stein, attending dinners in the Academy's dining room, reading on the couch listening to Brahms in the afternoons, and Italian wine by candlelight at night while hearing creative 'genius' Ollie Stein drone on about his unfinished novel that would one day be required reading on every beach in America. 'It's extremely gossipy, loaded with bizarre sexual encounters, and takes place in exotic locales where rules and morality disappear like an afternoon margarita,' he proclaimed on one evening walk to a reception being held in the Academy's Villa Aurelia Gardens. Then, she had seen his writing and saw why Narita and Judas had chosen him: He was good. In fact so good, she wanted him to finish the novel. They had revealed little of themselves to each other in the past few months, but traits seeped out now and then. And his writing ability opened up all kinds of questions. Did he study literature in college? Where did he go to college? His speech about Gibbon suggested college... Did he already *have* a PhD? Probably not, unless he had changed his name and appearance. Then again, he knew her under a false name, so... A Master's degree? Perhaps. They were a dime a dozen nowadays. Had he ever written a novel before? Was he a ghost writer for some big shot and the C.I.A. was just his day job? She'd probably never know. Was she attracted to him? Yes. They had held hands, snuggled, hugged, and had even shared the occasional kiss in public to present the happy couple to anyone who may have been watching. But, in private, it had been all business. There had not been a single moment of romantic tension since they'd been in Rome. She wondered what he thought about her.

She looked down at her own watch, an old gold Seiko given to her by the Company to wear. She'd have to return it when they debriefed, and, ironically, don her own Ironman Triathlon that was in some locker with the rest of Haley Girard's belongings. She watched the second hand reach the 12. There were five minutes left on the tape. As she dropped her hand to her lap, she wondered whose watch this had been before her. Was it stolen? Was it a dead agent's? A dead officer's? Her thoughts turned to Sari. Where was she at this moment? And what was in the envelope? The Station Chief in Rome probably had it by now and was examining its contents.

Her first summer working for The Company had mostly been spent in a locked room analyzing banker's box after banker's box of intelligence. She took notes, which were locked away at the end of each session, and eventually submitted three twenty-page reports. They had been accepted with a simple 'Thank you,' and she had returned to Rochester for the last two weeks of summer before school started. What had happened as a result of her reports? She had been informed when she was hired that she would never know. 'However, occasionally, you might see something on the news regarding an operation that took place because of what you submitted,' Judas had told her. 'Usually, though, whenever we make the news, it's because something went wrong.'

The fall semester had been the usual mix of engaged and disengaged students, triumphant and failed school initiatives, teacher's union conspiracy theories—'They're fucking hiding money!'—and conferences with disgruntled parents who on one hand would yell at their child for failing grades and on the other hand inform the administration that the family would be taking a trip the following week to Bermuda. Pretty soon, the only graph she was analyzing was the school's employee-alcohol curve: As the number of school days completed increased, the number of alcoholic beverages consumed by educators increased. Then, she had been contacted by The Company.

Movement across the room took her out of her ruminating. She watched as Turner removed his headphones and crept toward the tape recorder. He nodded at her, and she removed her headphones. Sounds of heavy panting filled the room. Then she heard her own voice, which always bothered her because she didn't think she sounded like that in real life. 'My *God*! Where did that move at the end come from?' her voice said. Turner's voice replied, 'I don't know, but it would make a great scene in a book.' Laughter came through the player's speakers, followed by her saying, 'Let's take a shower.'

Turner coughed loudly while carefully pushing the PAUSE button. Then, he said, "You first, my dear."

She replied, "Okay, but join me if you change your mind."

He walked with the tape recorder over to the CD player that sat on top of the bookshelf. He put in a CD by Stan Getz, and as "the sound" filled the room, he quietly ejected the tape and placed it back inside Dickens's masterpiece.

In the kitchen, she poured herself a full glass of ice water and then headed to the bathroom.

C.I.A. Officer Rose Wakefield entered the Rome safe house with the tote bag and was met by Rome Station Chief Ritzy Zimmer. Off to Zimmer's right was an officer Wakefield didn't recognize, although she knew exactly why he was there: extra security. An Uzi hung from a shoulder strap, and he also carried a 9mm with a silencer attached. Zimmer had her .44 caliber Magnum in a holster on her waist. 'Screw the noise. If the bullets start flyin', I'm pulling this sonofabitch out and lettin' loose,' she had explained to anyone who questioned why the station chief walked around like Dirty Harry. This bravado had not only earned her the love of her subordinates, but she had also become somewhat of a Company cult hero, nicknamed "Dirty Zim"—the hard drinking, chain-smoking, foul-mouthed card player. To a select few, including Wakefield, it was also known that Dirty Zim was the on-again, off-again lover of Rolfe Judas.

Speaking of the devil, Judas emerged from the safe house kitchen with three icy beers. He handed one to Wakefield in exchange for the bag. "Cheers, Rosey," he said. "Our kiddos did great."

"He's good," Wakefield said, referring to Turner, "and Lear was as calm as can be. Where did you find her?"

Judas shrugged. "You know they don't let me in on that stuff," he joked.

Zimmer took the other beer from Judas, and the three of them clinked bottles.

After they all took a healthy pull and let the beer cool their insides, they sat down on the living room couch. Uzi stayed by the front door and monitored his laptop's screen, which was split into four sections to account for the four feeds he was receiving from cameras positioned outside the house.

Twenty minutes later, the mood had changed from celebratory to serious. Judas was nursing his second beer and looking at a piece of paper from Sari's envelope. Wakefield was pacing the floor.

Zimmer inhaled from her cigarette and then exhaled smoke through her nostrils. "Does the word '*empire*' mean what I fucking think it means?" She sat back against the couch cushions and gripped Judas's shoulder.

Judas said, "Yes."

"Trouble," said Wakefield.

"We need to notify Narita and the DCI *now*," said Zimmer.

11

SATURDAY, JULY 1, 2006

Bay Harbor Lanes had been an after-hours working-class fixture in Bay Harbor for over sixty years. Twenty lanes of polished wood with glowing white bowling pins painted with fresh red stripes at the far end were meticulously kept up by owner Harold Steffins and his crew of assistants. Attached to the back, not by coincidence, was a bar named "The Lane" that ran the entire width of the alley. The bar was fashioned as one long lane with a bowling ball welded down at one end and a set of pins anchored to the other, and while it was stocked with the usual selection of alcoholic beverages, The Lane made most of its money from its famous endless pitcher deal. Steffins kept it simple like his father before him. And simple meant that if you're bowling after a hard day's work, you want cold beer and a lot of it. For the sixties, seventies, and eighties, you couldn't find an open lane or an empty stool at the bar after 6 p.m. Monday through Friday. But, as technology started to explode in the 1990s, Steffins saw fewer and fewer nights at the alley were packed; people had more options for distraction. He didn't know what it meant, but he knew that he didn't like it. Blowing off steam from a long day at work while having a few beers usually led to nothing but good things. There was camaraderie and lifelong friendships nurtured and preserved by the idle chit-chat and joking up and down the lanes. He also lost count how many times there had been a collection basket on the bar to help out someone in the community facing a difficulty or to buy school supplies or sports equipment for the local kids when times were tough. Right or wrong, he equated the diminishing attendance at the alley with the loss of his community. So, at the turn of the century, he renovated. The alley now had big screen TVs; the days of paper scoring were kicked to the curb and replaced by automatic bowling computers; the balls and bowling shoes for rent were all replaced with brand new ones. The Lane still stood sentinel at the back of the alley, but the wooden bar stools that swiveled were replaced with leather stools that spun, and the selection of craft beers increased, as did the selection of mixed drinks and high-end liquors.

And so the next generation of bowlers was born, and Harold Steffins was happy.

Iggi Hilliard led the way into the alley followed by Maria, Haley, and Cal. When his football, basketball, and track days were behind him, Iggi had stumbled upon the game one night with his fellow sports writers. 'Screw golf,' they had said. 'The alley is open no matter what the weather is like, and there are no pompous assholes who shoot 75 and think they are God's gift to the Country Club.' On his first roll, he had wound up and thrown a 12-pound ball down the lane and gotten a strike. The beer had started to flow and so had Iggi: His first game was a 242. After that, he joined a Tuesday night league where they would talk about the Monday Night Football game and the upcoming week's games. 'Don't you get enough of sports?' Maria had asked. 'Guys love to argue sports,' he said. 'We can talk about it all day and all night.' She had her book club—*um, boring*—on Tuesday nights, so it had all worked out. He needed his time with his friends, and she needed her time with her friends. One magical night, he had rolled an alley record of 278—the first 9 balls were strikes—and the place had gone crazy. The aftermath was a night that went into the wee hours of the morning, filled with beer, arguments about a playoff for college football (he hated the BCS, and the SEC), and bowling war stories that got more far-fetched with each telling: 'All I needed was 7 on the last frame, and I threw a fuckin' gutter ball!' 'Sonofabitch coughed right before I let go, and I lofted the ball ten feet down the lane—got thrown out.' 'He started talkin' shit in frame 3, and then I wiped the lane with him in frames 4 through 9.' 'Got him to commit to a third pitcher of beer and the shithead fell apart.'

His average hovered around 225, and there were thoughts of going pro, but every now and then he couldn't find the pocket and self-destructed in games of 134, 122...even one abhorrent 82. Minus those off nights, he had found in Rochester what Harold Steffins had created in Bay Harbor: a place to kick back and get away from the ridiculous pace of American life. He didn't like the word pretentious—he'd say dedicated—but he did own his own ball, shoes, and glove, which he now carried with care into Bay Harbor Lanes.

Cal said that the outing was his treat; the Hilliards had paid for the late lunch when they had walked around Bay Harbor's downtown area. They had all slept in and slept off most of their hangovers—30 was *not* the new 20. Still, why was golden boy Cal paying for the bowling? Maria gave him 'the look' and he relented. Forget it. Show him who is boss on the lane.

They got to their lane, and after balls had been chosen and shoes had been put on, two pitchers of beer arrived with four frosted mugs from The Lane. Haley poured, and Iggi entered everyone's name into the bowling computer. Then, the wings arrived—lunch felt like ages ago—and they all dug in.

Maria motioned Iggi to join her by the lane's ball rack. He licked barbeque sauce off of his fingers and walked over. Haley and Cal stayed at the table and

Landon Beach

continued to eat and drink and make small talk. However, he noticed that they were sitting closer to each other than at lunch. Maybe Maria was right and hook-up city was around the corner for them. All the better—Cal wouldn't be focused on hitting the pins, he'd be focused on—

"Hey," Maria said, interrupting his thought.

"What?" he said.

"I'm just warning you that Cal is one of those guys who is good at every sport he tries."

"What in the hell does that mean?"

She rolled her eyes. "It means that he'll probably be good at bowling, and I don't want you to get thrown off, baby."

He looked over at Cal. The bastard was smiling and already refilling Haley's mug. He was also refilling his own. Iggi returned his attention to Maria, "I'm not worried about Cal."

"That's my man," she said. "Now, gear up. I'm hitting the suds. You know I hate bowling," she laughed.

He winked.

To the right of the display mounted above their lane was a large screen TV that was playing the Yankees-Tigers game. In fact, every other lane had a TV with the game on. Being a lifelong Tigers fan, he knew he was gonna be outnumbered—they were in New York, for Christ's sake. No matter, he'd make his presence known, especially if Big D started to put runs on the board. There was something about this new manager, Jim Leland, that he liked. He'd never be the white-haired wizard that Sparky Anderson was, but this season was going a little too well right now. Any *real* Detroit fan was ready for it to crumble at any minute. Verlander was on the hill tonight, and this kid had some *heat*. Then again, so did Iggi's hook. He smirked and started to stretch. Yes. Bowlers stretched, damnit. Laughter floated over from the table as another Cal joke apparently found its mark. His wife's laugh was one of the most pleasant

104

sounds ever to grace the earth, and, he had to admit, Haley's giggle was magnetic too, but why did it have to be because of *his* jokes. He leered at Cal. The cop didn't see him—too busy studying Haley move her hair over her damn ear. Enough already. Let's get this started.

Iggi walked over to the table.

"Everybody ready to start?" he said, taking a swig of beer and then putting on his bowling glove. Notice, he had said everybody, not the dreaded *ya'll* he had heard a few tables over from some southerner who must have been visiting. 'Ya'll comin' over to this lane?' 'Ya'll don't have any sweet tea?' 'Ya'll gonna win that game tonight, bubba?' No. No. And, No.

"Lead the way," Cal said.

Oh, I will, my friend. "You got it," he said instead.

"Show us how it's done, big hook," Maria said.

They laughed.

"Where did he get that name?" Haley said.

"From all the sports fanatics he bowls with," Maria said.

Iggi smiled.

"Big Hook it is then," Cal said, toasting with his mug.

Iggi's smile became fixed. *God. Damnit.*

A roar from a lane over got all of their attention. The group with the southern visitor was looking up at the television. The Yankees had just scored the first run of the game. But then they heard, "Ya'll calm down. It's only the first damn inning."

Well, at least "bubba" was right on that account. You have to get to Verlander early. If JV settles in, it's over for the Bronx Bombers.

"Still early," Cal said. "Let's go, JV."

Great. It's me, Cal, and the southerner against the rest of these arrogant Yankee assholes. Still. Cal's not afraid to speak up for Big D. That was...something, at least.

"Let's go Yankees!" Haley said.

He stared her down. *Girl, it's on.*

Cal scooted away from her. "Boo!" he said, giving a thumbs down.

Iggi turned around, let the air from the ball return run over his fingers, and then walked to his preferred marks on the lane floor. He studied the pins, measured his breathing, and then gracefully stepped off toward the foul line while winding up and finally letting his ball fly.

Like all good right-handed rolls, the ball traveled down the right-hand side of the lane with a beautiful spinning motion and then, as if drawn in by a magnet, hooked into the pocket causing the artistic chain reaction that made all ten pins seem to fall over at once. STRIKE.

"Boom!" he crowed and then strutted back to the food and drink table.

"Nice ball," Cal said.

"Thanks," he said.

Maria gave him a pat on the butt right before he sat down.

Haley was next: gutter right followed by gutter left. "Next one has to be down the middle, right?" she joked.

"Maybe you should stick to baseball," Cal said.

"Oh, should I?" Haley flirted back.

Iggi seized his opportunity to refill everyone's beer, and then two more pitchers arrived.

Maria followed Haley with gutter ball right and then six pins with her second ball. She sat back down and tipped back her mug.

Cal rose.

Okay, let's see the *athlete*.

Cal grabbed his ball from the rack and wasted no time. He lined up, approached, and let it rip. Iggi watched as it traveled straight down the lane at a considerable speed. *He's going to leave a split.* Then, it eased just a bit to the right of the head pin and...STRIKE.

"Woo!" Maria shouted.

Haley watched, but the angle of her gaze pointed to the backside of Cal's jeans just a bit too long.

Everything became quiet for a minute as Iggi looked up at the scoreboard. Music had been playing since they arrived, but he hadn't noticed it until now. As if someone had turned up the volume and turned back the time, he heard George Benson's "Turn Your Love Around" start to blare. He looked back to the table and Maria was starting to shift back and forth to the tune. God, she looked hot. Take it down a notch, sweetness. I've got a game to win here.

Then he saw the owner, Harold Steffins, behind the main counter singing the song to himself. Harold had noticed his bowling skills one night and struck up a conversation. Apparently, Harold read his column and loved it. And the subject of music had come up. 'I may have modernized the alley, but I'm not modernizing the music. In my mind, we never left 1990. Everything before that is fair game; anything after it is garbage.' Iggi didn't agree with him, but he respected Steffins's decisiveness.

The song continued to play; there was something about this tune...

DETROIT, 1990

Head Football Coach Justice Benjamin Woodson entered his office followed by Dr. Jasmine "J.J." Jenkins, Iggi Hilliard's high school English teacher. She took a seat in one of the office's folding chairs, and Woodson closed the door.

"J.J., this is his third visit to the principal's office in the past two weeks," Woodson said. "I'm afraid that Weston is going to tell me he has to leave the football team."

"We can't let that happen," she said. "We know why he's acting out and so does Principal Weston. Iggi's father was just gunned down. He's in a dangerous place. We could lose him if we don't do something. Besides, academically, he's a great writer—one of the best I've ever had."

"No shit?"

"No shit," she smiled back.

Woodson rubbed his hand across his brown shaved head. "I know. I liked his old man. I can see Iggi's pain, frustration, and anger every time I see him—in the hallway, in class, and on the field."

"We've got to talk to him," J.J. said. "Do you know his mother?"

"No, but word gets around. She's in a bad place."

J.J. tapped her long slender brown fingers on top of Woodson's desk. "I think you should talk to him."

"He's in study hall right now," Woodson said.

"Ugh. The period where athletes' grades go to die," she said. "We've got to get him out of there."

"And put him where?"

"I think I can get Weston to agree to let him be my aide for that period. Then, I can keep an eye on him and help him."

Woodson looked at his wall clock above the door. "Who is covering your class right now?"

"Sharon," J.J. said.

Woodson nodded. "He's scheduled to meet with Weston in an hour."

"You talk to him now, and I'll go see Weston."

"Okay."

She exited, and five minutes later there was a knock at the door.

"Come in," Woodson said.

The door opened, and a skinny kid with closely cropped hair and a peach fuzz moustache entered.

"You wanna see me, coach?" Iggi said.

"Close the door," Woodson said.

Iggi did and took a seat in one of the folding chairs. "You kickin' me off the team, right?"

"No, but you're in a heap of trouble, son."

"Man, coach, I hear you. I hear you. But don't call me your son. Don't go there."

Woodson fiddled with the whistle at the end of the nylon cord around his neck. "I'm not trying to be your dad—"

"You're fuckin' right on that," Iggi cut him off.

Woodson leaned forward. "Watch your language."

"Man, fuck that! We done?"

Woodson exhaled. "Iggi, what happened to your dad wasn't right."

Iggi went to speak, but his lips and chin started to shake and his eyes welled up, so he bit down instead.

"Sometimes bad things happen to the people we love without any warning or explanation. Right now you're thinking it was the cops, right?"

Iggi nodded.

"Well, you might be right. Or, you might be wrong. There are racist cops, no denying that, but most of them aren't."

"How you know that?"

"Because *my* daddy and uncle are Detroit policemen who serve our city right now."

"You ain't never convincin' me that he wasn't gunned down. Those two assholes shot my dad and his best friend in a 7 Eleven—a 7 Eleven! This ain't the way it's supposed to be, coach!"

"You're right," Woodson said. "I don't think I'll convince you right now. Maybe down the road, you'll see it differently. You're hurting right now," he paused, "and are making some bad choices."

"It don't matter much now," Iggi said.

"Bull shit! It matters now more than ever!" He slammed his fist down on the table. "You've got a lot of talent on the field, and, I hear, in the classroom—where it *really* counts."

"Who have you been talking to about me? You don't know me like you think you do," Iggi said, and then stared at the floor.

"It doesn't matter. What matters is that you get straight. I'm going in to talk with Principal Weston in a few, and I'm going to argue for keeping you on the team under certain conditions."

Iggi's eyes moved from the floor to his coach.

"You're going to meet with me every day before and after school. We'll go over your schedule and make sure that you're keeping up with your classes."

"I hate class," Iggi said quietly, looking at the floor.

"Not true. I looked at your Junior High transcript. All A's and B's."

Iggi was silent.

"You might be switching out of study hall—"

"Naw! This is too much—"

"You don't do *squat* in study hall. None of you boys do. Hell, I'd get every one of your asses out of there if I could, but our jacked-up school system doesn't have enough places to put all of you, so they dump you there or in art or in a *second* gym class." He stopped, realizing he had just let out some of his personal views.

Iggi had the trace of a grin on his face.

"Don't tell anyone what I just said."

Iggi nodded. "But if you take me out of study hall, where am I goin'?"

"You might become Dr. Jenkins' aide for that period."

"She the one who told you I had academic potential?"

"Maybe. She did tell me that you're a good writer. That true?"

"I guess I could be okay being an aide for Dr. J. She's legit."

"Now you're talking sense," Woodson said. "I'm going to give your mom a call tonight and tell her of our arrangement. And...I'm going to ask if I can pick you up on a couple of Saturdays to work out with me and maybe get some lunch and watch a college game at my house. You okay with that?"

Iggi sat back and was silent for a long time.

Woodson kept it silent, waiting for him to speak.

"I used to watch Michigan games with my dad on Saturday." Then, the tears started coming. Iggi put his head in his hands and began to cry.

Woodson got up, moved around the edge of his desk, and put his big hands on Iggi's shoulders. Then, Iggi stood up, and Woodson wrapped his huge arms around the boy. "We're going to make it through this together." He pulled back and looked Iggi in the eyes. "Got it?"

Iggi shook his head in agreement—and then went in for one more huge hug.

Iggi tipped back a fresh beer as Haley got up to roll her ball down the lane. The song reminded him of Woodson. After serving thirty-five years in the Detroit Public School system, Coach Justice Benjamin Woodson would be retiring after the 2006-2007 school year; the fall of 2006 would be his last season as head football coach. Iggi had received an invitation to appear on the sidelines during the final home game of the year in a few months—the date was already circled and highlighted on his calendar. As for Dr. Jasmine Jenkins, she had retired in 2003, but Iggi still talked to her once a week. In fact, she was one of his beta readers for the upcoming tragic tale of the Detroit Lions, and he needed to touch base with her after the weekend at the cabin. *Where would I be right now if they hadn't stepped in to help?*

Another eruption came from a few tables down and took him out of his thoughts. He looked at the screen and saw that the Tigers had just tied the score with a 2-out double that drove in two runs. He stood up and clapped.

The noise in the alley lowered, and the members from the other lane heard his clapping and stared him down. He turned to go get his ball.

The first game ended with Iggi at 231, Cal 194, Haley 92, and Maria 121. Maria punched a button on the computer console, and the scores cleared for game number two. Eight frames in, Maria approached Iggi, who was sipping nervously on a beer while staring at the lane in disbelief. Like the Tigers, Cal had roared to life and had already passed the 200 mark with a 203 heading into the 9th. Iggi's big hook had become even bigger, and he had left two open frames; he was at 186.

"What's wrong?" she said, sitting on his lap.

Iggi looked behind her. Cal and Haley were still taking a bathroom break. He pointed at the lane. "This. Is. My. *Domain*." He said. "*My* alley. Your friend Cal is getting on my nerves."

Her eyes were glazed. *She's lit already.*

"I told you he's good at every sport," she said. "But c'mon," she stroked his beard, "you're the king. Get up and show it when it's your turn. You've still got the 9th and 10th." She saw Haley leaving the bathroom and got up from his lap. "Be back in a minute."

"Where are you going?"

"Girl talk," she said.

Iggi turned his head and saw Haley walking across the carpeted floor between the bathrooms and bowling area. Maria intercepted her, and they talked for a minute. He couldn't get a read on what they were saying. Then, Cal exited the men's room, and they all headed back to the table where he was.

"You're up, Cal," Maria said.

"On it," Cal said as he took a drink from his fresh beer.

Cal approached the ball return and picked up his ball. He became aware of someone right behind him.

"Hey there," Haley said.

Okay, he was interested. And it wasn't the beer talking at this point. It had started the night before at the fire and had continued this afternoon when they had sat by each other at lunch. He wasn't sure what it was. Yes, she was beautiful and smart, but there was a mystery that surrounded her—not in a standoffish or aloof way, just something different. "Hello," he said. "Trying to throw me off?"

She gave an innocent *who me?* look. "Just sizing up the competition from a different angle."

He looked up at the scoreboard. She had a score of 64. "Making your plans for game number 3?"

She moved closer and whispered in his ear, "Just trying to get some pointers. Still haven't brought out my A-game yet." She backed away.

He glanced back at the table where Maria raised both eyebrows. Iggi's eyes looked like they were shooting machine gun bullets through his skull. He turned around and started his approach. *I'll show you some A-game.* As soon as he released it, he knew he was in trouble. The ball went wide right, hanging on the edge for a second, and then plummeted into the gutter. Like most amateur bowlers who are having success but then do something like that, he tried to overcorrect on the second ball—*just play it safe, go for the center*—and hooked it left, knocking down only two pins.

Maria yelled from the table, "He *is* human after all!"

Haley grabbed his beer and delivered it to him. "Found out what I wanted to know," she said.

Before he could answer, Iggi approached him. "These lanes are bullshit sometimes."

All he could do was nod as Iggi strode by. A minute later, *Big Hook* delivered a strike. Then three more in the 10th.

* * *

On fire inside, Iggi remained calm on the outside as he saw the final scores go up for game #2: Maria, 143; Haley, 78; Cal, 225; and Iggi, 246.

"Good game," Iggi said to Cal.

They shook hands.

"Yeah, pull him, Leland!" shouted a Yankee fan from the other table.

Iggi and Cal looked at the screen. The Tigers had a 5-3 lead, but it was the bottom of the 7th, and Verlander had loaded the bases with two outs.

"Don't do it, Jimmy," Cal said. "Let him get the last out."

He stole my line. "He's got one more out in him. I know it," said Iggi.

They watched as Leland talked to the young pitcher and catcher. Iggi noticed that more and more players these days were talking into their gloves, and managers were covering their own mouths with their hands during these classic baseball discussions on the mound. There were all sorts of superstitions in sports, but baseball was in a category of its own. Now, apparently, teams were worried about opposing ball clubs hiring and planting professional lip readers in the stands to pass on information. Throw in phones with cameras, and it was only going to get worse.

"He's gonna pull him," Iggi said as the conversation on the mound continued.

"Don't do it," Cal spoke to the television.

Leland gave Verlander a pat and jogged back to the dugout.

Together, Cal and Iggi shouted, "Yes!"...

...and slapped a monster high five.

Surprised, Iggi just smirked, and they went back to watching the game.

* * *

Outside of Bay Harbor Lanes, Gregory and Vladimir watched the entrance from their parked car across the street. It was nearing 10 p.m., and they were restless.

"We've been sitting here for half-an-hour," Gregory said. "We'll need to move soon."

"You mean you want to kill her as she exits the alley?" Vladimir said. "Too public."

"I meant *move* as in *move the car.*"

"Oh. I see." Vladimir checked his watch. "They've been in there for three hours. Does bowling take that long?"

"Sometimes," Gregory said. He leaned back against his seat. "We'll wait until tomorrow."

"But if they are in there playing and drinking alcohol as you have suggested they are, then tonight is perfect. They'll have a slower reaction time, and we have more cards to play in terms of how we make it look. Let's eliminate them all when they get to the cabin."

Gregory was firm. "No. We now know that Cal Ripley is a Detroit Police Officer. I want to study the situation a little more before we commit."

The old man thought, then agreed. "One or two more days. We need to be out of here by the 4th. Our orders are clear."

"I know what our orders are, comrade," Gregory said. "Drive us back to the marina."

Vladimir started the car, and they drove off into the warm July night with the windows down. A few early fireworks could be heard as the car disappeared down the winding road.

Maria exited the master bathroom in a silk nightgown that barely went past her round behind. She turned off the light and started to walk toward the bed, where Iggi was sitting with his back against the headboard, looking out at Lake Ontario.

"Ahem," she said.

He looked over at her, but his eyes were not what she expected—they were watering. "My God, what's wrong?" she asked, sitting down next to him.

He turned toward her and gave a weak smile. "You look incredible, and I definitely could be in the mood, but I—"

"Is this the first time you have ever rejected me?" She grinned.

"I guess—"

"Don't worry. We have time. Haley and Cal are downstairs." She moved closer. "We're all good."

"Okay. Thanks," he said. Leaning over, he gave her a kiss on the cheek. Then, he sat back and remained silent.

What was it? Something she had said at the alley to him? Tension with Haley or Cal? Something more serious? She was a bit scared.

"I thought about my dad tonight at the bowling alley," he finally said.

"Your dad?" she said, partially relieved.

"And the day he died."

"When did that happen?"

"I heard this song—you know that the owner Harold only plays songs from like 20 or more years ago—and it just took me back." He put a hand on her thigh.

She settled in, her eyes welded to his. He had only told her the basic facts of his father's death over the years. "I'm right here."

"I know." His eyes drifted back to the lake. "But the truth is, I don't know a lot about what happened that day."

12

DETROIT, OCTOBER 1989

Jayvyn Hilliard walked into his 14-year-old son's room at 5 a.m. on Saturday morning. The room was tidy, and Iggi had placed his gym shorts, t-shirt, hooded sweatshirt, socks, and underwear on top of the worn wooden desk underneath the room's only window. Jayvyn had found the desk in a junk heap on a curb in Hamtramck. It appeared to have once been a beloved writing station—the wood was knotty pine—but its legs were splintered, and the drawer was missing a metal rail. Iggi's grades had been slipping, and Jayvyn knew the kitchen table was no longer a place for his teenaged son to hit the books. So, together, they had refinished and rebuilt the desk. It was now wiped with Pledge daily by Iggi in preparation for Jayvyn's two inspections—one at 5 a.m. and the other unannounced. He had noticed that his son had made it a routine to wipe the desk every night when he was done with his homework and then place the family's copy of *Bartlett's Familiar Quotations* back on top, opened up to the page he was on. Jayvyn peered over the clothes, clicked his flashlight on, and ran the beam down the page. His eyes stopped at an entry by John Adams.

I must study politics and war that my sons may have liberty to study mathematics and philosophy. My sons ought to study mathematics and philosophy, geography, natural history, naval architecture, navigation, commerce, and agriculture, in order to give their children a right to study painting, poetry, music, architecture, statuary, tapestry and porcelain.

Letter to Abigail Adams [May 12, 1780]

Jayvyn turned the flashlight off. His eyes rose from the desk and stopped at no point in particular on the wall. He closed them...and began to smell the damp rot of the jungle floor. Someone was hacking the bush in front of him, complaining. Suddenly, he heard a machine gun opening up on his right, and he dove for cover. There was screaming up ahead, yelling to the right, then Staff Sergeant Matthews was next to him shouting, 'Hilliard, give me your goddamned grenades. There's a bunker up—' and then the Staff Sergeant's body seemed to tense up as if someone was applying pressure to the small of his back. His eyes froze, and then his head hit the maze of mud and sticks on the ground. Jayvyn could now see the hole in the back of Matthews's head with blood oozing out of it. *Impossible—not Sarge too...*

Jayvyn opened his eyes and found himself lying flat on the cold wooden floor of Iggi's bedroom, flashlight gripped tightly in his right hand. Nothing in the room moved, and he relaxed—now knowing where he was. He stood up and wiped tears from his eyes. Iggi was still asleep. *Thank God.* His eyes worked their way back to the desk area, and he gathered his composure.

On the floor directly beneath the clothes were Iggi's new Nike Shark football cleats, each shoe perfectly lined up next to the other one with the laces pulled tight and the ends stuffed inside. The cleats had cost his son an entire summer's worth of mowing and edging the family's small yard twice a week.

They were the first pair of new cleats anyone in the Hilliard household had ever owned. When they had left the sporting goods store—after puzzling looks from the cashier after Iggi put down the cash from his own wallet to buy them—Jayvyn had stopped his son in the parking lot before they got in the car. He had said, 'Now you'll take care of them the proper way because you know what it took to get them.'

Jayvyn picked up the shirt, underwear, and socks from on top of the sweatshirt. Holding them above, he saw the large block 'M' on the front of the sweatshirt. He exhaled, "Iggi, you must be dreamin' if you think you're gonna play for Schembechler—well, Moeller after this year." He paused, remembering Iggi placing in the 100-meter dash at a home track meet last spring. "Well, maybe," he smiled and put the clothes neatly back on top of the sweatshirt. The big talk around the city was a junior over at Dearborn Heights Robichaud named Tyrone Wheatley. "You gotta come see this kid run," one of his co-workers at the GM plant had said.

The room's floorboards creaked with each heavy step as he approached the bed. His son's breathing was heavy, a heavy Jayvyn hadn't known for over twenty years. He stopped at the foot of the bed and watched as the covers moved with each breath. *Still a long way to go, but he'll make a good man one day.* He allowed himself a smile of accomplishment; the way his son was sleeping told him that Iggi didn't have a worry in his brain. *May he never see what I have seen of this world.* He put his hand on his son's right calf and began to shake it.

"Iggi," he said.

Iggi's eyes opened, and he stretched his arms over his head. "Yeah?"

"Inspection," Jayvyn said.

Iggi wiped his eyes and pulled the covers off. "Yes, sir," he whispered, and slid out of bed.

Jayvyn turned on the overhead light and then the desk lamp as Iggi made his bed—no wrinkles across the thin bedspread and hospital corners at the foot. When Iggi finished, he stood by his bed at the position of attention.

Jayvyn put a white glove on his right hand and began to search the room for dirt and dust: under the bed, in every corner, on top of the door, behind the drawers in Iggi's chest of drawers, under the shoes lined up in the closet, behind the nightstand, and even the entire surface of the desktop lamp's bulb. He found none. Next, he took a plastic ruler out of Iggi's desk drawer and measured the folds on the bed. The fold was supposed to be exactly six inches, and it was to be precisely twelve inches from the head of the bed; most weeks Iggi had it right on, but he had seemed a little cocky this morning by not using the ruler when he made the bed. Jayvyn looked at the ruler. The fold was a foot from the head. Good. He slid the ruler down and measured the fold.

He frowned. "Six and a half inches," he said.

Iggi didn't move.

Jayvyn removed the white glove and tossed it on the bed. Then he took the ruler and slid it back into the desk drawer. He turned to Iggi. "Attention to detail, boy. Gotta pay attention to detail. This mornin' you let one lazy moment ruin what was a decent job on the rest of your quarters."

"Dad, it's a half of an in—"

"Don't have the luxury of givin' half an inch up in this world. You still haven't learned it." He glanced at his watch. "Another one later today and then same time tomorrow morning."

"Yes, sir," Iggi said.

Jayvyn gave a nod of approval and then walked out of the room.

At 7 p.m., the door to the 7-Eleven store swung open, and Jayvyn Hilliard entered. Ever since he and his wife, Brianne, had settled back in Detroit after the war, he had made it his nightly routine to walk the half-mile down to the store, get a copy of the *Detroit Free Press*, a coffee loaded with cream and sugar, an apple fritter, and then walk home while eating the donut and sipping on his coffee.

Every single fellow soldier he served with in Vietnam had something he missed from home and swore if he made it back he would never take for granted again. For Jayvyn, it was fresh coffee and apple fritters—he dreamt about them on patrol, craved them on lonely nights sitting in a bug infested bunker—and he had almost not returned to ever enjoy them again.

Routine had become his ally. Get up, inspect the house and kids' rooms, have coffee with his wife at the kitchen table, leave to put in a full day at Detroit-Hamtramck Assembly, arrive home, lift weights in the garage, eat dinner, and then go on his 7-Eleven run. When he would get home, he would sit on the front porch and read his paper by the porch light; when it was too cold during the winter, he would sit by the space heater in his garage. The nightly ritual was a reminder that he *had* made it home, and it helped him deal with some of the nightmares. After reading his paper, he would come inside the house to shave, shower, and have family time. Then, came night. A flashlight and a full glass of ice water were always on his nightstand, and a small nightlight was turned on when he went to bed and remained on the entire night. Brianne had handled the task of telling the kids that they had to grow out of their nightlights but that daddy never had to, and that she would explain why when they were older.

Jackson "Jonesy" Jones stood at his usual position behind the 7-Eleven checkout counter, smoking a cigarette and sipping on a 44-ounce Big Gulp of Mountain Dew.

"Evenin', Jayvyn," Jonesy said.

"How were the geese this morning?" Jayvyn asked.

Jonesy had also served in the war. After his platoon had been cut to pieces in an ambush, the North Vietnamese Army soldiers started going up to each

121

member of his platoon and shooting them in the head. When they were just about to Jonesy, the geese in the area started honking so much that they annoyed the NVA soldiers to the point where they turned their weapons on the geese and forgot about Jonesy, who continued to play dead. When he returned stateside and settled back into his Detroit home, one of the first things he did was locate the local population of Canada geese—who annoyed the hell out of Michigan residents. After finding some that lived in a nearby pond, he started the ritual of driving over and feeding them every morning as a tribute to the geese that had died saving his life.

"Beautiful as ever," Jonesy smiled.

"Any good word, brother?"

Jonesy set down his Dew and started to run a hair pick through his afro. "Shit, in this town? Nothin'." Jonesy sucked on his cigarette and exhaled a cloud of blue smoke that rose in front of his face. "Nothin' except Barry Sanders. That rookie's got wheels, Jayvyn. Might actually win a few games."

Can't argue with a thing he just said. Jayvyn nodded and walked toward the coffee maker where he grabbed a large Styrofoam cup and started to fill it. He caught a glimpse of his reflection in the Bud Light mirror on the wall above the coffee station; he looked much older than he was—wrinkled forehead, gray 5 o'clock shadow, and eyes that had seen too much to keep their youth. He continued to pour.

"I've got your fritter and paper ready up here," Jonesy said.

"One squared away store, sir," Jayvyn said as he shook an ample amount of powdered creamer out of the Coffee-mate container into his cup. Then he did the same with the sugar container. The smell of his favorite blend reached his nose now. He looked to Jonesy. *Man knows how to make coffee.* He returned his attention to the drink station. About to grab a stirring stick, his left hand stopped as he heard the front door slam open. Full coffee cup still in his right hand, he turned toward the front door. Two men wearing ski masks entered and ran to the front register. Another blocked the door from outside.

"Open the cash register!" one of the men yelled at Jonesy.

Jonesy's hands started shaking as he raised them in the air; the second man had a handgun aimed at Jonesy's chest.

The ski masks weren't pulled all the way down, and Jayvyn could see that one man was white and one man was black. He started to calmly walk toward the men with his open cup of coffee in hand.

Jayvyn reviewed the situation. Jonesy had worked the noon to 8 p.m. shift at the store for as long as Jayvyn had been coming for his nightly routine. Jonesy's manager was a jerk who had fired the last two clerks when the store had been robbed. The robberies had taken place close to midnight, and both times the police had shown up close to an hour after the robbery, written down a few notes, promised to investigate, and then were not seen again until the next robbery. The manager knew the money taken would not be compensated for in any way because the perpetrators would never be caught. Therefore, he had mandated that a loaded Saturday-night special be kept behind the counter as a deterrent. The manager also refused to put cameras in the store—too much hassle. With the robber's gun aimed at Jonesy's chest, Jonesy would never be able to raise the gun behind the counter in time—he'd already be shot by then. Was there a chance Jonesy would keep his job? No, he'd be fired, which was why Jayvyn had to help him. Right. Now.

Jonesy saw Jayvyn approaching, and the robber with the gun must have seen Jonesy's eyes, because he now looked over at Jayvyn. "Stay right where you are, man," he shouted to Jayvyn.

The other man quickly stole a glance at him. Jayvyn continued to approach. "Don't you fuckin' come any closer. You hear?" the man with the gun shouted as his eyes alternated between Jonesy and Jayvyn.

Jayvyn took a sip of coffee and kept walking.

The third robber opened the front door. "We gotta split. Cops just around the corner."

The man without the gun at the counter replied, "No. I ain't leavin' here without my money." He turned to Jonesy. "Hurry the fuck up!"

Jayvyn made eye contact with Jonesy. He couldn't tell if his friend was saying, 'Yes, you jump the guy with the gun and I'll take care of this other asshole,' or, 'Don't do anything. Just let these guys go.' Jayvyn started to lower his coffee cup. He was within ten feet of the robbers.

Then, he heard, "Stop! Police!"

The robber outside tried to take off. Shots were fired. Jayvyn used this to his advantage and launched the coffee out of his cup at the man with the gun.

The hot liquid hit the man's mask and his eyes. He instinctively flinched and lowered his gun, which gave Jayvyn enough time to jump on him and tackle him to the floor. Jonesy saw the other robber reaching for a gun, so he jumped over the counter and joined the fight.

Jayvyn ripped off the man's ski mask and saw that he was a mid-twenties Caucasian with a goatee. But he was also strong, and soon he gained an advantage over Jayvyn, rolling him over and using his weight to pin Jayvyn down.

Jonesy went big and took a massive swing that whiffed through the air above the other robber's head. The miss gave the man enough time to pull his gun out, and he fired it squarely at Jonesy's chest.

The door to the 7-Eleven burst open, and two police officers—one white, one black—entered the store with guns drawn. The robber who had shot Jonesy turned around and attempted to fire, but both officers shot him dead before he was able to pull the trigger. Meanwhile, the other robber saw Jayvyn's hand reaching for the robber's gun that had fallen to the floor as he started to pass out due to the robber's chokehold on him. When Jayvyn finally grasped the handle, the robber let go and rolled off, saying, "Help!" to the police officers.

You're okay. He's off of you. You don't need the gun. You're safe. But, he was unable to stop his hand with the gun from rising up in time.

Both police officers fired center of mass—and killed Jayvyn Hilliard.

Jonesy, blood soaking his shirt and now also leaking out of his mouth, looked over at his friend's glazed eyes. "Jayvyn—" was all he could get out. He fell back against the counter, and then the life went out of his eyes.

The surviving robber thought quickly. He picked up the ski mask and threw it at Javyn's still body. "I was just mindin' my own business, havin' my coffee, when these two pieces of shit tried to rob the store. I was tryin' to help the clerk when this fuckin' thug tried to kill me."

One of the police officers checked the dead bodies, then called it in. The other officer looked at the robber and said, "It's over," he said. "You're safe."

"What about the one outside?" the robber asked. "I heard gunshots."

"Got him too," the officer replied.

The other officer got off the radio and gave his partner a look that said: *Let's get this cleaned up and over with as soon as possible.*

Not ten seconds had passed when the radio crackled to life with the report of another shooting four blocks away. Officers were being dispatched and back up had been requested.

13

SATURDAY, JULY 1, 2006

"So they told you that your father was trying to rob the store and that he aimed his gun at them?"

"My dad would have never robbed *anyone*," said Iggi, "Let alone the store he went to every night, and I mean *every* night. Jonesy was one of his best friends." He sat up a little straighter in bed. "The Vietnam veterans were treated like dirt when they got home. And the black ones? Even worse. But the guys I saw with my dad stuck together. Jonesy and Dad saw each other almost every night, and a few others used to come over to the house and sit on the porch late at night talking. I was never allowed to join, but I knew when they were out there. One night I snuck out my second story window, climbed across the roof, and listened to them. One time was enough. The stuff they talked about scared the hell out of me."

"When the police showed up to deliver the news, was that when you started to not like cops?"

"Maybe. I don't trust them."

"I always knew it had something to do with his death. You've just never talked about it in this much detail before, baby."

"I guess we all keep some things to ourselves."

She thought about the abortion that she had never told him about.

"I mean, we'll never know everything about each other, right?" Iggi continued.

"It's impossible, I think." She thought back to the years she had taught Joseph Conrad's *Heart of Darkness*. "Maybe Conrad helped us pose the question best: Do we ever really know anyone?"

Iggi pulled her to him. "Startin' in with the English teacher mumbo jumbo, huh?" He kissed her head and smelled her hair. "I hope I can say that I know you and that you know me."

She closed her eyes for a beat. "You know me," she said. He began to rub her hair, and she opened her eyes.

"What about Cal?" she said.

"What about him?" Iggi said.

"Do you trust him?"

"I don't know," he said. "I haven't known him long enough. But..."

"But?" she said.

"I admit that the weekend hasn't been a disaster so far."

"That's a start," she said.

"A start to what?"

She left the bed and walked over to the CD player, which was on top of the dresser. "A start to the rest of the weekend with our friends downstairs, and," she turned around and gave him a devious grin, "the start of this." She slipped out of her nightgown and turned on the CD player. Moments later, Chuck Mangione's "Give It All You Got" started playing—loudly.

Standing in front of him, completely nude, she said, "You know how thin these old walls are. We need Chuck to give us a little cover tonight." *And we need to get off the topic of secrets.*

He started to move his head side to side with the music. "You know what I can do when Chuck's on," he said. "The pendulum," he patted his belly, "gets into sync with that horn of his and you're in for a long night."

"I know," she said, stepping toward the bed.

"Is that Chuck Mangione?" Cal said.

"No idea," Haley replied.

They were heading up the stairs to go to bed.

"I haven't listened to him in years," Cal said. "One of my dad's favorites."

The music got louder as they approached the top of the stairway.

"I haven't heard this song before," Haley said. "Maybe if I heard another one."

"You'd recognize his song 'Feels So Good'. It was played in every grocery store, hotel lobby, dentist office, and radio station when we were growing up."

They arrived at the second floor and headed down the hallway. Cal's room was the first on the right and Haley's was at the end on the other side of the hallway. They paused outside of Cal's room.

Cal started with, "I enjoyed our—"

But the sound of moaning rising above the song stopped him cold. He looked at Haley. Then, they looked at the door to Maria and Iggi's bedroom.

More moaning and then, clear as day, Maria's voice commanding, "Hit it. Get it. Oh, fuck me!"

Haley and Cal looked at each other and then reversed their steps back downstairs.

✳ ✳ ✳

Gregory sat in the salon of the boat sipping his vodka in the dark. On the port cabin bench, Vladimir snored away, his empty vodka glass still curled in his hand like he was protecting a teddy bear. Up forward, the other two Russian men had gone to sleep half an hour earlier than the old man. The boat was quiet and so was the marina for that matter; the topside hatch was still open, but the noise from other boaters coming back to their berths after a night out had died down an hour ago.

He couldn't sleep. The mission was on his mind. His thoughts scrolled through the specifics. His thirst for information became insatiable; operations always went smoothly because of over-preparation, never because of under-preparation. That was what was nagging him right now. He felt the team was not prepared. They were better off than when they had arrived a few days ago, but there were still too many variables. Too many 'what ifs' for his comfort. If Vladimir had been in charge, they would have already headed to the cabin—inebriated or not—and started blasting away. Gregory had underestimated Officer Lear, and that was dangerous. Add a Detroit detective to the equation and now he was glad to have the additional two men up forward. He had wanted Viktor on his team, but Moscow Centre had sent him to eliminate the others. And when those assassinations were complete, he would be leaving for the safe house in Canada—and then the airport.

So, he would have to make do with Vladimir and the two others. He thought about the cabin where Lear was staying. Was there anything else he could do tonight? The answer was yes. If it came down to killing Lear at the cabin, then they needed to know more about the layout. They would have broken in tonight while Lear and the others were all bowling, but the owners had armed the cabin's security system before leaving for the alley. His team could have made it in and out before any police showed up, but the break-in might have alerted Lear or the detective that something was up. And he knew Lear was smart and capable. He took stock of the situation one more time and then decided that there was nothing stopping him from doing a little surveillance tonight.

He drained his vodka and scribbled a quick note. Vladimir paused in his snoring and rolled over, now facing the bulkhead. Gregory placed the note on the salon table next to the half-empty bottle of vodka. He took one last look at Vladimir sawing logs and exited the salon, emerging topside. The summers here really are beautiful, he thought while the crisp breeze off the lake hit his arms and face. He closed the cockpit hatch and then stepped off the boat and onto the dock.

The fire roared in the living room fireplace, and Cal sat with Haley on the couch, each with a glass of wine.

"So, you teach high school science and math?"

Along with the other job. "Yes," she said. "Boring right?"

"Not at all," Cal said. "I might be one of the few students who liked school."

"More than just for sports?" She paused. "Sorry, that came out wrong."

Cal waved it off. "Don't worry. Most guys *are* there for the sports."

"But you weren't?"

"I was there to learn. I've always been curious."

She took a sip of wine and let it sit in her mouth for a moment before swallowing. He was nice. Handsome. A little rugged, but what cop wasn't? And he was straight-forward, which she appreciated the most. No psychological games. No insecurity, just comfortable as a man. No pretentious flirting. After two days of observing him, she decided he was confident without being arrogant, quiet without being mute, and athletic without having to wear tank tops to show just how athletic he was. Actually, she was getting curious— curious to feel his shoulders. And that square jaw. She wondered what it might be like to put her hand underneath his chin and then bring her lips to his. Oh,

Maria. Up there having her way with Iggi. Her friend's exclamation had steered her thoughts in a different direction with Cal. It had been going just fine as new acquaintances. Now, she was thinking about touching him.

"Haley?"

Had she missed a question? *Damn* you, Maria. "Sorry," she said.

His grin was so disarming. It held no judgment. He was not keeping track in a first-date scorebook of any kind. She relaxed.

"I was just wondering if, as a scientist, there are still things in the world that you are curious about."

Like what does Cal Ripley do for fun? She almost laughed at herself out loud. "I'm curious about you," she said.

"I'm a cop. I'm boring," he said.

"No, there's more to you. There's more to everyone."

He took a drink of his wine. The fire light reflected off his glass making the red liquid look like he was drinking fire. A log fell over with a soft crunch and pop.

"Okay," he said. "You tell me something about teachers that I don't know, and then I'll tell you something about police officers that you don't know. Fair?"

She scooted closer to him, but they were still not touching. "You're on," she said.

"Intrigued," he said, concentrating on her.

Whether it was the beer at the bowling alley earlier or the wine now, she felt comfortable around him. In fact, she hadn't felt this close to her old self since—forget about that. Don't let it come back up. She took another drink, gathering herself. Then, she put on a smile and said, "So, it turns out that teachers have affairs."

"How do *you* know?" Cal flirted.

"Once every two years, I go to a conference in Nashville, Tennessee. We stay at The Gaylord Opryland Resort & Convention Center, which is probably the nicest hotel I've ever stayed in. And I've seen the bill; the stay costs a fortune. Regardless, the place *should be* named The Adultryland Resort & Convention Center. I had thought science teachers were pretty tame. Not the case. At all. Apparently, there are long-standing affairs and this is just one of the stopovers on their year-long schedule of conferences. It's almost like people become different couples for a weekend and then go back to their old lives. But that's not the crazy part."

"I'm waiting," Cal said.

"One year, I met a woman in her mid-forties, who had two kids, a husband of fifteen years—and was in a long-term relationship with a professor from the University of Wisconsin. They were all over each other in Opryland. But the weekend ended, and I'm thinking I'll never hear from her again. Wrong. We had exchanged professional information, just e-mail addresses, and I get an e-mail from her months later asking if I can give her a call. I do, and she tells me that her lover has attempted to commit suicide. She says that while he was in the hospital, his wife found all of her information in his Blackberry."

"Those things are pure evil," Cal said. "The hell with cell phones."

"So, she starts asking me if I think it is a good idea for her to tell *her* husband."

"What did you do?"

"I got the hell off the phone."

"Nice."

"But here's my real problem. Here I am, some science teacher at a winter convention who bumps into another *professional* who is messing around on her husband—and I know this, I even know the guy who she is having the affair with, and her husband, poor bastard, doesn't."

Cal sat back, and she felt the tenor of the room change. What had she said?

"I've been that poor bastard," he said.

DETROIT, 2004

Detective Cal Ripley sat in his parked Ford Bronco across the street from his wife's red Durango. He was parked across the street because the Durango was not parked in front of their house—it was parked in front of a house *five miles* from their house.

This isn't happening. This can't be happening.

The brick house was a modest two-story with black shutters. The homeowner, family friendly podiatrist Zach Augenbecker, drove a cobalt blue Mustang that was parked in the driveway. There were no lights on downstairs. One light was on upstairs. Cal had been observing for half an hour after watching her enter the front door.

He pulled his work cell phone out and stared at it. He'd gotten wind of the affair from a fellow police officer who had seen her car parked where it was now three weeks ago. Since then, he'd seen it here two times—both nights when he was working. He was supposed to be working tonight but hadn't told her that he'd taken time off. Almost ten years together were about to go away with a few pressed buttons. He started to tear up. When had it started to come apart? Since 9/11, he had been working longer hours—everyone in law enforcement had—and been under more pressure. If the civilian population knew how many tips the department received that 'something big' was about to happen, they'd never be able to sleep at night. Every threat had to be handled, every lead followed up on, and the rub was that, if at all possible, the operations had to remain behind locked doors. When a threat was neutralized, the accomplishment was celebrated with silence. Detective Cal Ripley had played a role in breaking up three minor threats but was not allowed to tell anyone, not even his wife. Perhaps it was living with those secrets that had put space between them. He didn't know. He hadn't thought about it until now, and that might have been the problem. Now, she had crossed a line. *Don't judge yet! It might not be an affair.* However, if she denied where she was at, then he knew it was. Why hadn't he noticed the gap? Why couldn't she have just talked to him when she started to feel them drift? He peered at the upper story window. Well, maybe she had and he had missed the signal. It was too late. He knew he could neither forgive nor forget an affair. He considered himself open and flexible, tolerant and forgiving, but having another man stick his dick inside your wife. Nope.

Stop waiting and get your answer.

He took a drink from his coffee cup. His bladder was starting to feel full. *Maybe I'll take a piss on his lawn—or on the hood of his Mustang.* He sniffled, wiped his eyes, and dialed her number.

It took six rings but she picked up. "Cal?"

He set his coffee cup down and watched the house as he talked. "Hey, I got off early tonight and thought we might get a drink together. Been too long since we've gotten out of the house. You home?"

There were a few seconds of silence. "Um, no. I'm at the store and should be home in around fifteen minutes."

Their house was ten minutes away. She's giving herself five minutes to change and leave. His stomach felt queasy, and he struggled to breathe. Anger was inside him, but it was losing to sorrow and despair. He hung his head, and tears filled his eyes once again. He wiped but could not stop them.

"Cal? Did you hear me?"

He gathered himself. "Yeah," he got out. "Since you're out, do you just want to meet somewhere?"

"No, I think a quiet night at home would be best tonight. I'm tired."

I bet you are. "What did you have to pick up at the store?"

More silence, followed by, "Just a few odds and ends. Where are you?"

"I'm just about home."

"Okay," she said. "I'm on my way and will see you soon."

She hung up.

He put the phone down on the passenger seat and waited.

Five minutes later, the front door opened. She emerged but stopped and turned back to Zach, wearing a bathrobe as he stood in the doorway. He reached out his hand and pulled her to him. They embraced and then kissed. *It's over.* She turned around and starting walking toward her vehicle. The man stepped back inside and shut the front door.

Cal got out of his car. She did not notice him and kept walking around until she was about to open the driver side of the Durango.

"That's a strange looking store," he said.

She froze.

He began crossing the street. "And what kind of store is it where the clerk wears a fucking bathrobe and kisses the customer?"

She turned toward him as he stopped at the end of the driveway.

He waited. She said nothing, but her hands were shaking.

"At least you're not trying to make an excuse." He said. "So, who moves out tomorrow? Me or you?"

She started to cry.

The front door opened, and Zach stepped out wearing jeans and a t-shirt now.

"Get. The. Fuck. Back inside your house," Cal said.

Zach looked over to her.

She wiped her eyes and said to him, "I'm okay. Go inside."

Zach nodded and backtracked, shutting the door after he was back inside.

"I'll go," she said.

"What about tonight?" Cal said, barely keeping it together.

"I can stay somewhere else if you want," she said.

"No," he said. "I'll sleep in the guest room." Then, emotion overtook him. "Why?" he said. "*Why?*"

She started to cry again.

He took a step toward her but then stopped.

She held on to the door handle while she continued to sniffle. Two times she attempted to speak but couldn't. On the third try she got out, "Not here. Can I tell you when we get home?"

"Home? We don't have a *home* anymore. It's just a house now." He paused. "And I want to know right now, right here."

She wiped her eyes with the sleeve of her coat. Shaking her head, she said, "Okay. Fine."

He immediately regretted pressuring her. He wasn't ready to hear what he had done to drive her into another man's arms and bed. It was control he wanted, and blocking the path of her Durango seemed the only way he was going to get it.

"It's plain and simple, Cal," she started. "Ever since 9/11, you've hardly been at home. On nights when I thought you were coming home and we'd have an evening together, I'd put out candles and try to make a special dinner. I'd even buy a nice bottle of wine and wait. Do you know how many times you never showed? Do you know how many times you never even called me to tell me you'd be late? Then, when you'd get home late, you never even noticed the table setting or anything. You were either amped up from what happened at work and wanted me to have sex with you on command, or you would crash so hard that you'd sleep in late, and I'd have the table cleared by the time you got up. If it was Saturday or Sunday, then you'd start working on a case of beer and watch football all day. I knew the pressure you were under at work and that you needed space to escape, but after a while there is only so much a person can give. I was tapped out a year ago and told you—"

"You never told me—"

"Oh yes I did," she shouted. "But you never listened."

He thought about fighting back but decided that she *might* have told him.

"You remember when I had that ingrown toenail?"

That, he did remember. She was a runner, but her left big toe got so bad that she could hardly walk. It was non-stop complaining for about a week until she could get in to see the podiatrist. Why could he recall that and not when she had warned him that he was drifting away? "I do," he said.

"Well, I went in and," her eyes then motioned toward the house, "Zach fixed it. That's where it started. Simple as that, Cal. After I told you what I needed and you did nothing to address it, I gave up. Zach was available on nights that you weren't, and a friendship turned into something else."

His frustration began to show as he clenched and unclenched his fists. He was pacing now, breathing in and out with each step. "So when were you going to tell me?"

"Honestly? I wasn't sure. If things went badly between Zach and me, then maybe I would have tried to talk with you again and see if there was a chance to save what we once had."

He stopped pacing. "It doesn't look like it's going badly."

"I've answered your question," she said.

She had. Then, the weight and clarity of the situation settled upon him. He spoke directly and without anger. "We're not going to make it through this one, are we?"

Her hand dropped from the handle, and she looked at the ground for a long time. When she looked back up at him, the tears had returned to her eyes. "I don't think so," she said.

He looked into her misty eyes and then over her head at the gray sky, which became vision after vision of their life together: standing at the altar waiting for her to come down the aisle on their wedding day, the crimson carpet beneath her flowing white dress and the look of hope and wonderment on her face;

making love in their stateroom aboard a cruise ship on their honeymoon, cuddling afterwards and talking about what they wanted their life together to be; holding her at her grandmother's funeral; the two of them arriving at the German Shepard breeders to pick up an eight-week-old Roscoe whose ears hadn't stood up yet; celebrating his promotion to Detective; taking a walk together along the beaches of Traverse City on a getaway weekend; the phone call from her on the morning of 9/11, reassuring her that everything was going to be okay; the sound of her laugh when he fell off the bed trying to make a move on her but slipped off due to the fact that he had had one too many scotches...

"Cal?" she said.

All gone now. Forever. He thought there would have been more conflict, but because she was direct—always had been—there was little else to say. "I'll see you at the house," he said. He turned and started to walk toward his car. Behind him, he heard the door to the Durango open and then close, followed by the sound of the engine turning over.

But, in a way, I've also been your science teacher conference friend. After she had moved out, he'd started his own fling before the divorce was a done deal. Payback? All is fair in love and war? She deserved it? No, the root of it was hurt, and even though his feelings were genuine for the woman he saw, it still didn't sit right with him. She had sensed this, and the relationship fizzled out and died a month after the divorce was final. Right now, Haley didn't need to know this. Maybe she never would. The important matter right now was that he enjoyed her company. Maria's *announcement* was a gift, like getting to stay up late an extra half-hour when he was young, because he was in no hurry to go to bed. Last night, he'd had nightmares from the operation in Detroit. The image of human appendages being blown across the basement had awoken him, and he still wasn't sure if he had yelled out loud. The house had remained quiet

138

while he stayed frozen underneath the covers looking at the ceiling and waiting for a knock on the door perhaps followed by a concerned voice. Thankfully, the knock never came. And no one had said anything during the day, which put his mind somewhat at ease, but not completely, because he didn't know if they had heard it and decided to not talk about it.

"Well, there you have it," he said.

"I'm sorry that happened to you," she said. "Have you adjusted to being alone again?"

"Well, I still have Rosco," he said.

"Who's Rosco?"

"My German Shephard. Had him since he was a pup." He paused. "There was no way in hell she was getting the dog."

"I'm more of an animal tolerator," she said.

He chuckled. "What in the hell is that?"

"It means that," she thought of a way to put it, "well, let me ask you. If you were at a veterinarian's office with your dog, and the vet asked you if Rosco was just your dog or a family member, what would you answer?"

"Family member. One-hundred percent," he said, as if on the stand.

"Ah ha," she said. "My answer would be *dog*."

"Ice cold," he grinned.

"Honest, Detective," she said.

He took a large sip of wine. "I can respect that."

She took a drink, and inched closer. He eyed her lips. Was it going to happen? Please, let it happen. *Should I be the one to—*

"Still up hitting the joy juice," said Maria.

His eyes left Haley, and he watched as Maria descended the staircase wearing a pink colored robe.

"Just a nightcap," Haley said and then locked eyes with Cal for a moment.

Her gaze told him that she had wanted to, which made his insides warm up even more. Just how long had it been since he had received *that* look? Too long, because when you get *that* look you never want it to disappear.

"I'm just getting a few bottles of water," Maria said, pausing at the bottom of the stairs. "Can I get either of you anything?"

How about giving me that moment back! "No," he smiled.

"Nothing for me," Haley said.

Maria nodded and entered the kitchen.

Good. Good. Get your waters and get the hell upstairs, Maria.

Haley rose from the couch. "I'm going to hit the hay, I think."

No, no, no, no, no. His insides went from a slow burn to a bare cupboard.

She came over and gave his arm a prolonged squeeze. "Thanks for the talk. See you in the morning."

Accept it, buddy. The moment is gone. "I enjoyed it too. Sleep well." *Because I won't.*

She walked to the stairs and headed up. A few moments after her door closed upstairs, he heard Maria say from the kitchen, "Cal, did you hear that?" She sounded uneasy.

He was off the couch in an instant and jogged to the kitchen. When he arrived, he saw her looking out the window at the deck.

"What did you hear?" he said, approaching her.

"I thought I heard a thump or bump outside."

He smirked, while looking out the window and not at her. "Yeah, there have been a few thump and bump noises tonight." He started to whistle the Mangione song.

"You rascal!" she said.

He winked at her. "Secret's safe with me."

Maria was blushing. "Did Haley..."

"No idea," he lied. "You want me to check outside?"

"Would you?"

"Sure. Watch me; when I raise my arm up, flip on the deck lights."

"Got it," she said.

He went into the living room and exited through the French doors.

The night was cool, and the wind came in off the lake and blew against his bare arms. He scanned left to right as if his head was on a swivel. Nothing in the woods, no movement in the backyard or the beach beyond, nothing in the water, and nothing in the woods to the rig—

Snap!

Cal's eyes searched the darkness where he had just heard the sound of a tree branch breaking. He stood motionless for at least thirty seconds. Should he motion for the lights? It would destroy his night vision. He listened. Nothing but the sound of the wind rustling the tree leaves and wave after wave breaking on the beach.

He raised his right arm. The lights came on. Cal's eyes were intense as he watched and listened, but the beams only reached the backyard up to the edge of the woods.

He frowned. If there was someone in the woods, he or she would have the advantage if he decided to approach. If he went inside to get a flashlight, then that would give the person time to get away. Maybe it was just a squirrel or even a deer. He searched and listened for a minute more and then headed inside.

"Anything?" Maria said.

"No," Cal said. "I think it was just nature at work."

She relaxed.

Just like he wanted her to.

"Well, I'm headed back up," she said, turning off the deck lights. "Looks like you and my girl were having a nice chat," she winked.

"See you in the morning," Cal said.

When Maria closed her bedroom door, he crept toward the window and looked outside.

Nothing.

He watched for five more minutes and then headed up to bed.

Gregory reached the edge of the woods and then kept running along the road toward the marina. Too close. But, it had been worth it. He had a better layout of the house and how their team should proceed the next day.

14

C.I.A. HEADQUARTERS, MCLEAN, VIRGINIA
JUNE 2004

The door opened to Deputy Director Leiko Narita's office, and Jennifer Lear was escorted in by Narita's secretary. Seated on the long couch were Officer Brian Turner, Rolfe Judas, and a woman that Lear had never met before. Director Narita sat in her usual chair across from the couch and motioned for Lear to sit down in the other empty chair. She looked at the coffee in the cups as she sat down and noticed that Judas's cup and the unidentified woman's were almost empty whereas Turner's was full—the heat still rising from it. She couldn't see into Narita's cup. *How long have they been in here?* The secretary exited, closing the door behind her.

"Officer Lear, you know Mr. Judas, Officer Turner, and myself," Narita said, and then motioned to the other woman. "This is Officer Zimmer, who will be working with your team on Operation Empire."

Zimmer gave a nod but that was it.

Lear reciprocated. *This woman looks like she could kick all of the asses in this room right now.*

Zimmer lit a cigarette and reached over and refilled her coffee cup and Judas's. Lear watched as Zimmer put in four full teaspoons of sugar into her black coffee and stirred. The spoon hit the saucer with a loud *clink* as Zimmer drank half of the cup in one gulp.

"We're gathered to hear your report on the data gathered from Sari," Narita said.

Lear had arrived right after school let out three weeks ago and had been confined to her windowless room with banker's boxes full of information regarding Operation Empire. After sifting through most of it, she had some rough conclusions, but there were still a few missing portions that would have given her a clearer picture. She and Turner were scheduled to go to Paris in August to meet with Sari again. The open borders of Europe were an advantage sometimes.

Lear gathered herself. There were no handouts—no point papers, briefs, summaries—and no PowerPoint presentation slides. She had been directed to type up a report, which she had (74 pages long), that the others could review after the meeting. The face-to-face sit-down meeting should just cover the essentials to orient the team to the situation so that they didn't go into the report blind. She had learned that this was how Narita worked; if everyone was given the brief beforehand, no one would read it, or maybe one person would read it but have so many questions that the meeting would get derailed and bogged down in specifics while losing the big picture. Narita liked to have the detailed document ready but wanted a human being to summarize main points for consideration and present them before anyone jumped into the brief. That way, the team members could be more active when they read the document. The meeting that followed the initial briefing would then bear the fruit she wanted in terms of creative problem solving and more pointed questions to attack. She had told Lear that she was the perfect person to deliver the brief because she did not possess the ego that the other team members had and would also not try to grandstand or pontificate on the virtues of her research.

She spoke. "Thank you, Director Narita. From the information that Sari has provided, I have concluded that the United States faces the threat of an Electromagnetic Pulse, EMP, attack."

No one reacted to the statement, which she expected. When she had examined the information that Sari had provided in Rome, the intelligence pointed toward this possibility.

"There is no specific timeline that I could make out, but something is definitely in the works," she paused. "Although I am sure that some, if not all, of you are familiar with the specific challenges an EMP presents, Director Narita has asked me to provide a quick review."

Narita nodded and then sipped from her coffee cup.

"There are many ways that an EMP can be delivered, and there certainly exists the possibility that more than one could be simultaneously deployed in an attack scenario. However, let's keep it to a single powerful EMP attack for the moment. Every country knows that our military's reach on the planet is second to none. We also have bases strategically placed all over our own country, eliminating any weakness because we are so spread out, making it impossible for any enemy to take them all out at once. Other nations also know that a large portion of our country's citizens are armed because we have that right according to our Constitution—another reason why we've never been invaded and a huge deterrent if our government ever became corrupt enough to think it could just steamroll over our citizens. So, any kind of conventional war with the United States would be lost by our enemies, and they know it. I'm not entertaining a nuclear threat because Mutually Assured Destruction, MAD, is still a good rule of thumb to operate under. We've all heard it a million times: The Russians would never start a nuclear war with us because we would retaliate with nuclear weapons and destroy them, meaning we would both destroy each other and no one would win. Obviously, we want to prevent any terrorist organization from acquiring nuclear weapons because that would complicate things beyond the MAD principle. We'd get hit, but it would be difficult to determine who to retaliate against."

She had their attention. As the words came out of her mouth, she couldn't help but think: *If only my physics kids could see Ms. Girard right now.*

"This leaves our potential enemies with only one option: Cripple the United States in such a way that the country turns on itself and falls from within. Enter the EMP threat." She paused. "Let me start with something that did happen."

Like a hungry wolf, Judas interjected, "We've never been hit by an EMP attack. And if it *had* happened, it wouldn't have been because we deserved it."

Zimmer elbowed him. "Will you let her finish?"

Narita lowered her cup and glared at him. "What's up your ass today?"

Judas sat back but kept his eyes glued to Lear.

She had an idea where his need to appear superior was coming from. *He thinks I'm going to come at this from some left-wing, sins-of-the-past angle.* In one of her first briefings, he had pulled her aside and said, 'Okie dokie, teacher. We're here to protect every American, and we don't need guilt trip speeches or time-wasting bullshit apologies. We're on a rock floating through fucking space, okay? And that rock we call Earth was lucky enough to be in the Goldilocks zone so that we could evolve into the self-centered assholes we are today. Every human being is inherently selfish, so drop the activist charade. Just focus on analysis and your job.' He had eyeballed her at this point. 'If you can't, then go back to your useless protests and marches—which you know, people only do nowadays because of some insecure need to *be somebody—look at me, I was there, take a picture*...blah, blah, blah.' He had inched closer to her at this point. 'And while this is going on, The Company will be busy fighting to keep you safe and probably keep you thinking that you're making a difference.' She had then closed the distance between them, getting in *his* face, surprising him, and had said, 'One. Don't ever lecture me again. You're the one who recruited me. Two. You don't know anything about me.'

Lear continued. "On March 10, 1989, a massive explosion on the sun shot a cloud of gas, a storm cloud, toward the Earth at a million miles an hour. Two days later, the storm created a visual spectacle in the night sky that awed people who happened to be looking. However, what went unnoticed was the fact that the geomagnetic storm had disrupted the Earth's magnetic field in this region, causing electrical currents to flow through the ground all across the continent. Just before 3 a.m. on March 13th, in under 2 minutes, Hydro Quebec experienced a series of overloads and trips that created a total power loss for Quebec. Let's focus on Montreal for a moment. Almost half of Quebec's residents live there. They had no electricity for almost 10 hours in 20-degree weather. Airport shut down, no heat, no lights, people stuck in elevators, losses in the millions of dollars for businesses. Thankfully, power was restored, and life went back to normal. In a successful EMP attack, power won't be restored, and life won't go back to normal."

Turner crossed his legs and took a sip of coffee. No one else moved.

"If a nuclear weapon was to be successfully detonated about 35,000 feet over the middle of the United States—use Kansas as a geographic center—then an electromagnetic pulse would be generated that could take down our very sensitive and fragile electric grids across the entire United States. Right now, we have some aspects of our electronic grid system that are hardened against an EMP attack. However, we are extremely vulnerable in most areas, and it is not clear whether most of our complex and intertwined systems would recover. So, let's go with the worst-case scenario. A nuclear weapon is detonated over Kansas. The electric grid across the entire country goes down for months or even years in one second. We are suddenly plunged back into the 1800s where, without the infrastructure that we currently have in place, our population would be around 80% too big to support. That means if power is not restored for a year, we're looking at an 80% attrition rate. First of all, every plane that is airborne when the EMP hits is going down. Next, even with emergency generators that we assume would miraculously survive the attack, anyone in a hospital or nursing home requiring electricity to live would be dead in less than a week. Then there's food and water. Local grocery stores only have enough food to feed a town or city for three days. The regional warehouses that supply those grocery stores only have enough food for a month. However, unless you own a car that is 50 years old or more and in its original configuration, aka, no modern electronics, every vehicle will stop literally in its tracks and be rendered inoperable the moment the EMP waves hit. So, without the ability to deliver the food and the fact that a lot of the warehouse food would rot without refrigeration, the warehouses would offer little real support in keeping people fed. Back to the vehicles. Think of good old I-95 or I-75 filled with cars. Beyond the death toll from the accidents that will take place when the vehicles lose power, you'll have hundreds of thousands of people stranded far away from home. Think about how long it takes to even walk five miles. So, now you have people who will flock to nearby towns and cities and deplete the limited number of resources they have, and we know that there will be no re-supply shipments arriving. Then, think about all of the people who require medication to live. Pharmacies will be raided in the first few days, which will give some people a bit longer to live, but many will die because they simply won't have their medication. Then there is the communication challenge. No one will be able to communicate with each other, so there will be no updates as to when things are going to be restored, when help is arriving—it isn't—and how to organize, adapt, and survive. Within a week, massive hoarding will start to take place, and people will start dying over a case of beer. In a month, even neighbors will start turning on each other if it means feeding their families. In short, it would be a catastrophic disaster."

Judas interjected. "But we do have the 2004 report, which is public knowledge. I mean, we are taking some precautions. Look at the prepper movement, for Christsakes."

"With all due respect, Mr. Judas, I think you're overestimating the steps the government has taken to combat this issue. I doubt if one in a thousand American households has read the report."

Judas sat back and rubbed his beard. Zimmer gave him a look that said '*Shut up.*'

Lear continued. "Now, in regard to the prepper movement you mentioned. Yes, there are some good old Americans who are not waiting for their government to act and are taking matters into their own hands. But, let's face it, fifty percent of this country thinks that government is the answer to solve our country's problems. Most likely, only a small percentage—let's be optimistic and say five percent—of them are prepared or self-reliant enough to live for a year independently. Then you have the other half of America that thinks government *is* the problem. But, optimistically, only around ten percent of those folks are prepared. This means *eighty-five percent* of our population is nowhere near ready to handle an EMP attack."

Judas couldn't resist. "What about the *Mormons*?"

"I would put the Mormons in the fifteen percent who are ready. The Mormon Church's guidelines are for each family to stock a year's worth of food and water in their home. Then, there are the massive silos containing grain, etc. for their community to use in the worst-case scenario that I just provided. However, even with a smart infrastructure like this, it doesn't mean that other groups of hungry human beings won't organize and raid the Mormon strongholds. Utah might do well for a while, but hungry plus guns plus the survival of your loved ones and we become animals very quickly. Look at what happens every time a hurricane threatens Florida. The coastal residents are ordered to evacuate, so they travel inland. Meanwhile, all of the residents in the interior towns and cities clean out the grocery stores of food and water before the unfortunate coastal residents, stuck in traffic, ever make it there. It's almost as if someone should stand by the highway with a sign that says, 'Welcome! We didn't leave you much, but we're glad you're here.' And that is just how greedy human beings become while weathering a 24-48-hour storm. And then there's the growing addiction to technology."

Judas's pants began playing "Eye of the Tiger" and he scrambled to shut off his Blackberry. Zimmer smacked him.

"Take a look at how dependent upon technology we are and you'll immediately grasp the gargantuan challenge we're up against if the grid goes down indefinitely—beyond the loss of entertainment and the other worthless and utterly empty distractions that technology provides. Our communications. Our transportation. Our health and human services. Our military capability. Our coordination, collaboration, and teamwork. We won't be worrying about what some dumbass put on the internet, what privilege someone grew up with, or who a celebrity is sleeping with—we'll be in the fight of our lives, and there will only be enough supplies for around twenty percent of us. There are your real numbers. Of course, the attractiveness of this scenario for our enemies is that they don't have to invade us or even face us on the battlefield. They just sit back and watch us tear ourselves to pieces. Game over." Lear took a drink of coffee and then eyed Narita. "This concludes my brief."

Narita set down her cup. "Thank you, Officer Lear." She turned to the rest of the group. "So, I think that accurately frames the stakes."

Turner gave Lear a nod of approval. Judas crossed his legs the other way. Zimmer looked on fire.

"I've seen Lear's report. It's damn fine work," Narita said. "I want all of you to read it in the next twenty-four hours. We'll meet back here tomorrow, same time, to discuss the situation in more depth. We know an attack is being planned. We have an idea of who might be behind it. We have no idea where they intend to launch it from, or when. All indicators from Sari say it is in the initial phases. I want your individual assessments." She waited a beat. "Dismissed."

15

SUNDAY, JULY 2, 2006

C al and Iggi paddled their kayaks along Lake Ontario's southern coast. They were fifty yards offshore and had been heading east for the past hour. Cal watched as Iggi's powerful arms drove the paddle through the water on the starboard side, propelling the craft forward and to port. Then, he lifted the paddle out of the water and brought it down the port side, and the kayak's bow went to starboard. The steady sculling rhythm—starboard, port, starboard, and port again—kept the boat on a straight course. Cal's arms were starting to tire. For as out of shape as Iggi was around the midsection, he was definitely in better kayaking shape than Cal. However, Cal would not be the one to call for a break. Twenty minutes ago, he had asked Iggi about his workout routine, and Iggi had replied with, 'Workout routine? What workout routine? The only exercise I get is from kayaking, bowling, and sex. Period.'

Cal mimicked Iggi's routine, and his kayak cut through the water with ease and paralleled Iggi's from perhaps ten yards away. There hadn't been much conversation. Every now and then, Iggi would point to a beach mansion on the shore. There was a Hollywood tycoon's summer house, a Buffalo Bills back-up quarterback's lake house, a New York Senator's five-thousand square foot weekend retreat, and an author's beachfront writing cabin. Cal figured that his entire house would fit in the garage of one of these mansions.

He paused from paddling, letting the boat glide as he checked his watch. It was 10:30, and the sun was starting to heat up the day. He watched as Iggi dipped a small bucket in the lake and then dumped it over his own head. The steady sweat running down Cal's neck had turned the collar of his gray t-shirt dark. He cupped his right hand and scooped out a handful of water and splashed it against his face.

"Feel like a break?" Iggi said.

"Works for me," said Cal.

They put their paddles down, and each man took out a large bottle of Gatorade. There were still a few cubes of ice that rattled around in Cal's bottle as he tipped it back and let the cold liquid quench his thirst. The waves were less than a foot and nothing more than a gentle nudge every cycle. Cal swallowed and put the cap back on his drink; he still had half a bottle left for the trip back. He peered over the side, and the sun gave him a clear view of the sandy bottom, perhaps fifteen feet below. There were no fish or other objects visible, just cold, beautiful water that, further out, deepened into darkness. He lifted his head and looked over at Iggi, who was still chugging from his own Gatorade bottle. Maybe twenty yards seaward of Iggi, the water turned dark blue. A power boat cut the waves in the distance.

After they had all enjoyed a late breakfast of eggs, bacon, waffles, toast, and coffee, Cal had been surprised when Iggi invited him to go kayaking. They had gotten along okay during the weekend so far, but Cal suspected that there was something that Iggi didn't like about him. But what? Maria had said nothing, and he was sure that Haley wouldn't know what it was. He could make it another few days without having to know, but the detective in him wanted to know. Where to start? Friendly turf.

"So you're a sportswriter?"

"I am," said Iggi.

"Your breakdown of the Tigers-Yankees game last night on the way home from the bowling alley was spot-on."

Iggi took his paddle and pulled a few strokes on the port side to bring his kayak around where he could see Cal. They both had sunglasses on, so there was no eyeballing, but that also meant that it would be hard to get a read on him.

"Thanks," Iggi said. "You're not too bad with a bowling ball. You on a league?"

"No," Cal said. "Who got you interested in the game? Your dad?"

Iggi paused for a few seconds—not an uncomfortable silence, but noticeable. "He wasn't much into playing sports," Iggi said. "But he liked watching football."

"Did you play?"

"Yeah."

"My dad ended up being the same way. However, before he went to Vietnam, he was a pretty good basketball player. There was a city league in Detroit where he could have played and also a cop's league, but he never did."

Iggi seemed to be taking a measure of him. His demeanor was neither aggressive nor welcoming. "My dad was in 'Nam too. A grunt."

"Mine was a platoon commander. Served one tour, got out, and became one of Detroit's finest."

"I know," Iggi said.

"You do?" Cal said.

"Well, about the cop part. I didn't know that he served in the war."

The way he said *cop*. That was it. He'd heard the inflection so many times, that he knew what it meant when the person said it. He wondered where it came from with Iggi though. Had something happened? He decided to stay away from it for now. "My dad never talked with me about his time in Vietnam. How about yours?"

"Never directly, but it was present every day that I ever knew him. He ran our house like a drill sergeant."

"Now *that* I can identify with. I can't tell you how many times he inspected my room."

Iggi gave a grin. "Same here."

"You ever wonder what happened to them over there? I mean, I've seen pictures and some video footage, but I just can't picture my dad in any of them even though all I've ever known him as was a man in uniform. But that was a policeman's."

"I never got up the nerve to ask him," Iggi said. "I don't know what he saw or who he lost over there."

16

12 MILES NORTHWEST OF KHE SANH BASE
SOUTH VIETNAM, 1968

Marine Lance Corporal Jayvyn Hilliard sat down against the muddy inside wall of the bunker he had spent the day digging out with his squad leader, Corporal Jeff Turnberry. He was on his fourth-to-last cigarette; the nicotine calmed his nerves, and the smoke kept the mosquitoes away. Above his head, there were logs and sandbags placed around the rim; if the other holes held, then the only way he and Jeff would be goners was from above—mortars, hand grenades, rockets. Outside the front of the bunker, the earth's surface sloped away over one hundred meters down the hill and rose hundreds of meters behind the bunker.

His unit, Alpha Company, currently occupied the western side of Hill 802, named after the elevation in meters shown on the map his Company Commander was using. The brass was calling the hill "Augusta." In pairs of two, the members of second platoon were stationed in fighting holes that were evenly spread across the western face. His bunker was somewhere near the middle. However, they shouldn't even be here. The company had been in the bush for over two weeks and was waiting to be relieved, but the fog had rolled in, and it seemed that every helicopter within 20 miles of the DMZ had been grounded. Supplies were running low, fuses on tempers were getting shorter, and no one was sleeping.

Jayvyn heard the sound of a body crawling over leaves, mud, and sticks on the ground just outside the bunker. Holding the cigarette between his lips, he raised his M-16 rifle. "Who is it?" he asked.

"It's just me, Jayvyn," Jeff said.

Jayvyn lowered his rifle and then set the butt of it on the bunker floor and propped the barrel up against a wall. Jeff swept his red-lensed flashlight across the open hole, and after locating Jayvyn, slid down into the open space next to his bunker mate.

"Everything's all right over in Bissonnette and Hall's hole," Jeff said while sitting back against the cool mud wall of the bunker. "Lieutenant Schiffer just finished his rounds checking on everyone. Gentry may have immersion foot, but there's nothing anyone can do without the damn helicopters." He opened his canteen and poured in a packet of grape Kool-Aid. "They're worried about Erlinger and Mattie down at the listening post tonight." He put the lid on his canteen, swished the mixture around, and then opened it. He took a whiff and smiled. "Only thing keeping me going over here." He took a sip, savoring the sweet taste.

"After what happened to Mason and Crist last night, I can't blame them," Jayvyn said. The memory felt like an uppercut to the chin: a flare shooting into the sky below, followed by the sound of AK-47s going off, then screaming for help, then silence—then finding the disfigured bodies of Glen Mason and Greg Crist in the morning. "We're up for patrol tomorrow, right?"

Jeff stared at the bunker wall in front of him. After another sip, he just said, "Yeah."

"You got another packet of Kool-Aid?" Jayvyn asked. "I'm out."

Jeff fished around in the front pockets of his soaking wet camouflage jungle fatigues, finally pulling out a folded pouch of Kool-Aid. "One left, my friend," he said and tossed it to Jayvyn. "Have at it."

As if receiving the sweetest mana from heaven, Jayvyn held the pouch protectively and carefully poured its contents into his canteen.

"Bissonnette is starting to wonder what in the hell we're doing on this hill?"

Jayvyn was busy shaking his canteen. "Other than waiting to be relieved, why *are* we here?"

"The NVA knows we're here to disrupt their supply line, right? So they're sending wave after wave of troops to mess with us and destroy our positions on the hill so that they can maintain their supply line to their troops in the south."

"And our government won't let us follow the gooks into Laos where we could really do some damage," Jayvyn added. He took one last marvelous puff from his cigarette and then stubbed it out against the muddy wall.

"Right," Jeff said. "It's this cat and mouse bullshit. We've been here *seriously* for three years. Why those generals won't let us take the gloves off and really hurt 'em is beyond me."

Jayvyn studied his canteen, then took a long drink. "All I know is that I got 283 and a wake up left until I'm out of this shit. Fuckin' don't matter to me." He screwed the cap back on. "What're you worried about anyway? You're short and you're white and I'm black, and if and when we set foot on the soil of the good old US of A, you're gonna be able to pick up the pieces and have a pretty good life. Me? I'm gonna have to scrap and fight for every motherfuckin' inch. I already heard of brothers who made it back and weren't treated any differently than before. And these brothers served their country."

Jeff exhaled. "I know you're right."

"Get the fuck outta here, man," he said playfully. The truth was, he liked Jeff. "You don't know nothin' about what I go through."

Jeff got serious. "Jayvyn, I'm scared tonight." The words hung in the air. "Bissonnette thinks there's a whole NVA regiment out there—heard the lieutenant talking to the captain earlier—and that it's thirsty tonight. They can't let us continue to have the high ground to pick away at their troops and supplies moving south."

"We're gonna be okay, Jeffy. We been through this before."

Jeff shook his head. "Not like now. The fog won't clear, and that means no helicopters. We haven't been re-supplied since we blew up the top of the hill to create the LZ. These gooks know that. The lieutenant says we might be winning the kill ratio battle, but these people don't quit no matter how many we slaughter from our bombing. They're gonna outlast us, Jayvyn."

"How many days you got left?"

"Sixteen and a wake up," he said.

Man, he's really short—"short" meaning that Jeff's tour was almost over.

"They were supposed to get me out of here a week ago. Now, I'm stuck in this hellhole for at least another night. I'm so short, that I'm startin' to worry that I won't make it out of here." He paused. Jayvyn could hear him breathing in and out, in...and out, in...and out. "I know you saw what I was looking at in my wallet last night."

He had. Every grunt kept a picture in his wallet of his girl—real or fantasy—that was supposedly waiting for him back home. He certainly did. Brianne was his high school sweetheart, and the last thing she gave him before he left was a copy of her senior picture: silky black hair done up, eyes that you trusted, a smile that made you smile, and a turtleneck sweater that, when you looked at it covering her smooth ebony skin, made you feel warm, comfortable, and safe. He had borrowed a roll of scotch tape from one of his brothers at the base before being helicoptered to this hill and had taped the entire picture to protect it.

The picture that Jeff had been looking at was not of a woman. It was of a man, perhaps in his thirties, with a receding hairline and a full black moustache. At first, Jayvyn thought the picture must be of Jeff's father. But the way Jeff concentrated at the picture—the longing, the sadness, the fear of losing someone—was not the look of a son wishing his father was there to give guidance or protect him. No, it was something more. "I did," Jayvyn said.

"You know then?"

"That you like dudes? Not my place to judge."

"You gonna turn me in?"

"Hell no. You fight as well as anyone in the platoon."

Some dirt fell from the logs above and rolled down Jayvyn's neck. He reached back and brushed it off before it slid down the inside of his fatigues.

"I met him when I was a senior in high school last year," Jeff sniffled. "I—I've never told anyone."

"Not even your folks?"

His composure returned momentarily. "God, no. They wouldn't understand and would never accept it."

Jayvyn opened his canteen and took a heavenly chug. "I guess that's somethin' we got in common then," he said.

Jeff straightened up. "Really?"

"No. What I mean is that we both have our challenges when we get back."

Jayvyn could see the shadow of Jeff's head move up and down in agreement.

"See me any differently?" Jeff asked.

"Nope," Jayvyn said. "We're good. But we're all different from who we were when we got here."

"How are you different?" Jeff asked.

"Human beings didn't become the rulers of this planet because we're kind, man. My time here has shown me what we can devolve into, and no one should ever have to find out who he really is inside. Fuck. We might pay the piper tonight, so I'll dump. I'm scared of what I've become. I'm hollow. Dehumanizing my enemy is the only way I'm gonna make it home. Don't know how much soul I'll have left if I get there. How's that for fucked up?"

Jeff took out his picture and focused his flashlight on it. "I don't know if I could ever explain any of this to him."

Jayvyn leaned his head against the barrel of his M-16. "I'm sure as shit not tellin' my girl anything. No, no, no. But your feelings for him," he pointed at the picture, "man, you shouldn't have to hide it when you get back. When you've seen what we have...friends getting their legs blown off, brothers getting burned to death because some asshole dropped napalm in the wrong place, just...the cruelty of *ending*. We're animals over here, but it puts things into perspective. People at home have no clue. The last thing they should be worried about is the color of my skin and who you love."

Jeff sniffled again. "Thanks." He put the picture away and turned his flashlight off. "I remember joking with Mason and Crist the other afternoon about how they've never had a real Philly cheesesteak sandwich, and then later that night, they're gone forever. I—I just had to tell someone about *who I am* in case I don't make it back, Jayvyn."

"Stop sayin' that garbage, man. We're gettin' out of here tomorrow."

It was so cramped in the hole that Jayvyn stood just to straighten his legs. "I got first watch, okay? Get some sleep."

Jeff said, "Okay," and Jayvyn could hear him slouch down and attempt to get comfortable.

His eyes looked through a crack in the logs. The night was black. He knew that the foliage that had been on the hill had been burned off by napalm weeks ago; he saw nothing move in front of the bunker. He squinted and then heard rustling as a cool wind blew through the jungle below and then came up the hill and through the crack. Jayvyn shivered. But his heart was starting to thump, and he swore he could hear it in his ears. He hoped Bissonnette was wrong.

At 0200 2nd Lieutenant Bill Schiffer spoke into his radio. "Jill, this is Jack. What's up?"

He listened as either Erlinger or Mattie responded with multiple keys of the handset from their listening post.

Schiffer looked at his radio operator, Lance Corporal Mike Wishbone, who had arrived in Vietnam the very day they left on this mission two weeks ago. Wishbone was shaking his head as if to say: *Fuck, not again.*

Schiffer keyed his handset and said, "Key your handset once for every gook you see, boys."

The keying took off...and then stopped.

The jungle below came alive with AK-47 fire mixed with M-16 fire.

"Jill, this is Jack, are you okay?"

There was no answer.

"Jill, if you're wounded, key the handset once. If you're not, key it twice."

Still no answer as Bissonnette's machine gun opened fire on the valley from two holes to the right of Schiffer's.

Schiffer went to key his handset again but the anxious voice of Trey Mattie beat him to it with the sounds of bullets hitting the logs and earth around the listening post and AK-47 fire in the background. "Lieutenant, Erlinger's dead. They're all around me, hundreds, thousands, get me out of—"

The radio went silent. Then, Alpha Company Commander Captain Mark Lefler came on the net. "All Lima Poppas, get back up this hill immediately if you can. Crawl. Do not get up and run. We'll cover you."

Then, NVA mortars and rockets opened up, and the hill became a flaming mess. Schiffer, followed by Wishbone, crawled out of their bunker and started to head toward the nearest bunker to coordinate fire. Ten feet out, Wishbone watched Schiffer's head explode from a rifle on full automatic. A flare shot into the air, and for a moment Wishbone saw a vision of doom: hundreds of NVA soldiers running up the hill with more emerging from the jungle behind them. He took the handset from Schiffer's dead hand and radioed, "All units, open up down the hill with everything you've got. We've got hundreds of NVA soldiers charging!"

Captain Lefler's voice replied, "Who the hell is this?"

Wishbone replied, "Lance Corporal Wishbone, sir. Lieutenant Schiffer is dead. We're about to be overrun. I'm—"

Wishbone fell to the side, exposing a long tear in his throat—black wires with blood pumping out the opening over them.

Jayvyn and Jeff launched hand grenades from their bunker at the approaching NVA soldiers scaling the hill. Off to his right, Jayvyn could hear the roar of Bissonnette's M-60, no doubt mowing down a section of enemy troops.

Another flare went up, and Jeff looked down the slope. A group of NVA soldiers to the left had spotted them and were getting ready to fire a rocket at their bunker.

"Out, Jayvyn! We've been spotted!"

Jayvyn was shooting his M-16 on full automatic at another group coming up the hill on their right. Jeff had shouted something, but he was giving his full concentration to the scores of gooks rushing up the western side of Augusta. Then, he felt the gun snatched from his hand, and Jeff pushed him out of the bunker.

"Get over to Bissonnette's hole!" Jeff shouted. "I'll cover you and be there in a minute."

Jayvyn formed his body tight to the earth as if attempting to become a part of it as bullets whizzed overhead and smacked the earth behind him.

Jeff slid the M-16 next to Jayvyn, and Jayvyn grabbed it. "Go!" Jeff yelled, and then opened up with his own M-16 down the hill.

Jayvyn slithered away, staying down. He could hear Jeff's M-16 continuing to go off behind him. *Get 'em, Jeffy. Then c'mon.*

A *whoooosh!* sounded in the darkness, followed by a massive explosion as the rocket found its target, and their bunker exploded behind him. Splintered wood from the logs sprayed out from the destroyed fighting hole and hit Jayvyn in the right leg. He shouted in pain, then someone was next to him. It was Bissonnette's bunker mate, Gordon Hall.

"I've got you, Jayvyn. I've got you," Hall said.

An endless volley of grenades started to explode below them as a few members of First Platoon joined the fight from up the hill. Fewer and fewer AK-47 bursts could be heard, and soon there was cheering from nearby holes. Someone shouted, "They're on the run! We beat the fuckers back!"

Jayvyn twisted his head around to see the bunker. There was no movement from the destroyed hole. He screamed, "Jeff!" and tried to crawl back, but his wounded leg was on fire. He felt the uneasiness of butterflies in his stomach, and a clammy sweat began.

Hall held him tight and said, "He's gone, man. I'm sorry."

Jayvyn's eyes let loose, and he began to uncontrollably sob into Hall's shoulder.

17

SUNDAY, JULY 2, 2006

"My dad was in D.C. in 1982 when they dedicated the memorial," Cal said. "My mom and I wanted to go with him, but he went alone." He opened his Gatorade bottle and took a long drink. "I remember when he came back, he spent a lot of time in the garage by himself. My mom told me to steer clear of him for a few days, which is hard for a kid to do."

"Did he ever go back and visit the wall?" Iggi said.

"Never," Cal said.

Iggi paddled a few strokes on the port side of his kayak, and the bow swung to starboard. When he was facing Cal again, he set the paddle down. "I don't think my dad ever went to the wall, but I can't be sure. He would go somewhere the last weekend of June every year."

"My dad would get away on some weekends to be all by himself," Cal replied. "But nothing as regular as that. Any idea where he went?"

"I never questioned him about it. Thought it had something to do with the war. Truth is—I don't know where he was and probably never will. No one in our family ever knew."

CHICAGO, SATURDAY, JUNE 27, 1970

The march started in Bughouse Square. Near the end of a group of one hundred and fifty people, Jayvyn Hilliard stood tall in blue jeans and a white t-shirt and walked down Dearborn Street. He knew not one person but could feel Jeff Turnberry in all of them. At the front of the march, two men held six-foot wooden poles that suspended a banner over their heads between them. The two men turned down Chicago Avenue, and the group followed.

"Where are we headed?" Jayvyn asked a fellow marcher who had his hair pulled back in a ponytail and wore a moss-colored t-shirt, jeans, and sandals.

The man replied through the opening in his thick black beard. "The water tower, my brother."

The marchers were mostly quiet but deliberate. No one was going to stop them today. There were parades planned for tomorrow in Los Angeles and New York City, but Chicago was first, and the marchers' pride and determination swelled with each step.

"You straight?" the bearded marcher asked.

Jayvyn looked him in the eye. "Yes."

The marcher smiled, gave Jayvyn a nod, and then his eyes teared up. "Thank you for standing by us today. Did you—"

"Know someone who was gay? Yes. Served with him in Vietnam." Jayvyn swerved to miss a bicycler riding though the marchers trying to disrupt them, shouting slurs. The marchers simply all said in unison, "Boo!" he continued. "He was a fellow member of my platoon who died saving my life. I heard about this event from a friend in Detroit, so I decided to drive over." Jayvyn exhaled, remembering the smoldering remains of their bunker—the stench. "I haven't found a way to..." he said, searching for words, "to...deal with his death. Thought this might be a start. Maybe a way to honor him."

The man put a hand on Jayvyn's shoulder. "I hope you find the peace you're looking for." Then, he wiped the tears from his eyes and became serious. "Work to be done, my brother. If this nation thinks we're going to forget June '69 at Stonewall, they're out of their fucking minds. We're a movement, and movements usually win out."

They had fallen behind a bit. Before he could respond, the man gave him a quick pat on the shoulder and then picked up the pace to rejoin the front of the pack. Jayvyn maintained his steady pace, taking in the surroundings and allowing himself to feel the loss of Jeff. The march was helping, but the revelation he had hoped for was nowhere to be found; he had wanted answers, or at least understanding, but most of all closure. So far, he had none of them. With each step, it was becoming apparent that he may never achieve any of these. Since his return home, there had been days at a time when his guilt would paralyze him. What if he would have pulled Jeff out of the bunker with him? What if they had thrown their grenades earlier? What if they had gone further up the hill and just abandoned the goddamned hole? What if the fog had lifted the day before? He'd heard the terms 'shell shock' and 'combat fatigue' but was told that shell shock was an old term for World War I soldiers who went crazy after the endless trench battles across the fields of France and that combat fatigue was something World War II veterans returned with after the war. On *his* way home, all the Marine Corps had done was thank him for his 13-month tour, tell him that his mission was complete, and explain that compared to what he had witnessed over 'in country' the rest of his life would be a piece of cake. They had also asked him if he wanted to re-enlist for another tour. Hell. No.

At least he was here today *doing* something. Although, he'd almost missed the event after driving four and a half hours on I-94 West this morning. Brianne had no idea where he was. All he had told her was that he needed to go out for a while, which was not uncommon for him since he'd been back. Long walks (good), meeting fellow vets at Detroit bars to get plowed (bad), sitting in silence for hours at the Detroit Public Library (indifferent). She knew he'd be home before bed; that was her condition to give him the time and space he needed to work things out after coming home.

As the group headed east toward the water tower, the two women marching in front of Jayvyn were hit with rotten eggs thrown from the sidewalk. They continued to march. Then, Jayvyn was hit with a small rock in the right shoulder. The rock dropped to the ground, and he started to massage his upper arm.

A man behind him said, "Don't give them the pleasure. Keep walking. You're doing fine, my friend."

Jayvyn nodded and kept marching.

At the water tower, he saw his bearded friend again. Two men lifted him up, and he addressed the marchers. "We're heading to the Civic Center!"

Jayvyn watched as some stayed at the base of the water tower, talking and hugging, while a large group broke off. He decided to follow the group headed south on Michigan Avenue.

The group arrived at the Civic Center, and, forming a chain with either interlocked arms or joined hands, the marchers made a circle around the 50-foot Picasso statue and started to shout, "Gay power to gay people!" As the chant went on and on, Jayvyn surveyed the plaza and the towering buildings around it. Then, his eyes focused on the blue sky, and his face felt the warm heat radiate from the sun above. Wherever Jeff was, Jayvyn was sure that he was not alone.

I will cherish the days of my life that you have given me, Jeff. I will be a good husband, a good father, and a good man. His eyes welled up. *Thank you for giving me the rest of my life.*

They were within visual distance of the cabin when Cal pulled up alongside Iggi. "So, I get the feeling that you don't like cops."

Iggi stopped paddling. "I think you're in it for the good of the people, Cal, but, unfortunately, I can't say that for all of your kind." He started to paddle again. "I don't think I'll ever fully trust the police."

He had been right. But *why?* "Why not?"

"Mostly because my dad was gunned down by two cops, and my dad was innocent. Not exactly a new story in America, right?"

"Unfortunately, it isn't, Iggi. And you're right, there are definitely prejudiced cops who should never even get near a uniform. I admit that I am biased due to my own dad's service and the men and women that I serve with. From what I have observed in my own department, the majority of them aren't prejudiced. I think we're fortunate to have a police force made up from our own citizens who volunteer to join the profession in order to protect others and uphold the law. In what other walk of life, minus the military, do you get called up by perfect strangers in the middle of the night who need your help...which may include *you* dying to save that person's life from a criminal?" Cal paused. "You're from Detroit right?"

"The one and only Motor City."

"My dad was killed in the line of duty. What happened to your dad?"

Iggi turned his head back at him. "I'm sorry to hear about your dad, but I don't want to talk about my pops." Then, he turned his head forward and started to pick up the pace.

"I understand, but let me ask you this: What would need to happen in order for you to trust that most police officers volunteer to help people?"

Iggi stopped paddling and said, "I don't know." He put the paddle back in the water and pulled. "Let me ask you this, though. When you go into a department store, do the cashiers and salespeople follow you around?"

"Not especially," Cal said.

"Well, I suppose we'll both get what we want when certain things change." Iggi started to pick up the pace.

Cal followed—a symbolic point and counterpoint to the central issue seeming to come with each alternating paddle as the men remained quiet and pulled.

Iggi was starting to grunt every few strokes.

Cal focused. His deltoid, bicep, and forearm muscles stretched and then tightened with each stroke. He realized that he needed exercise, and it felt good.

When they were within 100 yards of the water directly in front of the cabin, Iggi started to pour it on. Cal gritted his teeth and pulled hard, attempting to keep up with him. With twenty yards to go, Cal closed to within half-a-kayak length, but Iggi held him off.

They stopped paddling and glided, breathing heavily.

"Good run," Cal said.

"You too," Iggi replied.

He heard clapping and hooting off to his left. He glanced over and saw Maria and Haley standing next to each other on the back deck.

Maria shouted, "That was *hot*!"

Iggi and Cal shared a laugh in return and then paddled toward shore.

18

SUNDAY, JULY 2, 2006

Haley and Maria walked along the brick sidewalk in Bay Harbor's historic downtown. The cobblestoned Main Street ran three blocks before ending in a roundabout. The architecture and building codes had been fashioned after Nantucket Island: cedar-shake siding, black shutters, and white trim. Doors of color were allowed, and that is where each store displayed its character. Nothing else was allowed on the door, but they were allowed to be painted a solid color in the approved spectrum.

If one stood in the middle of Main Street and faced the roundabout in the distance, one would see a teal door for Margaret's Ice Cream Shop; scarlet for The Warehouse Theater; navy for The Spyglass Bar; white for Ms. J's Pizzeria; orange for Barringer's Shoppe—fine clothing and accessories; violet for The Windy Ontario where one could find local novelty items and all things Bay Harbor; black for Sterling-Mandock Properties; light blue for Beth's Pottery House; green for Outdoor Sports; yellow for Candy's Sweet Shoppe; and silver for The Reginald, the ancient downtown hotel. From the end of Main, which intersected with State Highway 250, one could see the clear waters of Lake Ontario, the state dock, and Casey's RV Park on the other side of the highway. Just down from the state dock was Billy's, a beach bar right on Lake Ontario, where fruity drinks flowed and music thumped on summer nights, tolerated by the seasonal residents of the RV park only because most of them were also the customers, along with the state dock overnighters.

"Ready to hit the best bookstore in the world?" Maria said.

Haley sipped on her coffee as they approached a beige-colored door with the words "The Last Book" painted on the store's window. A row of bestsellers lined one half of the window, and the other half featured a few books with stickers that said "Local Author" interspersed among timeless classics. "Ready," she said.

They entered the store, and the aroma of books, coffee, and a Yankee candle burning near the entrance filled the air.

"Let's get lost in here," Maria said.

They took a few steps forward through the narrow opening between two shelves, and Haley could now see the layout. The neat rows of bookshelves stretched the entire length of the store, and the shelves lining the walls rose all the way from the floor to the twelve-foot ceiling above. There were several ladders on wheels placed around the store, and, as Haley glanced around, she was impressed to see nothing other than books, stationary, pens, pencils, and journals. No games or toys or music or films—this was a bookstore. "Larger than I thought it would be," Haley said.

"I think it used to be two stores, but Millie bought out the other half."

A voice laced with honey and cheer came from across the store. "Maria!"

Maria swiveled her head above an interior shelf and saw the owner of the voice and the bookstore, 72-year-old Mildred Winfield Bailey. "Millie B!" said Maria.

"Come hither, dear," Millie said.

Maria took hold of Haley's hand, "Got to introduce you to my other mom," she said, and they weaved around bookshelves until they arrived at the circular checkout counter.

Reminiscent of Diane Keaton posing for a picture on the red carpet before the Oscars—hat, black suit, tie, and shiny black shoes—Millie stepped down three stairs from a section of her circular checkout tower that she had swung open. Her glasses hung from a cord around her neck, and her green eyes were soft but focused. Her smile displayed her white teeth rimmed by her scarlet lipstick. "Where have you been, radiant angel?"

Maria and Millie embraced. "No excuses worth your time," Maria said.

"There never are," Millie said. They stepped back but now grasped each other's arms. "And where's my favorite columnist and crush?"

Maria laughed. "Iggi's at home taking a nap, lady."

Millie grinned, and Haley could tell that she enjoyed the banter. Is it lonely being a bookstore owner? She had never thought about it until now.

"And who is this lovely companion?" Millie said.

Maria and Millie dropped hands, and Maria put her right arm lovingly and protectively around Haley. "This is my friend Haley Girard who teaches with me. She's staying at our place for the weekend to celebrate the 4th and her birthday. Girl just turned 30 today."

Millie offered her hand. "Enchanted, Haley. Thirty? I'd love to tell you that you've made it to the really good material, but they're still a few years away. Regardless, you're getting closer, my dear."

Haley felt how smooth Millie's hand was—like leather with soft pillows beneath it. "Thank you. I'm not one for books—"

"Science and math teacher," Maria cut her off.

"—but, you have an impressive store."

"I'm in the bout of my life," Millie said.

173

What was it? Cancer? Heart?

Millie seemed to pick up on her train of thought and put a reassuring hand on Haley's forearm. "Not *me*," she said and then used her hand, as if unveiling a row of new paintings, to guide their eyes around the bookstore, "Books."

Maria was quick to affirm the statement with, "Damn right."

"We need more readers, ladies. An integral part of our humanity, culture, and inheritance is disappearing and being replaced by inferior machines: Those phones with keyboards? Oh, heavens no, ladies, *heavens no*—"

Haley thought of the Blackberry in her purse. *Don't let her see it when you check out later. And, yes, you are buying a book from this woman today.*

"—the question is not whether the pen is mightier than the sword, it is now whether the pen is mightier than the keyboard or screen. Hence, I shall remain in my turret here," she motioned to the circular checkout and information counter, "ensuring that the value and power of books is not lost forever because of a few nincompoops from Silicon Valley."

"You are ruthless," Maria said.

There was a twinkle in Millie's eye that said, 'I will castrate anyone who threatens the livelihood of this bookstore without remorse.' "Oh, not me," Millie said.

"We're going to browse some, mother," Maria said. "But we've also got girl talk to accomplish. Miss Haley here is in the company of an attractive man this weekend, and attractive for all the right reasons. Although, he's something to look at too. Don't anyone dare tell Iggi I said that."

They all shared a laugh and Haley started to blush.

"Uh huh," Maria said to Haley. "I saw you checking him out when he got out of the water today wearing just his bathing trunks."

"I might have looked a little," Haley said. "And something might have happened last night if there wasn't," she looked directly at Maria, "so much *noise* in the house."

Maria's eyes opened wide.

"What noise was that?" Millie asked.

"Oh, nothing," Haley said. "I don't think Maria knew how loud she had the stereo playing upstairs."

"Tut, tut, Maria. You are entertaining guests, goddess," Millie scolded. Then a wicked grin emerged. "I just may have to tell Iggi what you have said about this other guest staying with you. Might be my big chance to lure him away."

"You wouldn't dare," Maria joked.

"Watch out," she replied. "Anyways, so there is a possible suitor for Ms. Haley, hmmm," said Millie, turning to her. "Make him sweat. Make sure he's worthy."

Who was this woman?! "Yes, ma'am," Haley said.

"He's worth it," Maria said. "But my girl here has to make up her own mind."

"Exactly," Millie said.

The front door chimed as a customer entered.

"Well, back to my perch," Millie said. "There are volumes to sell and acquaintances to make. Enjoy the store." Millie gave them both a hug, and they disappeared down an aisle.

Sure that they were out of earshot of Millie, Maria said, "You could hear us last night?"

Haley leered back at her. "You are many things, Maria, but *quiet* is not one of them."

Maria grinned back in defeat. "Point taken, lady."

"Was it as good as it sounded?"

"Look at you, you little gossip!" She looked up and down the aisles and then locked eyes with her. "Amazing," she said. "But, mostly because I know just what buttons to push when. He's just along for the ride!" She gave Haley a quick high-five. "You heard Millie," and she pointed a thumb at her own chest, "Goddess."

Haley nodded.

"Sorry if it threw you off your game last night," Maria said. "You probably guessed it by now, but I'm playing matchmaker."

"I knew what you were up to the moment I showed up," Haley said. "You're lucky I like you so much."

"C'mon. You know you're interested."

She was. After lunch on the back deck, she thought that they might hang out some more in the afternoon. But the boys decided on a nap, and Maria was anxious to get away for a little girl time. The main reason she knew she was interested in Cal was because she was already looking forward to returning to the cabin and seeing him again. "I am," Haley admitted.

"Hot damn, lady," Maria said. "I knew it!"

"Shhh," Haley said.

"Right, right," Maria said.

"We almost kissed last night," Haley said.

"Well, then it looks like the birthday girl might be making out tonight then."

"Maybe," Haley said.

"Maybe more?" Maria needled.

"Slow down," Haley said. "I only said that I was interested in him. That doesn't mean the other thing will necessarily happen."

"Okay, okay. I'm pushing." Maria said.

"Yes, you are," said Haley. "I've got this."

"You're right." Maria paused. "But," she grinned. "When was the last time you had any?"

The question jarred loose a memory, and she started to feel lightheaded. Her breathing wanted to pick up, but she fought hard to control it. *Answer her quickly and then start browsing.* She took a sip of coffee. "It's been a while," she said.

"Yep," Maria said—thankfully not noticing the change in her.

She winked at Maria. "Let's browse a little and then head back."

"You got it."

They parted, and once Haley was down an empty aisle, she let the memory start to play. That is what her counselor had told her: Let the thoughts come in and then let them go. She took a few cleansing breaths and tried to watch as if she was only an observer.

19

NEW YORK CITY, DECEMBER 2004

The holiday season had been a bore, Bryce Tucker thought as he approached one of the last independent bookstores left in New York City. He paused as the storeowner slid his shovel through the last clump of heavy snow and dumped it on the pile he had made to the left of the entrance. Further down the sidewalk, other store owners slid, lifted, and dumped snow from their shovels as flakes continued to fall; the wind whipped up snow on the street and blew it around as if to purposely confuse and frustrate the shovelers.

Speakers mounted underneath the bookstore's canopy played:

It's that time of year

When the world falls in love

Every song you hear seems to say

Merry Christmas

May your New Year dreams come true

Bryce concentrated while looking up at the speakers. The Christmas...Song? No. Andy Williams? No. He shifted his gaze to the window. An elderly gentleman—the only customer in the store—approached a shelf of books with the sign "Discount" on top of it and began to thumb through a paperback. *He looks as lonely as I feel.* Seeming to sense he was being watched, the man turned toward Bryce and their eyes met.

And this song of mine

In three-quarter time

Wishes you and yours

The same thing too

The Christmas...Waltz? Yes. Robert Goulet and Carol Lawrence? That was it. When, or rather, where, was the last time he had heard it? Perhaps, during the last Christmas holiday season that his family had shared together before his parents' divorce. That would have been, what, 1987? He was thirty-one, so...seventeen years ago. He recalled a vision of his mother curled up on their brown-cloth couch with wooden arm rests in her L.L.Bean pajamas and robe sipping on hot chocolate while his father brought the tree into the small living room and then anchored the metal screws of the tree stand into the pine's trunk. The tree's scent had begun to dominate the room. His father had yelled at him to bring in a pot full of water to fill up the stand. He had turned to head toward the kitchen when his younger sister had come barreling down the hallway dressed as a princess and missed him by inches before running into the tree. Then his father had yelled at Bryce's sister and then at Bryce's mother. Then his mother had yelled back at his father. Then his father had thrown the tree to the floor and walked out of the living room.

"Closing up in about twenty minutes, sir," said a voice from behind him.

Bryce swiveled his head in time to meet eyes with the bookstore owner, who gave him a soft pat on the shoulder before heading inside. Bryce looked at his watch. 10:40 p.m. He took one step toward the store, stopped, watched the old man inside start to amble toward the check-out counter, and then reversed his step.

He saw the reflection of her in the storefront window. He paused, brushing snow off the right arm of his coat while glancing at the window to see if anyone appeared to be watching or following her. If there was, then they had agreed that the signal would be for him to go inside the store. If everything was okay, then he would continue to stand outside the bookstore and then start walking toward the hotel.

They were not supposed to be meeting like this; he hadn't seen her since August when they had traveled to Paris to pick up the package from Sari. Like Rome the summer before, the operation had been smooth. The intelligence must have been just as good as the previous few exchanges because they were scheduled to meet with her again in Berlin this coming summer. What had complicated things, however, was the night after the exchange in Paris. After a mouth-watering dinner paired with French wine, followed by a nighttime stroll near the Eiffel Tower, the two officers became their cover roles as fiancées and made love into the dawn hours in the City of Light. She had been gentle and yet enthusiastic as a lover. He had felt something for her, too, which was dangerous. When they had awoken in the late morning, he was thankful that they agreed it had been a mistake. To his surprise, there was no awkwardness that ensued, and they had boarded the plane for home later that afternoon.

After the debrief with Narita and Judas in McLean, they had gone their separate ways as usual. She would never know him as Bryce Tucker—only as Brian Turner—and he would never know her as anything other than Jennifer Anna Lear. Who they were and where they lived during the rest of the year was never to be discussed. It couldn't be, and it shouldn't be.

And then October had happened. He'd been sent by Judas to Iraq to meet with an agent being run by a fellow Company officer who had another piece of the puzzle that Sari had given them the first pieces to. Just before the two

Humvees arrived at the meeting location, the Humvee, ahead of his, carrying the agent and officer, hit an IED placed in a road that had been cleared hours before. As his Humvee came to a stop near the decimated vehicle, AK-47 fire erupted around them and rippled the shit out of his Humvee, killing the .50 caliber machine gunner. The vehicle backed up and Turner had exited it with two SEALs and the Marine Corporal who had been the driver. By the time they had fought their way out of the ambush and made it to safety, Turner and one of the SEALs were the only ones standing.

He flew out of Baghdad that night and was in Director Narita's office the next day. In his five years with The Company, it was the first time he had killed or witnessed someone being killed up close. Judas persuaded him to take some time off, said he liked Turner. Because of nerves, bad dreams, or longing for the embrace of someone who might understand due to the nature of his work, he had asked Judas if he could talk with Lear. Judas had thought for a moment, and then, surprisingly, had approved. His reasoning was that the intelligence they were getting from Sari was so good that he didn't dare disrupt their team. Iraq had been a setback, but they still had Sari, and Turner and Lear were scheduled to meet with her in Berlin this summer under the cover of husband and wife again. 'Bringing back Professor and Mrs. Ollie Stein?' he had asked. 'No,' Judas had replied. 'This time your covers will be on their honeymoon.' He explained to Turner that a little stateside chemistry building couldn't hurt, but they would only get 24 hours. Judas would set the meeting up and would not tell Narita.

Which is why he now found himself, here, standing in the snowy shadows of New York City listening to Christmas music. And Jennifer Lear was across the street, wearing a charcoal colored overcoat with a scarlet scarf and beret. His heartbeat picked up as his eyes scanned the area around them. No one stood out among the gaggle of stressed-out Wall Street suits marching down the sidewalk after a long day with their cell phones welded to their ears. Other holiday shoppers were making last minute purchases, couples were arm-in-arm, rude New Yorkers were jostling for position to grab cabs, and New York's finest were sipping coffee while observing the spectacle.

As he turned to start walking toward the hotel, he saw her cross the street. In thirty seconds, she was by his side. He smelled her perfume—the same she had worn in Paris—before she spoke.

"Merry Christmas, Brian," she said.

"And a Merry Christmas to you, Jen."

He took his left hand out of his jacket pocket and lowered it. She took it in her right hand. If they spotted any trouble between here and the hotel, either would squeeze three times, and they would split up. She would get a cab to JFK and fly home—wherever home was—and he would go to the hotel and follow Judas's protocol to get him out of there safely and quietly. He had been informed that The Company used this particular hotel on many occasions, and everything was already in place if he needed to disappear. They continued to walk.

As the door shut behind them, the hotel room became a tornado of clothes flying off. There were no words, just action. She found herself much more aggressive than in Paris, taking control and using him to please herself. When it had happened for her first, she switched to concentrating on him, and over and over again, she would feel him near climax and back off. When she knew he could hold it no longer, she thrust harder—coordinating her second explosion with his first.

Now, he lay down on his stomach with his head turned to the side for conversation, while she lay on top of him, nibbling his ear.

"What happened?" she asked. They were the first words that either of them had said since 'Merry Christmas'. "What does Judas have us doing here?"

He slid his left hand up and massaged her left thigh. "I asked him if I could see you," he said.

She stopped nibbling. "I know what just happened, but I thought we had agreed that Paris was a mistake, and we aren't supposed to see each other between assignments."

He gently rolled her over and they now lay on their sides facing each other. "I almost died on a mission two months ago, and all I have been able to think about since then is you." His eyes became distant. Perhaps he was watching the snow fall outside of the window. "We lost people—good people—and I've been...struggling." He then told her what had happened.

She cupped his right cheek and chin with her hand. "I—"

"It's okay. There's not much else to say about it now," he said and refocused his attention on her. "And you're right. We're not supposed to be doing this. But I convinced Judas to set it up."

"I can't believe he agreed," she said.

"He can surprise sometimes," Turner said. "We'll be posing as husband and wife when we meet with Sari this summer. He gave me a twenty-four-hour window to meet with you. Thought it might help me and help our chemistry." He readjusted his position on the bed and rested on one elbow. "Judas doesn't know that we were intimate with each other in Paris. I told him that I wanted to talk with you because I feel comfortable around you, we have worked together, and that you might help me make sense of what happened over in Iraq."

"So there is no mission right now, correct?"

"Correct."

She admitted to herself that she was happy to see him. What had happened when they first entered the room? For the moment it was beyond her and made her feel uncomfortable. She was a perfectionist, a planner, and kept track of details. The call from Judas had been a shock. She hadn't been to New York

City since—since right after the attacks. It was the holidays. She was lonely back in Rochester. Some annoying, boisterous, and pompous co-worker had been calling her to see if she wanted to attend a political rally in D.C., and he had asked her out on a date. She knew which way she was leaning, but Maria had been her sounding board. "He's a complete idiot, lady." She stopped answering his calls.

She was not comfortable when her emotions overrode her judgement, but it happened the moment she and Brian had held hands. Could this ever be more? She almost laughed at the thought. She knew next to nothing about him other than the missions they had been on, the debriefs, and the fact that he was a C.I.A. Officer like her—who was not supposed to share anything that would even hint to leading to more. And why did he specifically need *her*? Over the past two years they had spent less than two months together and slept together once, now twice. What about his family? Were his parents still alive? Did he have any brothers or sisters? How old was he? She made eye contact. Why *me*? She decided to ask.

"Why me, Brian? We don't exactly know each other."

"Besides what I already told you, I admit that I have feelings for you. What just happened in here was something I don't do. I know nothing about you, but after working together, I care about you. Being a C.I.A. Officer is more lonely than I thought it would be, and now that I've killed someone and seen someone get killed a foot away from me, I feel...empty. But I was right. Seeing you has helped. But it will also end up hurting."

"Because we won't see each other for another 7 months?"

"And—" he exhaled. "And because we both won't know if what we have is due to our circumstances, or if we really have something. And we're not likely to find out unless we both quit The Company."

"Those words won't win you romancer of the year," she said.

He went to further explain, but she put a finger to his lips. "But you're lucky. I'm not much of a feely person, and I agree with you."

He grinned. "You're direct. I like that."

"Do you plan on staying in?" she asked.

"I was about to ask you the same thing," he grinned again. "Why did you join?"

"I lost someone close to me on 9/11, and a switch got flipped," she said. "I felt I had to do something."

He nodded. "Family member? Friend?"

"My college roommate. She died in the south tower."

He gave her arm a loving squeeze. "Is it eerie to be in this hotel, fifty floors up, just a few miles from where it happened?"

"I thought about it when I flew in today. I didn't think the skyline could change so much with that group of buildings gone, but after seeing it...it'll never be the same."

"Agree. The city is still working on what the memorial will look like." He looked out the window again. "What was her name?"

"My roommate's name?"

"Yeah," he said.

"Kelly Smith," she said.

His eyes lowered past her body to the white bed sheet. "I'm sorry," he said. The room was quiet for a beat. Then, he straightened his right leg, and the sound of his foot sliding across the bed sheet broke the silence. "I joined in 1996 right out of college. A recruiter showed up on campus during the spring of my senior year, and the next thing I knew, I was being indoctrinated over in Virginia."

She did the age math quickly. He must be 30 or maybe 31. A couple of years older. It could work. "But *why* did you join?"

185

"My grandfather was a World War II veteran, and I was very close to him. I grew up hearing about necessary wars and serving your country, and I guess something just clicked when I got approached by The Company recruiter. It kind of freaked me out because the guy knew so much about me—High School and College GPA, my history of playing contact sports, ACT and SAT scores, the fact that I had studied and was fluent in the Russian language, the works."

"You speak Russian?"

"Again, my grandfather. He introduced me to Dostoevsky and Turgenev, and I became fascinated with Russian history. Then, when I told him that I had joined the C.I.A. and was studying the language, the old warrior took me aside and said, 'You're learning Russian so the rest of us won't be forced to.'"

"Do you regret your decision to join?"

"No. Do you?"

"I don't regret it," she said. "I am surprised at what I'm doing."

"How so?"

"I started out as an analyst and thought that was all I would ever be. Then, one day I was escorted from the third-floor room, where I had been sifting through mounds of intelligence for Judas, to Deputy Director Narita's office. A few months later I met you. And now, here I am in New York City."

"I believe the work we've done has made a difference. The day that I don't, is the day I'll quit."

"You might also quit if you were interested in *me*, of course," she grinned.

"Yeah, about that," he said, moving closer. "We'll just have to see how *we* play out."

She started to move her hand down his chest. "How many hours do we have left?"

20

SUNDAY, JULY 2, 2006

"How in the hell did you manage that?" Iggi said as Maria walked into the dining room with a circular chocolate cake that had thirty lit candles spread evenly across the surface.

"Talent, sugar. Talent," Maria said.

"This is too much," Haley said.

"Now you stop that modesty routine right now, lady. If you're hittin' dirty thirty tonight, then we're doin' this right," she shot back.

Well, there it was. Thirty. Most years, it was just another year that had passed. After 21, the presents thin out, the cakes disappear, and grown up life takes hold. This year would have been no different, except that she had almost not lived to see thirty. And because of that, moments from her life came back to her as Iggi, Cal, and Maria started in with the birthday hymn..."Haahpee Birth—day to you...

She is a ten-year old girl, sitting in her 3rd grade classroom with her other excited classmates, watching the Challenger lift off into the sky. Then there is smoke, and the smoke trails off in at least two different directions; the camera shows the parents of the teacher who is aboard, and they look confused, horrified. Then her teacher is running to turn off the television set that is on top of the cart with wheels that they never get to have in class except for special occasions like this. And her teacher is crying, and then other students start to cry when they realize what has happened...

She has two zits on her forehead, and she has covered them with concealer. She is with a skinny boy with hair that needs to be cut; he is also wearing braces. They are on a date, and it is uncomfortable because she doesn't really like him. He parks the car on the side of a dirt road and tries to make a move, and she tells him to take her home. He frowns and starts the car. And then they hit a deer on the way home, and the car swerves and hits a tree. He breaks his neck and is in a wheelchair two years later when they graduate. She is unharmed, and the zits are gone...

She starts dating an African-American guy during her freshman year of college. She has strong feelings for him and tells her mother. Her mother tells her that she and her father are disappointed in her for dating an African-American. She hangs up the phone and shakes in front of the bathroom mirror knowing her parents are racist. She has sex with the guy—a lot—but they break up the following year...

She is a senior in college, sitting in the first row of a lecture hall, and some academic liberal is singling her out, telling her she has lived a privileged life and that no one gives a fuck about her first-world-white-girl problems. She wants to tell him that she was raped a week ago at an off-campus party, lost both of her immigrant grandparents within the past two months who had barely made it out of Nazi Germany before the war started, and now her mom is leaving her dad. Instead, she continues to sit and listen to him go on and on and on. She finds out he makes $125,000 a year, lives in a gated community, works mostly from home while a grad assistant teaches his one class a semester, and recently divorced his wife for a former student...

She has coffee with her brother and sister, and they talk about their parents' separation and how they saw it coming for years but no one said anything—not when their father hit their mother in the kitchen right before church, not when he hid booze in the garage, not when she cheated on him with her high school crush on a weekend when she was supposed to be on a mother's-only retreat, and not when their parents sat them all down on the couch and said they were going to try and make it work. She forgives her brother for being aloof; he forgives her for abandoning him. They both comfort their younger sister, who has lived through the worst of things at home while they were both away at college. They decide to keep in better touch and not make the same mistakes. After three months, their parents decide to stay together...

She's in Berlin with Brian, and he's yelling at her to run, and...No, she can't go there yet...

She pulls into the high school parking lot at 8:00 a.m.—class starts at 8:10—six months ago, drunk. She sits in the car, weighing the decision to go in and try and soldier through the day or head home. The nightmares haven't stopped, she's put on weight from the past few weeks of endless drinking and eating, attempting to numb herself, and she hasn't graded a single paper. She starts to cry. No one sees her. She drives home and calls in sick. She then leaves a message for Narita and falls asleep for the entire day. A knock at the door wakes her up; it is Narita. She invites her in and breaks down. Narita drives her to a counselor, and the healing begins...

"Haahpee Birth—day, dear Hay-lee. Haahpee Birth—day to youuu," Iggi, Cal, and Maria finish.

Haley leaned over the candles, feeling the heat rise up to her chin and face, and with one long breath, blew the candles out.

Maria clapped. "Impressed. What did you wish for?"

Peace. Rest. A long life. Cal? She smiled. "I don't want to spoil it," she said.

"Maria, leave the birthday girl alone," Iggi said, handing her the knife to cut the cake.

"Mind your own business, baby," Maria said with a wink.

189

Cal hung back, taking in the situation. She liked that about him. Then, he seized upon the moment of silence and said, "Happy Birthday, Haley."

A large piece of cake on a plate passed in front of her, and she moved her head around it to see Cal. "Thanks," she said.

Maria bent over, saying, "Oops, I'm droppin' stuff everywhere."

When her head was below the table, Haley felt a long pinch on her thigh. *That provoker!*

With her napkin recovered, Maria sat back up and started cutting the next piece of cake.

Haley wondered if she even dropped it or had it in her hand the entire time. Either way, it didn't matter. She watched as Cal dug in.

When they had returned from shopping downtown, she and Maria had found Iggi and Cal freshly showered, dressed, and talking by the fireplace. It seemed like they were getting along okay. On the ride home, Maria had told her a little about Iggi's father, and she now could sense the tension between the men because of Cal's profession. However, Cal was level-headed and calm, and that seemed to be helping out. On the other hand, she had to also give Iggi credit because he had visibly become more comfortable around Cal since the start of the weekend. Maybe the psychologists had it right: If you put two people in a room without any distractions and force them to spend time with each other, the things they have in common will overcome the gaps—if each person is willing.

"Should thirty feel old?" she asked the group.

Iggi jumped in first. "No, we're still plenty young."

Maria added, "*Hell* no. Thirty to forty is the buildup for the magic demarcation line."

"What do you mean?" Haley asked.

"Forty," Maria said. "I heard someone say that you spend your life up until forty trying to make sense of your history, but when you hit the big *four zero*, then you're free of it."

She liked it, for it bucked the conventional thinking that for men, forty was supposed to be the apex of one's masculinity and appeal, and, for women, it was the dreaded number that started the slide. The hell with that. Maria had it right: Thirty to forty would be the launching pad for freedom. Maybe this was what Millie had been referencing at 'The Last Book.' "Sold," she said to Maria.

"Let's hear from our elder here," Maria joked, looking at Cal.

"Easy on the 34-year old," Cal said, and took a drink of coffee. "There's still life left in these bones."

"Man can row a decent kayak," Iggi said.

"Back at you," Cal said.

"Well isn't this just a nice little happy birthday party," Maria said. "Look at my boys complimentin' each other," she shook her head.

Somewhat embarrassed, somewhat relieved, Haley estimated, Cal and Iggi focused on their pieces of cake, but they weren't frowning. Cal took the first risk and looked at her. Damnit, he's handsome. Would she let herself go a little farther tonight? Yes, if he decided to pursue. The question was: Would he? She wanted him to. But if he didn't, would she pursue *him*? A kiss was close to happening the prior night, so things *were* heading in that direction. She studied his mouth. She had never studied someone eating cake so intensely. The way he put the fork in his mouth and slid it out, seeming to contemplate the rest of the cake on his plate, then using the side of the fork to slice off a piece instead of the clumsy stab that so many people employed.

"You going to eat your piece?" Maria asked her.

Her cheeks were flushed, and she started to feel a warm sensation course through her body. If she was being honest, however, she was more like Princess Leia when it came to men; she *wanted* Han Solo but didn't *need* Han

Solo. Two years ago, she had attended a conference where a veteran principal had stood at the front of the room presenting the value of data with a few of her teachers. Five minutes in, the principal had said, 'You know, when these teachers started running the data meetings, I suddenly had the time to head out into the hall and have me a hot flash.' The room, mostly filled with other women, had roared and praised this no-nonsense deity. A minute later, she was back at the one-liners with, 'If you gentlemen will excuse me, these ladies are comin' for you—' she looked at the women in the room, '—and, bitches, don't be waitin' for them to lead.' She received a standing ovation. Right now, Haley wanted to infuse some of this woman's bravado and bluntness into her own body. Tomorrow was the 3rd. The 4th would be full of parades, barbeques, and fireworks, and they were all leaving on the 5th. The weekend was already going by too fast. And, yes, turning 30 had something to do with it. What was it? She spotted a family photo hanging on the dining room wall of Maria and her brother—Maria looked to be around ten—with her mother and father standing behind them. Her parents looked to be around thirty...

That was it. Thirty was her mother's age when Haley's first memories of her started. She wasn't anywhere near that phase of her own life. But, for some reason that she was unable to access right now, she felt vacant. Would she ever settle down with someone? Would it matter? What about the EMP? What if the U.S. went dark right now?

Her generation was coming of age and ushering in the switch from analog to digital, even though less than 50% of the world was online at this point. There seemed to be indications that something was not right with the housing explosion—the bubble was stretching, and, when it burst, the generation that would take the brunt of the force was X. Millennials weren't nesting yet, and the Baby Boomers were still riding the wave of prosperity from the 1990s—leaving Generation X right in the middle, bridging the gap, and about to be squeezed.

She took a long drink of coffee.

Get ahold of yourself. Enjoy your birthday. She saw Brian again, and heard him yelling at her. Oh, God. Not now. Then, it started to happen once more—a panic attack. Her chest went heavy, and she felt like she was being suffocated. *I need to get out of here.* She rose and gave her best attempt at a smile. She barely got out, "Be right back," as she headed for the first-floor bathroom.

Ten minutes later, she returned and informed the group that she was not feeling well and was going to call it a night.

Maria pulled her aside. "You serious?"

"Yes, I'm hoping that whatever this is will pass by tomorrow morning."

She caught a glimpse of Cal and could sense his disappointment. *Why now?!* But she knew that if she didn't get to her room and go through her calming ritual, another attack could spring up any minute, and, based on her experience the past few months, it would be worse. Her only salvation was that when an attack occurred at night, it usually passed by the next morning.

"Are you sure?" Maria asked. "Iggi's making a fire in the living room fireplace. We're just going to chill. You could rest on the couch."

God that sounded good. Maybe she could cuddle with Cal. Just to be held again. Her stomach tightened. "I'm sure," she said. "I'll soar with the eagles again tomorrow morning."

She said goodnight and headed upstairs. As soon as her bedroom door closed, Berlin entered her mind and she collapsed on the bed, shaking.

Vladimir lowered the binoculars, letting them rest against his chest while being held by the cord around his neck. "I think they're all in the living room. Well, at least three of them are—sitting on the couches; the other one might be on the floor," he said to Gregory. "Why don't we anchor and do it right now?"

They were in the stern of the cabin cruiser, which was twenty yards offshore, drifting with the running lights off.

How did this KGB shithead ever get selected for this mission? Yes, he was an old hand who had experience and had worked in North America before, but his suggestions were unorthodox, sloppy, and dangerous. "This is just a dry run tonight. The message today said that our man is in place, ready to carry out his missions tomorrow. If we were to act now, it might throw off his chance of getting Narita, Judas, and the others; if *he* acts now, then it might throw off *our* chance of getting Lear. No, we follow orders and do it tomorrow night."

Vladimir frowned.

He knows I'm right.

"Want to take a look? Might get to see your girl getting cozy with that cop?"

"No," Gregory said. "Let's go."

"Shouldn't we send one of the boys below ashore to get a better look at the cabin's layout?" Vladimir said.

"Not necessary. While you drunks were asleep last night, I did the necessary reconnaissance and have the information we need."

Lowering his head in what Gregory believed was the closest thing to embarrassment that he would ever get out Vladimir, the old spy said, "You came all the way over here?"

"Yes," Gregory said. He didn't wait for any more conversation. "Start the engine and take us back to the marina."

Vladimir nodded.

21

BERLIN, DECEMBER 2005 – PART II

L ear's gun was now in her hand. Behind her, she heard the door open and then the sound of two loud thumps. A series of shots rang out. Against her training, she turned around and saw three bodies on the floor—one was Turner's. Another man was sprinting toward her with his gun raised. She turned and sprinted, zigzagging as shots missed her, causing the rounds to spray the walls. In front of her, she heard the elevator *ding*, and the doors opened.

A man stepped out and raised his gun at her. She didn't hesitate and squeezed off two rounds. The bullets found the man's center of mass, and he dropped, clutching his chest. The elevator doors started to close. She zigzagged again to avoid more shots fired from behind her. With one quick pivot off of her left foot she cut between the closing doors and pushed the button for the ground floor.

Moments later, Lear exited the elevator with her gun back in her coat pocket. The lobby was empty, and she ran out the front door. It was snowing harder, and cold wind whipped across her face as she scanned for danger down the sidewalk in both directions. No one seemed to notice her. She sprinted back in the direction of the café, making a right turn down the nearest street and following it for two blocks where the car was supposed to be waiting.

Sari's eyes surveyed the sidewalk from behind the paperback she was pretending to read. It had been ten minutes. Maybe she was safe? Maybe she hadn't seen the man with the red scarf earlier? She was certain that she had lost him, but maybe she should have called off the meeting by not showing up. No. What she had to give her contact was more important, even if it meant risking her identity. She had thought about not giving the danger signal to her contact but had decided to err on the side of caution. Regardless, she suspected the enemy was closing in on her.

About to return to her paperback, she froze in terror. Across the street, the man with the red scarf stopped and stared directly at her. She turned around and looked beyond the café bar at the rear entrance—her only means of escape now. Too late. A tall man entered through the door and met eyes with her. She turned back toward the window. The man with the red scarf was crossing the street and hadn't taken his cold eyes off of her. His right hand was inside his coat pocket.

She reached inside her purse and removed a pill from a zippered compartment. The man's eyes opened wide as he watched her bite down on it. Her last thought: *I hope the Americans can stop it.*

Her dead body hit the floor before the man inside the café could reach her. The man outside paused and then began to meander down the sidewalk as snow continued to fall.

* * *

Lear reached the car and jumped in the back seat.

"Where's Turner?" Ritzy Zimmer yelled from the front passenger seat.

Lear started to tear up. "He didn't make it," she said.

A bullet shattered the driver side window but missed the driver.

"Go!" Lear said, ducking.

The car took off as more shots were fired. Lear hugged the floor with her body as the car made it down a block, and the driver took the first right. He pressed the accelerator, and the car sped through four blocks.

"I think we're okay, Zim," the driver said. "ZIM! Jesus!"

Lear's head shot up as the car swerved. "What?"

"Zimmer's hit."

Lear saw the slumped head of Officer Zimmer leaning back against the headrest of the front passenger seat—a mess of blood and gore leaking onto the tan leather.

"You know we can't stop at a hospital," the driver said.

Visions: Brian's worried face, his command for her to run ringing in her ears; the face of the man she had shot, blood erupting from his chest; the back of Zimmer's skull, blown away. She lurched over and vomited on the backseat floor.

"Officer Lear!" he shouted.

Lear wiped her nose and mouth with the sleeve of her coat and gathered herself. "I know," she finally said. "Just get to the safe house."

He nodded, and she took a wool blanket off the backseat and covered Zimmer's body. The mix of putrid smells began to fill the car's interior as cold wind and snow rushed through the open window. Lear thought of Brian Turner again and began to cry as the car sped out of Berlin.

197

22

MONDAY, JULY 3, 2006

The door to the deck opened, and Haley Girard walked out clasping a cup of coffee, still dressed in her pajamas.

Maria, Cal, and Iggi were seated around the large table where cups of coffee and breakfast plates that had only crumbs remaining on them sat.

"There's my girl," Maria said. She got up and gave Haley a hug. "Feeling better?"

She was. After working through the memory of Berlin, she had fallen into a deep sleep. When she looked at the alarm clock next to her bed, she realized that she had slept for almost 14 hours. It was a little past 9 a.m., and she needed food and coffee; most of all, she needed to get back into the swing of the weekend. "Much better," she said to Maria. Then, she spoke to everyone. "Sorry for being a party pooper last night—especially on my birthday—but I'm back in business."

Cal's eyes looked red. Jesus. Did he go on a bender last night after she packed it in? She hoped not. "Cal, are you up for a swim this morning?"

Cal took a long pull on his coffee. "Sure," he said. "Are you going to eat first, or do you want me to go get ready right now?"

"I think I'll go back in and make some toast. After I eat and have a cup of coffee, we can head down to the water. Sound good?"

He nodded.

She set her coffee cup down and was back in a few minutes with buttered toast.

"If you are looking for a great workout," Iggi said, "Then head straight out for Cedar Island. It's a mile out and a mile back."

Maria laughed. "Now, how would you know? You've never swam ten yards toward that island."

"Michael," he said. "You know, the guy two houses down? He swims out to the island and back when he's getting ready for those crazy Ironman competitions he does. What's the big one? Kona? Yeah, Kona. It's a 2.4-mile swim in the ocean, 112-mile bicycle ride, and a 26.2-mile run. Guy's crazy."

"What's on the island?" Haley asked.

"Not much. It's about 3 square miles of cedar trees packed next to each other like crayons in a box."

Maria cut in. "You'll see boats anchored out there, though, because of the two wrecks that divers like to visit. I've been down to both of them."

"You dive?" Cal said.

"I do," Maria said. "I'm a member of P.O.W., Preserve Our Wrecks. It was started about 25 years ago to keep thieves away from stealing artifacts off wrecks. We try to keep an eye on the state side, and S.O.S., Save Ontario Shipwrecks, which was founded in Toronto, takes care of the Canadian side."

"That's her big to do over the summer," Iggi said. "She dives every goddamn weekend except for her month away teaching."

"And you sit on the boat and drink Bud Light while I do, smart ass," she replied.

"I've got enough trouble breathing above water. Why in the hell would I want to complicate life and try to breathe one hundred feet below it?" Iggi said.

"How many wrecks does Lake Ontario have?" Cal asked.

"Around eleven hundred," Maria said. "And we have the claim to the first Great Lakes Shipwreck ever."

"The *Griffon?*" Cal asked.

"How do you know about the *Griffon?*" Maria said.

"Mostly because of my dad," Cal said. "When he wasn't busy being a cop, he was reading about Michigan history. I think it was the only hobby he ever had besides yelling at the TV when the Detroit Lions were on."

Iggi almost spit out his coffee.

Maria patted his back. "You okay there, big guy?"

Iggi nodded, wiping the coffee off of his chin with a napkin.

"Not the *Griffon*, Cal, although people always think the *Griffon* was our first shipwreck—mostly because it's never been found. Nope. The twin-masted schooner *Frontenac* was actually the first." She took a sip of coffee. "Wrecked around Thirty Mile Point on the state side of Lake O. But, there is a connection *to* the *Griffon*. Rene Robert Cavelier de LaSalle had both ships built."

"Now you've got her started, Cal," Iggi said. "I listen to this stuff all summer long."

"As you should," she winked at Iggi. She turned to Cal and Haley. "I'll give you a few more tidbits."

"Leave it alone already," Iggi pestered.

"Hey, they might like to know a little bit about the body of water they are going to be swimming around in." She did not wait for Haley or Cal to confirm or deny this statement. "So, originally, Lake Ontario had a different name. The major tribe in the area when explorers traveled here was the Iroquois, so they named the lake, Lake Iroquois. It's the smallest of the Great Lakes in terms of surface area, but it has a greater volume than Lake Erie because of its depth. Max depth is around 800 feet." She needled Iggi back. "See, that wasn't so bad."

Iggi eyed Cal and Haley. "That's the shortest her spiel has ever been. You're lucky."

Cal stretched. "Now that I know you dive, we'll have to go sometime together."

"Where do you go?" Maria said.

"Mostly in Lake Huron, but every once in a while, I head to Florida—the unofficial vacation spot for Michiganders—and do some diving in the Keys."

"Why the Keys?" Haley asked.

"Mostly sentimental reasons. Although, the diving there is incredible, and, hell, just the attitude and pace of life lowers your blood pressure when you arrive. We took a few trips there when I was growing up. The Keys were the old man's favorite spot on earth other than Detroit. Parents hate the drive down I-75, but every Michigan kid who has ever loaded up the car at the start of spring break and climbed in for the ride, loves it. And when you hit the Florida border, roll down the windows, feel the heat, and stop at the welcome center for a glass of orange juice, you never forget it."

"But your dad was a cop," Iggi said. "Didn't he hate Detroit?"

"No," Cal said. "I think some people have a love-hate relationship with Detroit. They hate it. They bitch. But, at least in the neighborhood where Maria and I grew up, Detroiters take care of their own and don't want to be anywhere else. From the police officers I talk to in New York City, it's the same thing. People grow up their entire lives in the Big Apple and never know what it is like to drive a car or have their own lawn, but they wouldn't trade city living for anything." He softened the statement with, "We all can't stand the

Lions, right? But we watch 'em every Sunday—we're still not good enough for the NFL to let us play on Mondays."

Iggi let out a laugh. "I hated Detroit, but you're right about the Lions."

"Okay, enough about the Detroit Lions already," Maria said, turning to Iggi. "I've already read more about them in your book than I ever cared to."

"You have your shipwrecks and literature. I have my sports," Iggi said.

"Think you'll ever go back to Detroit?" Cal asked.

"Only for a sporting event," Iggi said.

Haley finished the last bite of toast and washed it down with a gulp of coffee. She felt the caffeine pulsate through her body. Her systems were waking up, and she felt her energy returning. Last night was in the past. They all still had two days left together. "Well, Cal. I don't think I'm up for going all the way to Cedar Island, but we can certainly get a workout in."

Cal finished his coffee and stood up. "Ready," he said.

Haley followed him inside, and soon they were back on the deck—Cal in just swimming trunks with a towel over his shoulder and Haley in a bikini with a towel wrapped around her waist.

"Last chance to join us," Haley said to Maria and Iggi.

Maria said, "Get out of here already."

Iggi and Maria watched as Cal and Haley descended the deck steps and headed across the backyard toward the beach.

When they jumped in the water and started their crawl strokes, side-by-side, Maria said, "No workout today?"

Iggi moved his chair closer. "I said no to *that* workout," he said, pointing to Cal and Haley. "Let's go inside. I've got another kind of workout in mind."

"As long as you know that you're taking care of me first. This household runs on orgasm equality."

"Follow me into my lair," he said.

* * *

Cal came up for a breath and saw Haley smoothly stroking, five yards ahead of him. Christ, she was strong. He thought he was five yards ahead of her. He dipped his head in and began slicing the water with each stroke. *I need to be even with her when I tap her for a break.*

As he pulled his arms through the cold water and concentrated on his breathing, he began to relax. Was last night disappointing? Yes. Could today erase it? Yes. He was pretty sure she had snuck a few glances at him during breakfast; he knew that he had used every excuse to look her way during the conversation. He wished that he could just stare at her without it being awkward. There hadn't been any nightmares last night, and today, out here in the water, he felt a million miles away from Detroit and terrorists. He was existing, a part of the water, head up-breath-head down-stroke-stroke-constant kicking-head up-another breath—the sun was rising with no clouds. The talk of the Keys had brought his father to the forefront of his memories: his first Little League game with his dad watching, Christmas morning tugging on the old bear's arm to get him up because Cal couldn't stand it anymore, watching the Tigers together on the few summer nights when his dad didn't have to work, and seeing his dad relaxing on the beach in Key West—away from the stress, pressure, and danger of Detroit. Then, an episode of *Magnum P.I.*—his father's all-time favorite show—came to mind. *Magnum falls overboard and has to tread water, hoping to be rescued. While he treads, flashbacks of his father are cut into the narrative until the final cut where the audience learns that Magnum lost his dad during World War II.*

Cal pulled his arms through the water faster. Magnum wasn't the only one who had lost a father.

DETROIT, DECEMBER 1992

Police Officer John Ripley grabbed two Styrofoam cups of coffee from the Shell station counter. It was almost midnight, and he was hoping the coffee would give him and his partner the jolt they needed to make it the last 3 hours of their shift. Well, it would probably be longer than 3 hours. Something always happened after midnight in the Motor City, which meant by the time whatever situation was dealt with and the corresponding paperwork filed, it ended up being close to dawn when the shift actually ended. "Until tomorrow night, Chris," Ripley said as he put two dollars down on the counter.

The cashier, Chris Stockford, took the money, pushed buttons on the register, and the drawer opened with a *ching*. The digital readout displayed $1.03. Stockford took 97 cents out of the drawer and placed it in the slot of this month's donation stand: the American Red Cross's drive to cure children with cancer.

Ripley watched as the coins went into the small opening at the top of the plastic donation stand and rattled on the way down until all of the change had settled on the bottom. He gave a small grin which disappeared as fast as it had shown.

"Look more tired than usual tonight, John," Stockford said. "Everything all right?"

Ripley peered outside and saw his cruiser in the usual spot, engine running, with his partner George Graff in the passenger seat. Graff was black, 6'7" and around 250 lbs. and took up most of the passenger side—his head nearly touching the car's roof. They had worked together for the past six years. Like most partners, the pair had started out as just work acquaintances. But, over their time together on the job, a deep friendship had developed. They were both Vietnam veterans, had kids who were either in high school or college, and were past their mid-career points.

It was starting to snow outside. Ripley put the cups back down on the counter. "We're supposed to get four inches tonight plus freezing rain. Want to take any bets on how many people George and I will have to help get back on the road?" He was avoiding Stockford's question, and he knew why. Standing in the shadow of fifty was not something he wanted to discuss. Cal was in college, and his daughter, Lilian, was a sophomore in high school. The events in their lives he had missed because of his job were starting to creep into his daily thoughts, which had never happened before. He was becoming sad, regretful, and pained that he would never get the time back. Had the sacrifice been worth it? In the mid-1970s, when his career had started, Detroit averaged 3 murders a day. Last year, the rate was around 1.7 murders a day—still over 600 people. The number seemed to be decreasing, but so was Detroit's population. He had heard the figures at a recent meeting. At the peak in 1950, 1.8 million people lived in Detroit. 42 years later, just over a million people lived in the Motor City. The Michigan mystery of where Teamsters boss Jimmy Hoffa disappeared to after leaving his home in Lake Orion in July of 1975 might never be solved; the mystery of where in the hell almost 1 million Detroit residents had disappeared to already had been: The whites had fled to the suburbs.

"I'll keep a fresh pot brewed for you both all night," Stockford said. "And you haven't answered my question. Not lettin' you get out of here until you do."

Gotta give him something. "Old, Chris. Just getting old."

Stockford chuckled.

"What?" Ripley asked.

"Your partner said the same thing last night when it was his turn to come in here and get coffee for the two of you."

Made sense. They had been talking about it more and more on patrol the past few months. It was the holiday season, and family was always on his mind this time of year. He'd never admit it to anyone else, but he and George had even talked about being grandfathers one day. He couldn't see himself as one quite yet but was getting more comfortable with the thought. He had decided not to try and make up for his failings as a father—that would not be fair to Cal and Lily—but, rather, to be the best grandparent possible. He gave a short grin to Chris and motioned to the patrol car outside. "I'll have to give him shit when I get back out there." He picked up the coffee cups.

Stockford gave Ripley a pat on the shoulder. "Until later," he said.

"Thanks, Chris," Ripley said.

Stockford started to take a sip from his own cup of coffee but froze as something outside caught his eye. Before Ripley could turn, he yelled, "Oh no!"

Outside, two masked figures had sprinted toward the passenger side of the patrol car. Inside, Graff had spotted them with his peripheral vision but was too late. As he reached for his weapon, the roar of automatic weapon fire filled the night air. Graff's window shattered as bullets tore into him and the car's interior. His body shook as the assailants poured on more fire.

Ripley dropped the cups of coffee and pulled out his Glock. In an instant he had pushed open the Shell station's front door and was firing at the two attackers. One dropped, but still had his finger on the trigger, and bullets sprayed up into the air and then riddled the side of the Shell station until the body hit the ground.

The other assailant had enough time to swing his weapon toward Ripley. Bullets hit Ripley in the chest as he squeezed off his remaining rounds, one hitting the attacker in the face, which killed him. Ripley fell to his knees, blood starting to soak the front of his uniform.

Stockford ran to him and brought him carefully to the ground. "John, hang in there. Don't quit on me. I'm going inside to call the hospital."

Not going to make it out of this one, Chris. He looked over at the destroyed police car. *George.* His eyes became glassy. *This all has to stop.* He saw his wife and kids around the Christmas tree, years ago, and a younger version of himself smiling as they opened presents. *I was too tough on Cal and didn't know how to relate to Lily. I don't regret not telling them about Vietnam—the horror, the confusion, the lies, the bravery, the tremendous loss. I didn't spend enough time with my wife. I will miss my family.* With his right hand, he squeezed Chris Stockford's right arm, shook his head 'no', and then died.

Cal felt a hand squeeze his left arm, and he stopped his crawl stroke. His head came out of the lake, and he saw that Haley was next to him, treading water.

"You sure you're not trying to swim out to the island and back?" she said.

He looked back toward shore. They had to be at least five hundred yards out. "Whoa. Guess I got into a groove," he replied.

"No problem here. You shot past me, and it was fun staying up with you," she said. "I just wanted to check in."

The rush of adrenaline subsided, and he now felt the tiredness in his muscles. "Time to head back?" he said.

"Works for me," she said, seeming to tread effortlessly.

"I think we made some space for drinks later," he said. "Before you got up, Iggi and Maria were throwing around the idea of heading to some bar right on the beach called 'Billy's' tonight."

"Well, after my early exit last evening, I've got to make a comeback tonight," she said.

She went underwater and dipped her head back. When she emerged, her blond hair was slicked back. The look turned him on. "To comebacks it is then," he said. "Ready to free up some more calories? You're thirty now, remember?"

"Uh. Stop it."

"Make me," he said and then started pulling toward shore.

23

C.I.A. HEADQUARTERS, MCLEAN, VIRGINIA
JANUARY 2006

The door to Deputy Director Narita's office opened, and Officer Jennifer Lear was escorted in by Narita's secretary. On the couch across from Narita sat Rolfe Judas. Once Lear was in the room, the secretary left and closed the door.

Narita stood and walked toward Lear. They hadn't seen each other since right after the mission to Berlin. Without any words exchanged, Narita gave Lear a hug and then walked her to the couch.

Lear sat down and eyed Rolfe Judas. His usual pompous demeanor was gone, and he looked like he hadn't showered in a week.

"How are you holding up?" Narita asked, while offering her a cup of coffee.

Lear waved off the cup. "Got anything stronger?"

Narita exchanged glances with Judas. "Of course." She pulled open one of the coffee table's drawers and pulled out a pint of Johnny Walker. "Scotch?"

Lear gave a weak nod and grabbed an empty coffee cup from the table.

"Rolfe?" Narita asked.

Judas held out his cup.

Narita gave them each a few fingers worth and then did the same for herself. "Turner and Zimmer were both outstanding officers," she said. "In your field training—Lord, 2002 seems a lifetime ago—it was explained to you that this was a risk of the job. I've had to have these debriefs far too many times over the years, but we go on. When we entered the spy game in 1945, the Russians had already been at it for over two centuries. We've more than caught up—at least that's what I like to think—but every now and then their experience bites us. You know the game. You can't lie to everyone, and you don't always win." The words hung in the air as they all took a sip of scotch. Judas did not look up from his cup. "However, whenever *they* get a win, they almost always become overconfident instead of looking inward at their weaknesses, and we hit back harder." She sat up. "Now that we've got almost a month distance from the event, is there anything you want to add to what you told us when you returned?"

Lear took a second sip of scotch. "No," she said.

Judas uncrossed his legs and leaned forward, looking straight into her eyes. "I know this is difficult. Turner was your partner." He folded his hands. "But if there is anything else you can remember, it would help us as we go after those who did this."

Did they think she had something to do with what happened? Don't get emotional. They have to ask these questions. *Someone* wants more answers.

"Was Sari's information good?"

"Now why would you ask that?" Judas said.

"Because I hope it was worth the price we paid for it," Lear shot back. "One minute I'm giving you all a brief about the catastrophic aftermath of an EMP detonation above the United States, the next minute we're meeting with Sari in Berlin, and the next minute Turner and Zimmer are dead."

"Why do you think Sari was late?" Narita asked.

"I've already told you," Lear said. "I don't know."

Judas exploded. "That's not good enough! Think!"

"Screw you," Lear said. "I haven't stopped having night terrors since I returned. I'm barely able to make it through each day of teaching. I can't talk to anyone about this. And," she started to cry, "Fuck it. I had feelings for Turner, and now he's gone."

Judas went to speak, but Narita raised her hand. "Rolfe, why don't you leave us alone for a few minutes?"

Judas set his cup down in frustration and left.

Narita pulled her chair close to Lear's and handed Lear a tissue. "I believe you." Then she motioned to the door. "And so does he."

Lear wiped her eyes with the tissue.

Narita continued. "Don't mind Judas. He's reeling from the loss of Zimmer."

"What?" Lear said.

"You weren't the only one around here who was involved with a co-worker."

"You knew about me and Turner?"

"My dear, it's my job to know. Normally, I'd intervene, but because we paired you together as a couple, and it wasn't interfering with the operations—actually, it was making you both more convincing as a pair—I let it go on." She sat back and refilled her cup with scotch. "And there are dangers in doing that, but I knew what they were and was ready to answer for them. And so were you."

Lear nodded in agreement.

"What Sari delivered *was* worth it. I know that doesn't change how you feel right now, but I hope it helps some." She paused. "What will help more is that I'm placing you on administrative leave for the next six months. It's not punitive, just a break to deal with this and consider your future with The Company." Her warmth left. "If after those months, you believe you've had enough, then we'll start the separation paperwork."

Time away was what she *did* need. "Okay," Lear said.

Apparently satisfied with her answer, Narita's compassion returned. "And, if you need me during that time, I'm giving you my private cell number. Call me. I've grown kind of fond of you, Haley Girard."

Lear was taken aback by the sound of her real name; Narita had never used it with her before. "Thank you," she said.

Narita stood up. Lear followed her lead. The meeting was over.

"If I don't hear from you, I'll see you back here during the first weekend of August to see where you're at."

"While I'm on leave, do I turn my weapon in?"

"Keep it handy. There is no credible intelligence that you are in any danger, but the next few months will be tense as we investigate Sari's information."

"Yes, ma'am," Lear said.

Narita gave her another hug—this one was more of the *stay strong* variety than the initial consoling embrace.

Lear left the room.

Five minutes later, Rolfe Judas re-entered.

"Sorry if I pushed too hard," Judas said, sitting back down on the couch.

Narita stretched her legs and let him continue.

"I just don't know what happened. Everything checked out. I've gone over the debrief file a hundred times. Sure, Sari was a little late, but still within mission parameters. And she wasn't panicked when she met with Lear. The only plausible scenario is that when she did her surveillance detection run, she thought she was clear but someone had caught on and was following her."

"That was my assessment as well," Narita said. "The other possibility is that we had or have a mole, but that doesn't make sense because the meeting would have never happened if that was the case. Sari was able to pass on her information, and the meeting clearly wasn't an ambush because, if it was, Lear and Sari would have been killed at the café and we wouldn't have Sari's intelligence in our hands right now."

Judas nodded in agreement.

"Our only obstacle now is that we have to put the puzzle pieces that she gave us together without any more help from her."

"I believe she gave us enough to complete the puzzle, but the real question is: Can we? And, can we put it together in time? We don't know the delivery method, and we don't know the launching point. We're pretty sure who the players are, but we can't move until we're certain." Judas alternated moving his hands up and down. "But if we wait too long, then we're done."

"How long *do we have*, Rolfe?"

"From what we've decoded of Sari's information, it's going to happen within the next year." Judas motioned for her to refill his cup with scotch.

"You've had enough," she said.

He rubbed the cup with his hands and then put it down on the coffee table. "What's the DCI think?"

"He's made it a priority. The president knows now too."

"Well, let's hope that cowboy doesn't open his big mouth and start schmoozing to get information that he's not going to get."

"You don't like him?"

"I don't like any politicians," Judas said.

"I like him," Narita said. "He'll give us the resources we need to get this done. And he likes the DCI, which is the most important thing. *You* just make sure to tell me what *you* need."

"All over it," Judas said.

No, you're not. You look like shit, and you smell. Narita ran her right hand through her hair. "We're probably going to lose Officer Lear."

Judas tapped his feet on the ground, then stopped. "I don't think she'll recover from the loss. I've seen it before. But," he paused, "I've got another teacher in Connecticut in mind as a replacement."

Narita's eyes were cold. "I said *probably*. Don't write her off yet. Plus, do you think *you'll* recover?"

Judas's eyes twitched. "I'm fine," he said. "Either way, the program has been a success because of what we got from Sari."

"Until this is over, we meet at least every Thursday for lunch." She stood up and walked behind her desk. "Now, clean yourself up and get back to work."

Judas picked his cup back up and held it over his mouth, shaking it in an attempt to taste one more drop of Johnny Walker. It didn't happen. He put the cup down and walked out of the room.

Two hours later he was back along with a skinny kid who wore a short-sleeved collared button-down shirt with a tie that was tied too short. The youngster's hair was blonde and came down over his eyebrows. Judas appeared to be more awake; in fact, he looked on edge. He had a briefcase in his hand.

"Who's this?" she asked, pointing to the kid.

"Silman Russell," Judas said. "One of the techs working to decode the flash drive." He put his hairy paw on Russell's shoulder. "This tall skinny shit found something."

Russell's eyes searched the room for a place to hide.

She should say something but didn't have the time right now. "What do you have?"

Still looking like he was on the way to the guillotine, Russell walked over to the wall where he brought down a screen. Then, he hooked up his laptop to a projector.

Narita joined Judas on the couch, and they stared at the blue screen, waiting.

Russell punched keys and moved the mouse, eventually bringing up two photos that had been taken from the air. The altitude was too low for the pictures to be taken from a plane. It had to be from a helicopter, perhaps a drone. Russell dimmed the lights and enlarged the pictures so that they were side-by-side.

Judas spoke. "We would like you to take a look at these."

The first was of a mostly barren landscape, mountains in the distance but nothing else. Her eyes moved from the edges of the picture toward the center, and then back out to the edges again. There was nothing remarkable about the photograph. The terrain was so minimalist that it could be from a variety of places. She switched her attention to the second image. This picture looked like it was the same location, but now there was a building under construction at the bottom of the frame, and next to it was a long path that extended to the right and left of the building for quite some distance. Again, her eyes started from the edges and worked their way to the center and then back out to the edges again. Okay. What is the significance of the path and the building? What is the scale? Is this a garage being built or a soccer stadium? She sat back. "What am I supposed to be seeing?"

Judas rose and took a pointer out of his shirt pocket. He approached the screen. "Silman, wait outside."

The tech powerwalked out of the room.

Judas hit a button on the clicker, and a red dot appeared on the screen. He moved it over to the dirt path. "So, you probably guessed that we're seeing the same area in both photographs, just at different times. I had Russell estimate distances based on the height from which the photo was taken. The path is in the ballpark of how long a standard airport runway is for larger planes—757s, 747s, etc.—to land and take off. He took the pointer and ran the dot across the path's breadth. "The width is consistent too." He moved the pointer to the structure. "Based on Russell's measurements, this building is going to be huge." He walked over to the laptop and minimized the first photograph and then zoomed in on the building so that it took up most of the screen. With the pointer, he made an arcing motion at the building's superstructure. "This is just the start. See the beams going out into the open air here? See the trucks down here?"

She leaned forward. Damn. There were two trucks; one appeared to be a mixing truck, and the other was larger. A Semi? "I see them," she said.

"Well, I think what you have here is the beginning of an airplane hangar. We have a possibility for how the EMP may be delivered."

"What are the dates on the photographs?"

"That's the bad news. If the dates haven't been doctored, the first one was taken a year and a half ago." He rubbed his left hand through his hair. "The second, eight months ago."

"We have to assume that the runway and hangar are finished."

"Safe assumption."

"When did that kid decode these?"

"Ten minutes ago."

"Okay, so now we've got to find out where in the hell this is? How much of Sari's stuff is still unavailable?"

"Over half," Judas said. "What happened at the meeting and right after it is still a mystery, but she must have been rushed when she delivered this. The first few bits she gave to Lear in Berlin were easy to decode, but she must have just stolen the flash drive and not had time to decode it or take pictures of what she found. Russell is smart as shit, but even he says he's never seen anything like this."

"Chinese? Russians?" She exhaled, put her face in her hands, and then looked up from them. "Or both?"

"Your first two options are bad enough. I don't even want to think about the third."

"Me either, but Sari's intelligence is hard to argue with."

"Or it could be neither, and we are being made to think it is one of these two."

Judas took a paperback book out of his briefcase and held it up. "Besides the unhealthy habits I've indulged in lately, I have been doing some reading." He handed the book to Narita.

"The Clash of Civilizations and the Remaking of World Order by Samuel P. Huntington," she said. "This was required reading for all of us a few years back." She ran her thumb along the pages, watching them fan like a deck of cards being shuffled, and then set the book down.

"I never got to it then," Judas said.

"I'm not surprised," Narita said.

"But, I did get through it this past week. And I've got some ideas about why China and Russia may be ready to make a move—albeit the boldest ever made since Germany invaded Poland and the Japanese bombed Pearl Harbor."

"Let's hear it."

He sat down. "So we're tied up in Iraq and Afghanistan right now, correct? Bleeding billions of dollars over a war that we're not going to be able to kill our way out of. But we need the oil, and we're committed, so we can't back out. Yes, we've got global presence, but everyone inside this building knows that almost all of our focus is on the Middle East."

Generally speaking, he was right, but there were a few things she knew that he didn't. She nodded in affirmation. "Continue."

"First, the scenario that we all fear: China and Russia covertly team up to paralyze the United States with a devastating EMP strike. They make it impossible for us to trace it back to them, and they come to our aid in what amounts to a humanitarian invasion. They can't tip their hands by positioning their military forces around us before the blast because then we'd know it was them. And they wouldn't need to. They need our population to decrease by at least 50 percent to make room for their expansion—mostly Chinese expansion. As history has taught us, whenever there has been rapid economic growth for countries, the years that follow the growth are highlighted by outward expansion and imperialism." Judas coughed on purpose, "Ahem, the United States."

He is a loveable asshole.

"Right now, China is on track to replace us as the world's largest economy, and economic growth is the prime mover for military power. China's military has been growing exponentially since it went away from the defensive strategy of protecting its borders from an invasion by the Soviets and began focusing on projecting its power—regionally first, everywhere, eventually. And here's the irony. Where did they get their military equipment and technology? From the fuckin' Russkies!" He got up and started to pace back and forth. "More on that later. So, the Russians and Chinese wait long enough after the EMP— maybe a year—for America to fall apart on the inside, you know, the stuff Lear briefed us on." A Donald Sutherland smile came across Judas's face. "As for Lear's fellow academics, on day one after the EMP, they'll be lauding the virtues of utopian communal living, sharing, and suffering together. Day number two, they'll realize it's a fantasy. Day three, they'll be looking to survive—and for someone with food, water, and guns. Day four—" The smile widened and then disappeared, just like Sutherland's always did. "Anyway, their military forces come in, peacefully take over our country by helping the remaining survivors rebuild our economy and power grids—and never leave. After we're shaken like a rabbit in a St. Bernard's mouth, the Russians and Chinese will count on our will to fight back being broken. And, I don't know if you've been in any high schools lately where kids aren't standing let alone saying the Pledge of Allegiance anymore, they're probably right. Our spoiled young Americans are ripe for getting their asses wiped off the face of the Earth. They don't know that when you're kneeling to fascism, communism, or socialism, you don't get to stand back up. But this is a moot point anyway; most of us won't be around in a year after it goes off."

Narita smirked. "I don't remember any of that in Huntington's book."

"My private rant gone public," Judas laughed. He took a breath. "Next, why do Russia and China want to work together? China needs Russia's natural gas so it can reduce its use of coal. Russia would love a pipeline deal with China to align their economic future more with the east than with Europe. China also needs oil, so they've been engaging in a campaign with Iraq, Iran, Saudi Arabia, and others that goes like this: We provide you with weapons—some of which we bought from Russia—you provide us with oil. Russia has also sold submarines, fighter aircraft, and surface-to-air missiles to Iran. So on one hand, you have the Sinic and Muslim societies opposing the West—there's a reason why Huntington called it the Tehran-Islamabad-Beijing Axis—and on the other hand you have the Russian Bear aligning with the Chinese Dragon. Let's face it, their demographic destinies are already aligned. There may be more illegal Chinese migrants in Siberia than there are Russians."

She nodded. "Who does that leave *us* aligned with?" She already knew the answer; she wanted to know if he did.

"Ah, the ever-present questions. Who will be my enemy? Who will be my friend? This is where it gets interesting. The United States, Great Britain, France, and Russia combine to fight Italy, Japan, and Germany in World War II.

After the war, the Soviets start to gain ground, which pushes Japan and the United States to agree to a mutual security treaty; we become allies with our enemy. Meanwhile, the bear and the dragon start to get cozy. Then, Vietnam serves as the first post-World War II test. How far do you let a competing ideology spread? Vietnam becomes a proxy war between capitalism and communism—Russia and China supply the NVA and Viet Cong; the U.S. supplies the South Vietnamese army. Then, we push all of our chips to the middle of the table, except for the nuclear chip, and commit our own forces to winning an unwinnable war. We withdraw, and the NVA win. Then, an interesting thing happens in the '70s. The Soviet Union becomes so powerful that Nixon and Kissinger open up diplomatic relations with...China. Once again, our enemy in Vietnam becomes our friend in an attempt to neutralize the Russian threat. Then, Russia jumps into a huge mistake and invades Afghanistan; we do the proxy two-step again and back the Afghani forces, who win but then eventually turn on us and attack us on 9/11. This allows China to use the 1980s to grow its economy and build up its military. Throw Ronald Wilson Reagan into the arena and...boom! The cold war ends, and the common enemy of the United States and China is suddenly gone. And *this* chokepoint in history is what has led us to where we are now in year three of the Iraq war and year five of the war in Afghanistan. The '90s are commonly referred to as a *holiday from history*, but if you study them, they actually proceeded according to the natural course of history." Judas picked up the book and opened to an earmarked page. "I'll quote from good Doctor Huntington here: 'Economic growth creates political instability within countries and between countries, altering the balance of power among countries and between countries, altering the balance of power among countries and regions. Economic exchange brings people into contact; it does not bring them into agreement. Historically it has often produced a deeper awareness of the differences between peoples and stimulated mutual fears. Trade between countries produces conflict as well as profit.'" He closed the book and tossed it on the table. "How am I doing so far?"

"You left out the Korean War, but keep going."

"And so, it shouldn't be a mystery that every country on the planet is sitting at the racetrack wondering which horse to bet on. Take Japan for instance. We've been in an alliance with them for over fifty years now. But, if we don't stop our own internal decay and renew our nation, will Japan jump ship and align itself with China? This would be a disaster for us. No, we need Japan on our side to help balance China's power. But here's the catch: To do that, we'd have to help Japan rearm, which would mean Japan having more nuclear weapons. Now, imagine that happens and they *still* align with China. Think they might like a little payback for 1945? You can argue that when the cold war ended, well, shit, *suspended* might be a better term now, between the United States and the Soviet Union that a new cold war started between the United States and China."

"Any chance of us finding common ground?"

"You won't like my answer."

"Lay it on me."

He swiped the book off the table again. "The differences between China and the United States won't be bridged in our lifetimes." He flipped through the book until he found the desired page. After clearing his throat, he began, "First, China. 'At the broadest level the Confucian ethos pervading many Asian societies stressed the values of authority, hierarchy, the subordination of individual rights and interests, the importance of consensus, the avoidance of confrontation, "saving face," and, in general, the supremacy of the state over society and of society over the individual.' Now, the United States. 'These attitudes contrasted with the primacy in American beliefs of liberty, equality, democracy, and individualism, and the American propensity to distrust government, oppose authority, promote checks and balances, encourage competition, sanctify human rights, and to forget the past, ignore the future, and focus on maximizing immediate gains.' He sums it up for me: 'The sources of conflict are in fundamental differences in society and culture.'" Judas closed the book. "We'll never live under the same roof. The best we can do is to live peacefully in separate houses."

"Let's say an EMP does go off over the United States," Narita said. "What about our allies in Europe?"

"Are they our allies? Would France, Great Britain, and Germany take on Russia and China, or would they negotiate? Then it would be a case of the Asian hierarchy of power model against the European balance of power model, right? China knows that the bottom line is this: The United States could stop China's growing domination by either the balance/contain strategy or by going to war with the Chinese and defeating them. Huntington thinks that bandwagoning is a viable third option, but I'm not so sure. If we fight, we'll win but at a huge cost, and right now with the majority of our forces and money tied up in the Middle East, could our citizens stomach *another* war going on at the same time? I think the answer is no. Now, the balance/contain strategy. Have we truly committed to this? I don't know. And therein may be the problem: We have at least two options, and we are unwilling to commit. The United States of America has not made a definitive choice—China has."

Narita sat back. He'd come to the same conclusion she had. Bravo, Rolfe. The most dangerous time in any conflict is when the covert cover is stripped away, the lights come on in the room, and everyone realizes who they really are and who everyone else really is. She appreciated his conviction. And, now, perhaps, she had found another lever to manipulate him with—this time for his own health. Distraction can be a powerful ally when dealing with grief. In this case, it was easy because the distraction *was* his job—and the stakes could not be higher. "Let's meet with the DCI tonight. We're going to need him to swing those big brass balls of his and coordinate the satellites."

"Over Russia and China? Still a mammoth area to cover."

"That's where we start." She looked up at the screen. "But this place could be anywhere. Those mountains could have been put in there to throw someone off. The barren landscape—that could be a jungle. We just don't know; we have to find out. Get the kid back in here and start analyzing the photos. I'll talk to the DCI."

24

MONDAY, JULY 3, 2006

It was after 10 p.m., and the volume was rising at Bay Harbor's favorite outdoor watering hole, "Billy's", named after bar owner William Lyton Karpowski, Bay Harbor High School's only graduate to ever make a pro roster.

But on this warm summer night with a steady wind blowing in from the lake, liquor store owner Rick Dorne was holding court in a corner table near the bar; he'd been a regular customer for so long, he might as well be a part of the furniture. Surrounded by couples and singles half his age and twice as attractive, Dorne wore a charter captain's hat and had on a black button-down collared shirt, top two buttons unbuttoned, exposing a gray Brillo Pad of chest hair blending into his waterfall of a beard. After introductions had been made, he had caught one of the young ladies looking at his chest, and he unleashed his practiced line, 'A bird never makes a nest in a bare tree, darlin'.' At that remark, she had scooted her chair closer to him. *Maybe by the end of the night she'd be sittin' on Captain Rick's lap*, Dorne thought. Pitchers had been consumed, fresh pitchers had been ordered, and from across the bar, the owner, William "Billy" Karpowski, watched and smiled as Dorne told the bar's story.

"As a kicker for the Buffalo Bills, Billy set the single season record for field goals made over 50 yards in his rookie season," Dorne opened. "All of the local sportswriters nicknamed him 'The Bionic Leg', and Billy was lured into the lucrative sports-hero-of-the-moment TV commercial market at the end of the season."

Their eyes were glued to him. The pitchers arrived, and pint glasses were refilled. He took a healthy pull from his own glass and then continued. "So, *hotshot* over there," he pointed across the bar at Billy, who waved. They'd done the routine so many times that Dorne knew when he yelled 'hotshot', Billy's arm would already be starting its wave. Billy then raised a Collins glass in a toast; Dorne reciprocated.

One of the young guys—he looked like a rich kid from some northeast prep school—said, "You know him?"

Dorne rubbed his beard. *This kid's a doofus.* "I do," he said.

The kid nodded his head as if they now knew something that the others didn't.

Dorne held out his glass, and prep school boy gladly refilled it. The beauty on Dorne's right inched even closer. He resumed the tale. "So, Billy spent the spring and summer promoting Gatorade, American Express, and Tylenol. He purchased an expensive house right on Lake Ontario, threw parties until all hours of the night—" he paused for effect, "believe me, I was there—and reported to training camp thirty fuckin' pounds overweight. The preseason announcers changed his nickname to the 'The Beefy Leg', and Billy threatened to sue, claiming his brand was in danger." Dorne became serious, like he always did at this point in the story. "I would have too." He studied his beer glass while the table waited for the rest of the legend. "Anyways, distracted,

224

disgruntled, and rumored to be drunk before the season opener, Billy missed the first 7 field goals of his second season and was cut." Now he got pissed. "Piece of horseshit owner...it shouldn't have happened."

Lots of nods around the table. Prep school boy looked just as pissed off as Dorne. A hand touched Dorne's thigh and started to rub it. He smiled at her in thanks and then eyed everyone at the table for the climax. "But in America, tragedy can sometimes lead to triumph, and twenty years ago down-on-his-luck-ex-NFL-kicker Billy Karpowski's bank loan went through for a proposed beach bar a few blocks away from Main Street." His grin was barely noticeable, but then it widened into a full-toothed smile. Pointing again to Billy, he said, "Sonofabitch pulled it off...and here we are, friends." He raised his glass. "To Billy!"

A second later, they all followed with, "To Billy!"

Billy raised his glass again.

When they returned their attention to the table, Rick Dorne had company on his lap. "I'm Molly," said the girl, taking Dorne's captain's hat off of his head and putting it on her own.

"About time that hat found the rightful owner, darlin'," Dorne said. "Wanna head to an outdoor table, look at the lake, and hear some more of my bullshit stories?"

Molly giggled, exposing perfect teeth. She shifted her buns on his leg and his groin stirred. Jesus Christ.

"You've been demoted to First Mate," she said. "Now, follow your captain."

He could smell her fruity perfume mixed with cigarette smoke from a nearby table. *See? You were right to close the liquor store early tonight, you crafty old bastard.* "Yes, ma'am," he said. Out of the corner of his eye, he could see Billy shaking his head and laughing to himself. Dorne rose from the table and made an announcement. "We're heading outside. In half-an-hour, it'll be time for Billy to kick the bucket. I'll see you then."

The table cheered. Dorne had explained earlier that every night, at exactly 10:53 p.m., the bar patrons would crowd around a small makeshift football field made of AstroTurf in the corner of the bar next to the large stage. The mock football field included a yellow goalpost, an end zone, and yardage that extended out from the end zone to the seventeen-yard line.

Why? Because the last professional field goal that Billy Karpowski had attempted and missed was from the seventeen-yard line at 10:53 p.m. on national television. And so, each night, a bartender would serve as the center and hike the ball back to a patron, picked out of a ticket drawing, who held a bucket painted like a football. Billy would sweep his once golden leg through the air and kick the bucket through the upright. On the wall behind the goal post were various targets with specials listed on them—10% off the rest of the night, 5% off the rest of the night, etc. If Billy *missed*, then it was a free drink on the house for everyone.

Prep school boy frowned as Dorne and Molly shoved off with their glasses and a new pitcher.

The patio was packed. Iggi Hilliard and Cal Ripley navigated their way through the maze of tables and high tops with their two buckets full of beer and ice.

They rounded a table, and Cal felt Iggi pull on his shirt.

"See that guy standing against the railing with the girl wearing the captain's hat?" Iggi said.

Cal shifted to the left a few feet so he could get a look. The enormous bald-headed man dwarfed the young woman he was with. But whatever he was doing, he was certainly entertaining her—the girl was laughing hysterically. "Yeah," Cal said to Iggi.

"He's the local liquor store owner. He recommended that bottle of scotch we opened the other night."

Cal nodded.

Then, the man made eye contact with Iggi. He waved him over and shouted, "Brother! Brother! Come here!"

Iggi smiled. "Shit." He waved back, and they headed over toward the giant liquor store owner.

Not noticing that Cal was with Iggi, the man gave Iggi a surprise hug and said, "That scotch work out for that oinker you've got stayin' with ya?"

They parted and Iggi said, "Let's ask him."

Cal stepped forward and eyed the man.

Taken off his game, but trying to appear as if he knew that Cal was with Iggi all along, the man put out his hand and said, "Right, right, brother. The bottle meet your standards?"

Cal shook his hand. It was a chubby, large paw, and a sweaty one too. "Cal Ripley."

"Rick Dorne."

"Scotland shouldn't worry about losing my business anytime soon," Cal said.

"A gentleman *and* a scholar he is," Dorne said in reply.

"Neither," Cal grinned.

Dorne let loose a laugh. "I'd like both of you to meet someone very special to me." He put his arm around Molly. "My captain for the evening's revelry, gentlemen."

Molly eyed Cal in a way that made Cal immediately uncomfortable. Her look said, *I've just laid eyes on someone better than Rick Dorne.*

Dorne noticed it and stood up a little straighter.

"Molly Hillsdale," she said, shaking Cal's hand. It took some effort to get his hand loose from her grip. Then, she moved away from Dorne and closer to him. He looked down. Dorne's hand was becoming a fist.

We've got to leave—now.

Then, there was a tap on his shoulder. He turned around.

"We wondered where you two wandered off to," said Haley.

Thank. God.

Molly's eyes narrowed at Haley.

Cal enjoyed the show as Haley put her arm around him and gave Molly a gaze that was every bit the equal of the captain's stare.

"Yeah, get your asses in gear," Maria said, appearing to the left of Haley.

Iggi put his hand on Dorne's shoulder. "Gotta head back to our table. Thanks for the recommendation again."

Cal watched as Dorne relaxed. *He knows his competition is leaving.* "My pleasure, brother," said Dorne. He turned to Cal, "Enjoy."

They left. Behind him, he could hear Dorne, apparently regaining his old form, say, "Now, about that fishing pole we were talking about..."

As they weaved back toward their table, Cal couldn't believe he was out enjoying a fun evening with friends on the 3rd of July. It had been so long since he had a 4th of July off that he had forgotten the *early 4th* that started the night before and just kept going all day and all night *on* the 4th. Usually, he was in bed by this time in order to start his day, when duty commenced around 5 a.m. and concluded well after midnight. At the Detroit Police Department, they called it the 24-hours of patriotic obligation. Night shifts, bowl game security, and Memorial Day weekend had nothing on Independence Day. After every duty day on the 4th, Cal would launch operation 'Skip the 5th' and sleep all day and all night.

They arrived at the table and cracked open the beers.

"Was that the liquor store owner?" Maria said.

"The one and only," Iggi said. "I thought I recognized him, and he called us over."

"I saw who he was with. Did you make a friend, Cal?" Haley asked.

He tipped his bottle back. *Don't screw this up.* Swallowing, he lowered the beer. "Not *me*," he played.

She gave him a wink. "Good to know."

Iggi raised his eyebrows at Maria.

A band started to warm up, and then the lead singer took the microphone and told everyone that they had fifteen minutes until Billy kicked the bucket. The place exploded in cheers.

"What in the hell does that mean?" Haley said.

Maria explained it.

When the band started in with Marley's "No Woman No Cry", couples started to move toward the stage.

Haley chugged her beer. "Cal, wanna dance before Billy shows us his skills?"

He put out his hand, and she took it. They rose and headed for the dance floor.

GEORGETOWN, WASHINGTON D.C.

Rolfe Judas stood naked facing the foot of his bed. In front of him was a woman crawling on all fours across the covers toward his phallus. He had picked her up in a Georgetown bar a few months ago and only knew her as 'Star'. He should have followed protocol and checked her background, but his pain still ran so deep from the loss of Zimmer—her loss and his reaction surprised him—that he continued to bypass security for escape. He still had time for a quickie before he headed to headquarters to oversee the operation. Narita had told him to rest because tonight might be a long one. He was just following orders. Star had reached her goal and went to work on him. The only light on in the room was the bedside lamp, which cast a shadow across her perfectly round ass.

Behind her was their other partner, Jeremy Varga, whom Judas had been seeing off and on for five years. He was an accountant in his early thirties, a wizard with Judas's taxes, and had so far fulfilled every fantasy that he and Judas could think up. Jeremy entered Star, and she moaned in pleasure. Judas closed his eyes and drifted away into ecstasy. He did not hear the front door to his townhouse opening—it was unlocked because Star had received $1,000 the day before to make sure that it was unlocked, and she'd been promised a $5,000 bonus tomorrow—nor did he hear the footsteps going up the stairway, nor the sound of the bedroom door being opened.

The rocking of the bed stopped and Star's mouth jerked off of him. Judas opened his eyes to horror. Both Star and Jeremy were slumped on the bed, each with a part of their head missing. Brain, bone, blood, and gristle was sprayed across the sheets—away from the direction he was facing. He turned around.

Six feet away, a figure dressed in black—all the way from the ski mask down to the soft soled shoes that indented the luxury carpet of Judas's master bedroom—aimed a gun at him.

Judas went to speak, "I—"

And never got to the second word. A bullet entered the center of his forehead, and his body fell against the bed, bounced off, and dropped to the floor.

The masked figure backed out of the room and disappeared down the stairs toward the front door. *1 for 2.* He had barely missed getting Narita earlier— bitch had left her home fifteen minutes before he had arrived. He exited the house, walked down the block, and got into his car. He accepted that killing

Narita was a lost cause now, but he still had 2 more assassinations to carry out. His next target was forty-five minutes away, if traffic was good.

C.I.A. HEADQUARTERS, MCLEAN, VIRGINIA, 10:50 P.M.

Leiko Narita paced in the C.I.A. Headquarters Command and Control Center. "Where in the hell is Judas?" she said and took a drag from her cigarette.

One of the administrative assistants, Shelly Skowcroft said, "I tried him at his house, on his cell phone, on his car phone, and at that accountant's apartment. Nothing."

Narita checked her watch. The operation was scheduled to start in ten minutes—the helicopters were flying through the Altai Mountains right now. The DCI would be here in five. It would be a major embarrassment to not have her whole team there. "Okay," she scowled. "Send someone over to his apartment."

"On it," Skowcroft said. She picked up the nearest phone and gave orders to an officer on the other line. In thirty seconds she was done with the call and said to Narita, "Officers Corey and Sanchez are on their way."

Narita turned her attention to the state-of-the art displays in the front of the room. On display one was a satellite image of the large airplane hangar that had been constructed to hold the plane that would carry the nuclear bomb to be detonated above Kansas. A few days ago, Russell's team had finished decoding Sari's flash drive that gave them the estimated delivery time: 10 p.m. Eastern Standard Time on July 4th—just as fireworks would be going off all over the country. The hangar and air strip were located in one of the Altai mountain range's valleys, south of the city of Biysk, Russia, which was less than 300 miles from the border with China. Satellite images from the past few days had picked up helicopter flights back and forth between the city of Altay in northern China and the hangar. A Boeing 777-200LR had been taken at some point in the last 9 months—most likely from the closest international airport at Novosibirsk, 230 miles to the north of Biysk. That plane would be the one to carry the nuke. The timeline had been worked out as follows: The flight would take around 19 hours; Topeka, Kansas was 13 hours behind Biysk, Russia—if it was 9 p.m. in Topeka on July 3rd, then it was 10 a.m. in Biysk on July 4th; for a non-stop flight from Biysk to arrive over Topeka at 10 p.m. on July 4th, it would have to take off from Biysk at 4 p.m. on July 4th (3 a.m. on the 4th, Topeka time), crossing over the international date line going from west to east. So, right now it was 10:50 a.m. on July 4th in Biysk, which meant they had 5 hours and 10 minutes until the flight was supposed to take off. The war in Afghanistan, now mid-way through its fourth year, had actually allowed them to react quickly, as they still had members of Seal Team 6 in Uzbekistan. She and the DCI had briefed the President of the United States. Within twenty-four hours, two teams of SEALs were ready to deploy, and two drones were standing by to drop bombs and destroy the runway. But, POTUS wanted intelligence on just who exactly the enemy was. All signs pointed to Russia and China, but if the United States bombed the hangar and detonated the nuclear bomb on Russian soil without proof of Russian government involvement, then you had the start of World War III. The Pacific Fleet had been put on alert, and units were ready to intercept and destroy the plane before it made it anywhere near the western coast of the United States, let alone Kansas. Additionally, with one command, the runway could be destroyed in seconds by the drones; because of the C.I.A.'s decoding team, time was an ally again. Hence, the decision had been made to send in two teams to gather intelligence, disable the plane on the ground, and then destroy the runway. This would strengthen the POTUS's political position when he spoke with the leaders of the two countries. So far, he had not contacted them.

On display two was a split screen of the two helicopters carrying the SEALs en route to the hangar. They had considered sending the team in at night, when the use of night vision goggles could have given them an advantage, but they had not had enough time to ensure the power would be cut to the hangar. Plus, the heat signatures gathered via satellite told them that the hangar was relatively unguarded so as not to attract attention. There were no Russian forces or armament in the area, and no Chinese military units had crossed the border. It was simply the runway, hangar, plane, a few vehicles, and, at last count, a dozen human beings in or around the hangar.

The lights in the room darkened, and the main door opened. In stepped the POTUS, Vice-President, and Director of Central Intelligence, followed by a platoon of suits and military brass. The door closed, and the men and women took seats behind a long table. Narita was seated next to the DCI, who was in the middle next to the President. The chair next to her, reserved for Judas, was empty. Fresh coffee was then poured for each member at the table.

"You missing someone, Leiko?" The DCI said.

She exhaled. "Judas. We've got someone going over to his house."

The DCI leaned over and whispered in her ear. "I hope it's a good excuse. If not, fire him."

She nodded, and they focused on the screens.

The timer above the screens hit zero.

"Are we a go?" the DCI said.

Every member of the table except for the POTUS and Vice-President said 'yes' with Narita being the last.

The DCI said to the President, "Sir, we're ready to commence."

The POTUS sat back, and calmly said, "Commence."

One of the army officers at the end of the table picked up a red phone and spoke to the crew chiefs in the respective helicopters.

They all watched and listened as the crew chiefs relayed the information to the SEALs inside each craft.

The helicopters were now five minutes away from the hangar.

It was the third slow Marley song in a row, "Waiting in Vain", and Cal held Haley close. She felt like no other woman he had ever danced with. She wasn't forceful, and she wasn't delicate, but he could feel something underneath her pleasant manner that intrigued him. She was mysterious without *being* mysterious. Her hand felt right in his, and as each of the two previous songs had faded out, she had seemed in no hurry to end the dance. They just kept moving.

"Confession," he said.

"Yes?" she said, putting her head on his shoulder.

"This is my favorite Marley song," he said.

"Oh," she said.

Damnit. Nice small talk, idiot. What could he come back with?

"I thought you were going to say something different." She said.

Well, no. I wasn't going to—well, hell, yes, there is something I would like to say to you, but I don't know if I'm ready to...

She used her arm around his back to pull her body closer to his.

Don't wimp out. "In addition to liking this song, I am also enjoying the opportunity to get to know you." That's a start. Keep going. "I was having second thoughts about coming to the cabin for the weekend," he paused, "but I'm glad I did."

She lifted her head off of his shoulder and stared up at him. "Better," she said and put her head back on his shoulder.

"I know one thing. The weekend is going by too fast."

"I feel the same way," she said. "What do you think about the distance between Rochester and Detroit?"

"It's a ways for sure, but, not *that* far."

"Especially in the summer when I'm not teaching," she said.

"A fine point," he said.

The song started to wind down. *No. One more song. Please...*

The music stopped, and the crowd applauded. Haley and Cal broke their embrace and joined in. As the noise died down, the lead singer instructed everyone to fill their drinks and start gathering around the end zone because in three minutes Billy was going to kick the bucket. Lit's "My Own Worst Enemy" started blaring out of the bar's speakers, and the whole place seemed to be a massive wave of energy and anticipation. Cal saw Rick Dorne slapping high fives and leading a group of around twenty people toward the end zone.

"Want to go see Billy?" Cal joked.

"No thanks," Haley replied. "Want to join me back at the table?" she said, extending her hand.

Forget Billy! He took it, and they headed back to the table.

As they arrived, he heard Iggi say to Maria, "C'mon, it's my favorite part of coming here!"

Maria shook her head, "I'm not heading over there to see that weirdo kick the bucket. If you want to go, then fine."

Iggi got up. "Okay, okay. I'm headin'." He saw Cal and Haley. "You two want to go see this crazy shit with me?"

Before he could answer no, Haley had apparently already appraised the situation and made the right call. "Go with him, Cal. We'll hold your places at the table as long as you return from the mob safely."

"More beers?" Cal asked.

She gave his hand a squeeze. "I've had just the right amount." She released his hand.

Maria said, "Yeah, everybody up for heading home after my sports-nut husband sees the bucket get launched?"

Iggi and Cal agreed.

"Let's go," Iggi said.

The crowd was crammed eight to ten deep around the mini-field as homegrown legend Billy Karpowski walked onto the AstroTurf holding a Miller Lite longneck. Iggi and Cal had angled in on the far-left corner and were standing right in front of the end zone pylon; across from them in front of the right pylon was Rick Dorne, back to wearing his Captain's hat, with Molly, glazed eyes and all, hanging on his right arm. With his free arm, Dorne raised a pitcher to Iggi and then drank half of it. Cal watched as Iggi gave him a polite thumbs up.

Billy walked over to Dorne and Dorne shouted, "You're either the hero or the zero."

The crowd standing behind him exploded into laughter and then started the chant, "Bill-ee, Bill-ee..."

Billy responded by downing the rest of his longneck and then tossing it in a metal trashcan filled with empties. He bowed to Dorne and then asked the crowd for silence.

Cal chuckled to himself.

Iggi said, "I know. This is absurd, but it's addictive, man."

"Billy going to make it?" Cal said, mocking the whole event.

"I've never seen him miss," Iggi said.

When the crowd quieted down, Billy said, "It's time tooooo..."

"Kick the bucket!" the crowd yelled in unison.

The bartender, a three-hundred-pound monster, walked onto the field and picked up the bucket. Raising it above his head, he turned in a complete circle, showcasing it to the entire bar. The chants started up again. "Buck-it, Buck-it..." Walking over to their spot earlier, Iggi had told him that the bartender waited until after 10 every night to start telling the story to patrons that he was on the sideline the night that Billy missed his last field goal—'I was the back-up left guard.' And, 'If I would have been in there blocking, Billy would've never missed.' Some nights, he left with someone who believed him; some nights he got embarrassed when a patron called his bluff. Naturally, Iggi had been one of the ones to call his bluff. Cal had been amused: *This is the stupid shit I've been missing while on patrol or working security?*

Seconds later, Billy walked over and took the hand of a beautiful woman a few people to the right of Dorne. She started jumping up and down. Billy started bouncing too. When she calmed down, Billy said something into her ear, and she held up her ticket. The crowd went berserk. She would have the honor of "holding" the bucket for Billy to kick.

Cal shook his head. "Sure, *her ticket* got picked," he said to Iggi.

Iggi grinned. "What can I say, Billy's got it rigged."

The "lottery winner" strolled onto the field, and Billy—such a teammate— put his arm around her waist and guided her into position. Taking a deep breath, he took five measured steps back. The crowd quieted down.

Iggi said, "This is actually my favorite part."

Suddenly, the lights dimmed, and Billy's final game started playing on a massive screen to the right of the field. Cal, Iggi, and the other patrons watched as the camera zoomed in on the Bills's young placekicker, practicing on the sideline. The footage was fuzzy, but the nervous player warming up was without a doubt Billy. He did not have a helmet on and gave a laugh after every practice kick into the sideline net.

The audio started to blare through the bar's speakers.

"Fourth down and a foot, and you've got to believe they're going to run the ball. Karpowski has already missed twice. I mean, he's got the leg, it's just that no one knows where it's going."

There is confusion on the sideline as an assistant coach runs toward Billy and Billy starts looking for his helmet and he can't find it and the time on the play clock is winding down and then Billy is throwing a temper tantrum on the sideline and the assistant coach is yelling at him and anyone else close by. Finally, the camera accidentally does a close shot of Billy's face and anyone watching can see, plain as day, Billy say, 'Fuck it!' and then he grabs a helmet from someone, puts it on, and sprints onto the field.

"Finally, Karpowski gets a helmet on and they're going to have to hurry—they have no timeouts left—and...here we go, they're lining up..."

Billy takes five measured steps back from the placeholder and gets ready.

"Here's your ballgame, folks. If he makes it, the Bills have won. If he misses it, then we may have witnessed the end of the Bionic Leg's career. Here's the snap."

The screen went blank, the sound stopped, and the bar lights came back on.

"Man, he had it all," Iggi said to Cal.

Billy raised his hand, and everyone in the bar started to chug their drink.

"Tradition," Iggi said. "Everybody drinks until he kicks the bucket. Sometimes he holds it for 5 seconds, sometimes longer."

Cal watched as everyone around the field started to gulp. Rick Dorne almost had the pitcher finished when...

Billy shouted, "Ready!"

The crowd stopped chugging and watched.

The bartender got down into his stance, paused for one second, and then hiked the bucket to the beautiful lottery winner. She partially acted the part but instead of putting her right index finger on the top of the bucket, she held her right hand a foot over it. She looked back at Billy and winked.

With his eyes zeroed in on the bucket, Billy moved forward, right foot, left foot *plant*, and then swung his right foot—he was wearing a kicking shoe on it!—through the air and toward the bucket.

From the depths of his soul as a tortured life-long Detroit Lions fan, Cal yelled, "Choke!"

Whether Billy actually heard Cal or not would never be known. What came next would live in Bay Harbor infamy: Billy Karpowski's foot came down with extra energy (he would claim his patriotism got the best of him on the early 4th) toward the football-bucket, and he pulled it so far left that it landed on a patio table, sending a full pitcher all over the table's guests.

"Free drinks for everyone!" cheered Rick Dorne.

The place went ballistic. Bottles were opened and placed on the bar, Sinatra's "New York, New York" began to blast out of the speakers, and Billy, face redder than Ronald McDonald's hair, ran toward the table to apologize to the guests—and to retrieve the bucket.

"Ohhhh shit!" Iggi yelled, slapping Cal on the back. "I thought I had seen it all!"

Cal could not stop laughing.

Almost to the table, Billy went to pick up the bucket but slipped and fell flat on his ass.

Cal laughed even harder. Why couldn't his life be more like this? Humor, fun, not taking things so seriously all of the time. Human beings are better when they are able to poke fun at themselves. But then the answer to why life couldn't be like this came back: *Someone, somewhere, is out there right now, like he was a few nights ago, putting his or her life on the line in order for him to have a night like this.* Everything—*everything* has a cost.

Iggi was still hooting at the sight of Billy scrambling to get up from the floor.

A grin returned to Cal's face as he enjoyed Iggi's unbridled glee. Here they were, two Detroit kids, each with different experiences growing up, and yet, they had found something this weekend that had brought them together. He realized that it was going to be difficult to say goodbye to Iggi in a few days. And now that he thought about it, he had needed a weekend like this and should have made a weekend like this happen a long time ago—just the chance to enjoy the company of other human beings without responsibility, without roles to play, without judgment, without pressure.

"Man, you ready to go?" Iggi said, getting his breathing back under control.

Beyond him, Cal could see Maria and Haley heading their way. "Yeah," he said. "Who gets to tell the tragedy of Billy, though?"

The young Russian finished his beer and headed toward the exit. To him, the spectacle he had just observed was exactly why America no longer deserved to be at the top of the food chain. He looked at his watch. In less than 24 hours, America would be crippled for good, and soon food would mean everything to these spoiled, noisy, and annoying people. When the mission was complete tonight, they would have no time to lose. The cabin cruiser's fuel had been topped off at the marina earlier—the bill!—and was ready for the voyage across Lake Ontario to Toronto where they would leave the boat in its slip, take a taxi to the airport, and, if all went well, be home in Moscow when the EMP went off over Kansas. He had heard Gregory and Vladimir talking about all of this on the boat the other night when they thought that he was asleep. 'Loose lips sink ships,' he believed the American Navy phrase was. What he couldn't figure out though was why they were in the United States killing intelligence officers in the first place. This was usually a huge no-no, but he guessed that since the U.S. would soon be damaged beyond repair, it didn't matter and must be some sort of a personal KGB vendetta. Gregory seemed to be the catalyst for that, but the young Russian didn't know why. Maybe he should have just gone back to sleep that night and not listened to what they were saying. Maybe when this was over, he'd go on a Vodka bender himself and forget everything.

He watched as the target and the other three moved toward the door. The married couple was holding hands. The target and the Detroit cop weren't; they walked right next to each other, and there was something in the way they interacted—a touch here, a smile there, a pat on the back, a playful poke in the shoulder—that told him they were flirting. Too bad. The exit door opened, and they left. He stopped at the far end of the bar, took a plastic sword from the cup full of them, pretended to be interested in it for a few seconds, then tossed it on the ground and walked out the door.

Outside, he saw the two couples heading across the parking lot toward an SUV. He watched them pile in, and when the vehicle started to back out of its parking space, he walked around the far side of the building and took out his cell phone.

He punched the numbers and waited.

After two rings, Gregory's voice answered the phone, "Yes?"

"They just left," he said.

"Good, bring the boat over and wait offshore, no lights."

He acknowledged, and Gregory ended the call.

They were already in position outside the cabin, waiting. It would all be over soon. They would definitely kill the target, the others if necessary, and then swim out to him. The rest was easy.

He started his five-minute walk toward the marina. It was time for one last boat ride along the American shore where lights would dot the coast. After tonight, it would be darkness, then confusion, then starving, then panic, then murder.

25

ALTAI MOUNTAIN VALLEY

SOUTH OF BIYSK, RUSSIA

JULY 4, 2006, 10:58 A.M. (GMT + 7.00 HOURS)

The stealth helicopters moved swiftly toward the target. In Redbird One, SEAL Commander Jose Martinez, known to his fellow warriors as "Papa Grande", spoke into his headset. "Two minutes. Stand by for doors open."

The statement was acknowledged by every member—lastly by his old friend, Master Chief Petty Officer Rudolph Pike, who said, "Copy, Papa," into his headset. Then, Pike took the wad of tobacco out of his mouth and threw it into a plastic bag that was serving as the helicopter's garbage can.

Papa was forty-one, and Pike was thirty-nine, two years that Pike continually needled his commanding officer about. After tours in Afghanistan and Iraq, the men had become even closer. Both were within a year of retirement, and the other SEALs with them were all ten to twenty years younger. Martinez had a son in high school and a daughter in middle school; Pike had twin sons in high school. Martinez was divorced; Pike was still married to his high school sweetheart. Martinez ran four miles in 25 minutes and change; Pike could still dip below 24.

When Martinez looked into the eyes of Pike, he only saw blankness, and that told him that the US of A was still fine compared to the competition from other nations. The reason? *We've still got better animals than the other guys.* Better trained, better equipped, nastier. But Jose Martinez also knew that these animals were starting to stretch thin. Extend our elite forces any farther and we'll be in danger of giving away the circus. Our answer for every tough call cannot continue to be: Just send in the SEALs. You can only ride a horse for so long, and you always ride a better horse. He and Pike knew it because they had ridden better horses and been ridden. And, they had come to the conclusion that, in the end analysis, you're either a show horse or a work horse. Cable news channels and politicians liked to portray SEALs as show horses, but they got it wrong every time. The United States was still ahead for one reason: Its soldiers were all *work horses.*

Martinez checked his SIG 226 9mm. 15 rounds in the magazine, 1 in the chamber, check. Besides the SIG, the other members of the team carried an H&K 416 .223 caliber that had a 30-round magazine—the 10 ½" barrel had a silencer attached to the end. They were coming in during sunlight hours—the temperature would be around seventy degrees—but they did not want to make a lot of noise before they had to.

Another minute went by, and then the pilot came on the net. "Target sighted."

The helicopters banked to the left and began to swing around the mountain in front of them. Martinez wiped the sweat off of his forehead and then watched as Petty Officer Second Class Rob Kelly opened the door. The air felt good as it rushed over the arms of Martinez's fatigues and hit his face. The helicopter leveled off, and he saw the hangar up ahead.

Both choppers dipped down and hugged the surface as they split and headed for opposite ends of the hangar. There was no movement outside and no fire directed at them.

Redbird One set down on the dusty plain, and Papa was the first out the door followed by Kelly and the rest of the men. Pike brought up the rear. As soon as the men had disembarked, the helicopter took off into the sky.

Using hand signals to guide the men, Martinez motioned the men toward the door, and they arrived outside of it in under five seconds. The door opened, and a man with an AK-47 walked outside. Kelly put two rounds in his head, and the man crumpled to the ground. Martinez directed again with his hand, and a team member took the man's radio while two others moved his body out of the doorway. They listened and waited. No one came out.

They entered the massive bay and spread out. There was a stairway to the right that led up to a catwalk running across the entire length of the hangar. Below the catwalk sat the huge 777-200LR, painted white with the large gold letters spelling 'Emirates' along the side and the tail painted with red, green and navy stripes. At the far end of the hangar, there was a vehicle that resembled a large John Deere Gator, a crane, a set of stairs that could be rolled up to the plane and allow people to board, and a large house-like structure with a front door, windows, and a second story balcony. *Must be the living quarters.* To the left of the door they had just entered was a block of offices and the gigantic closed hangar doors. "Rudy, set up our sniper position above," he ordered Pike.

"Copy," Pike said, and then moved with two other members toward the staircase.

Thirty seconds passed, and Pike was back on the radio. "Sniper nest set up, Papa. No contacts."

"Kelly, you're up," Martinez said.

Immediately, three men followed Kelly across the open bay toward the plane's landing gear.

"Looks like we have a row of offices down here," Martinez said. "We're going to start our sweep."

"Roger that, Papa," Pike said from the catwalk above.

As Martinez and the remaining men reached the door to the block of offices, automatic weapon fire sounded from the other end of the bay.

The team from Redbird Two spread out while returning fire at the three AK-47s pouring lead down at them from the top windows of the living quarters. Lieutenant Commander Seth Decker, Martinez's Executive Officer, found cover behind the Gator right before a line of bullets sprayed the wall of the hangar behind him. One of his men was hit trying to make it to the staircase but had enough forward momentum to crawl behind the structure.

A voice came over the net. "This is Ramirez, I'm hit in the lower left leg. Won't be able to move on my own, over."

"Copy, Ramirez," Decker said. "Stay put until we burn these assholes." Then, he spoke to Pike over the net. "Rudy, we've got fire from the top floor. Does your boy have a shot?"

Pike replied, "Negative."

Shit, Decker thought. Next to him was Lieutenant Zach Brody. "Z, give me some covering fire. I'm going to throw up a couple of presents."

Brody nodded and readied his weapon. On Decker's command, Brody unleashed on the upper floors. Decker sprinted across the open bay until he was underneath the balcony. He pulled the safety spoons out of his grenades, waited, and then lofted them into the second story through the shattered window opening.

A second passed before two powerful explosions. Then, Brody was at it again firing into the second story. Two team members left their positions of cover and joined Decker. They moved toward the door, and, after a silent count, broke it down. Immediately, Decker threw in two more grenades. The explosions shook the building and rattled Decker's teeth. He and the other two men entered.

Inside, they found two bodies lying on the ground; the shrapnel had ripped into one man's chest and blown a leg off of the other man. Blood was splattered across the couch and television set that was somehow still hanging on the wall.

They entered the kitchen, cleared it, and then cleared a bedroom, completing their sweep of the first floor.

Brody came on the net. "No more movement upstairs, XO."

"Roger that," said Decker. "We're heading up."

"No more movement seen from sniper's nest," Pike said.

Decker led the men up the stairs.

Martinez opened the door to the first office and popped two men reaching for their handguns. A third man came out from behind a filing cabinet, and the SEAL behind Martinez wasted him. The team moved efficiently through the maze of offices and found no one else. They searched each body and found absolutely no identification. Then, they took pictures of all the dead hostiles. Every single one was light-skinned, male, maybe in his thirties, and had a crew cut. Not much to go on, and they didn't have any room in the choppers for extras. *Who are these guys?* "We've got a few laptops, some filing cabinets, and that's about it," said Martinez to Pike over the radio. "We're going to bag what we can and then we're headed to you, Seth."

"Copy, Papa," Decker said. "We're on the second floor. Got three dead hostiles up here and no one else. Just the living quarters. We've searched it.

Didn't find shit. Taking pictures. These guys all look the same. How about yours?"

Martinez described the men they had killed, and Decker replied, "Mine too. We're going to get Ramirez and—"

He was cut off by Redbird One's pilot. "Papa, we've got two birds inbound from the south. They should be here in fifteen mikes, so you've got less than ten to get outside for exfiltration, over."

Fuck. No time to enter the plane. "Roger, Redbird One," Martinez replied. "Break. All units, you've got ten mikes to be outside for exfil. Break. Redbird One, let home base know that we won't have time to check the plane or demo the runway. They need to send in Autobirds One and Two."

"Affirmative, Papa. Autobirds One and Two inbound."

Martinez and the men gathered what they could fit in their backpacks and then exited the office complex. In the hangar, they watched as Kelly and his team ran away from the plane toward them.

"Landing gear is set for demo," Kelly said.

"Good work, Rob," Martinez said. "Rudy, have your boys open up on the cockpit."

"Copy," said Pike.

A barrage of gunfire lit up the 777-200LR's cockpit. Glass shattered and bullet holes painted the area around the plane's windshield. After thirty seconds, the firing stopped.

"Electronics disabled," Pike said.

Then, the plane door behind the cockpit opened and Martinez saw a man in an airline pilot's uniform—holding a grenade launcher. Before he could give the order, one of Pike's snipers hit him and a red mist colored the air directly behind the man's head.

"Hostile is down," said Pike.

Kelly and his team reached Martinez. "Ready, sir," Kelly said.

Martinez went on the net. "Landing gear going bye-bye." He nodded to Kelly.

Kelly pulled out a detonator and pushed the button.

Simultaneously, the landing gear struts exploded, and the plane's fuselage landed on the ground with a BOOM.

At the far end of the bay, Decker's team opened up and shredded the plane's tail.

Martinez looked at his watch. Two minutes. "Begin exfil," he commanded. Both teams withdrew.

As Redbirds One and Two lifted off into the sky, Martinez heard Redbird One's pilot say, "Autobirds here in thirty seconds."

The helicopters gained speed and headed southwest away from the incoming choppers and drones. Watching on the helicopter's monitor, he witnessed the complete annihilation of the runway.

"Are we in any danger from those birds coming from the south?" he asked the pilot.

"No," the pilot said. "We're already opening up the distance and will be out of their airspace before they could send something else this way. And, I'm sure they're more worried about the hangar than who we are at the moment."

Martinez patted him on the back. "Agree."

Then, a new voice came over the net. "Papa, this is Ranger, over."

Pike raised his eyebrows at him.

Ranger was the *President of the United States*. Martinez cleared his throat and then spoke. "This is Papa. Read you loud and clear, Ranger."

"Roger." The voice paused. "That's a good day's work, Papa. Ranger, out."

Martinez swallowed. "Copy, Ranger. Papa, out."

As the net went silent, a whole barrage of cheers and whoops let out from the team inside Redbird One.

Papa didn't hear them. He could only think about what they had just prevented and that no one outside of a select few would ever know what they had done. He hoped the intelligence they had collected in the backpacks would lead to something, but he wasn't so sure. Something about the operation had been too easy.

26

C.I.A. HEADQUARTERS, MCLEAN, VIRGINIA
MONDAY, JULY 3, 2006

T he President and Vice-President had already left the room when Shelly Skowcroft hung up the phone in the C.I.A. Headquarters Command and Control Center. She walked over to Narita. "Judas is dead."

Still feeling the adrenaline from watching the successful operation, Narita snapped, "What?!"

"Shot in the head along with an unidentified woman and that accountant he was seeing. They were all in the middle of something in the bedroom when it happened."

Narita took a sip of coffee and tried to calm her nerves. *Rolfe, her trusted spook soldier and friend, gone.*

"We've got our forensics team on its way, and the D.C. Police Department has been notified," Skowcroft continued. "Judas didn't have a security camera, so we don't have any video."

Narita processed the information and allowed her brain to go to work like the gears in a clock. Connections. Find them. She pulled her pen out of her blazer pocket and began to write on the legal pad in front of her:

-Rolfe Judas, Head of the Office of Scientific & Weapons Research and co-coordinator and creator of Operation Socrates, co-coordinator of Operation Empire: dead. Killed at his home July 3, 2006.

She paused. Operations Socrates and Empire...she scribbled faster.

-Ritzy Zimmer, Rome Station Chief and support for Operations Socrates and Empire: dead. Killed in Berlin, December 2005.

-Officer Brian Turner, Operations Officer for Operations Socrates and Empire: dead. Killed in Berlin, December 2005.

-Sente Rahn, Agent, codename: Sari. Born in East Germany, raised by Soviet foster parents after biological parents killed in Stalin's purge, Senior KGB agent stationed in Berlin—turned in 2002: dead. Committed Suicide in Berlin, December 2005.

-Officer Rose Wakefield, Rome Station and support for Operations Socrates and Empire: transferred to Paris station.

She rattled the end of the pen between her upper and lower teeth. *Who else besides the people in this room knew about or worked on Operations Socrates and Empire?* There were the two other officers who offered assistance in Rome—Officers Meghan Trimble and Rod Pelham—who were back stateside and lived, what, Trimble lived in Frederick, Maryland, about forty-five miles northwest of Rolfe

Judas; Pelham lived in Annapolis—40 miles from Judas, around 70 miles from Frederick. The only other people were herself and...Officer Jennifer Lear.

Narita shot up out of her chair. "Shelly, get me Officer Lear on the phone—*now*." Then, she spoke to two other assistants. "Contact Officers Trimble and Pelham. Tell them to stay inside their homes and to arm themselves." She turned to a dispatcher. "Send teams over to their homes to watch—we might catch the assholes who offed Judas." She thought for a moment. "We don't know if there is more than one team operating here. If there is, then we're probably too late. If it is just one team, then we might have a shot. We don't know if they headed to Frederick or Annapolis first."

Skowcroft sat down in front of the phone and went to work.

Narita sat down behind another phone. She dialed the number quickly and then listened. It rang, and rang, and—

"Hello?" her husband's voice said.

He's okay. "Hello, dear," Narita said. "I'm going to get right to it. Do not open the door for anyone until Sylvia and Carl arrive, and do not go anywhere. We may have a problem."

Her husband caught on fast. "Got it. I'll keep my eyes open, but nothing out of the ordinary has happened so far. In fact, someone from that elementary school you visited a few weeks ago dropped by, but I told him you weren't here."

Her heart began to pound. "What? Tell me what happened."

"It was a young man I had never seen before. I didn't open the door and talked to him through the intercom. He said that he wanted to thank you in person for coming by his classroom. I told him that it was very nice of him to come by, but that you had left early to run a few errands and wouldn't be home for a while. You know, I used our errand code because I knew that you were at work. I almost opened the door, but I stuck to our protocol."

"Never open the door unless you know exactly who it is."

252

"Right. But, this guy seemed harmless. I told him the usual lie that I had a cold and apologized for not opening up. I even stood directly behind our bulletproof alcove too—kind of proud of myself."

Her mind was already racing ahead. "Good, it means that we have video from our porch camera. Sylvia and Carl will get a copy of the recording when they come to get you."

"You think this guy was trouble?"

"Yes," she said. "I never visited any classrooms that day."

"Oh," he said.

"Stay inside until they get there."

"Got it," he said, and the call ended.

Narita wrote down a note telling Skowcroft to send Officers Sylvia Cruz and Carl Decker over to her house to collect her husband and the video. She placed it on the table in front of Skowcroft.

Skowcroft gave her a thumbs up and continued working the phones.

Narita walked back over and sat down next to the DCI. She leaned toward him and whispered in his ear. "We may have a leak in respect to Operation Socrates and/or Operation Empire."

Then, she explained her theory.

The DCI nodded his head. "Could be," he said. "It doesn't make any sense though. Why off our people now? Someone plans an EMP attack but drops an assassination team in knowing that they might not make it out? The only thing that comes to mind is that those missions have somehow become *personal* to someone. But *who* and *why*?" He bit his lip and squinted for a moment.

She could envision his brain attacking the problem—the connections illuminating as each branch grew and secured itself to another branch in the spider web of his brain. He was a career CIA Officer who had walked the walk, and she respected his instincts, intelligence, and tenacity. Her brain was doing the same while she waited. Each of her branches was an endless maze filled with mirrors, and she could not navigate enough of the mazes to connect the pieces of information she had.

He shook his head. "I can't see it."

"Me either," Narita said.

"Do what you have to do to protect our people while we work on it." He turned to the man on his immediate left, Counterintelligence Chief Mike Lester, and started whispering to him.

Moments later, Lester stood up and walked over to Narita. "What do we have, Leiko?"

They went over to a corner, and for the next five minutes, Narita filled him in.

Skowcroft put down the phone. "Director Narita, I've got Sylvia and Carl headed to your house, but I can't reach Officer Lear."

"Where is she?" Narita said, walking over to her with Lester.

"I talked to our HR department," Skowcroft said. "She checked out for the long weekend. She's at a cabin owned by Iggi and Maria Hilliard—Lear teaches with Maria Hilliard—just outside of Rochester, New York. I've been trying the home phone number there, but no one is picking up. I tried both of the Hilliards' cell phones. No luck there either, so I left messages. I tried Lear's Blackberry, but it went straight to voicemail and I left a message. My guess is they are either outside or not at the cabin at all."

Even though Lear was technically on leave of absence, at least she had still followed protocol and had checked out for the weekend. "Who is close by?" Narita said.

"I checked. No one within two hours from the CIA side of the house. FBI is tied up with operations, inquiries, and threat assessments in all the major cities close to Rochester. It's a bad weekend, boss. July 4th. We're all overextended."

"Then contact the goddamned local police and get a car over there."

Skowcroft nodded and then began working the phones again.

The DCI walked over and joined Narita and Lester. "Mike, do you have a handle on the situation?" he said.

"Yes, sir," Lester said.

"Then let's get to work," the DCI ordered.

Lester marched off, already barking orders to his staff.

"I'm heading to Rochester," Narita said to the DCI. "I won't lose Lear. I won't lose another *officer!*"

"I concur," the DCI said and waved his assistant over.

"I'm hoping it isn't what we think it is, but I have to do everything I can."

The DCI's assistant arrived.

"Get Director Narita on a plane to Rochester," he said. "Now."

The assistant picked up a phone.

"Thanks," Narita said. "I'll keep you informed."

The DCI shook her hand.

He already looks older. I'm certain I do too.

"I'll make sure that I get any updates. I'm headed to both debrief the President on the operation we just ran and to brief him of the July 4th threats—number's up again this year."

He left.

Narita stared at Skowcroft, who had just slammed one phone down and picked up another. "You're coming with me. I want you calling the cell phones and the cabin until we get through."

The DCI's assistant got off the phone. "Your plane is ready, ma'am. This way," he said, leading her and Skowcroft toward the exit.

While hurrying down the hallway, she spoke to the DCI's assistant. "When my husband gets here, let me know. I'll call him from the plane."

FREDERICK, MARYLAND

The black government SUV sped down the highway. Inside, Officer Jason Easton kept dialing Meghan Trimble's phone number from the passenger seat. They were fifteen minutes away from her house. Trimble had yet to pick up the phone, and Easton was worried. In the back two rows were four C.I.A. officers dressed in body armor and carrying heavy weaponry. They had heard from the team heading to Ron Pelham's house. The Annapolis Police Department's S.W.A.T. team was onsite and had Ron Pelham protected.

Easton looked at the driver, Officer Beth Bennett, "She's still not picking up, Beth."

Before Bennett could respond, her cell phone rang and she answered.

Easton watched as he heard her say, "Oh...Got it...Shit...We'll be there in less than fifteen minutes...Okay. Bye." Bennett ended the call and said to Easton and the team, "Stand down, everyone. That was the Frederick police. The S.W.A.T. team they sent over just reported that Trimble is dead, shot in the head. They found her body just inside the front door. They've got the K-9 unit over there, and the forensics team is on its way. We'll do our own investigation when we arrive." Bennett took a breath and then exhaled. "Jason, call it in to headquarters. I'll call the Annapolis Police's S.W.A.T. team and our team headed to Pelham's and tell them to expect action."

ANNAPOLIS, MARYLAND

S.W.A.T. Team Leader Myron Wilkinson put the phone down and briefed his team on the headsets they were all wearing. "Bad news, Officer Meghan Trimble is dead. It looks like this could be the next stop for the assassin or assassins. Stay in position and be ready."

THE CABIN

The team had made sure that there was no evidence of their presence. The team vehicle had dropped them off with their gear and was now inside a pole barn, two blocks over. There was a sniper set up on the roof of the house across the street and one set up on the roof of the house behind Pelham's with a clear shot into his backyard and patio area. Inside Pelham's house, six team members spread out, covering the various entry and exit points. They had no idea if it was just one person carrying out the assassinations or a team of professionals. In either case, they weren't taking any chances; on the roofs along with the two snipers were two M-60 machine gunners who had been briefed to mow down any hostiles in their respective fields of fire. Pelham and his family had been taken away in a squad car and were safely on their way to the Annapolis Police Department Headquarters. There had been no time to evacuate the surrounding homes. So, an officer had simply told everyone on the block to go to their basements or closets and wait until it was over. The C.I.A. team was on its way, but it would most likely be serving in a backup role.

The sniper on the roof across the street got on the net. "Two blocks away, on your side of the street, I spot a person of average height wearing an oversized hoodie and sweatpants, bouncing a basketball and moving toward the house on the sidewalk."

"Man or a woman?" Wilkinson said.

"Can't tell yet," the sniper said.

"Right or left handed?"

"Hoodie is dribbling with both hands. Can't tell."

Wilkinson keyed his mic. "Okay, we know that Pelham's older son plays basketball and that there's a lighted outdoor court four blocks east of here. Hoodie could be a friend. If he knocks on the door, we'll tell him to go home. Update me as he gets closer."

The sniper acknowledged, and the net went silent.

Hoodie kept bouncing the basketball and walking along the sidewalk like he was in no hurry. He kept his attention focused on the ball and didn't seem to notice the houses he was passing in front of or the driveways he was crossing.

When he was less than a block away, the sniper jumped back on the net. "He's got his sleeves pushed up to his elbows...looks like hairy arms...man's watch on the left hand. I'm going with right-handed male, but I still can't see his face yet."

"Good," Wilkinson replied.

"He just switched to dribbling exclusively with his left hand," the sniper said. "I'm looking for a weapon—could be one underneath his sweatshirt. Okay, he's two houses away and starting to slow down. No other movement down the street. He just looked at the house and is studying it while he approaches. He picked up the basketball, got it in his left hand. Something's not right; he doesn't look like a kid. He turned at the house and is walking across the front yard. Ten yards from the front door...five...he's to you."

Wilkinson waited in the foyer, three yards from the front door. After a beat, the doorbell rang. Wilkinson whispered into his microphone, "If it is who we're looking for, I'm going to try and make him think I'm Pelham. I am not behind the door; I'm to the side. Be ready if he goes for a weapon."

"Roger that," said the sniper. "He just backed up about three paces from the door."

Wilkinson slid to the side of the door, his body in the dining room. Then, he raised his voice. "Who is it? I can't see your face behind your hood from the peephole."

"Mr. Pelham?" came a deep voice from the other side of the door.

"Yes. Now take off your h—"

He was interrupted by the sound of automatic fire as Hoodie pulled out an Uzi from underneath his sweatshirt and unloaded into the door. A dozen or more rays of light from the porch entered the house through the holes in the front door.

Then, the shooting stopped and Wilkinson thought he heard the smacking sound of a body hitting the entrance's pavement.

"Hostile is down," the sniper said. "One shot to the head. One to the chest."

Wilkinson immediately checked over the net to see if anyone was injured. They were not. "Copy that," he said. "I'm opening the door to evaluate. Keep your weapon on him."

"Roger that," said the sniper.

Wilkinson opened the front door.

Hoodie lay flat on his back, blood soaking his sweatshirt hood and the part covering his chest; a red pool began to form on the sidewalk entrance around the man's head. The Uzi lay on the ground less than a foot away from the man's right hand. The basketball was off to the left, resting in the mulched landscaping.

Wilkinson swiftly moved to the Uzi and put his left foot on top of the gun while keeping his Glock aimed down at the body. "Clear," he said into his headset. Seconds later, two more team members emerged from the front door and joined him.

After a thorough search of the body, they found a wallet with nothing but $500.00 inside and a set of keys. Within five minutes, team members had located the vehicle—a midnight blue 2002 Ford Explorer—two blocks away. The registration and license plate were already being run.

Wilkinson watched as the C.I.A. team's black GMC Yukon pulled up in front of the house. He walked over to the driver side where he met Officer Ariel Knight.

"Who in the hell is he?" Knight asked, following Wilkinson around the front of the SUV.

"We're working on it," Wilkinson said. "Let me show you what we've got so far."

27

MONDAY, JULY 3, 2006

Patrolman Jesse Heinrichs along with his partner Ernie Teagarden rolled down Beach Road in their patrol vehicle toward the address they had been given by the dispatcher. There had been some commotion over the radio about this being a priority visit. Heinrichs had rolled his eyes at that: Everything around the 4th of July was a priority. And if there truly was something going down, this stretch of expensive houses lining Lake Ontario would be the absolute last place it would be going down at. There had been so much chatter, in fact, that he had turned down the radio—but not before hearing that Billy's bucket kick had missed wide left. Dumb ass. *Gonna give him an earful when I stop in off-duty.*

He lowered the window a few inches more and tapped his cigarette against the top of the glass. The tip of ash fell away, and he brought the cigarette back down to his lips and inhaled. Teagarden had dozed off and was starting to snore. There went his peace and quiet. Well, he was a kid compared to

261

Heinrichs—twenty-one and still green. *Gotta do a top-notch mentoring job on this kid, or he'll never make it past writing parking tickets.* To Heinrichs's left, the trees opened, and a three-story mansion with the lights on in two rooms on the third floor rose in the distance. *What in the hell are we doing out here?*

By good luck or bad luck, they had been at the station just about to head out on their regular patrol when the dispatcher radioed them in the parking lot that they were to switch to the SUV and head out this way; all of the other patrol cars were on the far side of town. Hence, Heinrichs and Teagarden were the closest. When he had asked why they needed to switch cars, the dispatcher had told him that they would be picking up and transporting at least three people—Haley somethin' or other and the Hilliards—back to the Bay Harbor headquarters. Always something new. Since when had he become a taxi driver? Helping people change tires on the side of the road was one thing. But picking up some well-to-do folks that lived on Beach Road? What the hell? Now, if he was *arresting* the rich sons-a-bitches, then...

He'd never driven the SUV before, but now that he had, he never wanted to go back to the patrol car. This thing was a command center—a second computer screen up front, a second radio, and extra guns and ammunition in the far back. Maybe if he did well tonight, they'd upgrade him to this bad boy. He patted the steering wheel and took another drag from the cigarette. He was twenty-seven but considered himself an old-school cop already: two packs of cigarettes a day, perhaps a gallon or two of coffee, two donuts in the morning, and a trip to the barber every ten days for a fresh haircut. He also wore a full moustache, and that caterpillar was comin' off over his dead body. Who's gonna be chief of police? Who's got his shit in one sock? Jesse Heinrichs. He could absolutely Goddamn guarantee it.

A mailbox on the right-hand-side of the road appeared, and he slowed the vehicle; the driveway was on the left and marked with two red reflectors at the top of metal stakes.

"Wake up, rookie," he said, nudging his partner. "We're here."

Teagarden yawned and pushed Heinrichs's hand away. "I'm awake. I'm awake."

"Ready to storm the castle?" Heinrichs said.

Teagarden wiped his eyes and then reached for his department-issued coffee mug. His hand only found the empty cup holder. "Where's my coffee?"

Heinrichs turned into the driveway. "You leave it back in our patrol car?"

Teagarden's head slumped. "Yeah. Damn."

Heinrichs laughed. "You're useless. You know that?"

"Shut up, man."

"Take it easy," said Heinrichs, "we'll pick some up on the way back to the station. I'm buyin', all right?"

"Okay," Teagarden said.

The cabin's peaked roof took shape against the clear sky. "Doesn't look like anyone's still up," Heinrichs said. "You see any lights?"

"No."

"Maybe they called it an early night."

"Or they're still out."

Heinrichs took a drink of coffee from his mug. Kid had a point. Plenty of partying going on tonight, and he couldn't get too upset. That was what he used to be doing on nights like this...well, almost *every* night until he got his shit together and became a cop. At the rate he had been going, he would have made the consecutive hangover hall-of-fame. But Bushmills and weed had been replaced by coffee and cigarettes, and now he was right with the Lord again—kept his King James Version of the Bible underneath his patrol car seat. He slid his hand underneath the driver seat. Nothing but a tangle of wires. Small mistake. He had left the good book back in his usual patrol car. He took another sip of coffee. Well, if it was between forgetting his coffee cup like junior over there or forgetting Jesus, he figured Jesus would forgive him.

Two cars were parked on the pad that the narrow drive emptied into.

"Want me to run the plates?"

"No, let's just knock on the door," Heinrichs said. "Get your flashlight."

The vehicle came to a stop, and Heinrichs took one last drag from his cigarette. If no one was home, then this could work out well. They'd probably be told to stay and wait, so he could burn a few more and maybe pick up a west coast baseball game on the radio.

He turned off the lights, then the ignition. The white doors of the garage seemed to glow before them. Boring pattern, he thought. He peered over at Teagarden, who had a flashlight resting on his lap but wasn't moving; he just stared at the garage doors. "You okay, my young apprentice?" God, he sounded like he was in a *Star Wars* movie. How many times had he seen the first two prequels while baked, hoping they'd get better? *Stop it. Don't overdo the teacher-pupil act.*

"I gotta piss," Teagarden said.

Heinrichs pretended to be annoyed by bringing his right hand to his face and exhaling into it, but, the truth was, he had to drain the main vein too. He dropped his hand and looked around outside. Everything seemed quiet. "Okay, go drop your drawers behind the garage. I'll ring the doorbell. If they're home and they answer the door before you're done, we'll say you were just performing a routine security check. Got it?"

"Thanks," Teagarden said. "What if no one's home?"

"Then we'll radio it in and see what they want us to do."

"Shouldn't we check in and tell them we're here?"

"Just let me do the figuring, okay? Go pee."

They exited the vehicle, and Heinrichs put out his cigarette on the concrete pad and left it. Both doors closed, and Teagarden disappeared around the side of the garage while Heinrichs approached the front porch steps. *Again, why are we here?*

264

He reached the front door and pushed the doorbell. Thirty seconds passed, then thirty more. The inside of the house remained silent. He took a step back and looked up at the second-floor windows. Still no lights. As he went to turn around, he thought he heard the sound of a twig snap. Must be Teagarden. "Hey, Ernie, there's no one home. Zip up your dick and let's radio it in."

There was no response.

He walked past the vehicle toward the far side of the garage. "Ernie?"

He turned the corner and found the woods next to the garage empty. However, he could see the beam from Teagarden's flashlight around the back of the garage. He heard a cough. *How long does it take to empty your bladder for Chrissakes? It's like changin' diapers with this kid.* He neared the back of the garage. "Okay, dipshit—"

And those were the last words that Jesse Heinrichs ever got out. The bullet entered his skull from the end of a gun with a noise suppressor attached at a distance of no more than two feet. A man had been waiting, and when Heinrichs turned the corner, he blinded Heinrichs with the flashlight and fired. The police officer's body fell to the ground littered with twigs and leaves.

Vladimir holstered his weapon, and the other Russian was soon by his side. He knelt down and turned off the police officer's radio, as he had with the other man they had shot in the head moments before, and grabbed the vehicle keys from the officer's pockets. He rose back up and pointed at the two dead men. "Put these two side-by-side and cover them up."

The Russian started to move the second body next to the first.

Gregory arrived. "What in the hell were they doing here?"

"You don't suppose word has gotten out already from what our comrade on the east coast has been up to?" Vladimir replied.

Gregory paused. "I don't know. We should have time before another car gets here, but now we have little room for error." He stared down at the two dead police officers. "I don't like this."

"I'll drive the vehicle down the road and park it on the shoulder around the curve. They won't see it when they approach."

"Hurry," Gregory said. "Wait." He held up his hand for silence. The sound of a boat motor could now be heard. "That must be him," Gregory said. "Go," he ordered Vladimir.

Vladimir jogged to the police vehicle.

Should they just leave it, Gregory thought? No. The cop would sense something was wrong. Better to get it out of the way so they could ambush them the way they had rehearsed. The original plan—assuming the four people were going to stay in for the night—was more complicated because they would have had to assault the house. He guessed that both Lear and the cop had weapons inside, and if something went wrong, and they were able to get to their weapons, then it would be bad news. He didn't doubt Vladimir's tenacity, but he sensed that Vladimir's reaction time was not what it once was. The other two men? Unknown. They could be effective, but he had yet to see them perform in a real situation. Vladimir had taken care of the two policemen; the young Russian with him had just watched.

Gregory headed back to his position in the woods on the other side of the driveway. He heard the police vehicle's engine turn over. They'd be fine as long as Vladimir could get back here in time. They were fortunate that the bar "Billy's" was on the far side of town. He settled into his spot behind a large black oak tree and watched as Vladimir began to back the vehicle.

Then, a pair of headlights swung into the driveway.

* * *

"Okay, a quick fire in the living room hearth along with a nightcap," Iggi said. He patted the steering wheel with his hands. "We won't go too late. That's tomorrow night."

Maria rubbed his shoulder. "Your plans are getting better as this weekend goes on."

He took the compliment and continued to concentrate on the long narrow driveway. But Haley giggled, and he snuck a peek at the rearview mirror. There was no distance between her and Cal. *Well, maybe I'm starting to like these two, and maybe the introvert is going to get laid tonight in my house.* He grinned. *Oh, wel—*

"Iggi, stop the car," Cal said.

Without getting angry or questioning him, Iggi did just that.

"There's a police vehicle backing up towards us," Cal said.

As soon as Iggi spotted it, the vehicle stopped. "What the hell?"

Maria looked to Cal. "What do you think is going on?"

"You have an alarm system, right?"

"Yeah," Iggi said.

"Maybe there was a false alarm, and they came by to check it out?"

"But we would have been called on our cell phones," Maria said. She dug through her purse. "Damnit. I left mine at home. "How about you?" she asked Iggi.

"I never take mine with me when we go out. I hate that thing."

"I'm going to go talk to them," Cal said. "See what's up."

"Thanks, handsome," Maria said.

Cal went to open the door but then stopped. "Iggi, turn off the headlights."

Iggi did.

As Cal opened the door, gunfire exploded from the woods to the left of the vehicle.

28

Cal dove to the ground and pulled out his Glock 22. Aiming in the direction where the shots had sounded, he squeezed off two rounds. "Turn the headlights back on and get out of here!" Cal yelled to Iggi.

Iggi flipped the headlights on and went to put the car in gear when the driver side door to the police vehicle opened, and a man not wearing a uniform emerged and started shooting at Iggi's SUV. Two rounds found the top of the windshield and whizzed above Iggi and Maria's heads. The back-seat driver side door opened and Haley Girard pulled out a Glock 26 that she had hidden beneath the light sweater she had worn wrapped around her waist for the evening. Now the sweater was off and on the ground and Haley was aiming her fire at the man shooting from behind the police vehicle.

"Girl, what the hell?!" Maria said.

"Get to the back seat!" Haley ordered, and Maria and Iggi scrambled out of the front seats and onto the back bench.

"We're coming out there with you," Iggi said. "This thing is just a goddamned target."

Before either Cal or Haley could reply, Maria and Iggi slithered down the side of the car and over the running board, hitting the ground behind Haley.

Cal let three more rounds go and then moved around the back of the vehicle and was soon on the ground next to Haley. "I'm not even going to ask," he said.

"Don't," Haley said, firing off two rounds toward the police vehicle.

"What in the hell is going on?" Maria asked.

There was silence for a moment.

Cal whispered to everyone, "Okay, these guys are definitely not cops. Whoever showed up in that vehicle is either dead or incapacitated. It's just us."

"How much ammo do you have left?" Haley asked him.

"Two more 15-round magazines, and then I'm out," he said. "You?"

"Six shots left," she said.

"Let's make them count," Cal said. "We've got one behind the car and another in the woods off to the left."

"That's my count too."

"How can I help?" Iggi asked.

Cal's eyes darted back and forth between the woods on the left and the police vehicle while he thought. When he had worked it out, he said, "Haley and I are going to make our move in a minute. When we do, turn and run to the road—I don't think there's anyone behind us. Then, get to a neighbor's house, call the police and have them send more units." He looked back at Iggi. "Stay there until this is over." He eyed Haley, "I'm going to fire off a few rounds in each direction and then dart for the woods on the right. We haven't been able to see the sonofabitch in the woods to the left, so don't waste any ammo firing in that direction. If the guy behind the police vehicle gives you a look, take him out. I'll work my way up on the right."

"Got it," Haley said.

"Lady, you've got some explainin' to do when this is over," Maria said, voice shaking.

Haley put her hand back on Maria's shoulder and gave it a quick squeeze. Then, she brought it back to her gun and got ready.

More gunfire erupted from the woods to the left, and the windshield shattered, followed by a *pop, pop* as both front tires were hit. The front end of the SUV lowered to a few inches off the ground. However, the headlights were still untouched.

The firing stopped, and Cal said, "I'm heading to the other side. I'll count to three out loud, and then I'm going."

Iggi and Maria prepared to run as Cal moved around them and dove for the ground on the other side of the vehicle. "One, two, three!"

Cal rose and then fired two shots to the left followed by two at the police vehicle, while he sprinted into the woods and took cover behind an oak tree.

He glanced back and saw Iggi and Maria hauling ass down the driveway toward the road. *They should make it.* He returned his attention to the fight.

From behind the police car, a man rose and was aiming his gun in Cal's direction—a single shot sounded—when the front of his head jerked back and a red mist appeared above it. The body hit the concrete pad with a *thwack*!

She's a better shot than I am. He surveyed the woods to the left. One more to go.

Iggi and Maria ran down Jim and Rosemary Stetson's driveway. Reaching the porch, they bounded up the steps and Iggi knocked on the door while pressing the doorbell half-a-dozen times. His right foot tapped on the porch boards. *Come on...come on!*

A light came on inside. Perfect. He turned to Maria. "I'm heading back to help."

"Oh no you're n—"

"Yes," he cut her off. "Now, do what Cal said." He motioned with his eyes toward the front door. "You'll be safe here."

Without giving her time to say anything, Iggi jumped off the porch. He would go down to the beach and work his way toward the driveway from that direction. Before he disappeared around the side of the house he heard the baritone voice of Jim Stetson say, "Maria, are you okay? Some clown has been shooting off fireworks for the past ten minutes," and then Maria cutting him off with, "Those were gunshots!"

"What do you mean you've lost radio contact with your officers," Leiko Narita snarled into the phone. She and Shelly Skowcroft were in the back of an unmarked police car speeding down State Highway 250 toward Bay Harbor.

"What I mean, ma'am, is that they haven't checked in," Bay Harbor Police Chief Donald Blount said. "All of our attempts to contact them via radio and phone have failed. No one is picking up at the Hilliard residence either. Have you been able to contact any of them?"

"No," she said.

"Look, we're a small town. I've rerouted my entire force, and they're on their way, but you'll probably beat them to the house."

She wanted to flame spray this guy, but she realized that he was doing everything he could. Since 9/11, the world had changed. Departments were recruiting like hell, the police academies had relaxed some of the criteria to expand the force, but in the end it all came down to money. And when it came down to money, the big cities took priority. Small towns like Bay Harbor were way down the list, and, hence, had to overwork their forces to keep up with the increasing demands of a post-9/11 America. "Thanks, Chief," she said. "We should be there in five minutes."

"We'll be there as soon as possible to offer support," Chief Blount said.

The phone call ended.

Narita loaded her Glock then turned to Skowcroft. "You fired one of these since your farm training?"

"Not exactly," Skowcroft replied.

"Well, get your weapon ready. You may have to use it in a couple of minutes."

The driver, Sargent Brock Thompson from the Rochester Police Department, pushed the accelerator as they continued to weave around cars.

Will we make it in time, or will they all be dead? Narita pushed the small round button on her weapon, turning the safety off.

Gregory looked at Vladimir's lifeless body lying on the concrete. The old man had pretty much been useless, but at least he had been another body with a weapon. Russia won't miss him, and neither will I.

Minus Vladimir, it was still three on two. After the timeworn cold warrior had been killed, Gregory had radioed the man on the boat and told him to come ashore. Then, he had radioed the man hiding behind the garage and told him to take out the cop who was making his way toward him; once that man engaged, Gregory would take care of Officer Lear. He crouched low, ready to move.

Cal moved cautiously toward the garage. There were two large oaks about ten yards from the garage's side that would give him adequate cover and a good angle to pour fire across the driveway where the shooting on the left had come from. Maybe he could force the person into a mistake, and Haley would get another clear shot. He started to move when he heard a noise near the garage. His instincts saved him as he flattened himself on the ground while bullets tore apart the bark on the trees where he had just been standing. He could make out a shadow next to the side of the garage now, and he opened fire at it.

He heard a yell as the shadow fell, and he jumped to his feet and sprinted toward the garage. But as he moved, shots were fired from across the driveway, and he was hit in the left shoulder. Needles of pain spread down his arm, and Cal fell to the ground.

* * *

Gregory listened and watched for movement. He was sure that he had hit the cop but didn't know if it was fatal or not. He waited. No movement or sound.

He keyed the radio handset, "Unit two, report." The wind picked up and danced across the branches above, rustling the leaves. "Unit two, report."

There was no reply. The man by the garage was either dead or couldn't respond. He keyed the handset again. "Unit three, report."

"Almost to the beach," came the reply.

"Good," Gregory said. "Stay there and wait."

The man acknowledged, and the radio went silent. Gregory holstered his weapon—and unsheathed his knife. Now, it was just him and Lear, and he knew exactly how to approach her.

Haley was still in her position to the left of the SUV. She had not heard anything in a few minutes. Was Cal hurt? She had heard shots and the sound of breaking branches. Was he dead? Was he hiding, waiting to make a move? She wanted to call out. No, give it another minute; don't rush and make a mistake. She focused on the woods lining the left-hand side of the driveway. Was that person still alive? Had any of her rounds been lucky and hit the target? She hoped that Iggi and Maria were safely inside their neighbor's house.

She heard noise—off to the left and close by. Haley squinted and brought her weapon over to where she thought she had heard the sound.

Crunch.

"Who's there?!" she shouted.

There was no reply—just the sound of the wind moving through the trees.

"I have my weapon trained on you," she lied.

More cool wind rollercoastered through the maze of trees and blew across the driveway.

Who was it?

Then, she heard a voice that both froze her bones and ignited her nerves, which began speeding throughout her body like a circuit cable that had just been energized. "Jen? Jen, is that you?"

It...It can't be. He died.

"Identify yourself!"

"Jen, you know who this is."

She now heard the sound of footsteps approaching through the leaves, fallen branches, and dirt of the forest floor. Her eyes started to water, and her breathing became labored. It can't be.

She now saw the figure, still shrouded in darkness, approaching.

"It's me. I made it out."

"Brian?"

She stood up, but still kept her weapon aimed at the approaching figure.

He stepped out of the darkness and into the light of the police vehicle's headlights. "Yes. Brian Turner."

Her heart raced. It *was* him.

He put both of his hands up in the air. "I'm sorry I had to sneak up on you. I just took care of that guy you were shooting at on the left."

"What are you doing here?"

"I've got a lot to explain, believe me. But the short of it is that Narita and Judas arranged a prisoner exchange. The Russians had me, and we had one of their guys so they agreed to swap. I've actually been back operating with The Company for over a month now, trying to track down these guys who came here to kill you tonight. Looks like I got here just in time."

His hands were still up and her weapon was still aimed at him, but her posture had relaxed. "Why didn't anyone tell me?"

"Too much risk. We needed you to think I was still dead." He smiled. "Now, can you lower that thing so I can give you a hug?"

He started to move toward her, and she began lowering her weapon.

Then, a radio attached to Brian's belt crackled to life. "Gregory, there is a man coming down the beach."

His smile disappeared, and in an instant he was upon her. Strong hands wrenched the weapon away from her and then grasped her wrist, bending her arm behind her back. One hand let go, and in a second, a knife was at her throat. "Now, we're going to go make sure your cop friend is dead, and then I'm going to finish you."

She struggled to get loose. "Brian, why are you doing this?!"

He twisted her arm even more—her wrist and forearm felt like they were being held on top of a stove burner.

His radio came on again. "Gregory, he's almost to me. What do you want me to do?"

Iggi saw the boat at anchor just off their beach. Was that the same boat he had seen a few nights ago? His eyes moved from the boat toward the strip of white sand.

There was a man wading in toward shore, now in about two feet of water— and carrying something.

The man stopped, turned more toward Iggi, and started to raise whatever was in his hand. Iggi didn't wait.

He grabbed two handfuls of sand and began running at the man in a zig-zag pattern. The man was surprised by this, and fumbled whatever was in his hand; the item hit the water with a *sploosh*. The man shouted something in a language Iggi had never heard before and began to reach down to retrieve the item but realized too late that he would not be able to reach it in time as Iggi threw the handfuls of sand at the man's face and then form-tackled him into the water.

The man was strong, but Iggi leveraged his weight and was able to keep the man's head underwater. The man kicked and thrashed, trying to get a breath. Iggi held on, and the man's movements became even more erratic.

Finally, the man's strength lessened, and soon he was motionless. Iggi moved off of him and dragged the man's body ashore. Confident that he was out for the count, Iggi sprinted toward the driveway.

Cal stood ten yards away—his left arm bleeding and drooping—from the man holding a knife to Haley's neck. In the man's other hand was an MP-443 Grach Yarygin Pistol pointed directly at Cal's chest. Moments earlier, Cal had been forced to throw his Glock 22 to the ground in front of him.

"Who is this guy?" Cal asked Haley.

"A former CIA Officer named Brian Turner."

"On your knees," Turner said.

"Fuck you," Cal said. "Let her go and try and take me out like a real man. Cut the hostage bullshit."

"I'm going to tell you one more time," he said, but then paused. "You know what, I don't need you to kneel."

A blur came from Cal's right.

Iggi Jayvyn Hilliard jumped through the air as the gun went off, and he took the bullet that was meant for Cal Ripley.

Brian Turner lost his concentration, shocked by the man who had just saved the cop's life. The knife lowered, giving Haley an opportunity, and she brought her elbow sharply up, breaking Turner's nose. He dropped the gun.

Cal scrambled to get it, clawing at the ground with his good arm. The gun was just out of reach...

Haley Girard picked up the weapon just before Turner's hand came swooping down. She stood back and pointed the barrel at Turner's bleeding face.

He moaned in pain and went down on one knee—his left. "Please, please don't kill me. They'll kill my wife and kids." He began to cry.

"Your wife and kids?!" Haley shouted.

Cal crawled to Iggi.

"The Russians tortured me, and then they kidnapped my family." One hand went to his right knee. "Said they would execute them if I didn't kill you. Please, help me, Jen." All of this was true. He had to complete the mission and return to Russia or else they *would be* executed. Before Berlin, he had considered leaving his wife and children for Lear. But now, he had to save them.

Haley saw Turner's hand reach down by his ankle and before she could think she pulled the trigger twice, putting two rounds in his head. Turner's body fell back onto the concrete.

Haley jumped on the body and removed a small pistol from underneath the right pant leg. Sonofabitch. After verifying Brian Turner was dead, she rushed over to Iggi.

"He's still breathing," Cal said, "and his clothes are soaked. Where in the hell was he?"

Haley looked at the hole in the front of Iggi's t-shirt and felt warm blood coming out as she put pressure on the wound. "We've got to call an ambulance, now."

"Don't move," came a voice from the side of the house.

Haley turned, and saw a man approaching with a handgun aimed at them. "I'm going to jump him when he gets close enough," she whispered to Cal.

The man stepped to within a few yards, and Haley could see that he was drenched.

Haley started to shift her weight. *One, two, thr—*

Shots sounded. Before she could leap, the man's body shook with each bullet that entered and crumpled to the ground.

Cal looked behind them and found a tall Japanese woman holding a gun, still aiming it at the dead man.

Haley yelled, "Director Narita! We've got one down here. We need an ambulance!"

A police officer and another woman came running down the driveway and stopped when they reached Narita.

"Chief, get an ambulance over here," Narita said.

"You've got it," Chief Blount replied. He picked up his radio and started giving orders.

Narita knelt down and hugged Haley. Fireworks started to appear over the lake.

Haley started to tear up. "Look over there," she said, pointing at Turner's body.

Narita stood up and walked over to the corpse. "Oh God," she said.

Ten minutes later the ambulance arrived, and the EMTs began treating Iggi. Maria came running down the driveway. She made it to the stretcher and saw Iggi's unconscious body lying there. Haley went to hold her, but Maria was frantic.

Then, the machines that were hooked up to Iggi started to beep.

"We're losing him," one of the EMTs said.

Maria let out a visceral, shrieking scream that no one would ever quite be able to forget, "Iggi! Iggi!"

EPILOGUE

JULY 4, 2007

L eiko Narita entered her home carrying a banker's box in her arms. Using her foot, she closed the door behind her. There was no welcome home greeting, no television on in the other room, no music playing—just silence.

She kicked off her shoes and set her keys down on the small table to the left of the door. Then, she turned the deadbolt. Her husband was still at the store picking up steaks, onion rings, Caesar salad, and a bottle of their favorite red. It was Independence Day, and they would be watching the fireworks from their second story balcony later in the evening. But today was also something else: her last day of work. After almost forty years spent in the heat of the battle to protect the United States of America, she was returning home for good. The office cleanout had started last month and had ended an hour ago as she packed the last few things in the box she now set on the floor—she'd take it upstairs to the office and unpack it tomorrow. Or, maybe the next day.

Forty years of spies, lies, secrets, assassinations, friendships, teeth-grinding stress, wins, losses, draws, frustrations, regrets, and duty. The co-workers she liked, the co-workers she loathed. The shitbags and the shining stars. The climbers and the career torch bearers. In a way, she would miss it all.

She entered the den and sat down on the long couch, sinking deeper and deeper into the cushions. No more meetings. No more files. No more leading. She stared at the motionless ceiling fan, and her eyes became heavy. Her legs felt like lead, her arms weaker by the second, and her body clammy. One year ago, the United States had almost suffered a catastrophic—perhaps, fatal—blow, and her descent into retirement had begun. The country would never know how close it had come to eating itself alive—one of the prices of getting to know secrets was the burden of keeping them. *All great empires fall from within.* The question wasn't, *Did we stop it?* No, the question was, *How long did we postpone it?* She stretched her legs. There would be plenty of time to look back, although her superior had told her to try and not think about the losses as she settled into retirement. 'Think more about the victories. It makes life easier in your third act. The weight of memory can crush you if you let it. And, most of all, spend time with your family.'

She'd written the standard last-day-on-the-job Op Ed and saw it in the morning's edition of *The Wall Street Journal.* And like all of her predecessors and those who would follow her, Leiko Narita would be forgotten tomorrow morning along with her column.

The last party 'To celebrate the career of Dr. Leiko Narita and her extraordinary contributions to The Company' had taken place last week. Since then, she had rarely seen anyone as the C.I.A.'s new Deputy Director for Intelligence had moved into Narita's old office, and Narita was given a small space on the floor below to use until her last day. As her security clearances and building access slipped away, so had she. There were smiles in the hallways and light pats on the shoulder at lunches in the cafeteria, but that was it. Someone else was now in the crosshairs.

Alone in her quiet house, she felt relieved, but also...old, tired, and sad. She could deal with the defeats—had almost half-a-century of experience—but knew that it would be the missed signs, the missed calls, and the history of record that could not be re-written, mostly because it could not be written at all—that would stay with her. The intelligence gathered from the raid on the hangar had been minimal. Was there a nuclear weapon on the plane? She had to believe that there was but would never know for sure. No one would. And without knowing exactly who sabotaged the plane and runway, the Russians and Chinese were in no hurry to put out inquiries, which would, of course, be admitting that they had known of the plane, hangar, and runway. The DCI had hinted to her that the President had called his counterpart in both countries *out of concern* for them and asked if they had heard the same rumor that he had been hearing about some foiled plot involving a commercial jet loaded with a nuclear weapon. Apparently, they both said that they had heard about it, didn't have any more information, but would *look into it*. Naturally, they were concerned for the well-being of the United States too.

And so the great game of cat and mouse continued, although global relations had cooled significantly between the three superpowers since the raid. Would anyone have the guts to push pause on the game? Would anyone have the spine to say enough was enough?

Another book detailing the history of the C.I.A. had been recently released to wide acclaim. She let out a small laugh. It's not history when you only have half of the story. No doubt The Company would release a statement condemning the book. As a career officer, she knew most of the history, and there had been numerous embarrassing, devastating mistakes over the years. But there had also been triumphs that would never come to light. There were 87 stars on the Memorial Wall located in the original headquarters building lobby. And below the wall was the Book of Honor that listed the names of those Company employees who had died in the line of duty. 33 of the stars had no names listed; their deaths were still classified. To her, those stars were 33 reasons why all of the failures had been worth it. The burden of knowing what those 33 had prevented would always be with her, but, as a fellow retiree had told her, 'It will be a burden with the silver lining of gratitude.' She had attended the ceremony in May when 4 more stars had been added to the wall. Eventually, stars would be added for Rolfe Judas and Meghan Trimble. And then there was the star that had already been added for Brian Turner, which had no name next to it in the Book of Honor. Would it be removed? She didn't know. Haley Girard had asked her if Turner really was married and had children. She had decided to lie one last time and had told her no. Seeing the relief on Girard's face had made the deception worth it—Girard had suffered enough. Before the C.I.A. could locate Turner's wife and two young boys to protect them, their bodies were found in a car that had run off the road and burst into flames not far from their home in Pennsylvania. Narita suspected that they had been dead before they even got into the car.

She looked at her watch. Might as well get used to not wearing it. For the first time in forever, she had nowhere to be. She yawned. *Better get up now or else you'll be asleep when he gets home. C'mon. You're going to go take an endless shower, put on comfortable clothes—that would be another thing to get used to—and enjoy a dinner uninterrupted by cell phone calls.* For someone who had always found *an* answer, if not *the* answer, to the difficult questions posed to her over her career, she was bothered by the fact that she could not answer the most pressing question in her life right now. She opened her eyes, sat up, and looked out the bay window at her front yard. A bird flew by, maybe looking for home or food. *What do I do tomorrow?*

Haley blew a kiss to Cal from the swim step of their 33-foot Hunter sailboat—bought with the money from the sale of Cal's house in Detroit and her salary from the C.I.A., which she had placed in a mutual fund for the past 4 years. As far as money was concerned, they were in great shape. She was a saver, and he was a saver. Her grandmother had told her that relationships usually worked out if at least one person was a saver; if both people were spenders...watch out.

It was eleven a.m., and the sun had climbed high enough to beam directly on the surface of Lake Ontario creating a thin layer of steam which kept the surface perfectly flat. She entered the sapphire water in a vertical dive and descended straight down, pausing once to equalize the pressure in her ears, and then continued on until she reached the sandy bottom at around fifteen feet. The cool temperature was refreshing after sunbathing on the foredeck for most of the morning next to her husband.

They had started with coffee in the cockpit as the sun rose on the eastern horizon—Haley in a white terrycloth robe with her hair pulled back in a ponytail, Cal in his boxer shorts and bed head, which always turned her on. Breakfast had been skipped for lovemaking on the salon bench, and after showering together, they had put on their swimsuits and relaxed on the foredeck—him reading a paperback and her fading in and out of sleep.

She began to exhale as she ascended, and the bubbles steadily leaving her mouth and nose tickled her forehead. If this was day one of the honeymoon, she couldn't wait for day two. They were anchored a hundred yards offshore and would be leaving to travel further along the southern coast in the afternoon. They would anchor, take another dip, have dinner, then talk until the food had settled—and then make...no, making love was this morning, tonight would be sex. Another shower would follow, full of massaging and washing each other, and the night would end with snifters of brandy topside under the moonlight.

Her eyes were closed, but she could sense the light becoming brighter and brighter as she neared the surface. With the exception of the parts of her body covered by her turquoise-colored bikini, she felt goosebumps all over her skin. The school year was officially in the rear-view mirror, and they had two full weeks together, alone, before returning to their home in Rochester where Cal had transferred to the Rochester Police Department. His last day in Detroit had been difficult—from saying goodbye to lifelong friends on the force to pulling out of his driveway for the final time. They had talked about it, but she suspected that there was no way to ever really say goodbye to a childhood home—especially one he had lived in as an adult.

Her head broke the water perhaps ten yards aft of the sloop.

"How is it?" Cal asked from the swim step.

She splashed him. "Why don't you join me and find out?"

She treaded water, admiring his lean, hard body. He was already tan and had let his hair grow out; the sides had to be tapered and kept within regulation for his job, but the top was now wavy. His sunglasses gave his figure a mystique, but the smile below them betrayed his charm.

"They're on their way out," he said, pointing toward the beach.

Haley scanned the shoreline until she located the cabin rising in the distance. On the surface of the water, she could see two kayakers paddling toward them. After the endless wedding reception, she wasn't sure they would be recovered by now. A grin spread across her face, and she submerged, kicking to the stern. Her hand rose from the water and held on to the swim ladder that Cal had kicked down.

"I can't believe it," she said.

"What?" He lowered a hand and helped her onboard.

"When have they ever been on time?"

Cal laughed. "Well, it sure wasn't the wedding."

She gave him a kiss and then climbed up into the cockpit. Standing on the starboard bench, she closed her eyes and felt the sun's warmth pour down on her skin. A flock of seagulls flew by and rose into the sky, heading somewhere unknown. It was the Fourth of July, a time of celebration and remembrance. Her time in the CIA was over, and although she did not miss it, she awoke each morning thinking that someone, somewhere in the world, was 'Jennifer Lear'. She would never forget that—or her experience.

What a difference a year makes.

She opened her eyes and waved to the two kayakers.

Maria and Iggi Hilliard waved back.

AUTHOR'S NOTE

Thank you for reading *The Cabin*. As an independent author, my success greatly depends on reviews and referrals. If you enjoyed the book, it would help me out if you left a quick review on Amazon and then passed on the recommendation.

If you would like more information on upcoming books and discounts, please sign-up for my email list through my website (landonbeachbooks.com) or follow Landon Beach Books on Facebook, Twitter, or Instagram.

The Cabin proved to be a much more ambitious project than my previous works, and there was a great deal of research involved. A few books that stood out were: *The Best and the Brightest* by David Halberstam, *Dispatches* by Michael Herr, *Legacy of Ashes* by Tim Weiner, *The Clash of Civilizations and the Remaking of World Order* by Samuel P. Huntington, *Lights Out* by Ted Koppel, *Michigan: A History of the Great Lakes State* by Bruce A. Rubenstein and Lawrence E. Ziewacz, *The Great Lakes Diving Guide* and *The 100 Best Great Lakes Shipwrecks, Volume I*, both by Cris Kohl, *The Billion Dollar Spy* by David E. Hoffman, *Deep Undercover: My Secret Life and Tangled Allegiances as a KGB Spy in America* by Jack Barsky, and the *2004 Executive Report of the Commission to Assess the Threat to the United States from Electromagnetic Pulse (EMP) Attack*.

As far as the intelligence material in the book, much of what I present is actual tradecraft that has been declassified. Of course, I don't—nor should I!—have access to current methods being used by the C.I.A. or other government agencies. Using teachers as C.I.A. Officers is entirely my creation; although, from what I learned during my research, it wouldn't surprise me if a few educators are currently serving their country while on summer vacation. I wish I could say that the EMP material was all made up too. Unfortunately, it is not.

The Cabin is not meant to be a drop-everything-you're-doing-and-start-prepping call to action. However, I am a firm believer in self-reliance and think every American should read the report listed above. I hope the scenario that I describe in the novel never comes to pass.

In terms of politics, sorry, no agenda here. Now, that doesn't mean that my *characters* don't have political leanings (I think it makes them interesting and complex), but, alas, there is no overriding message. In fact, anyone looking for political schemas or viewpoints in my fiction will be disappointed; unfortunately, we are all already oversaturated with political manifestos in everyday life. However, call me crazy, I have a feeling that if our country was faced with a real catastrophe like an EMP attack, those partisan divisions would vanish very quickly. We wouldn't be asking our neighbors who they voted for; we'd be asking how much food and water they had and brainstorming how we could work together to survive. Wouldn't it be nice if this could happen without the doomsday scenario? Nate Martin's line from my novel *The Wreck* comes to mind, "Food, water, shelter. After that, human beings made up the rest."

Next up: *The Hike.*

Many thanks to MB, JB, EL, CG, and KJ who all provided helpful comments on an early draft and to my editor, ED, who always turns a manuscript into a novel—a difficult task! Beachreaders: Thank you for your encouragement, support, and belief in me. I can't wait to share my next book with you. Finally, my never-ending appreciation to my wife and two girls for getting me through each book, start to finish; these novels don't exist without the three of you.

Happy Beach Reading!

L.B.

If you enjoyed *The Cabin*, expand your adventure with *The Hike*, the next book in The Great Lakes saga. Here is an excerpt to start the journey.

THE HIKE

Landon Beach

PROLOGUE I

Springer Mountain, Georgia, Saturday, April 4, 2015

Rays of golden sunlight found their way easily through the bare, gray tree trunks rising toward the sky as Brad Cranston stood in front of the stone archway that marked the start of the Appalachian Approach Trail.

Last night, he had stayed at Amicalola Falls Lodge and been told by the front desk clerk that in a few months, the surrounding woods would be a lush green canopy of tree leaves. However, in April, it was as if nature refused to leave a deep winter depression and only a skeleton of the once vibrant woods remained with human beings hiking around her weathered-bark bones looking for flesh. Brad couldn't argue with the description, but he did see scattered patches of foliage, signifying that the forest was coming back to life and that spring was here, and summer was right around the corner. After a chilly morning with temperatures in the low forties, Brad's watch said the temperature was now in the upper fifties. Dressed in a red, long-sleeved, moisture-wicking Columbia shirt with tan Columbia pants and leather L.L. Bean Cresta hiking boots, he turned his forty-six-year-old body away from the stone archway, and a beam of sun shone on his face. He enjoyed the momentary warmth and then took a couple of steps forward, then stopped and scanned the faces of the half-dozen hikers wearing bright-colored windbreakers and lugging huge backpacks, heading his way. They passed by him, stabbing the earth with their trekking poles, without offering any greetings and without much chatter between them, seemingly lost in their thoughts about the task that lay ahead. Some earlier hikers had been louder, cracking jokes and laughing to ease the tension, which he had settled on as a strategy to use with his own hiking partner. He looked at his watch. It was 1 p.m. They were supposed to meet near the arch at noon. Brad's hiking partner, his loveable screwup of a younger brother, Conrad, was still nowhere to be seen.

Brad pivoted and watched the hikers go under the arch. For a while, he could hear the sound of the group's boots cracking the scattered branches on the floor of the trail, but soon the cracks and snaps faded until all he could hear was the occasional buzzing of the few bugs that had dared to brave the cooler April temperatures. For the twentieth time today, Brad looked at the red sign with white letters next to the arch signifying the beginning of the approach trail. Eight and a half miles later was the official start of his 2,181-mile Appalachian Trail (AT) hike with Conrad. If all went well, they'd summit Mount Katahdin in Maine's Baxter State Park and hug the sign on Baxter Peak sometime in September or early October. Months had gone into their preparation, all leading to today—day one.

He had picked the approach trail as their start instead of being dropped off where Forest Service Road 42 intersected the trail less than a mile into the AT. If Conrad, the king of shortcuts, had known about this option, he would have demanded that they start there. Brad figured the 8.5-mile approach trail would be an easy test to see if Conrad was serious or not. Once Conrad started something he was interested in, he had a surprising amount of drive and resiliency, which had been a powerful advantage at a few brief points during his life and a debilitating liability during other stretches.

They were from Michigan, so a handful of Michigan state parks had been their training ground for day hikes to get them in shape and get them used to carrying the load they would hump with on the trail. They had scaled up to overnighters and performed equipment research and testing, read a dozen books about the trail, including Bryson's inspirational account, and, finally, tackled logistics planning. Their support person would be their sister, Heidi, and she had bump boxes, containing specific items to replenish their supplies, all addressed and ready to send to them as they reached certain towns. Brad reasoned that if they failed, it wouldn't be because of a lack of preparation. In fact, they were so prepared that he was seeing visions of toilet paper, duct tape, and half-toothbrushes on the wall at night, including his stay last night at the comfortable lodge. He'd invited Conrad to fly into Atlanta with him, ride to the lodge, and stay with him there so they could start hiking in the morning, but his brother had declined. *"Look, I'll be standing with you under the stone-arch at high noon, all right? Don't get all uptight on me. Let things flow,"* he had said. Like always, there had been no changing his mind.

Brad looked at his watch again. 1:15 p.m. Another group of hikers, louder than the one he had just seen disappear into the woods, passed by and stopped by the arch to have their pictures taken before embarking on their journeys. Thankfully, they did not ask for his help. He must have seen over fifty people already and helped most of them with their pictures. *"Hello, sir. Could you help us take a quick picture?"*

Where in the hell was Conrad? That was the most pressing question. Another question slithering around in Brad's mind was: Why am I doing this? He'd been divorced for five years, so this wasn't a knee-jerk escapist mission. He was relatively happy in his life, so this wasn't an "I've gotta go find myself" remedy. He had never been out of shape, and so this wasn't some crusade with echoes from a doctor's physical examination that said, "Lose the weight...*or else.*" He hadn't succumbed to materialism, so the hike was not to get away from the empty distractions and excesses that contemporary life in America offered at every turn. *Why am I here?* His best answer was that he had helped his brother turn his life around, they had both always been the outdoors type, they enjoyed each other's company, and, although Conrad was much more competitive than he was, they liked a challenge. Any other positive that this half-a-year provided would be welcomed but not required. *What will the rest of the world be doing for the next six months?* Standing here, pissed off waiting for Conrad, Brad Cranston decided that he didn't really care.

He moved away from the archway and took a seat far enough away to not be asked for any more picture assistance. He'd give Conrad another half-hour or so, then he'd hike back up to the lodge and start making phone calls.

Don't start playing the 'What if?' game, he told himself. He picked up a twig from the ground and started bending it, testing its pliability. On the third bend, it snapped in two. He threw the pieces down. *Okay, what have I missed here?* He searched his memory for any hints that Conrad would be a no-show.

All of the milestones that, if not taken care of, would have triggered Conrad's early exit from the adventure had been achieved. They had already paid for the necessary permits, had plenty of money for fees, bought the equipment, bought the airline tickets, and registered for the thru-hike. Their trail names were as different as they were: his—Sandusky, because of his love of Cedar Point and the happy memories of taking his daughter Noelle there when she was young; Conrad's—Proust, his brother's favorite author. Brad had wanted to leave earlier, late February, to avoid the crowds. With so many northbound hikers, shelters and tenting areas ran out of space quickly. Conrad had said no, and Brad had given in to the April start date. So, the schedule wasn't a show stopper. Then, there was the cash issue. The general rule of thumb was to budget one thousand dollars per month each on the hike. Since the hike took five to seven months, Brad had saved seven thousand dollars, and Conrad had shown him his bank account statement two days ago—the funds were there. As far as travel, Conrad's flight had taken off early this morning from Detroit Metro and had landed in Atlanta on time. He had called Conrad a half an hour after the plane had landed, but the call had gone straight to voicemail. Brad had called Heidi next, but she hadn't heard from Conrad either. There could have been an accident on the way from Atlanta. If that was the case, he would hear about it at some point.

He laughed to himself. *This is ridiculous.* Brad knew that Conrad was probably going to show up any minute now with some lame excuse, which would be forgiven, and then they'd hike the legendary Appalachian Trail. It sounded like he was relaxing, talking sense into himself, but something about the situation didn't feel right to Brad.

Did Conrad try and bring a gun in his luggage?

They had talked about bringing one on the trail, but Brad thought they had come to the agreement that it was not worth it. The gun could be taken and used against them, it was heavy to carry, and, with Conrad's luck, an accidental discharge was highly probable. There were risks hiking the trail. There were also risks getting behind the wheel of a car and driving ten miles down the road each day to work. In the past two decades, there had been two or three major crimes on the trail. Other than those, three million people had safely traveled its winding path. When he calculated the odds, Brad saw the three million safe passages; Conrad saw the handful of major crimes. *"Somebody could take us right out, Brad!"* he had yelled in one of their early arguments. Christ, he hoped he was wrong and that Conrad had not attempted to bring a weapon to the Detroit airport. *Did Conrad even own a gun?* He didn't want to know.

After waiting an extra ten minutes past the half-hour he had already waited, Brad made his way up to the lodge and called Heidi.

"It's Brad," he said.

"He already quit, didn't he?" Heidi said. "I knew it."

"No. He still hasn't shown up."

There was a pause. "What?"

"I've been waiting at the entrance to the approach trail since noon, and he's not here. Have you heard from him?"

"No. Since the plane landed on time and he didn't answer, I just figured he was on his way to you. You know how horrible he is with his cell phone, if he brought it at all," she said, an edge to her voice that seemed laced with both sadness and disappointment. He knew that rage was just around the bend.

"Yep." He tipped his head to the right, sandwiching the phone between his ear and right shoulder, while he lowered his pack to the lobby floor. He then told her all of the scenarios he had thought through. "Other than waiting here to see if he shows up, the only thing I can think of is to call and see if he even got on the plane in Detroit. Can you check for me?"

"Don't you have your cell phone?" she asked.

"No. I didn't want it on the trip with me."

Another pause. "Okay, I'll call," she said.

"Thanks, and, hey, let's not panic. He's put too much into this thing to back out now. That big-hearted oaf will be here any minute, wearing his toothy grin and armed with a ridiculous story about why he was late. And while he tells me the tale, he'll be slinging his backpack around with his thick, hairy arms because he can't stand still."

Heidi's tone was serious. "He may still have a touch of his old charisma, and he's smarter than he deserves to be, but, Brad, he's thirty-eight years old. I'll call."

Five minutes later, one of the phones behind the check-in counter rang. An attendant waved him over.

"Heidi?"

"He never got on the flight. Didn't even check in a bag," she said. Her voice was a whisper, half-concerned, half-enraged.

After all Conrad had put the family through, Brad knew this would be the fatal blow with Heidi. She would now join their parents in the 'Done with Conrad' Club. After dinner with his family a month ago, his father had pulled him aside, eyes narrowed and more serious than a retiree's should be, and said, *"Don't bring him on the hike."*

If he lost faith in Conrad now, he'd never forgive himself. There had to be some explanation. *Had* to be. Even Heidi knew that Conrad was overinvested in the hike, and Conrad was never invested in anything—spent too much time in his own head, or, when he was heavy into every drug on the market, spent too much time out of his head. "It doesn't add up," Brad said. "I—"

"Stop, Brad," she said. "Stop. This is it for me. I'm through. I've got a *whole* bedroom in my house stacked with packages ready to send to you two along the way." He heard her start to cry. "He's gone, and you know it."

"Heidi, I'm sorry. I know how much you've done to help us. We wouldn't even be able to attempt this thing without you." He paused, searching for something to say to keep her on board. "Look, I'm going to stay another night here and wait. We owe it to ourselves and to him. There has to be a reason," he said, wondering if he believed what he had just said. "You know how to reach me. I'll call you in the morning, okay?"

She sniffled. "Fine," she said.

The next morning, he awoke to no Conrad.

And the next morning.

And the next.

Nothing from Heidi.

On Wednesday, he left the lodge and headed home to Michigan. Conrad had disappeared.

PROLOGUE II

Location: CLASSIFIED, Winter 2016

hief Petty Officer Allison Shannon could feel goosebumps on her
brown skin underneath her drysuit as she kicked forty feet below the
surface of the water. Her fin strokes were smooth as she swept her
underwater light from side to side, searching for anyone and anything that was
not supposed to be in the water at this time. Approximately ten feet above her
was the hull of the most technologically advanced warship ever built, *USS
Zumwalt* (DDG-1000). Costing approximately four billion dollars to construct,
the destroyer was six hundred feet long, nearly eighty-one feet wide, and had been
commissioned on the fifteenth of October in Baltimore's Inner Harbor during
Fleet Week. Now, the ship was in another port, staying the night to refuel and to
let a few select naval personnel at the base come aboard and tour the spectacular
vessel. *Zumwalt's* ultimate destination was San Diego, its new homeport. Before
and after commissioning, there had been intelligence indicating that attempts
would be made to destroy or damage the new pride of the American Navy before
the ship ever reached the California coast. Hence, at each stop, security was
tighter than a pair of spandex.

Chief Shannon had been a Search and Rescue (SAR) swimmer for most of her career. She was also a Master Diver, and when the Coast Guard established the diver (DV) rating in 2015, the commanding officer (CO) of the new program selected her to switch rates and help him develop and lead it. The maximum age for entry into the program was thirty-five; at thirty-four, she had outperformed over ninety percent of the new recruits—who were just over half of her age—in the physical fitness test. Now, she was a member of a Maritime Safety and Security Team (MSST), which provided anti-terrorism security for high-value vessels like *Zumwalt*. Her team had provided underwater security during the commissioning and for the two port visits so far as the destroyer made its way south from Baltimore. They were embarked until the ship made it through the Panama Canal; then, a west coast team would embark and take over security until the ship was safely moored in San Diego. Her CO thought that having the team embarked was a bit of an overkill—commissioning was one thing, but *every* port *and* when the *Zumwalt* was at sea? However, he saw the possible rewards of showcasing his top divers doing the job they had been trained to do, which was to make sure there were no divers in areas they shouldn't be—in this case, anywhere near the hull of *Zumwalt*.

Shannon checked the bright Luminox around her wrist: 2345, or 11:45 p.m. civilian time; fifteen minutes until her watch was over. Her pressure gauge indicated that she still had around twenty minutes of air left. *Take it nice and easy.* She rose a few feet and aimed her light at the hull. *Zumwalt*'s motto was *Pax Propter Vim*: Peace Through Power. From what she had observed the past month and a half in the Atlantic Ocean, this ship had power and then some. Up forward, she could see the light of her diving partner, Petty Officer First Class Matt Keller.

She pushed the button to talk on the full face mask she was wearing. "Fifteen minutes, Matt. See anything?"

Keller's voice came across crystal clear in Shannon's wet speaker that sat against her left ear. "Nothing, Chief. Cold, quiet, and dark."

Zumwalt's command duty officer (CDO), the engineering duty officer (EDO), and the quarterdeck watch also had communications with the two divers via a net set up on a surface station that had a transducer cable lowered into the water. The CDO broke in, "All quiet up here."

The quarterdeck watch radioed in, "Your reliefs are on deck suiting up as we speak."

Shannon said, "Good to hear. Didn't have to pull them out of their racks this time." She turned in a slow circle away from the hull and pointed her light into the middle of the basin's dark water. From the outer reach of her light's beam, a shadow passed by. *What was that?* She kicked away from the ship, her light in one hand, her spear gun in the other.

"See something, Chief?" Keller asked.

She brought the hand that held the light to her face mask and pushed the talk button. "Saw a shadow at the edge of my light's range. Checking it out."

"Roger that," Keller said.

Shannon appreciated his brevity. During the commissioning, she had been paired with Scroggins, who wouldn't shut the hell up. Plus, Keller was thorough and smart—a pleasure to work with. She stole a glance back at the ship and saw Keller's light moving aft along the hull.

She went to aim her light in the direction where she had seen the shadow but felt a surge of water from her right. Turning just in time, she ducked and saw an enormous white underbelly pass overhead. She raised her light and focused the beam on the creature as it swam past her. Perhaps twelve feet long, there was no mistaking the conical snout, large dorsal fin, wide pectoral fins, and huge crescent-shaped tail: This was a great white shark. Having never seen one underwater before, the length was not what impressed her the most—it was the girth. She watched as the large fish turned and headed toward the middle of the basin and perhaps out to sea. *Had it been circling her, waiting to attack, or was it just searching the port's waters out of curiosity?* There was no barrier to prevent sea life from entering the basin, but she had never seen a shark, let alone a great white, in the U.S. ports where she provided security. Dolphins and the occasional sea turtle? Yes.

She keyed her microphone. "We've got a great white shark down here with us."

"Where? I've got to see it!" Keller said.

She could see Keller's light change direction and start heading toward her. "Too late, sport," Shannon said. "I think he or she is headed back to sea."

"Damn," Keller said, arriving next to Shannon. "Think it will come back?"

She looked in his faceplate. "I hope not. Beast's enormous. It's one thing to see it from a distance and watch its beauty and grace. It's another thing to have that sucker come out of the gloom of this shitty-visibility water."

"How big?" Asked *Zumwalt*'s CDO.

"Around twelve feet—big enough. You should let *Carney* and *Hué City* know, sir," she said. "They have divers working who would appreciate the heads up."

"Roger that, Chief," the CDO said.

"Hey, at least you've got another check on your bucket list now," Keller said.

They had been talking for the past few weeks about all of the underwater sea creatures they had seen throughout their years of diving: blue sharks, bull sharks, mako sharks, oceanic whitetip sharks, tiger sharks, grouper, moray eels, stingrays, sea turtles, manta rays, etc. But neither of them had seen a great white. "Helluva way to do it," Shannon said. "I had envisioned checking that one off in the clear blue water off of South Africa or Australia, both of which I plan to visit when I retire." She smiled, her eyes betraying a slight hint of greed. "Now that I've seen one, though, I've *got* to see another one."

"Okay, stop rubbing it in," Keller said.

They both aimed their lights into the basin and moved them together, first up and down and then side to side. The shark was nowhere to be seen. "Let's do our last sweep," she said. Their lights were now pointing up at their masks, and they could see each other while they spoke. "You move forward to aft, and I'll move aft to forward."

Keller nodded, and she gave him a wink. Then, she put her spear gun under her arm and, with her free hand, made a fin and moved it toward Keller's mask. "You'll get your chance."

"Yeah, right," Keller said.

They kicked back toward the ship.

Standard procedure for turning over the watch meant that the reliefs would start a walk-through about thirty minutes before assuming the watch and then meet up with the off-going watch approximately fifteen minutes later. However, for underwater security watches, the reliefs only needed to be in the water with the off-going watch for a few minutes. There were either enemy divers in the water, or there weren't, and any other piece of information that the on-coming watch might need could be learned from the quarterdeck watch. If they were further south in warmer water, then the watches could be as long as three hours, but, thankfully, Shannon thought, because of the current water temperature, their watches had been reduced to two hours with a tank change at the one-hour point. The MSST had enough divers to ensure that they would get a solid seven hours in the rack before their next two-hour dive at 8 a.m.

Shannon spoke to the quarterdeck watch. "Making our final run. Except for the shark, everything has been quiet," she said. "We are ready to be relieved."

"And ready for a mug of hot chocolate and some sleep," Keller added.

On the quarterdeck, the two divers taking the next watch were almost suited up. Hearing the report, they gave a thumbs up to the officer of the watch, who said, "Quarterdeck, aye. Next watch getting wet in five minutes."

Shannon and Keller acknowledged.

The cool night air stung Lieutenant Marissa Avery's face as she jogged along the base's white strip of beach. The rest of her body was covered in cold-weather running gear, including a watch cap and a thin pair of gloves. Since she had been running for nearly forty minutes to clear her mind after having trouble falling asleep, her sweat seemed like it was starting to freeze between her skin and the tight outer garments she had on.

Twenty more minutes to go, she told herself. *C'mon legs. Don't abandon me now.*

The nearly full moon slid behind a cluster of clouds, and, to her right, the ocean water darkened from slate gray to black. She looked ahead. There was approximately a half-mile of beach left before she'd have to turn left, follow the seawall along the river that branched off into the basin, and then complete her loop around the perimeter before arriving at the base's Bachelor Officer Quarters, the BOQ, where she had a room. One more week of training left, and she'd be headed back to Norfolk Naval Station, where her ship was homeported. She'd checked in after dinner with her husband and toddler, who were back home in Virginia. It had been a trying three weeks away from them. Beyond the physical and emotional separation—no, the Navy had not and would never be able to bridge that gap—her training school schedule had been demanding. Up at 0500 and not returning to her BOQ room until dinner, day after day, was starting to wear on her. In fact, as good as the training had been, it was getting repetitive. But that was an area of Navy pride: repeating everything a million times in the name of safety and training. Her word to describe this philosophy? Overkill. However, she was in the home stretch now, and her spirits were rising. What had kept her awake tonight was worrying about what would happen two weeks after she arrived home. Her ship was leaving on a six-month deployment; it would be mid-summer when she saw her family again. *How much do two-year-old boys grow in six months?* She pushed the thought away and focused on her breathing as each footstep patted the sand.

About two hundred yards from the seawall, she noticed something moving irregularly in the waves off to her right. She slowed, eventually jogging in place, and focused on the spot of ocean that had caught her attention. She squinted.

Was that a boat out there? She stopped jogging. Yes, it was a boat. A cabin cruiser, painted jet black and around forty feet with no running lights on, bobbed at anchor about fifty yards offshore. There was nothing unusual about a boat anchoring close to shore. However, there was something strange about one that did it and *didn't* display anchor lights. *Maybe the boat was having electrical problems?* She could see no one topside, but the cruiser's dinghy was still secured up forward, so whoever was on board had a way to reach the shore for help.

After a minute, she started to walk, still keeping her eyes on the craft. Maybe there was nothing wrong. Perhaps they had a little too much beer, or, tired after a day of cruising, they simply nodded off and forgot to turn on their anchor lights. It had happened before. She started to jog. After a half-a-dozen strides, a little voice inside her head told her to report it when she got back to her BOQ room. *If you see something, say something.* It had become a cliché since 9/11. The wind started to chill her as she picked up her pace, but her body still felt healthy and strong as she welcomed the cold air into her lungs and then exhaled loudly through her nose.

She neared her turn and jogged backward for a few seconds. The boat was still there, no lights on. She turned and kept going. She'd call base security when she finished her run and make a report. It would clear her conscience even though—she snuck one last look—there were probably just a couple of yo-yos out there passed out below deck.

She turned and ran along the massive seawall. Up ahead, the basin full of ships loomed in the darkness.

The two men kicked slowly along the mucky bottom. They neither used nor carried dive lights. According to their dive computers, which had backlighting and integrated compasses, they should be in the center of the basin by now, where the depth was just above fifty feet. The man on the right had taken on the name of Bill Johnson, according to his forged passport, and the man on the left, Henry

Peterson. He, Bill, was the underwater demolition expert. Henry was there to make sure that he was able to complete the mission—Henry was expendable, but he was not. Tonight's target: the Americans' newest machine of death, the *USS Zumwalt*.

A man whom they had never met before, known only as Marcus, was on board a cabin cruiser, anchored off the coast, waiting to pick them up once the explosives had been placed on the hull and the timer had been set for an hour. This would give them plenty of time to climb aboard, weigh anchor, and travel down the coast for thirty minutes until they were directly offshore the beach house that had been purchased a year ago for the mission. Marcus would drop them off close to the beach, and they would swim ashore in just bathing trunks while Marcus headed out to sea to sink the boat in deep water. Then, Marcus would motor back in the dinghy, sink it in water approximately one hundred yards from shore, and swim in. They would all stay the night in the beach house, and in the morning, Marcus would take them by car to an airport. Twenty-four hours later, they would be back home across the Atlantic Ocean. Where would Marcus go after that? Perhaps back to the beach house. Perhaps elsewhere. Bill didn't know.

They approached using closed-circuit rebreathers, which reused the gas that the divers exhaled, enabling them to use the replenished air for their next breath. This gave them three advantages. One, because of the increased efficiency, they could dive longer. Two, because the rebreathers recycled all of the gas they used, there would be only a few bubbles that escaped, meaning their approach would be very quiet, and the lack of bubbles rising would not give away their position to someone looking at the water from above the surface. Three, because they were breathing gas that had already been warmed by themselves, the rebreather would keep them warmer, which was perfect for this cold-weather dive tonight. They had drysuits available on the boat but had decided to go with wetsuits since they wouldn't be in the water that long. Plus, Marcus had explained that if they were a little colder, then they would concentrate harder and be more efficient. Bill thought the logic was sort of sound, but now he wished they had chosen the drysuits.

There was nothing ahead, and, for a moment, Bill started to second guess himself. *Were they headed in the wrong direction? Was the compass not working?* His doubts vanished after a few more kicks. In the distance, two yellow beams swept along the hull of their target. He reached down and felt the bag with the explosive charges and timer. Everything was perfect. As he brought his hand up, he felt a pinch in his thumb. He tried to pull his hand up, but it was caught on something sticking up from the bottom. He grabbed Henry's arm, and they stopped. As soon as he got in position to see what he was stuck on, his hand popped free. At first, there was a kind of pulsating relief, and he rubbed his thumb with his other fingers. Then, he could feel warm fluid ooze from just below the knuckle. Blood. If he had a light to shine on his thumb, at this depth, the blood would appear green. *How bad was the cut?* He straightened and bent his thumb a few times with minimal pain. He'd be fine. *What in the hell had been on the bottom?* He looked down and saw nothing but darkness.

A foot away to his left, he could see Henry's right arm, the hand holding a spear gun. He couldn't see but knew that in Henry's other hand was a stainless-steel dive knife. He gave the right arm a squeeze, and they began to fin toward the ship again. Bill looked at his watch. If everything went as planned, they would have a few moments when the two security divers would swim together and exit the water behind the stern just after the next team entered. Hence, with all four security divers aft, this would give them the opportunity to quickly affix the explosives and timer to the hull near one of the seawater intakes located amidships. It would still be visible, but placed right next to the intake, it would take a slow, detailed inspection to see it. And from what they had observed on a dive earlier in the evening, the security divers didn't go slowly enough all of the time to see everything. The odds of success were good. They continued toward the ship, the golden yellow dive light beams of the security divers growing larger and larger. Meanwhile, green liquid slowly left his thumb, leaving a trail behind them.

"You ready to head up?" Shannon asked Keller.

"All good on my end," Keller said. He was at the stern, looking up at *Zumwalt*'s two enormous shafts and propellers. Shannon was forward, past the bow, turning around.

"I'm headed to you," she said. "Quarterdeck, we're coming up."

The officer of the watch acknowledged and then notified the two divers waiting on the pier. They gave a thumbs up and walked down, fins and dive lights in hand, to the sea ladder at the end of the pier.

Shannon finned up to a depth of twenty feet, and her dive light's lemon beam bloomed against the port-side hull. All of the appropriate equipment aboard *Zumwalt* that would pose a threat to divers had been tagged out after the ship had entered the port and switched from ship to shore power. Still, she kept her distance from any intakes, not wanting to get a part of her body sucked up into the hull. Even though she and Keller had verified the tags prior to diving, accidents had happened before. She descended back down to forty feet and swam toward Keller's beam.

The mammoth shark appeared on the edge of her beam's reach. "Keller! The white is back! Swim toward me." Shannon watched as the large fish ignored her and swam past, heading toward the bow of the ship.

Keller arrived next to her and aimed his light in the same direction as Shannon's. "I see it!" he said. "Let's follow it forwa—wait a minute, what's it doing?"

Suddenly, the shark bolted toward the bottom. Shannon and Keller followed, continuing to shine their lights in the direction the shark had gone. A few kicks later, they witnessed horror as the shark had snapped its jaws around a diver and was shaking its head from side to side as blood billowed out from its mouth.

"Jesus Christ!" yelled Keller.

"What's going on?" shouted the CDO.

Shannon swam down toward the shark. The diver's head and one arm hung out the right side of the fish's mouth, and out the left side was...nothing. She aimed her light and saw two legs with fins, bitten off just above the knees, lying on the basin floor—a cloud of blood rising from them. A spear entered the shark's snout, and Keller's beam found a second diver, a few yards away from the great white. The diver let his used spear gun fall as he swam up to the fish and started to bang on its skin with one hand and repeatedly puncture it with his knife in the other. The shark opened its mouth, and the diver's corpse slipped out—a bloody hulk of shredded neoprene, bone, and gore. The diver with the knife kicked backward, avoiding the agape mouth packed with white, serrated teeth. The shark made a few strong strokes with its crescent tail, cruised by him, and left.

Shannon said, "CDO! We've got two divers down here. One has just been attacked by the shark, and one is—what's he doing?"

She watched as he swam down to what remained of the other diver and started cutting a bag away that was attached to the corpse's midsection. She aimed her speargun at him and approached. Keller was holding his position in the water, approximately ten feet above and behind the man, his spear gun also trained on the diver. "Matt, I don't like it. Whatever he's cutting away is important. He'd be outta here by now if it wasn't," she said. "I'm going to get a closer look."

The CDO came on the net. "There are no other divers who are supposed to be in the basin right now. All divers working on *Carney* and *Hué City* have been accounted for. Bring this guy up, Chief. Your reliefs are on their way to help."

At that moment, both divers sitting on the edge of the pier put on their fins and jumped in.

Keller watched as the diver freed the bag. Holding it in one hand and his dive knife in the other, the man turned and looked up at Keller and Shannon.

Using her spear gun, Shannon motioned for him to surface. The man's head turned slightly to the right as if to get a look at something behind her.

Two lights were making their way down toward them.

The man opened the bag and reached inside.

"Is that a...it's an explosive charge!" Keller yelled.

Shannon aimed her speargun at the diver's center of mass and fired. The spear found its mark, and the diver threw his head back in agony. "Get that bag!" Shannon commanded.

She watched as Keller swam down to grab it, but the man stuck his hand inside one more time before Keller could get there.

An explosion erupted from the bag.

"Chief? Chief, can you hear me?"

Shannon's eyes opened. Both of her ears were ringing, and her right leg felt as if the blood inside had been set on fire and a million pins were stabbing her flesh. There was someone on top of her; her mask was off, but the image was blurry. The rest of her body felt cold and clammy.

Where was she?

Her left arm was lifted up. A wrapping had been placed around her biceps. *A tourniquet? Please, no.* She felt a squeeze and started to cry out.

Her vision returned to her, and she could see that it was not a tourniquet around her arm, but the black canvas wrapping used to take a patient's blood pressure. A navy corpsman was squeezing the rubber ball at the end of the tube while studying the gauge. She exhaled and looked up into the face of the CDO.

"Chief? Can you hear me?"

Her ears continued to ring, but she could make out what he was saying. She said, "Yes, sir, barely."

He gave a thankful smile.

"My ears—"

"You're going to be okay," he said. "We've got the base ambulance on its way."

"My leg," she moaned.

"Our ship's doc has got it stabilized," he said. "It'll need surgery, but you shouldn't lose it."

She tilted her head left and saw other *Zumwalt* crew members huddled around her. She looked for Keller. Not locating him, she turned her head to the right. Two rigid-hulled inflatable boats were speeding out the mouth of the river and into the Atlantic. The basin's water lay flat with moonlight shining down, making a silver-mirrored strip across the center. She was on the pier. There had been an explosion. Underwater. *Was everyone okay?* She locked eyes with the CDO. "The other divers?"

"They're in the water, making a sweep. Basically, every available diver in the basin is getting wet, searching."

"Keller?" she asked.

His eyes became moist, and he dropped his head.

"No," Shannon said, tearing up.

He lifted his head back up. "I'm sorry, Chief."

She closed her eyes, and the noises around her disappeared as the ringing got louder.

At the first sound of the base sirens, Marcus had weighed anchor and sped down the coast, leaving the two divers. Clumsy fools were on their own now. *Probably fucked it up because they were cold,* he thought. *Should've used some of my local boys.* He knew that if they had been the ones diving, then there would not have been any problems. As for him, he was too old to dive now and had survived too long to be caught. If the wealthy men overseas wanted better results, then they needed to start sending him better soldiers.

Throttling down after ten minutes, he raised a pair of night-vision goggles and scanned the water aft of him. There were two small boats motoring back and forth along the coast just offshore of the base. He was certain that he had not been spotted because they would be giving chase if he had been. However, it didn't mean that they wouldn't head this way soon, or that another more powerful vessel wouldn't emerge from the basin and chase him down. Following the original plan was too risky now. He checked his depth. Almost seventy feet. It would have to do. Cabin cruiser, dinghy, the whole thing was going to the bottom. Of course, this meant a longer swim, but he couldn't chance getting caught in the dinghy. He shut off the engine and looked down at his round tummy putting a strain on the front of the black wetsuit he was wearing. Even this adult girdle couldn't fully suck in his fat. He raised a hand to his heart and massaged his chest while looking at the shore dotted with lights, far off in the distance. He felt tightness in his left arm and pulled it away from his chest. Then, he shook his arm up and down to see if the tightness would loosen up. It didn't. He swallowed.

Stop it, he told himself. *You can make it. Going to get to the beach, take off this body-sized diabetic sock and be at the beach house before dawn. Gonna rest up, fork out some serious cash on a couple of whores tomorrow night, do some blow, and then watch as the two lovelies work their magic on me. Hell. Yeah.* Delivering the bad news could wait. Striking their adversary was a virtue, but so was relaxing after putting your ass on the line.

He went below, set the charges, and quickly emerged from the cabin carrying a pair of fins, a mask, and a hood. Taking one more look with the night-vision goggles, he saw no craft approaching from any direction. He threw the goggles into the sea.

The hood took some effort to put on as he pulled the neoprene sleeve down over his large head full of thick, curly, gray hair. Once it was on, he felt an annoying pain underneath, and he struggled to reach in and pull both of his ears up as they had folded over on the final yank to get the hood down. Putting the mask over his face, he could now hear his heart beating in his ears and decided that he did not like it one bit. Everything was calm topside as he walked toward the stern. A nagging feeling washed over him. *What am I forgetting?* A moment later, it finally hit him. *Oh, right, the cabin!* He turned around and padded back across the deck to the opening next to the helm. He shook his head in annoyance as he closed the fiberglass cabin doors, slid a Master Lock through the metal eyes, and snapped the lock shut. The timer had been set for two minutes.

Get going already.

Marcus stepped through the open stern gate and sat on the swim step, putting his fins on. A quick dip of his hand in the ocean told him that this was not going to be a pleasant swim. *Fuck it.* He stood up, said a prayer, and jumped in.

The cold water engulfed him, and he thought that this was how it must feel when you are buried alive under an avalanche. His arms and legs felt clumsy, like dead weights that would not listen to the signals his brain was giving them. He turned over onto his back and started kicking to warm up his body. This way, he could also keep an eye on the boat. *Smart*, he thought. Thirty seconds later, he felt vibrations in the water and watched as the cabin cruiser slowly slipped below the surface. He kicked and watched for another minute and then turned over and started a lazy crawl toward shore.

He didn't get far. As if a bolt of lightning entered his left thumb and traveled down an inner expressway to his heart, Marcus jolted upright in the water. Reaching for the heavy and tightening fist-sized section of his chest, as if his touch would relieve the pressure, his eyes became wide behind the tempered glass of his mask. He gasped and then died.

A month later, a morning jogger would slow to a trot as he approached what he thought was a large clump of seaweed. A minute later, he would be on his knees, vomiting in the sand. Behind him, half-hidden by an entangled mass of seaweed and feeding crabs, would be the hooded head, shoulders, left arm, and upper torso of a diver.

Chief Petty Officer Allison Shannon blinked her eyes at the roof of the ambulance as it sped toward the base hospital. A female paramedic sat next to her, rubbing her shoulder.

"You're going to be fine, Chief. Hang in there. Just a few more turns, and we're there."

Shannon tried to give a smile, but the tears coming out of her eyes betrayed the attempt at positivity and hope. All she could think about was Keller and the fact that he was gone forever.

I'll never get in the water again. I swear it.

Little did she know that the water would call her back...

ABOUT THE AUTHOR

Landon Beach lives in the Sunshine State with his wife, two children, and their golden retriever. He previously served as a Naval Officer and is currently an educator by day and an author by night. Find out more at landonbeachbooks.com.

Made in United States
North Haven, CT
18 February 2023

32810322R00195